COME HERE TO ME

Prickly Hawthorn Village #2

KAREN DEAN BENSON

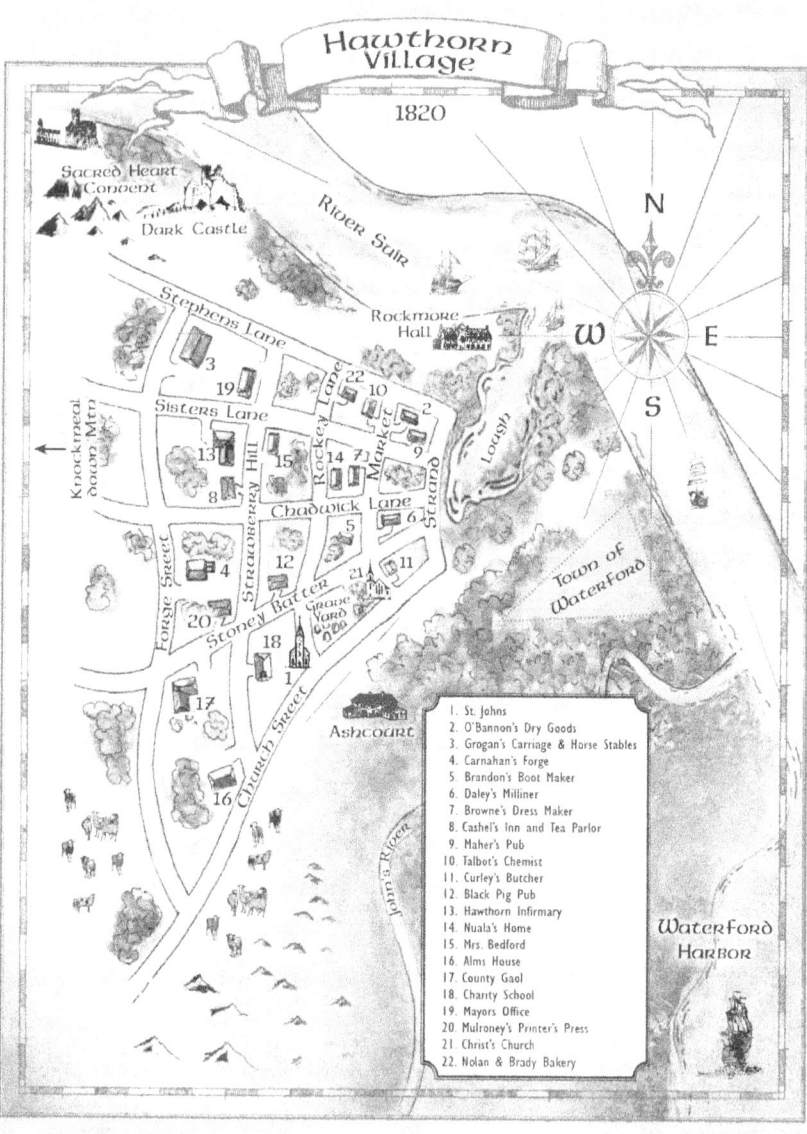

Hawthorn Village

1820

Sacred Heart Convent
Dark Castle
River Suir
Rockmore Hall
Stephens Lane
Sisters Lane
Knockmealdown Mtn
Chadwick Lane
Rockey Lane
Strawberry Hill
Forge Street
Stoney Batter
Market
Strand
Lough
Town of Waterford
Church Street
Ashcourt
John's River
Grave Yard
Waterford Harbor

N
W E
S

1. St. Johns
2. O'Bannon's Dry Goods
3. Grogan's Carriage & Horse Stables
4. Carnahan's Forge
5. Brandon's Boot Maker
6. Daley's Milliner
7. Browne's Dress Maker
8. Cashel's Inn and Tea Parlor
9. Maher's Pub
10. Talbot's Chemist
11. Curley's Butcher
12. Black Pig Pub
13. Hawthorn Infirmary
14. Nuala's Home
15. Mrs. Bedford
16. Alms House
17. County Gaol
18. Charity School
19. Mayors Office
20. Mulroney's Printer's Press
21. Christ's Church
22. Nolan & Brady Bakery

To all readers and lovers of historical romance!

Summer 1816
Hawthorn Village
County Waterford, Ireland

Christopher's attention was momentarily drawn from the gaping leg wound of a sailor off the privateer *Nomad* when a fierce pounding rattled the glass of his infirmary door. Before he could untangle his fingers from the scissors, the door opened, and a voice resounded from the front of his surgery.

"Ain't nobody here?" A heavy stride thumped down the hall. "What the bloody hell."

As Christopher glanced over his shoulder at the greasy tar in the doorway who grinned sly-like at the sailor on the table, a gush of blood from the wound splattered Christopher's vest and shirt sleeve. He quickly pinched off the source and reached for a cloth applying pressure.

His patient, grimacing in pain, managed to remark to his buddy, "Worried was ye?"

"Hell no. That damn kid's gone missin'—again! I ain't no bloody nurse maid." He slapped a well-worn strap against his thigh, obviously eager to put it to use.

Christopher's patience soured by the second as he tried to staunch the flow of blood on his patient's leg, his full attention honed on the intruder. He was a scruffy and unwashed gaunt man, straggly gray hair hanging out of a black cap. As he groused, his tobacco-stained teeth flashed in greeting. Fed up with the stench and the intrusion, Christopher barked, "Wait in the front parlor until I'm finished here."

"Ain't you I'm here 'bout, doc." His beady gaze swept the length of Christopher.

"Your friend will mend once I stitch the wound." Christopher's nose twitched with the briny stink of him.

"Ain't him neither."

Fast losing his patience, Christopher barked, "What then?"

The black hat with all the loose oily gray hair nodded toward the front of the surgery. "The brat ran in here. Damn him."

"Who?" Christopher glanced at his moaning patient whose jaw was clenched against the pain of his injury. "You?"

Through clenched teeth, the tar managed to sputter, "I ken he's pissed at Dino." There was a fiery shriek of *holy hell* as the doctor dug into the open wound and drew out a shard of glass. Christopher pressed the heel of his palm on the wound to stop the bleeding. His patient's lips were white against his clenched jaw.

Glaring at the intruder, Christopher barked, "Who is Dino?" He could have been talking to the wall for all the attention paid him. The sailor spun on his heel and stomped down the hall to the back of the surgery toward Christopher's private apartment. "You can't go in there. Come back here."

The tar on the table groaned, "He's gotta get that brat. Cap'n can't sail without his cabin boy."

Christopher gripped the man's hand and clamped it on the cloth over the wound. "Apply pressure," he growled and advanced on the intruder.

The filthy man opened the larder, grunting at the contents. He slammed it shut and muscled his way toward the bedroom.

"You are trespassing on my private property."

"I do as I want longs you mebbe harbor what's property o' the cap'n."

It took Christopher a moment to comprehend the slush of words. Standing perhaps a head taller than the sailor, and broader of shoulder, he advanced on him. "You get the hell out of my home, or I'll have the captain of your ship made aware of your trespass."

A whiff of foul breath washed his face as the sailor spat, "You think Redeye's gonna do without the brat—" his wrist swiped across his brow "—can't sail without his bugger."

Christopher grabbed him by the lapels of his leather vest and dangled him off the floor. "I'll say this once, so listen up. I've been here all morning, and no one has come besides your friend and you. Now you get out of my surgery, or I'll make trouble for you, your ship, and your captain. Got it?" He gave the man a good shake and set him free. Before the tar regained his balance, he fell back against the bed with such force the heavy wooden frame moved a few inches toward the wall.

In a split-second Christopher noted a small filthy foot under the bed slipping out of sight.

He yanked the tar off the bed pushing him down the hall. "You have a choice. You can leave my surgery peacefully, or I'll toss you out. What's it going to be?" Towering over the sailor, he glared down his nose at him. Shrugging off Christopher's fisted hold, he clomped down the hall and out of the infirmary.

Within minutes, as Christopher began sewing the gaping wound, he noted the man prowling past the window on the outside. He must have satisfied himself the *brat* was not about because he reentered the surgery, stench and all. "I can't go back 'till I find 'im." Casting a dark look on his friend, who moaned in pain, he said, "Ye'll have to 'elp."

Christopher, outraged that the child they sought was hiding beneath his bed, tried to rein in the violence descending on him.

Using a carefully controlled tone, he said, "Your friend's wound won't heal if he walks. I recommend sitting with his leg up for today and tomorrow at the very least."

The black-toothed one said, "An you'll serve tay will you now?" Both men guffawed.

Later, after they left his infirmary, Christopher gathered the filthy linens used to mop blood, and dropped them in a basket in the corner, took off his stained shirt and vest adding them to the pile. The woman, Darby, who came by daily, would return them clean.

Krysta, the cook, was off for a few days due to her sister's lying in. He had offered his assistance. However, midwifery was the way Hawthorn Villagers delivered their offspring, among other prevailing remedies to which they adhered rather than accept his professional advice. It was a struggle for him to bite his tongue when it came to the old ways of the Irish against everything he had learned at medical school in Edinburgh.

As he fixed dinner for himself, and a little extra for the foot under his bed, the sizzle and aroma of two slabs of meat searing in the pan made his stomach rumble. He tossed cut up potatoes in with the meat, stirring them with a long-stemmed wooden paddle, rotating the meat, soaking up the sizzling fat with the potatoes as they browned the juices. Then he cut up a leek and added it to the mix.

A knock at the front door, and Pete Waffer stepped inside. "What can I do for you, Constable?"

"It's what I can do for you, doc. Heard you had some trouble earlier. Anything I can help with?" His shabby green jacket was a leftover from the Battle on Vinegar Hill years earlier. It was Waffer's badge of honor, having lost two brothers in the battle, and himself wounded.

"All taken care of, and as far as I understand hopefully sailing with the tide as we speak."

The Constable took several steps forward his bright blue gaze flickering down the hallway. A scar left over from battle lined his face from his left ear down to his chin. The stitching used to heal him must have been done by a butcher, but on the battlefield, strange measures were necessary. The scar was showing signs of age, as it wasn't quite as red since he first met Waffer, who now asked, "You sure you wouldn't be with a firearm ta yer back now, would ye?"

"You are welcome to look about. I'm in the middle of fixing supper." Christopher wiped his hand on the towel and tossed it on his shoulder. Waffer always cautious, and diligent, used military tactics when investigating problems in the village.

The Constable took in a deep breath. "All's normal ta me. I'll be on me way. 'Bout time to check the lamps. Part and parcel of me keep you ken. I've got a dozen ta get lit. Hawthorn's a busy place in the dark of night."

It wasn't really a question, and Christopher nodded to him as he left. He locked the front door and with darkness coming on, lit two candles in the kitchen, then pulled the covers over the windows. After setting the table, he gave the meat one last flip, shoved the potatoes and leeks to the side of the grill further from the flame, and called out, "It's safe now, you can come out."

Nothing.

He listened for a shuffle, but his little guest hadn't made an appearance and it occurred to him perhaps he'd slid from under the bed and snuck out the back. "Dinner is ready, Dino."

Hungry as he was, he took his plate to the fire and laid it with a cut of beef and half the potatoes and onions, poured a tankard of ale then sat. Had the boy fallen asleep?

By his third bite and second pull on the ale, a sound came from the bedroom.

A cautious lad looking to be no more than nine or ten stood in the doorway to the kitchen, intense brown eyes set wide beneath thick black curly hair. His nose was too big for his face, but given a few years, his features would likely grow into a presentable blend.

His interest slid to the fire where a portion sizzled. "You are invited to eat with me if you choose." He gestured to the other plate on the table. "Fill it up then, lad."

The boy padded across the kitchen, taking the pewter in both hands, filthy as his feet, and bent toward the fire. Christopher's chair scraped the floor as he stood.

Dino flinched, the plate bounced and clattered to the floor as he backed into a corner, fists at the ready.

Christopher ignored the lad's defensive reaction and scooped up the pewter. "Why don't you scrub up while I get your food, there is a square of soap in a dish by the sink, and water in a bowl."

He filled the plate with what was left on the griddle, placed it on the table, filled the tankard with milk and sat. Dino wiped his hands down the length of his grimy pant legs. Casting a hesitant glance at the doctor, then slight as he was, he slid into the chair without pulling it out.

Christopher cast his attention to his own plate as the boy began to appease what must be a great hunger. He used his fingers to eat the potatoes and was about to pick up the slab of juicy meat when Christopher leaned across the table with the intention of cutting the lad's meat.

Dino fell back off the chair and sprawled on the floor. Jumping up, he leapt for the door. Christopher grabbed him by the collar hauling him back to the chair.

"Look, I'm not going to harm you. I'm a doctor, if I do anything, it will be to help you."

He focused on the boy, waiting for Dino to look at him. Christopher's knowledge of the world was broad, given his travels, and education. What he saw in the lad's eyes almost brought tears to his own.

"Do you understand what doctors are?"

A shrug answered him.

Christopher let out a long low breath. "You need to eat. So, how about I talk for a bit and you feed yourself."

No sooner were the words out, and Dino picked up the steak with his fingers biting into it. Eyes closed as he savored the taste. Swallowing, he broke off another piece and chewed with a look of contentment.

Christopher finished his meal, wiped his mouth with a napkin and sipped his ale. "A doctor isn't one to hurt others unnecessarily. As far as I can tell, from what your two friends had to say, you've been sadly mistreated. Perhaps it's why you ran away."

Dino set the mug down, a slash of white across his dirty upper lip. Swiping at it with a thin wrist revealed his left arm had been broken and not set properly.

"No friends o' mine, you can be sure o' that." Said in a firm, though childish tone, attesting to his youth.

"How long have you been aboard the *Nomad*?"

"Thinkin' four or five when they got me." He bit into the steak again and chewed a bit slower this time.

This interview was going to take all night at this rate. "How old are you now?"

"'Leven, maybe twelve."

Scrawny for his age, then. "Do you recall where you were born?"

"Seesly. I knowed it was the fire mountain. Mel said it was some volcano mountain, atnna. It's on Seesly." He gulped milk, then bit into the steak again.

Christopher nodded. "I've read about Mt. Etna and the destruction it has caused. And, yes, it is on the island of Sicily, off Southern Italy. You are a fair piece from your homeland, Dino. You might already realize that?"

The boy nodded as he chewed.

"Mel? Who is he?"

"The salt who came lookin' for me."

"You nearly got discovered, were you aware?"

His expressive awe opened wide. "I felt a blustery storm hit my chest."

Christopher smiled. "I bet you did. What are your plans for the future now that you obviously won't be returning to the *Nomad*?"

"As long as I draw breath, I ain't goin' back." His thin arms crossed over his scrawny chest, bare feet planted in such a manner, Christopher knew he'd bolt in a split-second if given cause.

"I heard a man come knockin'. What was he looking for?"

"Not you, lad. He's a constable. And was making sure everything is right. He protects villagers from bad people, and bad things like theft, and drunkenness."

"Ain't he kind of late with his help?"

Christopher chortled. "There is that. He means well."

৩১৫৩

The next morning Christopher tossed some coals on the embers in the grate, filled the kettle with water, hung it from the iron arm, then swung it over the coals. Glancing at the pile of blankets in the corner of the kitchen, a pair of dark brown eyes regarded him as the lad followed his every move, covers drawn to his chin.

"Rather than use the privy out back, I suggest you use the pot in my closet. For now, I think it best you don't show yourself during the day."

The boy's face softened. He threw back the blankets and padded off to the bedroom. A few minutes later he reentered the kitchen and sat.

Christopher leaned back against the counter arms folded over his chest. The boy sat hunched, digits clasped between his knees, an expectant look on his face.

It wasn't unusual for Christopher to dream when sleeping, then wake with solutions to problems. But he woke with dread this morning, not answers. He was surprised the lad stayed.

"I'm not sure what to do with you, Dino."

A flicker of fear clouded the lad's keen vision.

Christopher pushed off from the counter and drew the kettle

from the hearth, poured the water in a dish of tea leaves to steep and arranged two cups, milk, and a tin of biscuits on the table.

Dino inhaled a deep breath. "There's a pot of jam in the larder, in case you forgot."

Christopher chuckled. It appeared his guest had prowled about during the night. "Well then, make yourself useful."

J ust about when Christopher was to take a mouthful of the cherry jam and biscuit, he heard a loud banging on the front door, rattling the hinges. He jumped up glaring at Dino. "Get under the bed and don't show yourself for any reason until I come get you."

Quick as a mouse, Dino scrambled from the chair and leapt to the bedroom. Christopher grabbed up the bundle of blanket and tossed it on top of his bed, starting toward the door. "Just a minute!" He rushed back and fixed the table with only one plate and cup, then walked calmly toward the door growling, "Okay, okay."

He unlocked the latch, and an aged man looking more like a sack of potatoes fell into the room. Christopher caught him just before he hit the floor and dragged him to the examining table. Once he got him reclining on his back, he noticed an ashen countenance, shallow breathing, with no apparent open wounds. "Your name?"

"Schmitty." It sounded like he snored the word.

"What ails you?" Christopher asked as he prodded the man's stomach area with no response.

The patient's forearm fell away from his head dangling

toward the floor. Christopher lifted the limb folding it alongside his length. Schmitty's eyes were shut, he stank as bad as Mel and the sailor with the leg wound, making him think he was another tar. At sea, a storm might be the only cleansing a sailor got.

"Blazes and damn!" The fellow was out cold but did not stink of rum or ale. Christopher lifted the arm again and let it fall. Dead weight. "What the bloody hell am I expected to do with him!"

A small voice from the hall said, "He does that a lot."

Was anything going to go the way he wanted? "I told you to stay out of sight."

"I heard his name and figured he'd nod off."

"Explain please?"

"Cap'n Redeye says he almost gets himself killed all the time 'cause he can't stay awake. Maybe he sent him to you? Maybe Mel sent him? Or Gunther?"

"Maybe it's a ruse to discover you. If, as you say, you'll never go back, you damn well better get somewhere quick." Christopher suspected this man didn't arrive under his own recognizance. Someone dropped him on the doorstep.

No sooner had Christopher rotated to the man on the table when the front door banged wide. He guessed who the hefty, broad shouldered man of the sea might be. About Christopher's own height, though beefier, leather breeches, black boots, slick dark hair caught up in a ribbon, a tri-cornered black hat, and most notably, a knife in his belt. What named him was his marked red eye. Rings on his fingers flashed in the early morning sun falling through the open door.

Captain Redeye of the *Nomad*.

"Schmitty got here all right. Gunther said you had a way with fixin' folks." Redeye sauntered to the table and poked the sleeper in the gut. "Can you make him stay awake?" His gaze slithered about the room, catching sight of the hall that led to the rear of the building.

Lifting the sailor's eyelid, Christopher noted the redness, his iris rolling upward. "Within the last five or six months, is it possible you've been in Africa?"

The cap'n had sauntered to the opening that led to the back of the building. "Aye, South Africa."

"Your men, did they take leave?" He lifted the sailor's arm, and with his fingertips prodded the lymph nodes, repeating the gesture on the neck and groin.

"Those what earned it." He craned his neck looking around the corner.

"Schmitty one of them?"

He planted his attention fully on Christopher. "What the 'ell you thinkin'?"

"He might have what's called African sleeping sickness. You get it from the bite of a tsetse fly."

The captain's head snapped back to the figure on the table as eagle-like he inspected the gravely ill crewman. "It's been months. He's been able until mebbe two months or so."

"Symptoms come on slow, after the initial period of the bug bite, painful and sore like a chancre. Then fevers begin, severe headaches, and the fatigue. Has he complained of not feeling well?"

"Never shuts up about it. Ye'd think he was a child nursin' off his mam."

The remark made Christopher think of Dino, hiding under the bed. He poured alcohol over his fingertips and rubbed them together, wiping with a cloth. He leaned back against the counter. "This man is in the last stages of the disease."

Redeye lurched near the table, taking a good look at his sailor. "You say he's dyin'?"

He let the question hang in the air. This man didn't give a damn about anyone who could not serve him in one way or another.

Taking heed of each other, the pirate placed the cup of his palm on the shaft of his knife. "Satan's sins! The fourth crew to die on me. Counting that bastard kid, makes it like I'm cursed."

He wanted to react, but prudence kept his mouth shut. He watched in disbelief as the hulking pirate strode to the hallway, spun about, and growled, "How many will I lose?"

"How many got off your ship?"

"Jasus! Hades!"

He figured the captain mentally counted the number of his crew and appeared unnerved as he strode to the door reaching for the latch.

Christopher shouted, "Wait. You can't just leave him here. I haven't the help or the time to care for him. He's your responsibility."

His large head swung around, honing his red glint on Christopher. "You keep the brat and I'll call it even." He flung the door wide and stomped along the path to Sisters Lane bound for the cobbles on the Strand and hopefully the lough and his anchored ship.

Schmitty's labored breathing suggested his time was growing near. Christopher raked his fist through his hair and stared out the window. What in blazes was he to do? Not in Hawthorn Village barely four months and he encountered more mayhem for which medical school had not prepared him. A sense he was being watched, he swung away from the window.

"I ken 'elp."

"How's that?" He glared at the urchin who caused him much mischief.

The boy slowly moved to the table, touching Schmitty's arm. "He's my friend. Only one I got."

"You heard everything?"

"Aye."

"Then you understand what's to come of your friend?"

He nodded mournfully. "If yer a medical man, you could help 'im."

A deep sigh stirred his own feelings toward this lad who had encountered far more of life than any child should have to deal with. "I wonder if we could come to some sort of arrangement. How would you feel about working for me?"

His jaw gaped. "You mean gettin' paid?"

"More like, I'll provide you room and board, and you run errands and such."

A small dirty paw extended to him. "You got yourself a deal, doc."

Mindful of the dying body on the table, Christopher added, "As it appears rather quiet right now, let's look at a room in the back, maybe it will work for you." Dino followed him beyond the kitchen on the far side of the fireplace and lifted the latch on a creaky wooden panel. The dank scent of musk spilled out as Dino eagerly stepped within then sneezed.

Had he ever had a room to himself? A window on the far wall was partially covered by a huge cabinet, and a cot tucked in the corner could use a thorough cleaning. Christopher hadn't really looked in this space since he took up residence.

"You are givin' me this?"

"You'll have to work for it, but yes." The wonder on Dino's face nearly brought Christopher to tears. He coughed into his fist.

"Can Schmitty use the cot and I'll take care of 'im, till he…" His smudged features cast downward as if expecting answers somewhere near his filthy feet, but he didn't finish his question.

"The minute we shook on it you were hired. I need you to run an errand."

Christopher gave him a note to deliver to Darby, his laundress. "Do you read?"

"Yup, a man o' God what taught me when the cap'n gave him passage. The best. Didn't ken what I was missin'."

He chuckled at Dino's enthusiasm for reading. "How old were you?"

"Maybe seven or so. He was a friend, almost a year." A cloud flickered in his dark stare and he looked away with remorse, or was it shame.

Christopher considered once the preacher was gone, Dino's life may have changed drastically. He waved the piece of paper at him. "Darby lives on the second floor above Curley's on Market and Church. There is an entrance with stairs; you don't have to go into the shop. This explains who you are and asks her if she can help clean out the room for you."

"I can clean this, doc."

He brushed the boy's head. "I think your duty is to Schmitty right now. We need to make him comfortable."

Imbued with purpose, Dino left through the door at the back of the infirmary. Christopher noted his stealth as he warily snuck around the corner.

3

Christopher checked in on the dying man in his examination room. His breathing was consistent, but shallow. Assuring himself Schmitty wasn't going anywhere. He hurried to the room in the back and began putting some order to it by moving the cabinet to the opposite wall away from the window. Propping the window with a stick allowed a warm summer breeze to freshen the inside. He grabbed up a blanket off the cot and took it outside shaking the dust, then laid it across the railing on the back porch where the sun rested. Someone pounded on the front door. Why patients didn't use the doorbell was beyond him.

The local bootmaker waited on the other side of the partially glassed door. "Good morning, Mr. Brandon. What can I do for you?"

"I've come with an offer of dinner this evening. Miranda is trying out a new recipe and I thought perhaps, given your circumstance, you might enjoy a good meal."

The man meant well, and Christopher didn't want to ignore the fact he also owned this property and had leased it for use as an infirmary, but he had no interest in being set-up. "I thank you kindly, sir. Please extend my regrets to your daughter. I have a very sick patient who can't be left."

"We had our minds set you would jump at the offer." Mr. Brandon flapped his hat against his thigh.

"Duty calls."

Mr. Brandon nodded, placing his top hat on fluffy sun-lit hair. "Miranda is going to be put out. She intended to impress you with her culinary expertise."

"Give her my sincere regrets, please."

Darby wasn't long coming in the back door, calling out, "Yoo-hoo. I'm here, Mr. Curran."

He closed the door on Mr. Brandon and made his way down the hall toward the back of the infirmary. "Dino isn't with you?"

"In a hurry, the lad was. Slapped the note at me and took off on a leap and bound. I haven't noticed him about. New, is he?"

"That would be the size of it." He took the pail and mop from her and set them aside. The woman, though plump and well-rounded, was fleet of foot and energetic. "Can you make the room presentable?" He nodded to the open door.

"Ah, taken in borders are ye?" she said, fists on her ample hips.

"Not all patients are able to ambulate right away. And I have taken in Dino to run errands. This room should work as a sleeping room. As you can tell, it needs a feminine touch."

Her big smile leeched at him. "Ye'd be better off marrin' then, wouldn't ye?"

He grunted and shook his head. This wasn't the first in his four months she'd thrown the idea out there. He suspected if his mother were alive, she'd do the same. "I'm of no mind for *that* sacred ritual. Now, can you make sense of the dust and dirt?"

"I'll have it to rights soon enough." Her gaze shifted to the front of the infirmary. "Yer patient, he be all right out there?"

Pursing his lips, Christopher nodded as the bell at the front door rang. Refreshing for a change since most folks pounded. The post slid beneath his door was from his absent partner, Johnathan Burke Wallington, Lord Tremaine, his medical school cohort and life-long friend. Tremaine married his third cousin last fall and she, Lady Mairéad, accompanied him to Edinburgh as he finished up his last year. Christopher understood that after graduation they planned to travel on the continent before returning to County Waterford, and their family and medical practice.

Christopher settled into his desk chair, a fresh cup of tea simmering, and broke the seal of the letter. Tremaine's graduation was a mirror image of Christopher's, so he wrote. There were fifty men in his class, most of them off to London and several to Glasgow. The Tremaines planned a few months in London, on to Paris, and eventually making their way back home sometime this late autumn.

Christopher got caught up in a reminiscence of Lady Mairéad. Left on a convent doorstep as an infant, and as luck would have it, she was discovered to be the legitimate granddaughter of the Sixth Earl of Darnley. With a sparkling wit, and quick energy she was literally made-in-heaven for Tremaine. If only he, Christopher, could find a similar kind of companion. Ah, but it wasn't in the cards as he had discovered with Caroline Hammond; the face of an angel—the soul of a conniving witch.

He'd fallen hard after a few months of companionship, thinking, for the first time in his life, perhaps he had found his near-perfect match, until he accidentally interrupted a compromising situation with their professor. It took him a long time to resolve. She begged forgiveness, but it wasn't a predicament for which he could summon tolerance.

Darby stood in the doorway, clearing her throat. "What's next?"

After folding the letter, he left it on his desk and followed her down the hall. Night and day difference. She worked her magic and he drew in a breath smiling. She offered, "Lemon oil, doc."

"Ah. Well, I'll bring Schmitty in and give him some comfort." Near dead-weighted, together they moved him. Christopher had him under the armpits; Darby held his feet as they struggled down the corridor, through the kitchen, and into the room.

She'd put fresh linen on the cot and done wonders with the

pillow. It looked to be new as it was fluffed up and comfy, although the patient wouldn't be the wiser.

"What'll you do with him, then?" she asked as he tucked the blanket around the man's legs.

"The poor man has a sleeping disease; he's in the last stages. He'll dwindle until he's gone. The pain comes from the joints, so less movement means less pain. He takes a few sips of water now and then, but no appetite. He might beckon with a curve of his fingers not much else from him."

She patted the man on his shoulder and swept the hair off his brow.

Christopher got as far as the door and glanced back over his shoulder. "Tell me again how Dino acted."

Her brows rose, lips pursed as she recalled. "Nothing remarkable. Gave over yer note. In a terrible rush he was. Face flushed, he fluttered this way and that, like he expected someone to tap him on the head."

Christopher beckoned her to follow him into the kitchen. "He was kidnapped from his homeland and lived aboard the *Nomad*."

"How did you come by him?"

"It's a mess of intrigue, suffice to say, I discovered him under my bed."

"And you became his savior, no doubt." She swiped a wrist across her beaded forehead. "Ah, doc, you're a rare man, you are."

Christopher drew his head back, annoyed. "The man in the other room was his friend. The lad wanted to care for him in his last days. Now what will I do?"

The chair scraped as she stood. "You can follow yer inclination, go search the paths. Someone down at the Black Pig might have seen him. Go on with ye. I'll watch over this one, though I suspect he won't be given me any trouble a'tall. Bring me a pickle or two from the pub and I'll be content."

Christopher took the long route to the pub up Stephen's Lane, crossed over to Forge, then east toward the lough. He hoped if the boy was in hiding, he might take notice and come out.

It was easy to spot the *Nomad,* the beakhead emblazoned with the name. The timbers swayed gently with the tide. It wasn't a particularly extravagant Baroque style which surprised Christopher knowing the manner and excessive dress of its captain. He took note of the twenty-gun ports on the starboard side confirming Redeye dealt with more than plain cargo. If Dino had been nabbed, Christopher didn't relish rowing out to the ship and challenging the captain.

Conversation and hearty chuckles could be heard as he approached the Black Pig. A breeze off the lough thinned out the heavy atmosphere. The doors to the pub were thrown wide to clear the stagnant air. He walked up to the planked oaken bar and backed into a stool, his right arm extended over the well-worn oak as he glanced about. Conversation dimmed a bit with his presence. He didn't much frequent the place, keeping to himself, probably more than he ought. They impressed on him a sense of being judged and it did not sit well.

Several elderly men glanced at him as they lifted their mugs. He nodded at Danaher, hefty fellow, bulbous nose, shining red right now. Most likely a barometer to the amount of ale in his gut. Mulroney, a lantern jaw with a grin in the middle of it, owned the print shop in Hawthorn. And Carnahan, proprietor of the forge; all three occupied the very same table at the same time of day; Christopher could only guess it was an ingrained habit by now. Probably been doing it for years and years.

"Finally found yer way over, did'ja now? We've placed bets on yer hardly darkin' the Black Pig's threshold." Carnahan drew on his mug, then swiped his sleeve over a grinning lip as he regarded the doc. A burly, red-haired ape of a man, he never failed to take note of Christopher's presence.

4

Wishing he'd not stepped foot in the place, Christopher tossed five-pence on the bar. "I'll need a couple of dills to go." He grabbed up the tankard plunked in front of him as he headed over to the table. The men scraped their chairs aside accommodating him.

Setting his tankard down, he said, "I'm looking for a lad about so tall..." holding his hand out to Dino's height. "...he ran an errand for me and never showed up again. Last I knew he was barefoot, dirty, dark haired."

"Was coin involved?"

A couple of paws slapped the table causing ale to spill, a chorus of jibes regarding the stupidity of paying a ragtag to run an errand.

"Yup, spied ten o' 'em this morn alone, wouldn't you credit."

Christopher scanned the faces of each man, nodding in agreement. Comfortable in their own skins, a nice enough group. Above their heads, shelves circled the upper three feet of the walls in the rectangular room filled with stuffed squirrel and little red deer heads the likes of which only Ireland could lay claim. A cryptic sign here and there, painted no doubt by a Christian woman attempting to goad her husband into a modicum of temperance; *possess prudence*; *do not despise advice*; *lean heavily on God*. A tad surprising the owner allowed them considering the very nature of the Black Pig. He concluded must be Padhraig's wife who put them up, though he had no notion if the owner was married.

Still chuckling over what they considered his folly, he finished the tankard, thanked the men for their help and was ready to leave when a clap on his shoulder kept him in the chair. "A lad about this tall, you say?" The bearded fellow spoke, deep creases spreading out from the corners of his mischievous focus, leathery skin, pointed about chest high.

Christopher narrowed his gaze shrugging off Mulroney's clutch. "I'd say so. Why?"

"Just checkin' in case I come upon a barefoot boy." His lantern jaw nestled in a wide grin.

They cackled like hens. Christopher stood, irritation scratching. "Look, you may find amusement, but the lad could be in trouble."

Mulroney's face softened to a modicum of sympathy. "I can do a write-up, paper won't go out until tomorrow though," he said, no longer chiding. As the owner of Hawthorn's printing press, he would be aware of the seriousness of a child's disappearance. They may be a poor old Irish village, but children and people mattered. The ships at anchor coming and going didn't have any loyalty to one of Ireland's oldest villages and its population.

Glancing at the assortment of interested faces dotted about the pub, he guessed about an eighth of the men had been into the infirmary for one ailment or another. And most all of them had taken exception to his medical advice, several returning to impart their displeasure.

Maybe it was the dying down of the breeze and thickened heavy air, but he felt it oppressive in the pub. Cloying. They didn't send a message of hostility; it was more a sense of dismissal. Slapping his top hat on, he grabbed up the pickles for Darby and walked out, half considering their indifferent smirks, reminding himself they couldn't possibly understand Dino's horrific background. And, *he* had no intention of enlightening them.

He might have had a friendlier reception if Padhraig or his brother, Ian, had been in attendance, but someone he'd not met was behind the bar. The McCarthy brothers also owned the local funeral parlor, came by it as third-generation inheritors along with The Black Pig. Christopher, the only medical man in the village, would always have need of their daytime services, which drew him to think of Schmitty, who was already on borrowed time.

The sign on the back wall, over the bottles of liquor read, *we'll wine you and dine you, and bury you. Hopefully not on the same day*, was testimony to the prevailing tongue-in-cheek of the owners and their clientele. His problem was, *he* took life too seriously.

Arriving back at the infirmary, he came in the back door. Darby was asleep in a rocker next to Schmitty's bed, who showed no signs of having moved since last he saw him.

"Any luck, doc?" Darby asked, rousing from her doze, her voice quieter than usual.

"None, sorry to say. What can you tell me of the pub's owner?" He bent over Schmitty and felt a barely discernable heave in his chest.

"Padhraig? He's a hard worker, can't say the same for Ian. Unreliable as they come. Leaves most of the work to his elder brother. Ian has a sour disposition, can't hold his Guinness. A lot like their pa. Imagine 'im behind the bar every day? Padhraig keeps Ian busy with building coffins and such." She shifted in the rocker to glance at Schmitty. "This lad has not uttered a sound." Her gaze drifted to the small package Christopher clutched.

Having forgotten part of his mission, he quickly handed her the pickles.

She swiped the opened package under her nose, savoring the briny aroma. "Did anyone have anything to say about Dino?"

"No. Basically it was brought to my attention he looks like every other lad in the village, so what's to notice."

"They're a lot. Sittin' in judgement all afternoon, nothin' to rouse their minds to an honest day's work. Mulroney depends on old man Haggerty to set up the paper and such at the printers." She scratched her arm. He watched her do it several times lately.

He was about to make mention that at least Mulroney and Carnahan were actively employed, instead he asked, "Is it a rash?"

"It's nothin'."

"Will you roll up your sleeve and let me look?" It occurred to him they were in daily contact, yet *he* had to ask *her* about her arm. She kept the same distance he felt with most of the villagers. What was it all coming too? Why had he insisted on the infirmary in Hawthorn Village and not the more progressive village of Waterford?

"I'll rub vinegar on it." She rolled up her sleeve and thrust the inner part of her arm out for his benefit.

He stretched the skin on both sides of the golden-crusted eruptions. "How is your remedy working?"

"Stings like the wrath o' God."

"And, your thinking is, the more it hurts the more it heals."

"Ye'll make a good doc yet." Grinning at him, she rolled the sleeve down over the boils.

"Keep your arm covered until they are all gone. Right now, they are contagious. In time the boils will dry up and be gone. It's good you scratch through your sleeve, otherwise your fingers would become infected as well." He leaned into the basin washing his hands and reached for the towel.

"So, doc, what fancy name do you give it?"

"The Latin term is impetigo, which means *to attack*. It's a fungus attacking you and will spread if you touch it and then touch another part of your body or someone else. You will need to wash your shirt very well, and consistently keep the arm covered. You might get some relief spreading honey over the boils."

"Honey." She squinted in disbelief. "Easily done. I thank ye."

Schmitty let out a long sigh as if he heard them and understood. It was a long moment before he took another breath.

Glancing at the doc, Darby washed and dried her hands then sat in the rocker, leaning toward his inert frame. "We're right here. The doc and me. Your little friend should be along soon enough." She patted the quilt.

The bell rang.

Darby said, "Let me get the door. You take a minute. I put tea on the sideboard earlier."

He glanced at the copper pot as she closed the door between the back of the building and the infirmary. Where would Dino have gotten to? Had he been nabbed and taken to the *Nomad*? The thought made him ill. He wouldn't panic, but if the lad was taken, Christopher had no notion how long the ship would stay in the harbor. He'd have to find a way to get onboard.

The cruelties of life that would harm a child, a victim of neglect with alcohol and drugs usually the driving force. Walking the slums on the outskirts of Edinburgh had shown him the dire lives of those less fortunate. He'd been part of a group working to set up places with cots to bring them in off the streets. Their league was able to offer soup and bread most evenings in the winter.

When he and his lads graduated from med school, the group passed the reins to the undergrads. He wasn't going to let Dino slip through the cracks if he could help it.

Sipping a cup, he heard the low murmur of voices and another ring of the bell. It was stacking up to be a busy afternoon. What likely complaints might he listen to? Surely nothing so serious as to compliment his adeptness after years of medical learning.

Darby came into the kitchen just as he felt refreshed from the tea. "Well, ye've got a full waiting room," she warned. "Getting on to a mighty busy day for you, doc. Hardly past noon."

Grunting, he strode into the waiting room. A short stocky man bounced off the chair. "I'm first, doc."

Christopher stood aside as he walked into the office taking a chair. "What can I do for you, Mr.—"

"You can call me Shorty, doc. I've got a cow won't drop her milk and I need to have you look."

As ridiculous as the problem was for him, he still couldn't muster humor. "Is she with you?"

Shorty guffawed. "Got spirit in you, sir. Naw, she's in the barn waitin' on you."

Christopher stood, took the man's information. "I'll be to your place when my office closes for the day, I'll stop by."

He escorted Shorty back to the waiting room and glanced at the next man. "In my office please.

"Now, what can I do for you, Mr.—"

"Dooley, we're neighbors, sir. I'm over on Church. Wonderin' if you got a minute to help me fix the wheel on my wagon. I need someone to hold it whilst I pound pegs in the axel. Figure you for a big strappin' fellow might do the trick."

D isbelief washed over Christopher, setting his blood boiling. He rubbed the back of his neck, attempting to calm the irritation springing to life. "Mr. Dooley, I am not a handyman. I am a Doctor of Medicine. I have never fixed a wagon wheel in my life and have no desire to begin. Aside from the fact, I run the infirmary for those who need assistance with their health."

Dooley shot out of his seat. "I ken you make house calls. All I'm askin' is you make good on your promise."

Chastising himself, Christopher had allowed the comment to get the better of him. After all, the man said they were neighbors, though it was four lanes between them, he guessed that might still make them neighbors. "I make house calls after hours."

Dooley smiled. "Well, we'll have you to supper then. The missus will be mighty pleased, then won't she?" And out the door he strode.

Christopher would have run after him to get an address but was certain Darby knew where they lived. Glancing out the window facing Sister Lane, a long slow breath fogged the glass as he watched Mr. Dooley move left toward Forge. What was it going to take?

Out of the corner of his sight a woman was running up from

the direction of the Strand, her skirts held high, shawl sailing outward, hair falling from the pins. He watched as she scurried up his walk and arrived at the door. He met her in his outer room.

"Doc, a tragedy," she gasped, a palm to her chest, as she sank into a chair.

"Catch your breath, calm down."

Her face blotched with the struggle of her haste, she gushed, "They're gone, my babes are gone. Taken from me."

Darby having no doubt heard the commotion, entered with a mug of water. The woman's work-worn fist received it and she greedily drank.

Darby informed the doctor, "It's Mrs. Brandt. Her babes are sixteen and seventeen."

Christopher took the chair next to Mrs. Brandt. "When you are able, please explain."

She finished her draw on the mug and handed it to Darby. A trio of villagers came into the infirmary, gasping, wild-eyed. "Evie, what happened?"

He glanced at the small group realizing it took a crisis to fill his waiting room. He pointed to the empty chairs. "Sit." As they did so he gave Mrs. Brandt his full attention. "I'm listening."

She had gained a measure of calm and primly folded her hands in her lap, took a deep breath and began. "I woke this morning and both girls were gone. Mind you, they're good girls, Sarah a mite better'n Cassie. So, kidnapped I says. What else. I've searched those on my street, and none so aware they saw anythin'. Which is a bit strange being as how they usually got their noses in *everything*. So's, I march to the girls' friend up on Church, and the mother won't let me speak to her daughter to inquire. Says I'm not fit." Her face flamed red. "Not fit, says I. Not fit! Who the bloody blazes point's a finger at a grieving mother at the loss of her daughters'? says I." Evie's storytelling required she catch her breath and glanced about the room as she did so, noting her neighbors trying hard to appear as though they were not eavesdropping.

Christopher ignored them. "If you were to make a guess, Mrs. Brandt, where do you think they are?"

Her eyes blazed with concern. Her lips snarled, and she said, "Well, if I knew, I'd be there, now wouldn't I?"

A voice from across the room tossed out a possibility. "Could be one o' them tars they was mighty cozy with last eve down on the Strand."

Christopher glanced over his shoulder at the mid-sized man who rolled his hat between his knees. "What exactly are you saying, sir?"

"I'm sayin' her girls are likin' the company of a couple of lads off the *Seasurf*. Got into port yesterday mornin' loaded with mahogany and marble for some lord up near Kilmacthomas."

As irritated as Christopher was, he tried to comfort Mrs. Brandt. "Have you sought out the help of Constable Waffer?"

"I've been there, then, wasn't I? He's stuck his nose elsewhere."

Christopher leaned toward her again. "What would you like me to do, ma'am?"

"Jasus, go and fetch 'em. What is it you think I'd like you to do, have a pint at the pub? Like my old man would if he was about in time o' crises."

Combing fingers through his dark red hair, exasperated, Christopher asked, "Is it you think they were kidnapped, when in fact, they may have gone willingly?"

She sucked in a breath at what that accusation would cost should it be true. "They'd do no such thing, sir. Good girls they are."

A snigger from across the room, then an elbow from another to shut the companion up. Christopher turned away from the lot. Morally he could not ignore the implication here, whether the mother's or the neighbors. "I'll take care of it, Mrs. Brandt. You can wait near the quay, or I'll come to your home with news." He'd take a dory out and wondered if he'd be welcome on the *Seasurf*. Blazes and damn!

Mrs. Brandt cast her angry regard at the three across the room and swung her shawl over her shoulder. "I'll be on the Strand watchin' for you, doc." Chin in the air, she strutted from the waiting room, slamming the front door to the brink of shattering the glass.

Christopher informed Darby he had to leave again. She took it in good stride. "If Dino shows, keep him here. I'll be back as soon as I figure this out, *if* I can figure it out and get the daughters to come back with me." Why-oh-why did matters of this sort flood the infirmary? Did the villagers think this is what he was educated for? Was there no one else in Hawthorn who could tend to such problematic situations? He intended to have a talk with the constable.

Darby set the rocker to creaking on the floorboards as he grabbed up his hat, tailcoat, and a scarf off the rack. It would be chilly on the water.

Christopher stopped by the county gaol to seek the advice of Constable Waffer, who was still out. A man, face down on a cot in a cell, snored. A dull-witted replacement glanced up from separating a tangle of keys on a wire. "He ain't here, and I've no clue when he's comin' back, doc."

Christopher looked at the man whose words flapped through the gaping, toothless opening of his mouth. He was fairly certain he wouldn't get an answer, but asked anyway, "Who has jurisdiction if I were to row out to a boat and demand to be let onboard? Does the captain have the discretion to deny me?"

"And why would you do such a foolhardy thing, doc. If you don't mind me askin'?"

"It's Mrs. Brandt's…"

"Them lassies gone off again. Must sure like them lads." He fiddled with the keys, several dropping into a copper pot at his feet with a jingle. The noise woke the drunk, who demanded his bottle.

Christopher couldn't take another moment of doltish passivity and left. About to walk to the quay, he made a last-minute decision to stop by the Black Pig *again*. Thankfully, Padhraig was behind the bar. "What can I do you for, doc?" He was busy lining up washed mugs on a towel to drip dry.

"I'd like some advice before I make a decision."

"What might that be?" Padhraig stopped in his labor and gave the doc his full attention. Bright blue keen regard, ears too big for his head, and a shock of bright red curly hair, he faced Christopher with his full attention, looking somewhat like an elf. It occurred to him Padhraig looked a lot like a taller version of Pete Waffer—a holdover from a bygone era still believing in his dreams of when he was younger.

"Mrs. Brandt came by the clinic and said her daughters were kidnapped and taken to the *Seasurf.* She's asked me to bring them home. I personally have not dealt with a captain in a situation like this before and need a bit of advice."

As it happened, Danaher, Carnahan, and Mulroney, a trio of monkeys if ever there was such a thing, acted like they hadn't heard him when his gaze slid to their table. In unison, they put their mugs to their mouths, and set their attention on the contents; willing to eavesdrop, unwilling to offer a solution.

Padhraig scoffed. "Yer not going out to that damn rig. They'll come home. They always do."

"Then why was Mrs. Brandt in a fit?"

At the table of monkeys, Danaher broke the silence. "She's rantin' at you because she ain't got a husband to nag. She's come to all of us with her bluster one time or other. Mostly about this same thing. Heck, those girls want out as much as 'ol Henry wanted out."

Carnahan elbowed him, "'cept old Henry took the easy way. You fight a woman with your hat. He did just that, he grabbed it and ran like 'ell. Ain't seen hide nor hare of him since."

Christopher pulled his hat off and ran his fingers through his hair. Clearly bewildered as he soaked in this new bit of information.

The third monkey assessed, "Maybe she's got feelin's for you, doc. Trying to snare you into her spell."

Christopher glared at Mulroney and didn't trust himself to dignify answering him.

Padhraig cupped Christopher's arm as it rested on the bar. "You can go on out, dory is tied up at the end of the pier. But you might not get onboard. You're a man o' principal, doc. Who's to say he won't allow you, but what will you do if those lassies refuse to leave? You'll have gone out for nothing."

Danaher spoke up again. "They always come back, doc, isn't the first, nor the second this has happened."

Christopher had heard enough and pushed off from the bar, slapped his hat back on his head. "Thank you." He nodded to Padhraig, and then at the monkey table. "I'll take your advice into consideration."

As he neared the quay, Mrs. Brandt, her back to him, obviously scanned the river and came to rest on the towering masts of the *Seasurf*. He couldn't fault the fact she loved her daughters. Raising them without a father must be a burden.

"Mrs. Brandt."

She swung about her expression grim. "I was afraid ye'd not come."

"I gave you my word, ma'am. Have you a description of the two sailors your girls were with?"

Her cheeks pinkened. She stammered and shifted her gaze to the ship at anchor. "I've not seen 'em. They daydream its love. Foolish, simple-minded girls they are. What would they ken at their age?"

"If I might ask, when you and Mr. Brandt married, how old were you?" He followed her gaze to the far side of the lough, water rippling like diamonds in the late sunlit afternoon. The wind had shifted, the tide was coming in; the *Seasurf* wouldn't leave against the tide. They'd wait until morning.

"What's it got to do with them out yonder?" She twisted away from him, hugging her shawl close.

He hoped to calm her by saying, "I'm concerned they might have made an attachment of the heart and if I go out there demanding they return, rather than allowing them to come back on their own, you will lose that special something mothers and daughters share. It's a bond like no other, so I've heard."

He saw a shudder course through her, and drew away, allowing her the grief she must be feeling.

"What am I to do, then?" she asked, rubbing her chin with the ends of her shawl. A wind off the lough caught at strands of her hair, she looked miserable as she weighed his suggestion, broken in spirit, he thought.

"The captain won't sail with them aboard. When ship's ready, welcome them home with the love you feel. The ambience of your home should be accepting, conducive to productive conversation. Once you allow them freedom, your relationship will change for the better."

She locked a piercing inspection on him. He realized she was so frazzled with parenting she couldn't soften herself. "You're askin' I be the one to change, when they've run off, *again*?"

He tried not to scoff. "Give it a try, if you don't succeed, you can always fall back on the way things are done at present. You're a good mother, Mrs. Brandt. You just need to tweak your care of them."

A doubtful scowl on her rounded face, she gathered her shawl in a tight grip. "*Devil* take it, then!"

He bit his cheek rather than snicker as a war raged within her. He also sensed her great love for her daughters. "Good day to you then, ma'am." She nodded and gave the *Seasurf* one last scathing glare before tromping toward home.

If only his concern for Dino was as easily solved. He walked away from the lough up the Strand toward Market Street. The rolling hills of County Waterford stretched out beyond the village, mirroring the sun lowering in the sky. Vast expanses of golden light spread out over the emerald green grasses swaying with the song and drift of the wind. Beautiful country this, he recalled when he couldn't wait to set up practice here. A natural habitat for medical needs, Hawthorn Lough spread its deep waters northeast pouring into the River Suir an ancient waterway connecting County Waterford to the Celtic Sea and beyond.

Thanks to his partner, Tremaine, the financial outlay was shared. Though Christopher didn't have the income Tremaine came by with his aristocratic pedigree, Christopher's father had planned well. He and his two sisters were financially secure due to Morgan Curran's careful attention to finances. Christopher was born in Carrick-on-Suir where his father was a prominent council member and business owner.

The village of Carrick was roughly seventeen miles upriver on the Suir to the west from Hawthorn Village.

Christopher walked slowly up Sisters Lane hoping if Dino was hiding, he would feel comfortable enough to come out. He walked all the way to the Forge, Carnahan waved at him and Christopher stepped within the overhang where the man, protected by a leather apron, was fixing a horseshoe.

"Find the lad yet?" Carnahan called out.

Christopher shook his head and smoothed the neck of a well-muscled cob. They had several such in Carrick-on-Suir when he was a lad. He knew them to do very well for children as their disposition was gentle. He had learned to ride at the age of four on just such a horse. He remembered her to be a skewbald, Maggie was her name.

Carnahan barked above the hammering of metal on metal, "I wasn't aware you had a son."

Drawn from memories, he cast a blank look on Carnahan before it hit him what he asked, "I don't. He's an orphan off one of the ships. I thought to help."

"Ah, bad business that, doc. You'll have a houseful before you blink." Carnahan continued to slam the horseshoe with a mallet, shaping it.

"I'll get on my way, thanks for your advice."

"Anytime, doc. Anytime." His attention fully on the mallet smacking the shoe.

Christopher walked all the way to Church Street, hoping

against hope if the lad spied him, he would come forward. Walking down Strawberry Hill toward the infirmary, he saw nary a hint of the lad. So many little places, he could be anywhere.

Darby greeted him as he came in the back entrance. "No change, doc."

"Nothing. No sign at all." He hung his hat, then shrugged out of his tailcoat.

Checking on Schmitty, he listened to his heart and checked his pulse. Vital signs were slow, as to be expected given his diagnosis.

The rocker Darby vacated continued its motion for a bit, and for a moment, he again thought of Dino. Darby must have caught his thoughts because she said, "I sensed a distraught lad. Reminded me of a rabbit about to be caught in a snare. If he's able, he'll do what's in his best interest. You'll see."

Christopher nodded. He poured a cup of tea, took up two of Darby's scones, and retreated to his office. Though it was getting on to five o'clock, the front door rattled and in walked Mulroney.

"Wondering about the lad. I am. Has he come back?"

"No." Christopher twisted the book he was reading over on the desktop.

"I've written a piece for tomorrow's paper, wanted you to okay it." Mulroney placed it on top the book Christopher had been reading.

A young lad, Dino, is missing. Black hair, dark brown eyes, barefoot. About four feet tall. If you've seen him about, leave a message at the infirmary care of the doc, Mr. Curran.

"This is more than kind, Mulroney. You could add he was wearing a dark blue shirt, a cap, and brown knee-britches. You could also add his age, say eleven."

Mulroney reached over and took the paper from him. "I'll be glad to. Just trying to be a good neighbor." He folded the paper then added, "Sad thing these kids no homes, no family. Dino will be one of the lucky ones if he shows up, especially with you willing to care for him."

This was high praise from one of the elbow benders at the pub.

Christopher stood. "Thank you wholeheartedly, Mulroney. If this helps find him, I will be greatly indebted to you."

"Nah. It's Christian, it's the right thing to do. We're all in this life together, now aren't we?"

Christopher mulled over Mulroney's late afternoon visit. It brightened his soured attitude as he sat at his desk, absentmindedly reading a letter a professor from medical school wrote to him on the merits of mixing philosophy and medications for the betterment of his cliental. Which left Christopher with a smile on his face. The villagers appeared to need far more of the fundamental nature of living than of sound medical advice.

And then he remembered his promise to Shorty and Mr. Dooley. He donned his tailcoat and grabbed up his top hat. Then reached for his black bag and with disdain set it back down. Even though these were house calls, he would not need the contents of his medical bag.

He advanced directly toward Shorty's lean to. The cow was inside. Shorty, fists dug deep into side pockets swayed on the balls of his shoes. "Thought ye'd forgot."

"When did she stop giving milk?"

"Late yesterday. I noticed the calf didn't have foam after milking and tried to hand milk her."

Christopher sat on a stool, running his fingers over the udder which appeared to be congested. When he pressed with his fingertips, they left an indentation. "What happened when you milked her?"

"Nothing. I've had a milk cow forever. This one's new to me. I can't figure it out."

Christopher continued to evaluate the cow. "Have you tried a warm cloth pressed against the udder prior to milking? Sometimes doing so induces the milk to drop. Massage and warmth, then hand milk."

Shorty murmured something, then took off toward his cottage leaving Christopher alone in the shed with the cow, and a pesky calf eager to get to her source of food. He knew from his young days on their family acreage cows could have problems with udders. They had another milk cow to feed the calves. It looked to him as if Shorty had just the one, and one hungry calf.

Slopping a pail of water in his jaunt to reach the shed, Shorty's pants were soaked by the time he reached Christopher. "Here's yer warm water and some rags from the missus."

Christopher got up off the stool. "How about you sit here, wet the rags and apply them to the udder, which I believe is overfilled."

Grumbling, Shorty bent to the task. "I'm not one for milking."

"Must be your wife who does this then?" He glanced about the shed, tools stacked against the wall, hay neatly piled up.

"Yup. It's part and parcel of our agreement when I wed her. She said she'd take care of the stock if I took care of the land."

Christopher tried not to chortle. "Who agreed to do the cooking?"

Shorty tossed him a sullen look. "She does."

"The laundry?"

"What is it you were tryin' ta do here, doc, set us up a new agreement?"

"It might be fitting if this farm and cottage belong to both of you, you would share equal, and in times of trouble."

Shorty dipped the rags into the warm water again, squeezed the excess water out and continued rubbing the udder. The cow appeared to be enjoying the attention as she began chewing her cud once more. He groused, "She wanted to get wed. Me, I could have done without it, now couldn't I?"

Ignoring his caustic remark, Christopher said, "My next notion once you are done relaxing the udder, is to put the calf on the other two teats, and you milk the two on your side. She might let her milk down."

Within five minutes, it was obvious the maneuver worked. Foam formed on the calf's mouth proving she was milking, and Shorty was filling the pail with milk. "Yer not all that bad, doc. What do I owe ye?"

Christopher untied his apron. "Yes, well, thank you. Don't let word get out about this and I'll call it a partial payment." He tossed the apron over the stall door. "For the rest of the payment, how about you treat your wife as kindly you would like to be treated, and I'll call it even up."

Leaving the man with his mouth agape, and evening coming on, he walked a few streets over and knocked on Mr. Dooley's door.

"I'd about given up on you, doc. Susan set a place for you."

He took his tailcoat and hat off and rolled up his sleeves. "Let's get the wheel back on before it gets too dark."

"Follow me." Dooley strutted to the back of the cottage where the damage had occurred. A two-wheel cart on its side didn't exactly look like a two-man job to him.

"This is it?"

Dooley shrugged. "The wheels are special, fashioned with iron castings. I need help lifting it onto the axel."

"Have you the pins to hold it in place?"

Dooley scooped up two pins off the floor of the cart. "Right here, doc."

Christopher leaned over and grabbed one end of the wheel. "Let's make short work of this."

Dooley grabbed the other side, and they slid it on the point of the axel. Christopher balanced it in place and Dooley slid the pin in, and then hit it with a mallet to further drive it through the axel. Then he slid the second pin in and did the same.

Together they rolled the cart right-side up.

Christopher clapped his palms of the dust, rolled his sleeves down, and reached for his coat. "I'll be on my way."

"No, no. Doc, Suzy's got the table set, she'd be madder than a wet hen if you didn't join us. I can smell her roast chicken from here."

He smiled benevolently at the man. "You do not need to feed me after two minutes of work."

"She's just being friendly. As a favor to her then."

Christopher shoved his arms in his tailcoat, took his hat in hand and followed Dooley up the steps and into his cottage. He certainly didn't want to be judged as the patrons of the Black Pig had taken to doing. Perhaps he could do himself some good in company with this nice couple.

It became clear to him the whole wheel-off-the-cart, supper-as-thanks when he was introduced to Suzy's cousin, Jillian. A delightful young woman, she had flaxen hair and heavy brows over sparkling green eyes. She cackled like a hen, which she did a lot of every time he made a comment. As if he was the wittiest of conversationalists, which he knew he was not. He bordered on dull socially, far too serious.

Dooley obviously took note of the disparity early on and did his best to make Christopher comfortable. Until Jillian inquired about his medical education, asking, "Are you the kind of doctor who questions his patients about every little scrape and rash before you treat them?"

Suzy chimed in, "Jillian is from Cork where medicine is very much the vogue. Medicine is elevated to a science in her society."

Puzzled, Christopher said, "Medicine is clearly a science." He glanced over at Jillian. "Are you taking exception to a doctor inquiring of his patient's medical history?"

Raising her chin, slanting her gaze at him, she said, "I think it an intrusion. An utter disregard for one's privacy."

He dug deep for a sense of humor, realizing she had to be bating him. What possible purpose would she have otherwise. "I prefer to treat sick people who do not talk. Then I can be done with them in minutes and get on to something else."

Jillian sat to his left. She held a fork in midair and a knife in her right as she had been speaking. They clattered to her plate, and she engaged the use of a napkin to her pouty lips. "You deliberately misunderstood my initial question, sir. How careless of you."

"I apologize, ma'am."

Dooley was slowly shaking his head. His wife's cheeks were flushed with what? Surely not embarrassment?

Jillian retrieved her fork and knife, bent to the task of cutting into her chicken leg and ignored him as best she could, considering their proximity at the table.

To his way of thinking, Christopher decided Dooley knew the woman was a surly sort because he introduced a new subject. "Have you formed an opinion of Hawthorn Village, now yer settled in?"

"I was surprised to discover the number of sailors off the vessels who use my services. I don't understand why ships wouldn't employ a doctor."

"What kind of doctor would want to spend months on end sailing the seas?"

"Surely, not I," said Christopher before his next bite of a potato mash sprinkled heavily with butter and an herb he thought to be parsley.

Dooley claimed. "We are mighty fortunate to have Hawthorn lough allowing ships safe harbor thus giving them easier access to our village. There's talk of developing the Strand to accommodate more commerce." Dooley leaned in and inquired in a soft voice, "Did I read in the paper you lost a child?"

Christopher set his mug of watered wine down, giving thought to the question. "He is not from here, a child off a ship. I was providing him with shelter when he disappeared. Mulroney offered to put a notice in the *Tattler*."

Susan inquired, "Have you heard anything about the poor lad?"

"I am hoping he is in the kitchen waiting for supper."

Jillian came out of her funk and said, "If he's off one of the ships, he could be virulent with disease."

Christopher chuckled. "It is certainly a possibility, but I assure you he is not." He hoped the curator of this match-making dinner would realize her intention was *not* going to be fulfilled.

6

Renata Fitzjames walked the short distance to O'Bannon's Dry Goods for more suitable material for gowns. At home in Portugal, the village of Obidos to be specific, it was customary to wear a shawl over her head but noticed a better dressed woman in Hawthorn would wear a hat.

Hawthorns lanes were dreadful. She thought much worse than Obidos'. When wet, the lanes became a clay like substance. Since she and her mother arrived in the village, they had been leaving their shoes in the hall rather than track muck through the apartment. The maid, Lea, God forbid she should have to clean the floors.

The wardrobe Miss Fitzjames brought with her was thought quite fashionable in Obidos, but she was keenly aware it didn't suit in Hawthorn. A touch of ribbons and lace would spruce up her gowns. Perhaps O'Bannon's would have someone with whom to inquire about fashion.

The sky was filled with puffy white clouds, a slight breeze ruffling oak leaves and low-lying pink and lavender heather. Away from their apartment she calmed, not so anxious. It was difficult and conflicting living with her mother, Louisa. Renata often wondered if her father hadn't been more than willing to leave this world.

A donkey cart splashed through a puddle causing her to step to the boardwalk, just in time, too. A man with a long stick herded his flock of sheep around the corner with the help of a black and white collie. The dog dashed through the muck causing others to give them a wide berth as the four-legged shepherd performed his spirited duty.

The moment she opened the door of O'Bannon's, her spirits lifted with the wonderful colors of summer and displays of merchandise. Several women gathered around one table inspecting yarns. She headed toward the back of the store where shelves were filled with bolts every color of the rainbow. A luminous teal satin and a robin's egg blue in a twisted muslin, caught her eye. This would not be an easy decision.

She removed her glove and touched the silk. It was flawless and cool to her touch. A voice asked, "May I be of some assistance?"

Renata spun about and noticed a woman crowned with a braid of dark auburn hair streaked with gray. A bit taller than she, Renata was struck by her green eyes, sparkling with interest. "I'm in need of a gown or two." She patted the length of her skirt. "I've traveled for weeks in this gray outfit and it's had better times."

"Nuala O'Bannon at your service, I'll be very happy to assist you."

"Pleased to meet you. I'm Renata Fitzjames. My mother and I are recently arrived in your quaint village."

Nuala's gaze traveled over the gown she wore. "You're not so terribly out of date. Follow me. I've had a recent shipment from London." Nuala led her to the back of the store behind curtains separating the two spaces. "I hear it's the newest design—printed muslin. Renata ran her fingertips over the design, green leaves and multi-colored flowers. "Oh, so pretty."

Nuala offered, "Your English is very good. Do I detect a hint of Spanish?"

"Portuguese. I've been told I have remnants when speaking your tongue."

"Your English is near flawless." Nuala lifted a bolt of fabric. "Once I put this out front, it will be gone. My daughter wrote it's all the rage where they've been travelling."

Renata couldn't help but notice the modest pride in Nuala's voice. How lovely she had such an endearing relationship with her daughter.

Nuala said, "She and her husband, Lord Tremaine, married and traveled to Edinburgh to finish his education. After he graduated, they toured the continent. I expect them back in a month or so."

"You must miss her?"

Nuala's face lit up. "I do. It's quite a story, and someday I'll bore you with it. Your remaining family is in Portugal then?"

"My mother's family. But she is with me. My father was born in Carrick-on-Suir, and his desire was to be buried there. So, we've brought his ashes back. We preferred to stay in Hawthorn Village until we accomplished our task." A bit sheepish, she added, "My mother was adamant we would not stay in Carrick-On-Suir but refused to explain herself."

Nuala drew out a bolt of pale green sateen, with darker green dragon-fly embroidery to be used as the hem of a skirt. Renata thought it youthful and far too lovely for a twenty-seven-year old spinster.

"The color was made for you." Nuala unwound a length and draped a corner of it across Renata's shoulder then twisted her toward a full-length mirror in the corner. "Lovely against your olive skin. And compliments your green eyes."

She blinked then giggled, though it came out as a snort. She'd never worn anything so becoming. Surprising herself, she said, "I'll take it."

"Sally should be arriving any minute. We could enjoy a cup of tea if you have time?"

"I would like that very much."

A young woman entered from the back door, and Nuala

introduced Sally who promptly hung her coat and bonnet then put on an apron. Nuala said, "You take care of the front and I'll be out after tea." With a nod, Sally left them.

"Burying your father must be hard. How long has he been gone?"

"We would have arrived in the spring, but my mother felt it necessary to keep his urn on the shelf for others to notice." She sighed. "I'm revealing more than I ought. Sorry. I'm likely to bend your ear with none other to talk to these past weeks."

Nuala winked at her. "If you knew my past, you would rest assured I won't be holding you to any silly notions."

They smiled at each other and Renata hoped it might be the beginning of a friendship. "We'll see over time then, will we not?"

"Are you settling in?" Nuala drew the tea to her lips.

"I would be indebted if you could point me to an herbalist."

"You must begin your search at Mr. Talbot's apothecary shop. If anyone knows it would certainly be him."

A full hour passed with their chatter until Renata glanced at the bob she pinned to her gown. "Oh my, I've kept you far too long. I do want to purchase enough of the green sateen to make a gown. And the printed muslin. Perhaps you have the name of a seamstress?"

"Madam Browne, down a bit and across Market. The only seamstress I would recommend."

"I noticed the sign in her shop. We live above in the apartments."

"How convenient for your fittings."

As she left O'Bannon's Dry Goods, a feeling of ease engulfed her with the budding friendship. She was finding Hawthorn a friendly village and pleased they'd settled here for the time they would be in Ireland.

She crossed over muddy Market and made her way to Madam Browne's. The bell tinged as she opened the door. A full-bosomed, heavy-set woman flew through the drapes that concealed the back of the shop. "May I be of service?" Her curiosity fell to the package in Renata's arm.

"I would like two gowns using this material."

"Will this be for madam?"

"Yes."

"If you will follow me, we will retreat to my fitting room where I will take measurements. Do you have a design in mind?"

"I…something more stylish than I am wearing. Your suggestions will be considered, as I am unsure. Mrs. O'Bannon sent me."

"She's Lady Rutledge but won't go by it." Madam Browne reached for her cloth tape and a pad and pencil.

"I didn't realize. She never said." Renata eyed the writing utensil madam used.

"That's her way, she wouldn't. She's as modest as can be. Some say stubborn."

"May I ask what you are writing with?"

Madam smiled. "First time I saw one of these, I was surprised, too. They are called pencils. They write with a substance called graphite. A gentleman from Germany gave me several."

Once they fixed on a more modern style, Renata promised to present herself for a second fitting in three days. Pleasantly surprised the woman could work so fast. "I live in an apartment above your shop."

"I think I noticed when you moved in. Was it your mother who sat in the carriage until the last of your goods were taken in, two weeks ago now maybe?"

On that precise, horrid day, her mother threw her latest fit. She could barely look at the seamstress wishing she could claim the woman was another. "Yes, that would be my mother."

"Well, it is a pleasure to meet you, Miss Fitzjames." She folded up some lace she looked at and obviously discarded. "I recall my mother when we moved. It puts a strain on them as they age."

Renata felt relieved. "Yes, for sure. And we'd just come off the boat. She was most uncomfortable. Even Lea, her maid, couldn't console her."

Mrs. Browne gave her a quirky grin. "Disagreeable?"

She smiled.

"Lookin' at you, I'd say you're from Spain, maybe Portugal?"

"Yes, Portugal. A small village with miles and miles of rolling hills filled with grapes. Would you be familiar with Obidos?" She was a bit flattered by the question.

"No, but there's a look about you, and I love maps when I come by them. My late husband was a captain. Once in a great while I sailed with him, until I opened this shop. I guess I could say anchoring myself to it." A sheepish look came over her. "I go on, sorry. Give me three days with this printed muslin. I've not seen a pattern that's not embroidered. Something new in textiles."

Then she swept her fingertips over the embroidery of the darker green sateen. "This will look perfect on you. I'll edge the hem with the dragonflies."

Done with taking Renata's measurements, Mrs. Browne folded the green sateen, placing tissue between the folds. She swept her palm across the dragonfly embroidery once again. "Nuala's been holding out on us. Will a week from today be convenient for a fitting?"

Renata fairly skipped out of the seamstress' shop and strolled along the boardwalk. It was such a lovely day she really didn't care to return to the apartment and looked for the apothecary sign instead.

She hadn't far to go when she encountered a cream-colored sign reading Old Town Apothecary, Est. 1750. The blunt end of a pestle jutting out of a mortar offered further proof she'd found what she was looking for.

The bell jingled as she entered the shop, and was immediately struck by the pungent medicinal odors, spices, and aromatics. A man she would guess in his fifties, glanced at her. He had an abundance of dark hair streaked with gray, glasses perched on his nose, and lots of freckles.

"Good morning, ma'am. What can I do for you?"

"Miss Fitzjames, sir. I would like to talk to you about an idea I have."

He looked down at her over the top of his glasses. "What might that be?"

"Quite recently I moved here from Portugal. I have an interest in herbals, and Ireland boasts a vast array of such." She set her reticule on the counter and wished she had brought the book her Tia Agnes gave her. "My question, sir, is it possible you could use some assistance, anyway I could possibly help and be of use in your shop?"

He pushed his glasses up further on his nose and gave her all his attention. "Now why would a pretty thing like you want to work here?"

She had never been acknowledged as pretty. The comment almost made her blush. "I—I wouldn't expect you to pay me."

"Besides your interest, what would draw you to a dark, cramped space such as I have?" Was he attempting to provoke her? Did he think her too fragile to work in a place like this?

"I have a great interest in medical herbs." She glanced about the small stacked drawers each with its own label, and shelves with numerous jars of medicines. His counter space housed an immense brass scale and balance pan, all shown to advantage with the six windows against the far wall spreading light. "This is a lovely space. I envy your talent and could learn much I'm certain."

With a sour look, as if he didn't believe her, he asked, "You want me to believe your *interest* in herbs and medicine is enough to warrant working here?" His palms were spread on the counter, fingers spread wide as he leaned close.

She dug in her bag. "I have proof of classes I've taken. Will that help?" She drew out several papers stamped with the University of Coimbra's seal and showed them to him.

He began reading, pushed his glasses up on his nose, looked at the next page, quickly glanced at her with narrowed sight then back to the pages. She doubted he could understand the language in Portuguese. But the seal might be impressive enough for him. And the basic courses in medicines had root words in Latin—surely an apothecary was familiar with Latin.

"You attended the University, then?"

"I wasn't allowed to enroll, but I could sit in as long as I didn't cause a commotion."

"Whatever sparked your interest in science?"

"Tia Agnes, my mother's sister, was the influence. Their father taught at the University. He took my Tia with him when he taught his science classes. When I began to show an interest long after my grandfather was gone, the University allowed her to bring me. It was a privilege I treasure."

The doubt on his face soured her confidence, she anticipated a resounding *no*. "Follow me, miss." Talbot led her to a curtained doorway into a back room. "This is the only workspace I have."

She glanced about the musky room. Though dusty with only one window, she spied a fireplace and a door that probably led to the alley. Several tables held stacks of big clumsy strainers; shiny pill tiles and a bolus knife; spatulas protruding from a jar; and another apothecary scale with its odd little weights stamped with scruples, drams, and ounces. Empty jars of various colors were stacked on shelves.

"I could make this do. Would you possibly consider my request?" She tried to keep her dignity and not beg.

He scratched the back of his head, then tucked his freckled hands into the pockets of his apron, rolling on the balls of his feet. "I don't really need anyone. I manage quite well on my own."

When there wasn't a *but*, she pleaded, "I won't be a bother if you fear I might."

"What would be your purpose, then?" He walked over to the curtain dividing the front from the back and drew it aside ensuring he didn't have a customer.

Renata said, "I live in a small apartment with my mother and have no occupation as such. It is on my mind perhaps I could bring my herbals and books in here and come in each day—or if it would be too disruptive for you, every other day and do my reading. Perhaps I could dry my herbs on the stakes in those beams?" She pointed above.

He followed her direction and scratched his head again. "I suppose there's no harm. We could give it a try, Miss Fitzjames."

She wanted to hug him but felt he was on the brink of a refusal and didn't want to push her luck. She curtsied instead, causing him to accentuate his freckles with a blush, of all things.

"I'm so grateful. And I'll sweep up and dust if you like."

His gaze set firmly on her. "I don't see a woman before me who has done much if any cleaning. More like you've been well kept. What does your father have to say about all this?"

"It so happens my father is the reason we've come to Hawthorn. He has passed, and we've brought his ashes to bury in the town where he was born."

"Fitzjames, is it? Here in Hawthorn?"

"No, he was born in Carrick-on-Suir; but my mother preferred to stay in this village."

"I don't recall the name, but if he lived in Carrick, it might explain why."

Eagerness trilling in her mind, she asked, "When would it be convenient for my trunk to be delivered?"

"Trunk, is it?" He scanned the room. "I shouldn't be surprised you'd have a library now, should I? You're an organized and dedicated lass."

Now it was her turn to blush. "It's been a fascination of mine for a long time. And with our settling here for a while, I didn't want to be without my research."

"All right then, Miss Fitzjames. We'll give it a try. Bring your things over and begin when you want. I'll make some sense of all this." He half-heartedly waved at the tables smattered with the paraphernalia of his profession. "I can't abide keeping you from something you hold with such reverence. I'll say this much, you've quite an education to guide you."

Embarrassed at his enthusiasm, she gave him a slight curtsy

and fairly skipped out the door but not before she promised he wouldn't regret his decision.

She walked across a grassy expanse not a block from the lough and its park with benches and majestic pines, ash, and oaks. She was grateful for Mr. Talbot's generosity. and pondered the next few weeks and months filled with her passion. Ireland was such a lush land, green hills, blue sky, birds chirping. Obidos was dry and hilly. Her homeland was parched compared to Hawthorn.

Renata was suddenly overcome with the last few days, their arrival and settling in, and calming her mother. Drained of energy, she sat on a bench taking in the bustle of Hawthorn's villagers going about their daily routines. The lough rippled with a low wind coming in off the mighty Suir. A family of wild geese wobbled their offspring across the grass and cast her a beady glance probably looking for assurance she meant no harm.

A sense of freedom washed over her. Was it the distance from her grim mother and the ever-fawning Lea? Or was it the beautiful sateen green? She smiled at the thought.

"Everything all right, ma'am?"

A stocky man, ears big enough his helmet couldn't contain them. His frock coat had seen better days. A belt held his sword in place. "I'm fine, thank you."

"Constable Waffer, ma'am." He gave a slight nod. "You must be new, then?"

"Yes, two weeks now. My mother and I."

"You're not loitering. Never fear. I like to ken folks livin' in my jurisdiction is all. If you are ever in need of help, my office is at the gaol up on Stoney Batter. You can leave a note under the mat if'n I'm out."

"That is kind of you, sir." She shooed a butterfly fluttering at the brim of her hat.

He gave her another nod and appeared to be making up his mind to linger or walk on. When suddenly he said, "You don't walk out after dark, I'd be thinkin'."

"I haven't had occasion to, why do you ask?"

"Not to worry you, ma'am. But there's mischief afoot in Christ's Church graveyard at night. I'd keep my far distance if'n I'd be you. Haven't had the chance to catch the culprit. But I'm on it, rest assured."

Quite surprised, she glared at him. "Why would I have reason to be there at night, or at all, for that matter?"

He adjusted the belt holding his sword, his chin rose, and he met her gaze. "I'm just doin' my duty, ma'am. And you're new to the village, I thought to be neighborly." Tipping his military hat, he meandered on his way.

She sat for a while longer, fussing over the real reason the constable stopped. Could he possibly know her plans were to settle the remains of her father? She bristled at the notion. Arguing with herself how on earth would he? She was not confident about dealing with her father's ashes and allowed herself to think he could see through her.

Clouds lazily floated past in the light blue sky, and her thoughts settled on her father. Born and raised in southeast Ireland, she wondered why her parents had ever left this lush green paradise.

Arriving at the apartment she stopped at the neighbor's knocking on their door. Mona Cooke, quite ponderous expecting her second child soon, puffed as she greeted her. "Good day to you."

"I hope I'm not bothering you, Mrs. Cooke, Would your husband know of two lads strong enough to carry a trunk of mine to Mr. Talbot's apothecary?"

"He surely would. When he gets home, he'll come over."

Later, during supper Renata's mother, complimented the maid, Lea, on the salmon and greens purchased at the market earlier in the day. It was clear she was attempting to encourage Lea to learn the English/Irish of the locals. The maid was a stubborn girl resisting her mother's efforts.

Renata thought it was a waste of ship's fare bringing the girl. But her mother had insisted. "Why is she so set against learning at least a few words in English?"

Louisa patted the sides of her mouth and placed the napkin on her lap before addressing her daughter's remark. "Because she knows we will not be long in this country. Today's market was filled with local peasants, rags holding their hair in place, children barefoot."

Renata took a long time chewing her fish. If she reminded her mother their homeland also had barefooted children and women in rags sarcasm would drip from her words and that would not do.

Lea carried a hot dish with pads to protect her fingers and set it in the middle of the table. Her dark inspection shifted to Louisa, who asked, "What delightful dish is this?"

With a curtsy, Lea replied, "It is spinach and bacon to remind you of home," and twirled on her shoe toward the kitchen sending her veils in a swirl.

Renata knew what she was up to, and quickly put another bite of fish in her mouth, ever thankful for Mr. Talbot's generosity in allowing her a space in which to retreat.

Louisa cast a dour glance at her daughter. "She is lovely to think of us yearning for home. I am grateful she agreed to accompany me. I don't intend keeping her here long. She'll suffer so." And with that, she brushed crumbs from her bosom and dug into the dish of spinach and bacon.

Renata fished a bone from between her lips. Her visits around Hawthorn, making a friend, and the thrill of new gowns were such a delight, she tried not to allow her mother's longing for home overcome her recent good fortune. "Please excuse me, I've reading to do."

Her elder looked down her nose. "What reading would force you to your dreary room?"

"I made it my goal to learn of the herbals in this part of the world. And the book Tia Agnes gave me is a great help."

"Bah! That silly sister of mine, always with her head in the clouds. What possible interest are those dirty little plants?" Her mother's heavy arms bulged at the seams. She might need Mrs. Browne's sewing expertise for a new gown.

"Oh, Mother, please. It is a hobby I enjoy. While I was out, I shopped at O'Bannon's and discovered some lovely material for gowns. You might want to do the same."

"Not in this village. There would be nothing here to satisfy me." Squinting at her daughter, she grumbled, "I've the finest silks in all of Portugal at my beck and call. Why ever do you think I could be satisfied with crude materials from this dirty little place?" The spinach dish finally cooled, she scooped a spoonful into her mouth, making a noise of satisfaction.

"You're wrong, Mother. Irish handiwork is truly fine. Wait until you see the creation Mrs. Brown is sewing for me." She put the napkin on the table then stood. "If you'll excuse me."

"Bah!"

She held a smile until her back was to her mother and opened the latch to her room. The small window seat drew her, and with enough light still in the sky, she had the perfect spot to read. She sat on the ledge, peering into the distance, over rooftops and tall trees to the mountains far away into the west. Just dark enough, the purplish ridges were beginning to blend with the blue sky.

The part of her that was her father's daughter must be why she loved Ireland. Her mother had made it known through the years, she was never so happy as when they left the island in their early marriage and sailed to her family in Portugal.

Later, during the times her parents argued, she heard it all as their marriage soured even more. The accusations, the dissatisfaction, disharmony. But, of course, since her father's death, their household quieted. If Renata treated her mother with respect and kept her distance from serious personal sharing, their relationship was usually sanguine.

Birds flew in the air, settling into their nests for the eve. Constable Waffer was in the process of lighting the lamps. If she strained a bit to the east, she could just make out the sway of ships' masts poking the sky, reminding her of their journey to this place.

This quaint village was so unlike her homeland. It was a lush green not dusty and dry. They planned to return to Portugal as soon as she carried out her father's dying wish. She still didn't know how to accomplish *that* but vowed she would find a way.

Her father hated Morgan Curran with a vengeance. His intention was to bedevil him through eternity by having his ashes buried as close to Morgan's grave as possible.

Mr. Cooke's rap on the door interrupted her thoughts and she quickly walked into the living area just as Lea bade him enter.

He nodded at her mother seated in her corner chair where she had already established the habit of looking out over the street below in the evenings. Renata greeted him. "Thank you for stopping. The trunk is here in the corner."

He grabbed a leather strap on the end and lifted it a mite. "This should be no problem a'tall. Tomorrow, early if possible, we'll drop if off on our way to the docks."

"I am so grateful. What will I owe you?"

He smiled at Mrs. Fitzjames, whose attention was firmly set on the street below, then to Renata. "A neighborly favor, miss. Nothing more."

7

The next day, Dino had not returned. Christopher saddened by his absence, and with Darby in attendance on Schmitty, he hurried to the chemist to replenish a few items before the rain clouds loosened their hold. He hadn't given up Dino might come out of hiding and once more walked up on Forge toward Stephen's Lane where a thick woodsy growth could conceal a lad. He also realized he hadn't inquired of Darby if she used honey to calm down the impetigo.

The chemist's bell pinged as he opened the door.

"Good day, Mr. Curran." Christopher nodded and advanced to the back of the shop glancing at the shelf full of bottled labels in meticulous alpha order.

"What'll it be?" Mr. Talbot, glancing over the rim of glasses, stuffed his hands inside the pocket of his white apron.

"I'm running low on colchicum and myrrh."

Mr. Talbot reached across Christopher, plucking a jar off the shelf. "Colchicum, enough to treat a dozen folks. And will keep quite nicely in this container." He gave it over and moved across the room behind his desk. "I keep myrrh over here. I've misplaced some of my inventory and thought it better to put it where I could keep watch."

Christopher considered Mr. Talbot wouldn't outrightly claim theft. He knew some favored it as a pleasant perfume, otherwise he could think of no reason why anyone would steal it. As he waited while the chemist wrapped the items, he asked, "You wouldn't have noticed a young lad, new to these parts, would you?"

Talbot shook his head. "I can't say. Then I don't get on the lanes much until after hours." He gave over the package adding, "I'll put this on your bill. Must be a bit of gout to be cured, eh?"

"Surely. At university, one of the professors swore to its healing power when blisters present in the mouth. I have an unusual case and might consider this if the situation doesn't calm down soon."

Leaving the chemist's, his long legs stretched out toward the strand, he thoughtfully scanned the ships in the harbor. Masts gently swaying with the tide, the *Nomad* was one of five in port. He blew out a breath of relief and headed home.

Darby fried up a mackerel for dinner. He checked on Schmitty whose breathing hadn't changed, his facial features in peaceful repose. Feeling the patient's forehead, his body temperature appeared normal. Christopher moistened the patient's lips without getting a reaction.

Back in the kitchen, he asked Darby, "Did you put honey on the impetigo?"

"I did, and the itch is near gone."

"Glad to hear it." He grinned at her. "The cure didn't come from any medical journal I've read. My late aunt used to put honey on rashes of any kind, and I never forgot it. Any hint of Dino?"

Shaking her head, she swung the griddle with the fish, its fat crackling and spitting, away from the fire. "Ye've got it in yer head to get on that vessel, haven't you now?"

Christopher's attention drifted to the dense oak and hawthorn, framed by the window, wishing Dino was hiding within the thicket. Christopher's routine had taken a complicated twist. He enjoyed the challenge of solving illness, but somehow, he'd become more deeply involved with the small lad in a very short span of time, hours in truth. Confronting the ruthless Captain of the *Nomad* seemed the only probable solution. "There's no other course of action."

Darby divided the mackerel into two servings sliding each on plates along with potatoes and a leafy concoction of greens and tomatoes. "Will you manage if I wash up and leave for the night?"

"To be sure, Sean will be after me if you spend any more time here." He forked a good-sized bite of the mackerel, enjoying the sauce she sprinkled over the top. "Is this gooseberry?"

"Ye've a good nose, doc. Sean's happy as a clam on the boat for a week, and glad for the work, believe me. I feel like I'm on a break right now. Ye're easier to pick up after than that old goat."

A faint groan came from the bedroom. Schmitty's arm flopped off the bed and somehow the coverlet was on the floorboards. Knowing periods of a rally could occur, Christopher had thought Schmitty was deeper into the disease. He had not wrongly diagnosed the symptoms he'd swear to it. He tucked the blanket in place, washed his hands and returned to the kitchen.

Darby finished her mackerel and was at the washboard cleaning up. "I'll keep a watch out for the boy. If he's afraid, he'd avoid my home, yours too, mayhap he's keeping low." She turned to look at him. "Did you notice the *Nomad*? Was it in port?"

He nodded.

"Ye'll not be satisfied 'till you go out there?"

He nodded again.

She continued her duties. "A nonsense thing to do, doc. Confronting the likes of them with yer suspicions. I've heard it said, they take people like you 'cause of all the things what can happen on the seas."

Christopher bristled. "I won't be labeled a coward."

Her jaw gaped. "I would'na think such a thing. Hawthorn Village needs you a sight more than that floating mess of filthy..."

"Whoa." His palms shoved the air between them.

She wiped soap from her hands and then folded the cloth and laid it over the washboard. "Let me check if he's hiding at my place before you go out there. You can make your decision in the mornin' when I come, then." When he didn't respond, she spoke up. "Hear me?"

He glanced up from the table, his gaze shifted to the bedroom, a dying man within. "Dino called him his friend, the only one he had. I find it hard to believe he's not here unless he's been taken. The only way to be certain is for me to go out to that rig and confront a heinous man."

Darby rolled her eyes. "As I said, give it a night before you do. I'll come around mid-morning and stay."

Scraping his chair back, he said, "You're a Godsend, Darby."

True to her word, Darby came through the front door mid-morning, basket filled with carrots and greens slung over her arm. She stopped at the open door to his office. "How goes the patient?"

Christopher shuffled some papers together and set them on the corner of his desk. He stood, put the cap on his inkwell and shut the pages of a ledger, and said, "He got through the night with little commotion. Unbelievable stamina. What I do know, he's on borrowed time." He came around the desk and followed her down the corridor to the kitchen.

Leaning against the sideboard, he inquired, "I take it you saw no hint of the lad?" Pursing her lips, her head shook, the gray scarf tied to keep her long dark hair off her face. "Wish I could say so."

"I'm off then." Christopher grabbed his hat off the hook and left through the back door. Anxious to confront the captain of the *Nomad*, he headed straight to Padhraig's dory down on the Strand when, much to his surprise, he noticed the unmistakable shapes of two women rowing toward the dock.

He waited until they climbed out of the dory, anchored it, and came up toward him. "You would be Mrs. Brandt's daughters?" Rebuffing him they sauntered past exchanging glowers, the same round faces as their mother. "What of it?" sneered the shorter of the two.

"I'm Mr. Curran, and your mother has been quite worried about you." Stronger than usual this morning, the smell of saltwater pinched his nose. Clusters of kelp slapped against the shore with each pulse of the water.

"So, you be the doc, then?" At his nod, the elder of the two narrowed her gaze. "She stirs up everyone. We're sick and tired of it all. Easy to see you've stuck your nose into our business, then." It wasn't a question.

His jaw clenched as he looked at the self-satisfied lasses, smug with what they thought as a solution to the future. Did they truly believe they could spend several days aboard a ship filled with men and not compromise their health, and not contemplate the possibility of a resulting pregnancy?

The shorter one mimicked him. "You think you ken it all, but we've got our future to consider and it won't be including' that one." Her gaze shifted over his shoulder and he looked back to observe Mrs. Brandt hastily approaching, the ends of her shawl sailing behind her. "She's already run off our da…he got out when the gettin' was right."

"Mother of God!" Huffing, Mrs. Brandt practically cried out the words. "I'm so glad to see you, welcome home, come now, I've plenty food, you must be starved. Did they feed you then?"

Like a bolt out of the blue, their mouths slackened with disbelief. Mrs. Brandt slipped an arm about each, and as the three rotated toward home, she winked at him.

The morning sun glistened off the lough all the way to the inlet where the lough met the River Suir. A deep sigh cleared his lungs as Christopher rotated from one more problem solved; and took on another as he noted the *Nomad*, shifting gently with the tide.

He knew what he had to do and stepped into the dory. Short of an hour later, he came alongside the *Nomad* with a distinct feeling he'd been spotted earlier as the direction he rowed would take him to this vessel for the others were at anchor a bit upwind. "Ahoy!"

"What can I do you?" An old, leathered face with a faded red bandanna wrapped about the tendrils of greasy hair peered over the ships' rail.

"I'd like a word with your captain."

The tar squinted at him. "Who might you be?"

"Mr. Curran. He knows me."

Captain Redeye stepped to the rail, looking down at him. His baritone reaching the dingy. "I take it Schmitty's dead?"

Christopher seized the suggestion. "He's alive, but barely."

"You came all this way to tell me?" He noted the captain knew better from the sarcasm in his voice.

"No. I've come about the lad."

"What of him?"

"Is he onboard?"

A vigorous guffaw emitted from the foul man. "Hightailed it, did he." His dark face screwed in a sneer, he leaned over, grinning as if he knew where the lad was. "If he's onboard, it's by choice."

Christopher calculated the captain hadn't found Dino because of the immediate delight. Yet, he couldn't totally forfeit the possibility Dino wasn't aboard. Feeling at a great disadvantage to demand anything of this man, he asked, "Is there anyone to be notified when Schmitty dies?"

The captain had withdrawn from the railing, but the old leathery face of the tar peered at him. "We're the only family 'e had. And cap'n already told us about 'im not bein' long for this 'er life."

Christopher shook his head in a fleeting gesture as he gripped the oars and began the row back to land. The prow pointed toward shore his gaze riveted on the *Nomad* as he stroked the blades through the water. But for Redeye's last comment it would appear a certainty Dino remained in Hawthorn Village. But where? And why did he avoid the infirmary? He noted Redeye climbed the helm scanning the horizon with a glass. It dawned on Christopher he would be aware if Dino was out in the open. Christopher realized Dino was aware of it.

With each squeak of the oarlock, Christopher prayed Dino was not on the ship. He had a sense the *Nomad* would pull out with the tide later in the day.

When he stepped into the infirmary, Darby informed him there had been no change in Schmitty. A stew bubbled in the pot over the fire, and his outer office was empty. He was grateful for both and sat at his desk shuffling some papers about, his mind full of the whereabouts of the lad. In all the years of medical school, he still wasn't prepared to accept the abduction and forced degradation of a small lad. Running free must be a Godsend to him —no longer enslaved. Prudent as Christopher was, he couldn't let go the word *if.* Because he wasn't convinced Dino wasn't being held against his will in the bowels of the *Nomad.* Maybe it was his pessimism dwelling on the worst.

Late evening and before Darby headed back to her place, Christopher stood on the Strand. The Nomad's sheets were up and stretching with the wind drawing the ship south beyond the harbor toward the Celtic Sea. Darkness descended upon him, knotting his stomach.

He walked the entire length of the Strand, then on to Church Street, his mood pensive as he reached the marshy land south of the village. Glancing over the reeds and limestone rocks dotting the area, he wondered if Dino had ever caught frogs, or tossed a ball with someone. Things he, Christopher, had done as a lad.

Constable Waffer came up to him, his matches and wick on a pole already about the business of lamp lightning. "Wavin' someone off, doc?"

Christopher shrugged. "Ah, no. I pray not, anyway. On your walk about, would you keep watch for a lad, barefoot, dirty, comes up to here about," he noted above his waist.

Waffer's skepticism shifted to kindness. "That I'll do, doc."

Darby had her pail, mop and satchel sitting on the back step when he opened the door, greeted by a dour look.

"I should have come back sooner. Sorry." He hung his hat on

the hook and used his palms as a bracer against the washboard and leaned.

From the table she gave him a questioning glance. "Sorry, are you? I'm sure as rain lookin' at sorry. Your face is hangin' like a dog without a bone. All over the lad? Or 'tis the bunch at the Pig got you down?"

A long minute ensued where he thought of an answer, then decided against mockery of her sincere inquiry. "Nothing of the sort. A bit tired perhaps. A long day, and yet I don't have much to look back on."

Her skeptical glance showed she wasn't buying it. "I've had the pleasure of knowing you since when your pa let you tag along when he was on business in Hawthorn. I'm not a stupid sort. It's that lad, Dino, and you've got to get over it. Whether he's on the ship or not, he's no concern anymore. He's had to shift for himself and has no other way. He's more like a wild animal, it's his own kind of freedom he lives, not the way you live." She slapped her hand on the table, indicating she'd spoken the truth and that's that.

He couldn't help but smile. "I've known you for as long as I have memory. You've not changed one bossy bit." He pushed off the washboard and peeked in on Schmitty.

"I'll be getting on, then. A couple of the women are demonstrating tatting tonight, and I've been eager to learn." The chair scraped against the wooden planked floorboards as she pushed it under the table.

He swung back into the kitchen, intending to show his appreciation for her kindness. "Your friendship means a lot, Darby."

Her hand on the door latch, she answered, "I'll drop by mid-morning and check how things are going with him." She nodded her head toward the bedroom.

Christopher's choices for the evening were ledgers, Schmitty, or pour himself a few drams of brandy and catch up on his reading. The brandy won, the reading maybe not.

8

C hristopher woke from a night filled with action and cruelty, exhausting him. He didn't pop out of bed immediately but thought about the children without parents, and the hungry and uneducated in the world. Obviously, on some level, the dream was about Dino, but he couldn't fix what he couldn't find. He blamed it on the Irish in him.

His parents were industrious. His mother easy going, quiet. His father was a hard man who didn't suffer fools. As a lad, he knew they were respected by the village folk. His father helped build the foundation for the town clock in 1784. As a youngster, he had been impressed with the shiny brass plate on the foundation of the clock Morgan Curran etched in big letters.

His father also created the toll road out of Carrick toward Dublin, which was still maintained to this day as a major thoroughfare and among the biggest at almost forty feet wide with gutters on each side.

His mother, Lucille Butler, came from a family heavily involved in the fishing industry, which expanded to include the growing woolen industry as the last century ended. Christopher was raised in a household with two older sisters. Molly, the eldest, lived in Dublin with an elder aunt. Rose married James Hawley and now has three lasses, and two lads and they live in Lillybrook, the family home in Carrick.

Christopher rolled over and lifted the curtain at the window. The fog wouldn't last long once the sun was up. As his feet dropped to the wooden planks he drew on breeches and pulled on a clean white shirt tying the collar closed then padded to the kitchen. A groan from the patient's bedroom drew him to the doorway rather than boil water. He stood there in complete and utter disbelief.

Curled up on the bed with Schmitty was Dino, his arm and leg thrown over the sick man as if protecting him from the world. Christopher's intense relief caused him to smart with emotion. He stood there for a long time drinking in the sight of the boy wrapped around the only friend he had in the world. Dino's devotion to someone who had been kind to him aboard the *Nomad* was beyond anything Christopher had ever witnessed. He silently backed away.

In his office with a cup of tea, he pondered the remarkable ability of one so young to be so kind, especially considering the way he was abused. At such a young age, he was remarkably adept at discernment.

Deep in thought, Christopher concentrated on his twiddling thumbs, when he became aware of someone else in the room. Dino stood in the doorway as if unsure he should enter the office.

Christopher asked, "Are you hungry?"

The young voice, sounding as if it hadn't been used much in the last few days, graveled, "I could eat a horse but there's no jam."

With a hearty laugh, he pushed back his chair. "Were we robbed? Are you absolutely certain?"

The weary down-cast child confessed in a remorseful tone, "I was dastardly afraid."

Christopher's heart clutched and he bent to Dino gripping his shoulder. "I'm guessing you waited until the *Nomad* sailed."

He answered with a short nod, those piercing, child-eyes locked on Christopher.

Christopher's heart clutched as he considered the suffering and abominations in his short life. Periodically they were bound to burst out of him like thorny reminders of what he endured. Christopher had long since made up his mind to strive for normalcy with Dino, yet never deny him his revelations. He prayed that over time they would diminish as Dino grew into a different way of life.

Christopher pinched his nose and sighed. "I'll have to say something to Darby. She keeps us in jam. Hopefully, we'll never run out again."

Dino's dirty face flashed a grin. "Me too, doc. I expect to never get trapped again like what I was."

The pain Christopher felt scorched his soul. "If it's within my power, son, you will never have to fear torment of any kind. And, now you've come home, let's get something to eat. I could eat a horse, too, but not with jam on it."

Cakes fried up a golden brown, bacon crisp, and a rare orange cut in pieces served as their breakfast. Syrup, an earlier offering from Darby replaced the jam Dino craved. Christopher warmed to the sight of the young boy literally diving into what might be his first meal since delivering the message to Darby and then taking himself into hiding.

Sipping hot tea laced with honey, Christopher sat back in his chair and enjoyed the presence of this youngster. "I looked everywhere for you."

Swiping a drip of syrup from his chin, Dino didn't glance up as he pierced another fried cake. "I saw you, several times. Figured what you were doin'. But I couldn't take a chance."

"I rowed out to the *Nomad*. Talked with the captain. He left me with a sense you might be aboard."

"A wily man, he is. I wish you hadn't gone out there. I worried mightily when I saw what you were doin'."

Christopher drew on his tea watching the lad make short work of the cakes.

Dino set the fork down, swiped at his mouth with the towel puddled on the planked table. "I've got an ache in my heart for the next one. I wasn't the first, so I won't be his last." His gaze cast downward. "I'm grieved."

"That's because you have God in your heart. And look where He led you, to a man who needs a friend. God watches over all of us. And someday, the captain will reap destruction. It's kind of a law, *Ye reap what ye sow.*"

The lad took a deep breath and let it out slow. His eyes razed from the empty plate before him to Christopher. "You're a good man, doc."

Scraping back his chair, Christopher stood gathering the plates from the table. "You might not think so, once I've told you what's in store for you."

Dino's jaw dropped a bit, his Adam's apple bobbing in his skinny throat.

Christopher continued as if he hadn't noticed the distorted fear. "There will be school for you, and chores, and cleanliness, and studies to adhere to. And, most importantly, you will tell me if you *EVER* get a notion to slip away from this home—your home, or *EVER* feel threatened by someone."

Dino jumped up from the chair and threw his arms about Christopher's waist, snuggling his face into the tall man's stomach. Christopher stroked his head, feeling wetness on his cheek. They stayed huddled until Dino loosened his hold and swiped at his face, sniffling. "This God sure knows what I want."

"Yes, it's kind of the way He works. Now, first up, *you* are in desperate need of a bath. We'll put water on to boil and haul in the tub from the shed. Schmitty isn't going to care if we set it up in his room. I think Darby put those clothes she got for you in the cupboard."

Christopher, at his desk, twiddled with papers, opened then

closed a medical journal. He heard a heart-warming distraction of a small voice humming a tune from the back of the infirmary.

The humming was replaced with splashes of water hitting the floorboards then quiet. Soon enough the likes of which he'd not noticed since meeting Dino, a handsome lad, black hair smoothed back with the use of a comb, clean short pants, a white cotton blouse almost too large, sleeves folded up to his wrists, and laced at the collar, woolen hose and sturdy shoes.

"What have you done with Dino?"

A chuckle mixed with his little voice. "He's a puddle of mud in the tub. I'm what's left."

"Darby will be along soon, then you and I will go meet Mrs. Hurley. She's the teacher at Hawthorn's charity school."

The chuckle left his voice. "I don't want charity."

"It's a name given to the school when it was built years ago, meant to say all children are welcome."

"Oh." He slowly walked about the room as if inspecting it. Christopher knew he hadn't taken consideration of the infirmary early on; he had been far too concerned with saving himself from Redeye.

The backdoor opened, and Darby's voice carried down the hall. "Hello, I'm here."

"You've got some explaining to do, Dino. I suggest you scoot in the back and give that well-meaning woman some good news."

What Christopher heard from his desk in the front of the building was delightful. One second her thrilling *oohs* and *aahs* another the edgy scolding of which he'd never heard from her. He joined them in the kitchen. Darby was suffocating the lad with a bear hug, which only her ample self could be worthy.

Dino's dismay caused his eyes to bulge. She released him from her motherly affection, and he stepped backward, drawing in a long breath. "Well," said she, "the pants are a good fit, but the sleeves are a bit long. How do the shoes feel? Being as how you preferred bare feet."

Dino flashed Christopher a questioning glance, as if he looked for guidance. Christopher shrugged. "She asked you, not me."

"I'll get on. I'm thinkin' it'll take a bit gettin' used to."

"Be sure to always wear stockings. They'll keep from letting your toes and heels blister."

"I've had blisters. Ain't no fun."

"Ah, so you've worn shoes before." She was busy folding a towel and hanging it over the drying rack.

"They came from the strap. Are they the same as from shoes? 'Cause maybe I don't want to wear shoes."

Christopher narrowed his gaze from the lad and glanced out the window. "The blisters from the strap, have you got any on you now?"

"A couple on my back are bothersome. It takes a lot of time to not feel them anymore."

Christopher sat in the chair. "Let me look. I've got an ointment might just be the cure to hurry the process."

With the sincerity of youth, Dino had revealed one of the uglier sides of enslavement. Christopher squelched his anger as the lad pulled the back of his shirt up presenting himself.

It was a good thing Dino was unaware of Christopher's reaction. The small patch of olive skin was crisscrossed with several layers of scars horrifying him. The child had been whipped on at least three different occasions. When Christopher's gaze lifted to Darby, her mouth gaped, and she immediately fastened on the sink full of dishes attempting to hum a tune except frightfully awful sounds came out.

"Doc, can you see what I'm tellin' you?"

"Two small ones, festering. Do you recall when you first felt them?"

"Aye. I surely do. And being here with you makes it all worth it."

Christopher scraped back his chair. "I'll get my salve, be right back."

Darby was making lots of noise with pots and tableware when

he reentered the kitchen. Dino drew his shirt up again and presented his back. Christopher swabbed the open wounds with a cloth causing Dino to flinch. "It'll quit burning in a second and start to heal."

Pulling down the shirt over his bony back, Christopher added, "We'll do this twice a day until they quit smarting, so remind me if I forget."

Darby fixed a smile on her face. "What have the two of you in mind should you be faced with no patients to worry about?"

Dino piped up, "I'm goin' to try the charity school."

Christopher objected. "No!"

Startled both Dino and Darby looked at him as he said, "You aren't going to *try* the school, you are going to *go* to the school until you graduate."

Darby tittered. "Scamp you are, all ready to skip out and haven't even begun."

A faint blush crossed the olive skin of his cheeks. He looked askance Christopher. "I'm...it's..."

Christopher ruffled his dark hair. "You've not been to school and are unsure. I can promise you, son, you are going to enjoy the experience. It's there for just such as you, a smart and eager lad."

As Christopher led the way down Strawberry Hill past Stoney Batter, he shared a bit of history with his new little charge. "This school is currently taught by Mrs. Hurley, she stepped in when Master Gotsford was transferred up near Kilkenny. I expect there to be another replacement soon. Hawthorn folks prefer a Master to a Mrs."

"There'll be lads my age, will there?" He walked with a quick stride trying to keep up to Christopher's, who realizing this, shortened his step.

"Surely. And others younger and older. It's one room, what with the village not as big as others. You're a sharp lad, Dino. Once you settle in, I think you'll enjoy the experience. Didn't you tell me when we first met, you'd been schooled by a man of the cloth when aboard the *Nomad?* Do I recall you enjoyed the experience immensely?"

Dino flashed him a big smile. "You've got a good memory." He kicked at a rock on the path sending it into a flowering bush. A white-tailed bunny scampered away. "I'm ready to do this. I haven't given you any grief over it?"

"Fair enough."

As they approached the school, he pointed out to Dino the tapering conical of St. John's Church poking through the oaks on the corner of the school yard. The school was set off by a copse of trees with a large play area. A bell hung from the front of the building and there were steps that led to windows on each side of a red door.

Music reached their ears, and as they approached the school, they realized it was coming from within and quickened their pace. Standing just inside the doors, Christopher's hat in hand, they waited for the teacher to notice them. Mrs. Hurley was at the piano and a man guided the chorus of students, who were standing at their desks.

The teacher's desk was at the far end, a piano to the left and four rows of desks on both sides of the aisle. Two students to a desk. Christopher and Dino stood at the threshold of the coat room lined with hooks and shelves. Dino slid his hand into Christopher's and took a deep breath.

This environment was a far cry from the hedge schools prevalent in the county. The structures were usually built in a ditch on the roadside. A front sidewall, maybe a gable to add light. A window on each side of the door and then clay or sod laid in rows making up the walls. A thatched roof completed the structure. Teachers were always men, most of who claimed more knowledge than the students, and thus were the overseers of learning. When in truth a student or two would have as much good sense or more than the man who pretended to teach.

Thanks to benevolent funding from His Lordship, the Earl of Darnley, this school offered a more refined educational experience.

Christopher felt for Dino, but his intuition consoled him that the lad would get a grip on his fright and calm to a whole new experience with those of a similar age.

Mrs. Hurley finished playing and came quickly to where they stood. "Welcome Mr. Curran. And, what have we here? A new student?"

"Dino…" he glanced down at the lad, "…Curran?"

A big grin dwarfed the size of Dino's nose as he nodded in agreement.

Mrs. Hurley said, "Welcome, Master Curran. Do you read? Write?"

He nodded to both, as he took in the rows of desks, students glanced to the back of the room gaping with plenty of curiosity about his person.

"Can you count and do sums?"

Again, with eyes wide he nodded as all the students had turned in their desks to see the new arrival.

"Well, then I'll put you with several others at your same learning level." She led the way to the front of the class. Curiosity followed them, as she said, "Class, we have a new student, Dino Curran. Please give him a warm welcome."

Lots of clapping, the bigger boys making quite a loud gesture with the effort. "You can share this desk with Emil. He reads and writes, too." Her smile was lovely as her fingers tapped Emil's side of the desk. "Please make sure Dino realizes about the slate and chalk. And raising his hand." Emil nodded with a look of supreme importance.

Whispers began as she gestured for the man in the front of the class to follow her back to where Christopher stood. "Mr. Curran, this is Master Carleton. He has just today begun as the new teacher. I'll stay on a day or two until he is acquainted with students and routine."

"Welcome to Hawthorn Village, Master Carleton. If I can assist you in any way, I'd be quite willing."

She added, "Mr. Curran is Hawthorn's doctor. He was new to us about five months ago." She flashed him a grin. "Am I right?"

"Just about. I'll let you get back to the children. What time of day do you begin?"

Master Carleton answered, his voice mid-tone and firm, "I'll be changing things up a bit. As of now Mrs. Hurley starts at nine. I'll be changing the time to eight, Monday through Friday. No need to coddle our next generation. Your son will be duly informed, Mr. Curran. Do not worry."

Christopher gave a short nod, glanced at Dino who was engaged in a whispered conversation with his seatmate and then walked out of the school feeling quite paternal, and content.

9

Christopher heard the clatter of pans and pots from the kitchen and surmised Krysta was back. He rolled out of bed and splashed his face with water, dressed for the day, and wandered into the racket.

"Good to see you're back. I hope your time off was enjoyable?"

With her back to him, she shrugged.

"Have you seen Darby?"

She spun from the business of stacking the pans at the sideboard. "She's already come and gone."

"Well then, you'll be about breakfast, I take it?"

"Yes sir. Same as usual?" Krysta was a flaxen-haired, broad shouldered young woman whose torso narrowed to a thin waist. Her height was in her long legs. Her cheeks were red, and she'd done something different to her hair but what he couldn't decide.

He glanced about the kitchen, then peeked into the bedroom shared now by Dino and the dying Schmitty whose breathing indicated he was asleep.

He closed the door and said, "A young lad, Dino, lives here now. Given it's his room and he's sound asleep and as it's Saturday, he doesn't need to get up just yet. I have a patient,

Schmitty, who is in there too, quite ill." He brushed his fingers through his hair avoiding the shocked look on her face. "He's in the bed until..." leaving the sentiment to dangle in the unsaid word.

"Six ways to the *devil* then, you've been a busy man. Whatever I make for you, it'll do for the boy?"

"He eats like it's his last." He reached for the teapot and poured himself a cup. "Oh, and when at market, always make sure we have jam in the cupboard. Please..." he glanced at her over the rim of the cup. Her cheeks looked like she smeared raspberries on them, but why in the name of God would she do such a thing? "Is this a rash on your face? Does it itch?"

She stammered, "Ah...no itch." She swiped at her left cheek and noted a smudge of red on her fingers. "Ah, I've been destemming raspberries." The blush spread to her neck and up her ears.

Her embarrassment obvious, he felt uneasy and looked askance. "Glad it's not a rash. Thanks for making a pot."

"It's what I do, doc. So, how'd you get the boy if you don't mind my askin'?"

He thought a moment. What gossip did he want all over town? "Let's just say he was in need of a home, as the ship he came in on left without him."

"And good hearted you took him in?" She'd clamped her red-stained fingers on her hips waiting for more.

He sipped his tea. She wasn't going to give up until she was satisfied so he told her all. "Let's just say I couldn't refuse to offer shelter, and besides, the sick one is a friend of his. They both need nurturing."

"You're a wonder, doc. Sure wish them bunch at the Black Pig could understand you as I do." She slapped a wooden spoon against her skirts, inadvertently wiping it of pancake mix.

He almost chuckled but wasn't sure if it was her remark or her ignorance of what she'd just done with the spoon. He raised his cup. "Think I'll have a fill and work in my office until Dino gets up. Then we'll have breakfast together."

"Right you are, then."

An hour later, Dino stuffed himself until he could eat no more, and with almost all of Krysta's curiosity about him satisfied, Christopher took the lad to O'Bannon's Dry Goods. The owner, Nuala, was Lord Tremaine's mother-in-law, and Christopher respectfully referred to her by her rightful name, Lady Rutledge.

The bell tinkled as they entered. Sally was behind the counter. "One moment, I'll tell Nuala you are here."

Wiping her hands on an apron, Lady Rutledge came forward. "This is your new lad, Dino, is it?" She smiled at him. "You'll keep the good doctor hopping, I'm sure of it."

Dino glanced up at Christopher. "It's him keeps me hopping, my lady. I hardly get a moment's rest."

A delightful smile lit her countenance. "What can I do for the two of you?"

Christopher's inspection skittered over the shelves. "He's in need of clothing, especially now he attends school."

Her dark gaze slid to Dino. "Wonderful. What a grand time you will have with Mrs. Hurley."

"We've got a Master Carleton now. Mrs. Hurley was inter...."

"Interim?"

"Yup, and I only had her two days, so don't miss her as much as the rest of the students. Master Carleton is grand compared to her."

Christopher gripped Dino's bird-boned shoulder. "Be kind."

Dino sighed. "Yes, sir."

Lady Rutledge grinned. "Follow me, we'll fine what suits you the best." She glanced down at his shoes. "I'm thinking we might find a better fit in new shoes, what do you think, Dino?"

An hour later, and with numerous packages, they left O'Bannon's and headed to the infirmary. Dino hummed a tune as they walked up Sisters Lane, probably remembered from his younger years, perhaps his mother sang to him. Christopher was not familiar with the cadence. Christopher's heart warmed to think of Dino comfortable enough to fall back to a time he was secure.

As luck would have it, two men waited in the outer room. Nodding to them Christopher said, "I'll be right with you." He carried the packages into the back with instructions to Dino to unwrap and put the clothing in the drawers in the bedroom he shared with Schmitty. "When you are done, check with Krysta and see if she needs help with anything, will you?"

He shut the door between the private living quarters and entered the waiting room for the infirmary. "What can I do for you, Mr…"

"Wallace. Willy, and this here's my brother, Dilly. He has a problem needs fixing. I'm his voice."

"He doesn't speak?" Christopher held out his hand to Dilly, who firmly shook it.

"Doesn't hear either."

"I take it you have learned to communicate with Dilly in some manner, then?"

"Yup, all these years. We're gonna be fifty soon."

"Twins then?"

"Yup."

"Mr. Wallace, what is your brother's need? He appears in good health."

"You can call me Willy, doc. And, he says his mouth is givin' him fits. Hurts inside."

Christopher had read and listened to the suspected communication between twins in one of his classes at Edinburgh. This might appear to be solid proof of the hypothesis that they share an uncommon understanding. "Come into the examining room and have Dilly sit on the table for me."

He searched for a tongue depressor, washed his hands at the bowl and dried them before facing the patient opening his own mouth as wide as he could.

Dilly followed suit, and Christopher used the depressor to move his tongue from one side to the other, noticing white patches on the roof of the mouth, inner cheeks, and along the lower inside lip. It was enough to make an instant diagnosis.

"Ask him if he has had bleeding from the mouth. And if the patches are painful."

Willy communicated with hand signals and talking slow. Dilly's eyes, of course, glued to the words forming on his brother lips.

"Yes, to the bleeding, yes to the pain."

"How frequently does he brush?"

"Twice a day sometimes, depends on visitors."

"Are you talking about his teeth or his hair?" Christopher shook his head in meek despair.

Willy guffawed. "Ah, his teeth, and never."

"It looks like thrush mouth to me. Usually happens because of poor hygiene. It's basically the growth of a fungus. The fungus is allowed when we don't keep our mouths clean. Drinking of ale and eating bread, which are made with yeast, will need to be stopped for a time." He tried to think of Willy and Dilly's lifestyle. "Once the white patches and pain abate, I think Dilly can resume both ale and bread. But for now, he should do what he can to lessen the discomfort."

Christopher folded his arms leaned against the wall. "And he can try gargling with saltwater after each meal. He will find that soothing."

"I ain't gonna tell 'im he can't have his ale, doc. I ain't gonna do it."

Christopher put the tongue depressor into a long thin receptacle filled with vinegar, washed and dried his hands.

Dilly's regard was glued to his every move. Christopher wished he had other news, but the fact it was thrush and not something worse gave him a sense of relief. He took a small brush of his own, mimicked dipping it in soda powder and brushing his teeth. Dilly smiled at him and nodded. Christopher pointed at him, shaking his finger and very slowly said, "Do it, twice a day," holding up two fingers. "Mr. Talbot sells these brushes."

Christopher pulled a small vial out of the cupboard. "This is an oil made of myrrh. Have Dilly put a tiny bit on the end of his finger and rub it on the places that hurt. Take care not to overdue this. Never enough that he would have to swallow any." As he handed Willy the vial, the man assured him he would instruct his brother correctly.

Strong as an ox, Dilly slapped Christopher on the shoulder in affirmation, sending the doc forward a step.

After they left, his office quieted. He sauntered back to the kitchen. Krysta was nowhere to be found, and he looked in on Schmitty. Dino was reading a book given to him by Master Carleton, *Young Reader for Beginners*. Dino appeared to be nearing the end of it.

Schmitty's chest barely moved, his color ashen, his skin sunken to the bones. Christopher swabbed his mouth with a wet cloth and tucked the blanket over his arms. He glanced at Dino who raised his attention off the pages of the book and watched the doc minister to his friend.

"He's not long to go, you do understand, right?"

Dino nodded. "He'll go to a better place. I remember the parson telling stories about where we go if we are good. Schmitty was the best. He'll go to a nicer place than where he's been."

"You surprise me with your wisdom. Your parents would be proud of you."

The angelic look on Dino's face caused Christopher's chest to tighten, and he coughed into his fist. "I'll be in my office if you need anything." Dino nodded and focused his attention on his school reader.

After making a list of supplies for the infirmary, Christopher informed Krysta he would be back within the hour. She nodded as she pulled greens from a basket. A chicken with its neck wrung would be defeathered. Dinner tonight no doubt, fresh from the market.

A wind, gusting in from the east, had a decided chill to it and he drew his great coat across his chest, noting the lough rough with white caps. A sheet of newsprint sailed through the air like a specter. There had not been a hint of a blow earlier when he and Dino shopped.

Reaching the apothecary's, he gripped the latch of the door forcefully so it would not slam against the wall. The gust blew into the room and papers flew off the counter before he could shut the door.

He encountered a slender woman, whom he'd not noticed about Hawthorn, her mouth forming an O as papers took flight. The peacock feather in her jaunty blue hat waved at him. Her expression soured. In the moment, she attempted to grab the sheets as they scattered. Mr. Talbot dove over a stack of notices, grabbing at them with no luck.

Before Christopher could shut the door, he attempted to grab up sheets that flew near him, the door escaped his clutch and banged against the wall. He immediately grabbed the handle and shut the door using the force of his strength.

The woman bent to gather papers at the same moment Christopher leaned over. Their heads bumped, her hat dislodged, feather and all, and she fell backward with a wallop to the floor. Her dark auburn hair came partway unpinned from the vigorous fall, and her green eyes were fiery with accusation.

Mr. Talbot cringed. "Well, well, well, if it isn't the master of mischief himself blowing in like some great calamity."

Christopher offered the lady his hand but with her awkward position on the floor was going to need more of a boost. He leaned down, put his hands about her waist, lifting her upright. "My apologies, miss." He glanced at the windows. "Quite the wind churning out there."

Clearly aghast, she stepped back, brushing at her woolen skirts. Her thick, dark tresses in disarray about her face and flashing eyes that narrowed with disgust gleaming like a cat about to pounce. "You, sir, are an abomination."

He had the worst timing. Of its own accord, his face lit into a smile. "I'm sorry, I didn't plan this." He tried to appear somber.

"Likely not, but nevertheless, you've caused both of us turmoil." She faced Talbot. "Excuse me. I need to repair the damage to myself." She trotted off, shoulders squared, hat in hand, toward the drapes dividing the front of the building from the back.

Christopher began scooping up papers scattered to every corner of the room. Talbot huffed, "What is it you need, doc? Then you can be on your way."

"Bittersweet, marshmallow root, and white willow bark if you've gotten some in since my last call."

He bent low under the counter and pulled out a package. "Right here, this is the willow bark. The bittersweet is on the middle shelf—you can get it. And marshmallow root I'll have by day after tomorrow, *maybe.*"

Christopher dug in his pocket for coin, but Talbot waved him off. "Easier to put on your bill. If you've got what you came for, I'll bid you good day, sir."

Christopher had the distinct impression Mr. Talbot was eager for him to leave. He nodded and just as he spun on his heel, the woman appeared from the back of the shop. He would have offered another apology, but Mr. Talbot hurried to her side already in attendance on her. Gripping the latch, Christopher barely opened the door, eased through it, and made very sure the latch caught. His top hat flew off and he ran after it, no doubt confirming her earlier opinion that he was a dolt.

Making a brusque decision, the medicine tucked under his arm, he walked up Market toward the Black Pig rather than the infirmary and Krysta with her painted face. The water rising in the lough churned white caps. Though he couldn't see River Suir from where he stood, he imagined it roiling with greater intensity as it was very large and deep. Several days earlier more than ten seagoing vessels were at anchor. The wind was beginning to howl with an evil portent. This would not abate any time soon.

As he walked up the lane toward the pub, he noticed several of the shop's shutters were closed against the weather. His thoughts centered on Dino, innately kind, smart as a whip, and without a mean bone in his body. He still suffered from acceptance, something Christopher could identify with. The lad stayed in the background more than children would his age. Christopher knew it was going to take him time to reconcile and come to terms with the abuse he suffered. Hiding until Captain Redeye sailed was one form of rebellion where Dino asserted himself. Time would change him, time and affection. It gave Christopher an idea and he made a mental note to surprise Dino with a gift.

Schmitty only had a matter of days, could even be hours. All Christopher could do was keep a close watch and try to gauge Dino's acceptance of his friend's inevitable demise.

The howling wind raced across the village, churning the lough and pushing it toward the embankment of the Strand. Trees bent and litter sailed about. This was no ordinary change in weather, and he sensed there could be injuries involved. Even quite serious accidents.

Christopher changed his mind about the Black Pig and hurried back to the infirmary.

Krysta had left dinner in the pot to simmer over the fire. The scent of chicken and gravy filled the kitchen. Dino informed him Krysta was concerned for her mother in their little cottage and she planned to return in the morning as usual.

Christopher and Dino sat in the kitchen. Dino shared his thoughts about school and Master Carleton and the great difference between him and Mrs. Hurley. Christopher tried to think back when he was a lad about the same age, hoping to recall how he felt about his teachers. He would have been in his first year at Eton. Mostly he recalled there wasn't a moment to give thought to who taught him what.

He tried to keep up and stay out of the way of the older bully students as best he could. Once he'd gotten some flesh on himself and grown a bit, he hadn't a worry in the world. It was all about size in those early years. The memory brought a chuckle as he glanced across the table at the slight lad.

Dino said, around a mouthful of stew, "Krysta's a really good cook. The food on the *Nomad* filled your belly but little else."

Christopher could imagine one of the older tar's Dino was in company with making that statement. He put his fork down. "It would be nice if you told her how much you enjoyed her cooking. Women love compliments."

Chewing another mouthful, the lad nodded.

10

Christopher wasn't surprised when Krysta dropped by to say she needed to stay with her mother until this blustery blow ceased. The sound outside was fearsome as it whipped through the trees and around the wood framed homes. He encouraged her not to linger as the rain hadn't begun but when it did, they could expect a deluge.

Fishermen were anchoring their vessels, tying down the sheets and coiling the ropes. Bird song ceased.

He was sipping a cup of tea having checked on Schmitty who was barely breathing. He considered the sailor wouldn't be alive more than an hour or two.

Mulroney came by, using his shoulder to shut the front door. "Doc?"

Christopher sprang up from his desk and walked to the waiting area. The scowl on Mulroney's face suggested a problem.

"What is it?"

"In retrospection, the talk yesterday afternoon at the pub was a bit naïve considering the night just spent. Water's rising in Waterford along the quay. Hawthorn's river and lough are spilling over. Thatch is peeling off some roofs. This weather isn't near over. Should have realized a disaster was on its way when bird song was no more, and the catch had fallen off. I believe the worst is yet to come."

Having heard the same from Krysta, Christopher raked a hand through his thick hair and sucked in his lower lip. "What should be done? What can I do?"

"I wanted you to be aware. We've had blows before but not the likes of what this appears to be. Danaher has gathered a group of the men and they are going house to house making sure our elderly have peat enough and supplies to last a week."

Christopher offered, "We may need a building safe enough to house those folks whose roofs blow off. What about The Church of Christ, or the school? Or the forge for that matter?"

"Carnahan already offered his place, should we need it."

Dino shuffled into the office, knuckles twisting at the tears spilling from his eyes. Christopher knelt in front of the boy. "Tell me, lad."

"I think…Schmitty could be…" Christopher wrapped his arms about the small frame and glanced at Danaher. "We've a sailor, a friend of Dino's whose gravely ill. He's in the back. I need to…"

Before he could finish, Danaher jumped in. "It's okay, doc. Catch up with us when you can. The important thing is the infirmary's ready for problems if needs be." He patted the top of Dino's head. "Sorry, lad. I'll say a prayer for your friend." He slapped his tam on his head and reached for the door, yanking his collar up.

Dino led the way to the back, touching Schmitty's arm as it lay on top of the blanket. Christopher felt for a pulse, put his fingers over Schmitty's nose, then gave a nod to Dino. "You're right, his time has come."

The soft voice choked on sorrow. "He's gone to that special place in the sky."

"He has. Heaven."

Within the house, silence took over, except for the wind buffeting the roof and a shutter that wasn't tied tight. Dino sniffled and let out a long soft sigh as he slid his hand from Schmitty's and shoved it in Christopher's palm. They stood there looking at the emaciated remains of a man who had been kind to a child.

Christopher made a promise to himself. If he could raise this lad to be a man worthy of honor, he would have accomplished a wonderous thing. "Do you grasp what happens to the body of someone you love when they die?"

"Cap'n Redeye tossed 'em into the deep blue."

"At sea, that's acceptable. On land, there's another procedure. First thing, we would need to lower the lids over his eyes, but Schmitty died with them closed. Next, we need to pull the blanket up over his face to signify his passing. Then we will make plans to bury him, which we should try to do quickly considering the bedlam stirring outside."

Dino held Schmitty's face a moment, then grabbed the end of the blanket and pulled it over his deceased friend. His palms ran down the length of the sailor, tucking the blanket around his feet. Christopher was struck by the lad's efforts to comfort.

"I'm going to talk to Padhraig. Won't take me long. He owns the mortuary. You can come with me or stay."

Tears had begun again. Dino sat back in the chair next to the bed. "I'll stay by Schmitty."

Christopher nodded. "Shouldn't take me long. Either they have a plot or not."

At the Black Pig, Padhraig was behind the counter serving up a pint to Mike Cooke whose wife was home and preparing for childbirth any day. Christopher nodded to the man who had vocally refused his help with the delivery about a week ago here in the pub. Mike had already engaged a neighbor who had a reputation for midwifery. Months ago, Christopher had reconciled himself to the ways of Hawthorn's villagers.

"What can I do for you, doc?"

"A patient of mine has just died. I'm hoping you can arrange a quick burial. With the weather coming on worse, I'm in a bit of a quandary as to what to do."

Padhraig poured another ale for Mike and came back to where

Christopher leaned against the shiny mahogany bar top. "I can take the body to the morgue until the storm passes, or we can do a really fast burial this afternoon. I'm not sure what we're looking at here with this blow."

"Will he keep in the morgue?"

"Should. I've prepared corpses more than five-days old. They kept well enough to have an open casket for the family. Surely, this system will have moved on by then."

Mike, several stools down from their conversation, snorted. "This ain't passin' any time soon, feel it in me bones. This is the one we've been avoidin' for years." He took a long gulp, swept his arm across his mustache, burped and nodded to them with all the assuredness of one who accounts for the weather better than God.

Christopher glanced across the bar top at Padhraig, who was busy stacking glasses. "I'll take you up on the offer to use the morgue. I sure do appreciate this. We'll be wanting a coffin rather than the shroud. No viewing will be necessary. When this weather system passes, we'll have a graveside service of some sort."

"Good enough then, doc. You take care of that lad. He's lucky to have you."

Christopher held Padhraig's thoughtful gaze for a moment. "Thank you. But it's the other way about. I'm finding it's me who's fortunate."

Giving one last swipe of the bar top, Padhraig groused, "As soon as Ian gets his lazy carcass in here, I'll come by with a cart."

Dino was nowhere in sight when Christopher fought his way back to the infirmary. Within the hour, Padhraig appeared with his donkey cart. Together they carried the body outside and respectfully laid him in it, folding his legs inside.

Christopher asked, "You didn't happen to spy Dino about, did you?"

"Wasn't really looking but can't say as I did." He cocked his head at the back of the cart. "Don't worry about this un.' He'll be in good shape when this system rolls over. I can fix him up to show the boy when we get ready for burial."

"You're an understanding man, Padhraig. I thank you."

Christopher glanced about the kitchen realizing how hungry he was. Hoping Dino would show up soon, he fried up some bacon, cut a thick slice of bread from the loaf Krysta baked yesterday, and slathered it with fresh churned butter. He folded over two strips of crisp bacon. His stomach growled in anticipation.

A cup of tea in one hand bread and bacon in the other, he walked into the bedroom. Dino would have a room to himself now. As he glanced about, he pictured a bookcase filled with a young lad's interests. Maybe a drawing or two attached to the wall, and a hurling stick in the corner. He'd enjoy teaching the boy how to play. Maybe he could get a team up and teach the lads in the village. The pane in the window rattled. In the kitchen, he found a small piece of heavy paper. Folded it over three times, he stuck it between the glass and the wood frame. Pleased the window no longer rattled, he glanced about the room.

It felt as if he was waiting for the sky to drop with the unpredictability of the weather and Dino's whereabouts. Good men were out shuttering windows against the wind and gathering sheep into enclosures. Women plucked gardens of their produce in hopes they could save food that will surely be needed.

Finished with breakfast, ledgers, and musing, the next time he glanced at the clock it was two in the afternoon. It had not begun to rain, and he went the room Dino will now occupy and pulled the sheet and blanket off the bed, setting them in a bundle in the corner for Darby to wash. Then picking up the mattress and pillow, he took them outside on the back step beating both with a wire he had used when they first cleaned the room, a month or more now. How time flies.

The wind helped clear the air when he bashed them. Satisfied he'd cleaned both well enough, he brought them inside and put a clean sheet and pillowcase on. When Dino arrived, it would be his to occupy.

He glanced down the hall to the infirmary. His life had certainly taken a turn for the better since the lad's arrival. He was more interested in the daily routine; even meals had begun to taste better. Surely that wasn't a nod to Krysta, she fancied herself quite a cook, but some of her concoctions were experimental.

From his stance at the end of the hall, he saw a shadow through the glassed-in entrance to the door to the infirmary, and quickly made his way. "Come in, come in."

By the time he reached for the latch, the shadow drifted. Upon opening the door, he was presented with a woman, on her knees panting with labor. He stepped over the figure, grabbed her beneath the arms and hoisted her up. "Can you stand? Can you walk?"

"I got here, didn't I now?" *Aaaarrgghh.*

An instant assessment suggested she was in deep labor. "How far apart are they?"

"I'm near ready, doc. Can't go on much longer now."

He straddled her from behind, walking her to the bedroom. "I'll put you to bed, but it's in the back."

Her legs carried her until another pain hit. They stopped until it passed. A quick calculation told him she might be less than an hour, and for all he knew perhaps minutes, from delivery. "Is this your first?"

"I've got a wee daughter at home." She talked between gasps of pain.

"Whatever brought you out in this weather and in labor?"

"You'll see soon enough, doc. Get me to the bed quick like," she said—talking and wheezing at the same time.

They entered the kitchen. "To your left, Mrs…"

"Cooke." They were at the door to the bedroom where she headed toward the bed. "Thank God."

"Mike's your husband, then?"

"That bastard is. Now you get this babe out of me quick like before he shows up all fire and brimstone."

He knew women said odd things during labor, but this was a first. "I don't think I understand."

"It'll be clear as a fresh cleaned windoooooow…*aaarrrggggg…*"

They waited for the pain to finish then she sank to the bed, and he swung her legs over, slipping off her wooden clogs. "I need hot water and linens. Are you all right just now?"

"As I said, not my first. Do what'cha gotta do, doc. I'm not goin' anywhere."

The ground shook—he felt the floor shudder, and glanced at Mrs. Cooke, who appeared oblivious. The wind must have knocked something over. It's all he could think as the baby's entrance into the world was fast approaching. A far more urgent matter.

The water was heating up, clean linen at the ready on the dresser, he took her pulse, which was high, but considering the duress of labor, was within the limits of healthy. He put a cool cloth on her forehead. "Are you comfortable with my examination, considering my cleaning lady is not here?"

"Doc, do what you gotta do. I'm countin' on you to deliver me a son, otherwise I wouldna' be here."

He chuckled, thinking she was injecting a sense of humor into the mix, when something slammed against the infirmary door. He poked his head around the wall of the bedroom and looked down the hall. Mike Cooke stood on the other side of the glass. The fury on his face was quite distinct from this distance. "It's your husband, Mrs. Cooke," and Christopher withdrew to open the door.

"Where is she, where's that bitch? In here is she, hidin' from me, is she?"

Drunk and hell-bent to cause great mischief, Christopher put his hand to the man's chest. "You hold up a minute Mr. Cooke. I think you've sufficient ale to sink a ship, and your wife is getting ready to deliver any moment. I can't allow you to talk to her this way or infer any harm toward her."

"She's my wife, goddammit." His breath could sink a ship.

"Right now, she's my patient."

He brushed off Christopher's fist. "Get outta my way."

Christopher grabbed Mike's left arm and spun him around so quick, Mike fell to the floor on his knees, and Christopher pressured his knee into Mike's back. "Look, you'll do this my way, or you'll live to regret your actions. I haven't got a fight with you. But your wife needs immediate care, and I'm not going to waste precious time convincing you of *THAT*."

"Right...right..." Mike slackened his body and quit fighting Christopher.

Not convinced Mike wasn't bluffing, Christopher slowly let go and stood. Mike straightened up still on his knees, huffing and puffing with the fall he'd taken. Then, he stood, a bit wobbly. "Can I see her?"

"Your wife doesn't need you acting like a buffle-head right now."

"Who's with her?"

"That's my point, no one. And I'm out here protecting her from a foxed, dicked-in-the-nob yahoo who claims to be her husband."

"'Pon my oath, I'll calm down. But it's unseemly a man looking at her—down there."

Christopher groaned, "Honest to God, is that what's behind all this? For the sake of Heaven, man, she needs assistance, and I'm a medical doctor. Who, by the way, has delivered half a dozen babies. In Scotland."

"Did they live?" Mike, still gasping for air, leaned against the wall, probably due to the vast amount of ale he'd imbibed.

Christopher raised his fist. "I should..."

"Okay...okay..." Mike's palms shot up in surrender.

Christopher ran down the hall. Mrs. Cooke flinched as he drew her gown up to her knees. The baby was crowning. "You've got a red head, Mrs. Cooke. You're doing fine." He plunged his hands into the water, wiped them and took up clean linen prepared to hold the infant. "The next push, you'll have your..."

Mike ventured close to his wife, petted her cheek, then picked up the cloth that had slid off, wiped her face. "I'm an ass."

She had just enough time to agree when the next contraction hit.

Within seconds, Christopher said, "Oh, my, a healthy baby... boy." He took the caterwauling infant, who quieted as soon as his fist found his mouth, and laid him on the linen between her legs, cut the cord, clamped it, then wrapped him up and placed him in his mother's arms.

Mike cried. All the ale, no doubt. His great beefy shoulders shook with emotion. His wife cooed to her son. A picture-perfect family.

Christopher waited a minute for the afterbirth. From experience, once the mother held her child, it came quick.

Mike sobbed. "I got a son. *Me*, I did this." His wonder apparent in his voice, and sobered demeanor.

"You damn fool, you can't take credit for a few minutes of scratchin' your itch. The doc's the one what delivered him—no thanks to *you*."

She caught her breath, her features distorted. "Doc, this isn't right."

He stepped close, feeling her pulse. "What?"

"I'm having another pain."

"It's the afterbirth, the placenta. Do you want your husband to hold his son? It might be a bit easier for you."

Mike held out shaky arms, ready as he could be. Christopher asked him to sit in the chair and then he inserted the bundle into the crook of his arm. "You okay?"

The smile on his face was answer enough. A pair of bright blue eyes, and a shock of red hair kept dad busy with the miracle of the birth of a son.

Christopher focused his attention on Mrs. Cooke. "How are you doing?"

Weary, she laid her head back on the pillow, rubbing the sides of her stomach. "Somethin's different, not like when Mary was born."

Christopher pressed on her belly as the cramp eased, catching the end of the contraction. He checked her vaginally, and of a sudden grinned, just as she was about to have another contraction. "Mr. and Mrs. Cooke, you are about to have another."

She gasped, red faced with effort. "Oh my, oh no. Dear God in Heaven."

Dad was so mesmerized by his son he barely got the drift. "What? What's that?"

She shouted at him, "You fool! How will I feed two? With Mary at home, I'll be beside meself."

He glanced at Christopher who nodded as the next contraction began. "It won't be long now. A minute or so."

The wind howled and branches flew by the window. Christopher noted it still hadn't begun raining, but when it did, it would prove to be thunderous for certain. Of a sudden, his thoughts fled to Dino. At the same moment, Mrs. Cooke's next baby crowned. Another russet head of hair. Twins, and in a second, they would behold a daughter or another son.

She panted as before, but not with as much gusto, poor woman, she was very tired. "Soon to be over, your next push should do it, Mrs. Cooke."

"God's sake, call me Mona—*aaahhhhh*."

And behold she delivered her third child. "Congratulations, both of you, you've another son. Identical to the first I'm thinking."

From his chair, Mike said, "He's gonna' wake the dead, Jasus, Mary and Joseph…just like his brother."

Christopher cut the umbilical cord and clamped it, then wiped him off. "Another pair of bright blue eyes."

Mona was going to be an extremely busy mother keeping them fed with a small daughter at home, too. He placed the infant in her waiting arms. She sagged back into the pillow, tears streaming down her face. Christopher wiped her face with the cloth, telling her to breathe deep and try to relax.

"Is there more?"

He placed pressure on her stomach and shook his head. "No more babies, just the afterbirth."

Mike hummed an old Irish lullaby, and it comforted Christopher. He thought, a death and two births in this room, and on this bed. Not a bad rate of exchange.

With conviction, the new mother said, "Didn't I tell you we needed a man doc to deliver us?"

Mike grunted, a grin on his unshaven face.

Christopher said, "You get it, right? My delivering them has nothing to do with their gender. You are jesting, right?"

"We'll see how your business gets on now, won't we then?" Mona took in a deep breath of her newborn's scent a watery smile on her pinkened cheeks.

He left the Cookes and sought the calm of his office, stopping at the cupboard in the hall to pour himself a libation, which he wasn't planning to share with Mike because he'd had enough as it was.

Dino still hadn't shown, not a good sign. The windows rattled, all manner of debris flew in the air, and now the spattering of rain. The next twenty-four hours were going to be hell.

Done with his few minutes of relaxing, he checked the cupboard again, this time looking for food Krysta stored. He found jars of peaches and cherries, a sack of flour, a brick of sugar, two jars of molasses, and several jars of applesauce. A ham and a slab of bacon hung from the beam in the corner, all wrapped in burlap, along with a bin full of potatoes and onions.

On the top shelf he noted a jug of Irish poteen he had taken from old man Grogan when he found him in a ditch several months ago. A few smaller jugs of Tullamore Dew were next to the moonshine.

With enough in the larder to ward off famine, he closed the cupboard and checked on Mr. and Mrs. Cooke.

Mom, dad, and babies were sound asleep, for which he was grateful. He needed a quiet moment to consider sleeping arrangements for the infants for a day or two. Mr. Cooke would need to care for his daughter at home.

He took a moment to walk out on the back porch. The howling wind whipped the trees like they were straw, the sky had gone ebon dark. Though he was sheltered by the walls of the infirmary and the porch roof, gusts of mizzling steady and washed over him. No doubt this night would receive a ferocious rebellion from the skies; he also thought of the russet haired angels in the spare room and the confused, broken-hearted lad somewhere out there in the torrent of the storm hiding from hurt and a past he was determined to put behind him.

11

Next morning produced a weather system that reached into the high eighties with plenty of humidity even with the wind blowing. None of it was rare for August. Neither were thunderstorms and winds prevailing at near hurricane strength. The difference with this one, it hadn't abated in two days, it increased.

Christopher hunched out of his slicker after a walk about the village. The lough with its roiling mass was spilling over the strand. Damage was going to be costly. Hawthorn's lanes were beginning to fill with water. Massive waves splashed the eastern Strand of the village churning water along the doorsteps of most on Church Street, Stoney Batter, Chadwick and Sisters Lanes and up Stephen's Lane.

The villagers most in danger lived in cobb buildings made from subsoil water and straw, that were not built to withstand the battering. Though most cottages were more or less a hundred years old and had strained against many blusters over the years, this was an unusual and masterful storm. Hawthorn's villagers felt it in their bones. Thatching twisted over roof tops, windows, where the occupants had been able to afford the luxury, smashed. Rubble from chimneystacks tumbled into the lanes.

The shudder Christopher felt the day Mrs. Cooke birthed her

twins was the steeple of The Church of Christ as it toppled to the ground. He also learned some of Hawthorn's lovely birch and ash trees had been upended at the same time.

Mrs. Cooke and her infants were safe and comfortable in Dino's bedroom, attended to by a steady stream of women who braved the horrendous winds. Though worried about Dino, Christopher counted on the lad's resilience in spite of his heavy heart at the loss of Schmitty. Christopher's duty was to remain where he was as injuries, one upon another, were appearing on his doorstep.

He finished stitching a wound on the forearm of the Bryn's fifteen-year-old daughter. A tree limb had smashed through their window. Christopher led the young lady to the back of the infirmary. "Sit here and wait for your mother to return. I'll get you a drink."

A woman, leaning into a cupboard, who he'd not met, said, "We'll take care, Mr. Curran, you go on back to doctoring. Don't you worry about us. And Mona is doing just fine with her russets."

"I'm grateful for your help," he said to the backside of the woman. There were two other women, one kneading dough, the other mixing a bowl of something or other.

The woman in the cupboard finally came out. "I'm Mrs. Kneely, this is Greta, and Mary."

He nodded with gratitude. She passed him a cup of tea, and he asked, "You've not caught sight of the lad, Dino?"

With a chorus of no's, and a last glance at Miss Bryn who sipped tea with her good arm, he retreated to the infirmary when three men appeared. Two, arms crisscrossed, carried an injured fellow, who sat on their arms as if in a chair, his head lolled to the shoulder of one of the men. Christopher held the door wide as they sidled in. The wind howled down the hall and into the kitchen, to a chorus of women reacting to the gusts.

Christopher pointed to the table and they gently laid the injured man down. His left leg below the knee bent almost perpendicular to the thigh; obviously broken. The skin in the right upper thigh bled from a wound. Both legs were damaged.

"Hurts, does it?"

"…the 'ell, doc."

"What's your name?"

"…Asia Malcolm."

His friends fidgeted, squeamish and eager to return to duty. "I may need you to help with him. Give me a few minutes to assess the damage and figure out how to move forward. There's tea in the kitchen." Spinning on their heels, they retreated to the back of the infirmary.

Christopher washed his hands, grabbed up his scissors, and began cutting the trouser leg away from the wound. He rotated the leg back to what should be its original position, wondering how much damage to the knee there might be. Asia hissed with pain. The wound in the thigh looked clean and he washed it with alcohol and dressed it.

Turning his attention to the other leg, he considered the best way to set the break in the lower part of the leg. It appeared to be a clean break. He could feel the ridges where it had snapped.

"Do whatcha gotta, doc. Man ain't no use without his legs."

His friends poked their heads into the examination room mumbling about the 115 mph winds, so said the experts at the quay, and those at The Church of Christ worried about the toppled steeple. "God's showin' his wrath. The church was full of folks at the time and not a one dead. Yet they still feared the wrath of the almighty."

"Anyone hurt?"

"Nope. Water's comin' over the lough onto Market Street like a funnel all pushed up through River Suir. Ain't seen the likes of such since '89."

Christopher left for a minute returning with a jug of Tullamore Dew and popped the cork. "If you will assist me with Asia, he needs to take a good long swig of this."

Asia's face screwed with pain as he inhaled a ragged breath

then drank a very healthy slug. His two friends would no doubt have liked to do the same, but they refrained from asking.

Christopher soothed, "It'll be okay, Asia, a moment or two of discomfort, then it'll be over. If it sets right, you'll have many years of service out of your leg. How about one more good gulp." Asia's eyes were beginning to swim in their sockets.

Then he directed the beefier of the two men. "You mind the other leg." To the smaller fellow he said, "And you take hold of Asia's shoulders to keep him down."

Asia cried, "Doc, doc, I'm in mortal pain."

Christopher reached for the jug again. "This'll help." Christopher hefted him up from the shoulders as he drank another slug, came up for air and gulped another. The two men assisting followed the moment, their eyes growing larger with the amount Asia consumed.

Christopher maneuvered to the other side of the examining table, and noted two women standing in the door, a bundle of clean linen filling their arms. The dark-haired woman was the one from Talbot's who called him an abomination. The other one said, "We've brought supplies from the school; where there is a temporary supply place to house the donations of clothing, water, food, and doing whatever is asked."

"Leave the linen on the table, please." His gaze shifted to his patient. Asia's eyes were closed, a soft snore came from his parted lips.

"You men ready? I need you to lean hard, keep him steady. And you," he said, nodding to the other chap, "hold his good leg as still as possible, I don't need a kick in the head."

"Aye, doc."

As he wrenched the shin bone down into place twisting it a tiny bit, Asia's scream filled the room, causing each man to grimace. He let go of the leg and using his fingers felt if it had meshed or not. The tension in his patient's leg was gone and Asia was out cold. He took advantage of this and probed deeply on the flesh making certain it was in place; waved at the two men their work was done.

He removed Asia's soaked footwear releasing the most noxious rotten-egg stink, knowing the man probably hadn't taken his boots off for days on end. He reached for a jug of vinegar and several clean rags and began washing his feet.

As he did this, his gaze drifted to the dark-haired woman, who apparently had watched the whole procedure. She stood with linens in her arms, intrigued by his ministrations to the patient. Her friend had disappeared.

He asked, "Have you time to cut ten of those linens into five-inch strips? There is a pair of scissors in the cupboard over there."

Without a word, she placed the bundle on the cupboard, laid out one of the pieces and began cutting.

Because the patient hadn't gained consciousness, Christopher was able to wrap the leg without any tension of muscle. He prepped it with a tincture of myrrh and wrapped it in the linen the woman from Talbot's cut in strips.

Finished for the moment, he asked the men who had stayed in the room, "Does he have family?"

They glanced at each other and back to the doc. "No wife. He's off the *Winddrift* about a month or so now, wanting to stay in Hawthorn. I think he has family somewhere about."

"It was his lucky day you were with him. Has he a place to stay?" Christopher asked.

A shrug of a beefy shoulder was answer enough.

"Aah. Well, I've a cot in the back room where Mrs. Cooke is with her infants. How about you men get it and put it in a corner of the kitchen."

"We need to get back to the quay, doc. Will you be finished with us then?"

"Help me transfer him to the cot and I thank you for your assistance."

They nodded and retreated to the back of the infirmary. He glanced at the dark-haired woman who stood quietly near Asia

Malcom. "Would you be so good as to help me bind this leg? I'm Christopher by the way." He granted her a thin smile as he wasn't sure of her motive to watch his work.

"You may call me Miss Fitzjames." Her dainty chin rose as she watched him. A slow smile spread across her full lips.

The patient groaned, and he asked, "Asia, can you hear me?"

Blinking and groaning he slurred, "I hurt like the *devil*. Where am I?"

"In the infirmary. Two men brought you in. Do you recall being carried in?"

"Somewhat…leg hurts like 'ell."

"It's fractured. I've set it, and think you'll have full recovery. You can thank the Almighty it hadn't broken through the skin. I would be forced to amputate. As it is, time will tell. Until then, you'll not use it for several months at least. It's imperative you do not stand on it. It will crack through the skin if you do."

Christopher wondered how much Asia heard, as he began a soft snore.

Miss Fitzjames said, "You're a surprise, considering how we met."

"First impressions are important. Tell me, Miss Fitzjames are you a squeamish sort of woman, who doesn't like getting her hands dirty?"

"I do like a challenge if that's your inference. I'd be glad to assist in this poor man's recovery."

He placed a slat on each side of Asia's leg and looked at Miss Fitzjames. "Hold these in place while I bind his leg with the strips you cut."

Within minutes he was finished and pleased his patient hadn't reacted. He glanced at Miss Fitzjames. "You don't appear the least bit squeamish. Your gender doesn't usually abide hands on medical care."

"Fortunate for you, you've just widened your knowledge of *my* gender. I'm glad to have been of some use."

He glanced from the bundle on the side table to her. "They'll be put to good use here. You must be new to Hawthorn?" He stayed by the table afraid Asia might roll off as the liquor loosened its hold.

"A few months, now."

"Where is home, then?" She was as lovely to look at as he remembered when they bumped heads in the apothecary's shop though she'd been mad as a wet hen at the time.

"My father requested we bring his ashes back and bury them on Ireland's soil. We came from Portugal. Obidos, a small village. My mother's home."

"A true man of the sod, then." He laid a hand on Asia's shoulder, thinking he may be waking, but then the tar settled, and Christopher inquired, "Had your father a lengthy illness?"

Her lovely eyes darkened, and she nodded. "Painful, too." A minute of silence ensued, and she asked, "Are you curious because of your profession?"

"No. The Catholic Church is against cremation, and you mentioned his ashes. In the case of a length illness, or plague, I know the Church does allow it. That and also why would your father want you to bury him here when he died so far away?"

The question obviously bothered her; she began backing out of the infirmary. "I mustn't forget my other duties. I need to go."

"Before you leave, allow me to apologize for the mess I made of your papers."

Her eyes narrowed. "It was my bonnet and hair falling awry that grieved me almost as much as being knocked to the floor, if you must know." With that, she spun on her heel and marched down the corridor toward the kitchen.

◌❀◌

The kitchen bustled with energy and Renata found her friend Siofra in conversation with a woman making up the cot in the corner next to the fireplace, another at the sideboard peeling potatoes. "I'll peek in on Mrs. Cooke and meet you back at the school."

Siofra glanced at the two women with whom she'd been visiting. "Thank you for allowing me to rest, but duty calls."

Renata noted a tiny fluff of red hair at Mrs. Cooke's breast. It was a sweet scene. She took the chair next to the bed.

"You must be content with your boys. Thrilling news for all of us in the apartments. How you managed to arrive on the doctor's doorstep is a mystery. You couldn't have chosen a worse time. It's absolutely horrid outside."

She nodded, as her infant suckled his fill. "I was determined. And Mike is on a cloud. My poor Mary. I hear she wants to see her babies, as she's been telling her da. But he says wait till the blow is over."

"The doctor appears quite capable."

"Mr. Curran? He's why I've got my boys."

Renata's breath caught upon hearing the name *Curran. Had she just met...? No!* Curran was a common enough name. Her fingertips spread across her lips, stifling the urge to shriek. *Curran,* could he possibly be related to Morgan Curran? He *must* be. A nephew, a *son.* Oh, my! Her father's arch enemy, the reason she was in Ireland. His dying wish was to be buried close to a man he hated more than anyone else in the world. He intended to irritate Morgan Curran through eternity with his proximity.

She caught herself from blabbing to Mona and leaned over the infants makeshift sleeping drawer. Her mind in a whirl thinking of her father and that Mr. Curran might be related to Morgan Curran. Beset with conflicting feelings, because for a moment in the infirmary Mr. Curran's kindness and soothing manner to an injured man appealed to her.

She had noted compassion, even if she also suspected he was a trifle overbearing. A little smile came to her as she considered she'd worn her newest frock and knew Mrs. Brown had made the most of her curves with the creation. What was wrong with her?

Mona's voice broke through her musing, "What? I'm sorry. Tell me again."

"Would you take Michael from me and bring Patrick over. I'll put him on my other side."

Renata took the warm little bundle from his mama. Already sound asleep, his tiny lips mimicked his nursing effort. Savoring the feel of him in her arms, she reluctantly placed him in the makeshift crib and picked up his brother who was beginning to fuss, tiny fists grinding into rosebud lips. Would she ever have children of her own? At twenty-seven, and well on her way to spinsterhood, she was resigned to her future.

Mona settled her son against her full breast with its swollen veins. Renata watched as he eagerly latched onto his nutrition. Something deep inside, almost like lightning, pained her.

Humming a lullaby, Mona caressed the tiny russet-haired infant, giving as much love to him as she had to his brother. The miracle of it all. Mona spoke softly, "Have you met Christopher?"

"On the way in. He was setting a broken leg. I'm afraid I was a bit too inquisitive, I found myself staring at the procedure."

"You, Renata? I'm surprised. You are so composed."

"As it is, we met in Mr. Talbot's shop. Bumped heads attempting to pick up papers scattered in the wind yesterday." Her cheeks heated at the remembrance. "I think I was a bit of a fishwife."

Mona chuckled. "He's a calm sort. Very friendly, but the village is not accepting of his way. Learned in Scotland, he did. Brought us his know-it-all. Those rascals in the pub give him a hard going, they still do. Mike tells me of it from time to time."

"So, how did he end up delivering your babies?" She wandered to the makeshift crib absorbing the miracle therein.

"Call it fancy, but I wanted a son, and my old auntie told me 'have a man deliver you, then'. We ken how that worked out, now didn't we. I daren't tell Mike, he's such a hard-headed lump. When I wasn't home, he set off to his ma's place, and she can't keep her mouth shut to save a life, told him what I was up to. He muscled in here like a bull."

"Tell me you jest. You actually suggested the gender of a child is whether a man or a woman assists with delivery? Tell me you grasp the truth of it."

A sly smile came over Mona as she snapped the bottom of her son's foot with her finger. "Well, show me the proof of it, then. I got more than I wanted truth to tell."

"What did you just do to his tiny foot?"

"These wee critters already have patterns to them. This one falls asleep after a little bit, I want him full-fed. Snappin' his foot keeps him suckin' more so in his sleep, but he responds. Now, my Michael, is different. He gulps his full then falls asleep. Kind of like his father if I were to compare."

Renata couldn't help but ponder the sense of her remark as she took a chair. "What a life you have. And the things you know to do. Your family is fortunate."

"Mike understands. In his way he shows it." Obviously drowsy, she worked at staying awake, herself.

Renata suggested, "When he's fed, I'll take him and let you get some rest."

She intended to avoid an encounter with Mr. Curran when she left the infirmary. Mona and babies asleep, she closed the door to the bedroom, and nodded to Mrs. Kneely, Greta and Mary, whose morning work was displayed on the large table as they enjoyed a cup of tea. The scent of yeast bread rising was welcome as Renata pulled a shawl over her head and left through the kitchen door.

Her mother would worry if she didn't check in. Their apartment wasn't too far from the Strand, and she kept watch of the rising water before going back to the school where a makeshift kitchen had been set up, and blankets strewn about the floor for families to make do until the force subsided.

Her skirts billowed as she skittered about puddles making her way. Fallen branches, signs hanging from store fronts, a bedraggled dog meandering the street, an overturned cart another sodden dog sheltering within. The clean-up was going to take a great deal of time and effort.

The air was surprisingly mild and humid, a phenom hard to understand. The blasting rain was losing its intensity. Last eve it had been dark as a cave. Nearly every candle and lantern had been snuffed by the wind. and then night came on. It was horrid. Renata was grateful for today and the brightness and the softer wind that would dry the land.

12

Through the night the full force of the wind died to a rustling of treetops. The earthy scent of rotting wood, humid air, mold, mildew and rotting fish permeated every crevice and crack.

Villagers peeked out broken windows, and looked skyward at gaps in the ceilings, thankful to be alive.

Hawthorn folk were beginning to understand the totality of the tempest's fury, as they viewed the bleak and utter devastation wrought by the storm. Constable Waffer hustled through town ringing his bell, yelling out there was a gathering at the Black Pig for those able to help.

Before Christopher left for the village meeting, he spoke to Mrs. Kneely about Asia Malcolm's needs. "Plenty of water and soft foods." Grabbing his hat off the peg, he added, "Asia is not to walk, *at all*. I'm not sure what he'll recall from yesterday and try to stand."

"We'll take care of him, doc. Don't you worry. You need a bigger place, though. The kitchen is getting a bit crowded."

Mary and Greta were busy cleaning carrots and potatoes. Asia on a cot in the corner appeared to be taking in all the commotion, Mrs. Cooke and her infants were in the only spare room, which wasn't really a spare room anymore.

Mrs. Kneely inquired, "Is the lad off somewhere, then?"

He didn't want to hazard a guess with this woman, yet she deserved an answer. He picked up a piece of carrot top fallen off the table and dropped it in the trash pail. "I'm not certain of his whereabouts. His friend died and he took it pretty hard. You might add a prayer to your recipe for dinner." Christopher knew the dead man was Dino's last link to his abduction. Schmitty befriended him all the years since. It wouldn't be easy to give up that connection.

"*Ahh*. So be it then, doc."

Christopher grabbed his hat. "I'm going to the meeting at the Black Pig. I'll be back within the hour."

The damage to the village was enormous, multiple trees upended, most boats capsized, masts snapped in two. Thatched roofs had been torn off, and several deaths were some of Hawthorn's sad statistics. One could only guess what Waterford's devastation was considering its closer proximity to the River Suir.

Everywhere he looked Hawthorn was in a shamble, nothing spared. Folks stumbled about in a daze trying to make sense of it all.

Trees bordering Hawthorn's lough were either bent to the water or floating in it. Pale daylight beamed through sodden roofs illuminating wreckage. Fallen fences allowed livestock not slaughtered by the horror, to run free. Tall grasses flattened the landscape as the deluge pummeled the earth. Eerily quiet, Christopher knew it would take the birds and geese time to return.

Dwellings and boats, the livelihood of many fishermen, could require months to recover. Laying waste to dreams, loss of income, and death was going to take brute strength to overcome and require faith in tomorrow. The Irish had plenty of both. But the raging turbulence touched the entire village; and so, the question is who is left to bring a bit of cheer and hopefulness?

Village folk gathered at the Black Pig to determine how the inhabitants of Hawthorn were to dig their way out of Mother Nature's wrath.

Tossing a coin on the bar, Christopher waited for Padhraig to draw off a pint and slide it over the bar top. The pub was filling, men with disbelief etched on their faces mothers with children straggling behind, huddled in corners. A plaintive melody played on a concertina in the corner to his far right. Perhaps it was the only thing in the world the man possessed on this day after the fierce torrent moved on across southern Ireland to the Atlantic Ocean.

A table had been erected against the south wall with four chairs. Sitting in the chairs were St. John's Catholic Priest Father Riley Ryan, The Church of Christ's Reverend Alcott, Constable Waffer, and Mulroney owner of the printing press.

The Constable banged his gavel against the oaken tabletop, and the roar of conversation dropped to a murmur and then silence.

"We are here to discuss what's to be done with our village. I've received a note from the Magistrate in Waterford and can say their damage is perhaps more than ours.

"Our first concern is the repair of roofs. And cattle run off to someone else's property. Many of you had already gathered in your crops and stored them; for those of you who have not, we will need your names on a roster." He pointed using the gavel at a table near the end of the bar, where Carnahan waited.

Someone in the back waved. Waffer nodded, "Yes, Dennis?"

His tam crushed between big ham-like fists, Dennis asked, "Well, seein' as how I was already livin' in the barn since my cabin burned last year, would I get some help rebuilding?"

The Constable cocked his head toward Father Ryan and whispered in his ear. Then the Constable said, "It's been brought to my attention you refused the offer of help several months ago. Is that right?"

Dennis nodded his head, his gaze glancing sideways from right to left.

"Is your barn still standing?"

Barely perceptible, Dennis nodded.

"Is that where you sleep, then?"

Dennis shifted his gaze to the floor with a barely perceptible nod.

"Then I suggest you share your temporary home with those who have lost theirs. Under the extreme circumstances of the last few days, we've families needing immediate assistance. You'll have to makeshift for a while longer, Dennis, as is the whole of the village."

Someone from the back of the room yelled out, "You tell 'em constable, sir."

"I've got a tree in my house."

"What's to do with me boat upside down in the lough?"

"My chickens are dead."

"My husband is gone."

"My hay-ricks are blown to smithereens."

"The bones of our people are showin' through the sod."

"Birdsong is no more. The silence is deathlike. God has forsaken us. What 'ave we done 'ere that our land is now barren?"

Reverend Alcott stood. "Don't allow yourself to be forlorn, Mrs. Walker, and all the rest of you who have suffered. God didn't make this happen, and if you look around, you are not alone in your loss. This is precisely why we've gathered together, to figure out how to climb out of the confusion and destruction *together*."

The elder Mrs. Walker set up such a wail another woman drew her shawl about the shaking frame and led her to a corner in the back of the pub.

Constable Waffer banged his gavel again attempting to get on with solving immediate problems. "Who would be willing to organize the burning of rubbish and fallen trees and such?"

Several hands shot up, Christopher's being one of them.

The din increased and Waffer shouted, "Well, now, Billy-boy, and Cameron, and you two leaning against the wall, Tommy and Gar, the four of you will organize the effort."

Then Waffer cast his full attention on Christopher. "Doc, do you think you'll have the time, what with our needing you to hold down your surgery and all?" He pointed the blunt end of his gavel at Christopher and lowered his chin, glancing over his optics.

One of the two men who offered to help, said, "We'll come get you if needs be, doc, but Constable Waffer is right."

Christopher shrugged his shoulders. "I'll assist any way I can."

With a wide grin, the same man added, "Strappin' man that you are, I'm sure you'll get offers." A slight murmur interspersed with chuckles filtered through the pub, and a glance from several unmarried women didn't go unnoticed. Even in the face of the aftermath of the storm, humor prevailed.

The Constable took command again by banging his gavel. "No need to tease the doc, Billy-boy. It might be you needin' his efforts and you wouldn't want him finding it funny, now would you." He didn't waste a moment and added, "Those of you who volunteered, follow Billy-boy to clear debris and trees from the lanes."

A low rumble, a roar, and then a loud swoosh shuddered the air around them. Alerting everyone to a serious problem. With sudden renewed fear of the last days, folks glanced at each other as the fire bell set off a fierce clanging. Half the occupants of the Black Pig charged outside and ran toward a billow of rising smoke.

Women sobbed, mothers were forced to hold onto their children, who wanted to follow their fathers. With everything in Hawthorn so sodden how could a fire catch? Black smoke curled in the air eating up someone's abode.

The Constable, who remained inside the Black Pig, banged his gavel and yelled, "Order, order. By my authority, we'll end this discussion until tomorrow at the same time." As everyone had vacated, nary a soul heard his decision.

Padhraig and Ian glanced at one another, their hope being the fire wouldn't mean another death. Several deceased had been brought to them late yesterday and they had worked through the night to ready them as best they could. In two instances, clothing wasn't available as the storm poured rain into the cottages making a sodden mess of everything. The pair of morticians had to make do with what the deceased was wearing at the time of their death. Terrible business this when dignity was forfeit for the beloved who passed on.

Later in the day, after the fire was contained to smoldering ash, Waffer and Mulroney discovered it was a barrel of poteen that caught aflame from the hearth and blew up the O'Cleary's cottage. It appeared Mrs. O'Cleary's husband, Earl, whose charred body was found beneath the stones of the chimney, had brought his illicit whiskey-making device inside during the storm. He was pronounced dead at the scene. Women were able to salvage a few items and took the missus away. Several men carted O'Cleary's remains in a wheelbarrow to McCarthy's Funeral Home.

Christopher climbed the steps to the infirmary after being called to pronounce Mr. O'Cleary dead at eighty years of age. The poor man gone to his reward and now his widow had no one. Christopher understood their three grandchildren sailed to America several years earlier.

Mrs. O'Cleary would be well cared for by her loving neighbors and Christopher thought once again, how compelling life was in this small village. He had also heard the mutterings of many of the men who depended on Earl's whiskey. It was left for the young doc to shake his head at the incredulity of drinking the *poteen* and rotting one's insides or simply being blown up by it all.

Talbot locked up his shop before scurrying up Stephen's Lane. Rounding the corner onto Forge he saw Mr. Martin leaning against a shed with half a roof gone that had withstood most of the savage storm.

"You're late," growled Martin as he shoved his watch into his vest pocket.

"Cut to the chase. I had to close my door on two patrons." Talbot had a hard time liking Martin, a defrocked doctor, if one could think of such a thing. Talbot didn't suffer fools readily, but the coin was good.

And Talbot knew Martin to be a fool. Two years earlier he bled Lord Darnley after suffering a stroke. Martin defied Lady Darnley's express command not to inflict the barbaric procedure on her husband. Her influence was such Martin was banned from practice and practically run out of town.

After having his practice besmirched, Martin retired to his estate. He began writing and illustrating a book about the human body, and its functions, thinking to reinstate himself with the community. His aspirations were that Hawthorn and Waterford folk would perceive him as a brilliant doctor in spite of Lady Darnley's declaration.

His research required he perform autopsies on corpses. With his need, Martin leaned in, clearing his throat, his harsh whisper threatening, "I need an adult female. A fresh one."

Talbot's Adam's apple bobbed as he swallowed. "It's a dangerous time with the ground swollen from the rains and folk trying to bury their own."

Martin straightened up. Spit and spittle mixed with his threat, "You'll do what I want, or I'll take my business elsewhere. You've been greedy enough these past months."

"What if Waffer's keeping an eye on the graveyards. I'm not taking a chance."

Martin snorted. "You've given an idiot power over you."

Talbot swallowed hard thinking yes, he'd given *this* idiot power over him. But the gold he dangled in his face was worth it. What he said to Talbot was different. "Idiot or not, I don't want to take the chance getting caught. Everyone's riled up—"

As quick as a lizard, Martin grabbed Talbot's upper arm, shaking him. "Which makes it the perfect time to get me what I want." With a grunt he loosened his hold shoving the chemist back a step.

Talbot brushed off the sleeve of his coat as if brushing off Martin's demand and stood tall. "I'd keep my hands to myself if I were you, doc. You'd do well to realize the favors I've been doing you."

Martin yanked down on the hem of his jacket, straightening it. He squinted with anger. "You get what I want, or my funding is quit."

Talbot hissed, "You still owe me for the last two."

"Then you best be about business." Martin spun on his heel, not a moment too soon. Two sodden men each with a barrel full of debris rolled up Forge on their way to empty carts in the bog west of the village.

The stench of their lode assailed Talbot's nose. Curse Martin. He'd a mind to go to Waffer himself if it weren't for the fact he was as deeply involved as his nemesis. Though he wasn't the one defiling corpses, he would still be at fault.

❦

Christopher made his way through the debris on his way to the infirmary. He saw Talbot and another man, Mr. Martin, a doctor who used to administer to the His Lordship, Earl of Darnley, and some of the villagers. The two appeared to be arguing.

Martin angrily jabbed his finger at Talbot. Christopher couldn't make out the gist of it, but he knew enough about Mr. Martin's reputation, he guessed it would be unsavory.

Christopher recalled hearing that Lady Darnley had banned Martin from the estate, ruining his reputation. Villages were nothing if not purveyors of gossip.

He dreaded the idea that someday he could be on the wrong side of a rumor.

Thinking of the Darnley's, word filtered through the village of the damage to their ancestral home, Rockmore Hall. The earl suffered the loss of his picturesque wall of green that surrounded most of the park. Gone were many of the ash, oaks and firs that made up the copse where stood the ancient Celtic chapel. In the

1300s, once the invading Normans learned of Christianity, they built the chapel as a benediction for their barbaric marauding.

Without its shroud of mighty forest, the little chapel now stood in the northeast corner of Rockmore park reclusive and estranged, like a vagrant.

13

The second day after the storm passed, Renata hurried along the path to the infirmary. Mr. Cooke had asked her to check in on his wife and babies. She made haste and avoided the village meeting at the Black Pig surmising anyone who could walk would be there, the doctor included. She picked her way around uprooted trees and puddling in the lanes.

It was a relief mother nature's violence moved on, even though she left a mess few had witnessed the likes of in many a year.

The air was heavy with a musty decay. The sky overcast with heavy streaks of gray that allowed intermittent glimpses of blue sky. They had neither lost a window nor suffered any roof damage on their side of the apartment and counted themselves fortunate. So many folks were not so lucky.

Mr. Cooke knocked on their door late last night asking if they were all right. Part of his roof had torn off. Renata offered to shelter him and his daughter. He declined though asked if she would visit his wife and tell her what had happened. He was taking their two-year old daughter, Mary, to relatives up near Portlaw so he could fix the roof without worry about her.

At the infirmary, Renata was greeted by Mrs. Kneely and introduced to another young woman in the kitchen, Krysta, who apparently regularly cleaned and cooked for the doctor. Flaxen-haired and pleasant though with a quirky demeanor who asked quite boldly, "What's your business here? If I might ask."

"I'm on a neighborly mission, and if you'll excuse me, I'll get to it." Renata could feel Krysta's narrowed inspection burrowing into her back as she opened the bedroom door.

Mona was awake. The infants lay in the make-shift crib sound asleep. Renata sat in a chair near the bed, whispering, "How was your night?"

"Well enough. Mike came by earlier with Mary. He's taking her to family. She threw a hissy when she saw me. The babes meant nothing to her. I guess until the roof is fixed, we're better here."

"It could be worse. It's just the roof, not your home. There is destruction everywhere."

Mona threw off the blanket. "I got an earful this early morn when Krysta came in, didn't she now. She's been with her mam until the worst of it blew over. What a nightmare, kept me awake most of the night, but then died right off. Did you have trouble sleeping?"

Renata would be inclined to say yes, but her reason for not sleeping had nothing to do with the weather. Her problem was Mr. Curran and how to avoid him. She said, "Not really. The roar died down considerably, and I was very tired which always helps."

She lifted a hair brush off the dresser. "Would you like me to brush your hair?"

"I think I'll get out of bed and sit in a chair a while. It'll keep me busy for a change. Somethin' other than changin' nappies and feedin' little 'uns."

Renata handed her the brush after Mona situated herself, then said. "I'll get us some tea."

Mona pulled her long brown hair forward over her shoulder and began drawing the brush through the ends. "Take your time. I'm not going anywhere, and I ken how occupied you've been with your mam. Visit with Mrs. Kneely a bit."

Renata closed the door behind her, put the kettle over the fire, and retreated outside to a thicket in the back of the infirmary. In the short time she'd been inside, the sky brightened a bit more. She meandered through the path of stone, drips of water falling from the bushes, and was surprised by a bench in amongst tall shrubbery. The heavy scent of musk and wet earth was everywhere. It might take more than a few days of warmth and wind to dry things up.

A dark-haired lad appeared up the opposite path and stopped in his tracks when he noticed her sitting on the bench. His olive skin and dark eyes had her guessing he was not Irish. She thought he had the look of an Italian, maybe Portuguese about him and said, "Hello."

He flashed a guarded glance at her and muttered, "I didn't know anyone was about."

"Out for a walk, are you?" She smiled at him.

Hands jammed in pockets, he assessed her.

Undaunted, she inquired further, "You must live here about. Did your family suffer much with the storm?"

His vision narrowed as if she taxed him with her question.

"I…I live with the doc."

"You do? Well, then I already know your home didn't suffer as most others. You are fortunate."

He glanced at the earth and kicked at a rock with the toe of his shoe. "Lucky I am."

"You don't sound convincing." She patted the bench. "Would you like to sit a while?"

His gaze lifted just enough to look at her, as if he was calculating his options. Coming to a decision he shared the bench.

"You've been out walking, then? Observing the aftermath and troubles, no doubt."

He didn't answer her immediately and she waited. "You aren't hurt, are you?"

He shook his head, his voice soft as he spoke. "I'm sad my friend died."

"Sad at God or your friend?" Her hands clasped in her lap, she stilled, waited to discover if she could help him.

"Mostly Schmitty. He was my family. He got sick, and the doc said there was nothing to be done for him but make him comfortable."

"I am Miss Fitzjames. What may I call you?"

"Dino." Barely a whisper as his throat clutched.

"Dino, when someone we are close to dies, it is quite sad, heart rending. My father died, and I'm still sad. My mother and I came all the way here from our home in Portugal to bury him because he wished it."

He searched her face for something. Suddenly, he mustered, "Schmitty could have called anywhere his home."

"Is the doctor taking care of his burial?"

His head of dark wavy curls nodded. "The ground has to dry up first." His hands clasped, he bent forward dropping them between his knees.

Her heart quickened for him, and she suggested, "When your friend is buried, you can honor him by thinking about a favorite story, maybe the very first day you met him, and how he became your friend. A story to fill your heart with gladness when you think of him." She put her arm about his shoulders giving him a squeeze. He was skin and bone. "You do understand he is going to a much better place."

"That's what doc said." A tear slipped down into the dirt on his cheek. "I stayed away cause if the cap'n saw me he'd follow me and hurt the doc. The doc's good. He fixes people. I hid till the boat pulled anchor."

She puzzled over this a moment. "Are you telling me you've run away and are just now returning?"

The wavy head of hair nodded as he remained fixated on his dirty hands folded between his knees.

She couldn't account for Mr. Curran, but she could certainly imagine his concern over this young boy's absence. "I bet he's terribly worried about you."

Clearly startled, his regard centered on her. Then he shrugged his bony shoulders

Withdrawing her arm, she said, "You may keep your secrets, Dino. But please give some thought to easing the burden on the good doctor by letting him know you've returned. He must be quite worried about you."

Renata left the lad to ponder her words and returned to the kitchen. The tea tray was ready, and she picked it up to take it into Mona when Krysta entered. "Let me get that door for you, ma'am."

Hand on the doorknob, Krysta smiled politely, showing a row of little white baby teeth as if she wasn't old enough to have lost them yet. Though Renata had a sense she was in her thirties.

Before Krysta turned the latch, Asia said, "You're the lady what came in yesterday?"

"I'm Miss Fitzjames. And you are Asia?"

He nodded. "I'm hearing a wee one in there. It cries enough for two."

Renata could hardly contain her chuckle. "You would be right in that, there are two of them. If the mother permits, I'll bring one to show you before I leave."

"I'd like that. I haven't spied a newborn ever as I think on it. It'd be a feast for me eyes." He looked as though he was trying to stay awake but wasn't managing very well.

Krysta opened the door. Asia smiled at her before he nodded off, and Mona's voice could be heard. "What's going on out there?"

Within the room, Renata said, "The infirmary is overrun with workers and a patient. Yet everything appears to go smoothly. Asia is a patient on a cot outside your door."

"This place buzzes like a beehive. I think the doc inspires folks. Asia must be the one they got the cot for. It was over there under the window yesterday." She nodded toward the corner.

Renata stood at the make-shift crib glancing at the beautiful infants, tuckered out, no doubt with full little tummies. "You are right about the beehive. The doctor carries on well enough with all his duties."

"Inspired you, has he?" Mona's lips curled into a mischievous grin.

A bit ruffled, she said, "The doctor? Hardly."

Mona giggled. "Do I ken a bit of vexation?"

Renata bestowed a smile on one of the infants in the makeshift crib. She was not going to burden this new mother and friend with *her* dilemma concerning Mr. Curran.

"I've touched a nerve." Mona adjusted the cover over herself.

Renata took a deep breath before she glanced at Mona. Why was she nettled? What is it about the doctor that upset her? The fact that her father carried a vengeance against his father shouldn't bother her a wit.

What she said was, "It's not the doctor. It's my mother. Our purpose in coming here was to bury my father in his homeland. Then the storm hit. We're both a bit overcome."

"The storm has put off your plans, then? Your mother did appear to be out of sorts the few times I've met her."

Renata tried not to scoff. "Her maid keeps her occupied. My mother has taken it upon herself to teach the girl a smattering of words to help her purchase from the market. Truthfully, I think it's a disaster. That maid has no desire to be here. Why would she put effort into learning the language?"

Mona glanced at the make-shift crib. "I wouldn't mind a maid."

She grinned. "You wouldn't want this one."

Mona threw off the blanket and crossed over to her sleeping babies, a dreamy look in her eyes.

Renata inquired, "Did Mike tell you The Church of Christ's cemetery had some graves uncovered with the flood?"

"No, he was all about cooing to his sons. He even changed Patrick's nappy."

Renata smiled at the thought. "And you were pleased as could be."

"I pinched myself. Could hardly believe my eyes." Her thoughts wandered to that singular incident. She sighed and continued, "I'm hoping you won't leave any time soon. I want to keep you a bit longer. I'm grateful for our conversation. Takes me outside myself, it does."

"If my father were alive, I do believe we would settle here. But with mother's family in Obidos, she's not given a thought to remaining in Ireland. Half her things are still in the trunk, proving how eager she is to leave."

⚘

Christopher was amazed his building sustained only minor damage after all the horror stories he heard this morning. The railing on the front porch was loose. He made a mental note to fix it, and in the meantime scrawled a note and pinned it to the wooden rails so folks would know not to put their weight on it.

Mona and the twins, with Mrs. Kneely's help, were doing fine. Krysta busied herself wiping crumbs off the counter as she mentioned her mother's anxiety caused her to hide under their bed the entire four days. No one saw her come out, but she must have from time to time to eat and use the pot.

Christopher poked his head in the back bedroom to check on Mrs. Cooke and her twins. He couldn't help the grin on his face as Miss Fitzjames glanced up at him from the chair, she was rocking the other baby. Mrs. Cooke, modestly covered, obviously nursed one of the infants.

He said, "Just checking in. How you are doing?"

"Pampered as all get out, doc. When do you think I can leave here?"

"What has Mr. Cooke to say?" Christopher flicked a glance at Miss Fitzjames, who settled one of the twins in the crib.

"He's thinking another day and the patches to the roof will be made."

"You and your babies are doing fine. There is no rush. I don't need the bed. I'll leave it up to you to decide."

Miss Fitzjames picked up her reticule and leaned over kissing Mona on the forehead. "I'll say good day. It's getting late, and you know my mother."

Christopher opened the door for Miss Fitzjames and followed her out. "I'll walk you home."

"That won't be necessary."

It was obvious Krysta heard his offer when she glanced up from chopping an onion. "Oh, but it is, Miss Fitzjames. It grows darker and the lamps are damaged."

Surprised at Krysta's reinforcement he added, "If it would make you more at ease, I'll stay five paces behind." He chuckled.

With a crisp voice, she complied. "As I said, that won't be necessary." She turned away from him and marched down the corridor to the front door.

Christopher grabbed up his coat and hat, then stepping out of the office, he picked up the lantern on the step. Miss Fitzjames was on her way and it didn't take him long to catch up. Grinning down at her, he said, "I'm not walking you home. I'm out for a stroll."

Despite the destruction everywhere, a calm, temperate evening was upon them, much different from the past week. Because of his lantern, they were able to avoid low-hanging branches, heavy with rain, and stray limbs still aground.

When they reached her apartment on Market, she surprised him. "Would you care to come up and meet my mother?"

He tried to cover his astonishment. It wasn't as though he was meeting the monarch. "Very much."

He shuttered the lantern and followed her into the apartment. An elder, he supposed it was Mrs. Fitzjames, rocked in a chair near the fire, her legs covered in a shawl as she worked on some sewing. She was taken off guard with his appearance and quickly hid her work in a basket on the floor.

"Mother, this is Mr. Curran. He has been kind enough to walk me home. I'll fix some tea. My mother, Mrs. Fitzjames."

Hat in hand, lantern on the floor by the door, he nodded. "My pleasure, ma'am. It is getting dark, and I didn't want your daughter to walk alone."

Grim faced she forced the words, "She's capable. Doesn't need to be cosseted."

For a single moment he cringed at the coldness in her voice. "Most of the lamps didn't make it through the storm. Navigating the fallen limbs and water-soaked lanes, she needed a light." He couldn't help adding. "I think of it as a safety measure, ma'am."

Her eyelids lowered and she pushed the rocker with her heels, as if he needn't have explained. He inquired, "How long have you been in Hawthorn?"

"Mid-July. Enough time to settle in before this fiendish blow struck." Her gravelly voice was thickly accented. She hadn't offered him a chair. He stood near the door where it wasn't so stifling.

The scrunch of her brow unnerved him. He said, "Quite a shock to us all. We've not had such a storm since I can't recall when."

He saw Miss Fitzjames preparing tea in the little alcove to his left where the kitchen was located.

Mrs. Fitzjames was agitated. He couldn't imagine over what unless she hadn't wanted her daughter to visit Mrs. Cooke. The woman barked from across the room, "I didn't catch it. Your name again?"

He stepped into the center of the room. "Mr. Curran, ma'am."

"Would Morgan Curran be a relation?" She continued to push the rocker.

"As a matter of fact, that was my father's name. Why do you ask?"

Her jaw gaped, and she did nothing to hide her astonishment.

Miss Fitzjames came into the room with a tray carrying tea and scones. "Please sit, Mr. Curran. Have tea before you leave. I understand you haven't eaten since noon."

So, she noticed his habits, did she? The thought brought a twinkle to his eyes. He took the only other chair between the two women and turned a raised brow on her.

Answering the raised brow, Miss Fitzjames said, "Your housekeeper, Krysta. She demonstrates an avid interest in you." She handed a cup and scone to her mother, then sat next to Mr. Curran. "I notice how well liked you are with all the women who run your kitchen." After handing him tea, she picked up her cup and sipped not quite hiding her smile.

He chuckled before drinking. "I think of the infirmary as a place of healing and friendship. Mrs. Kneely and Krysta get on well. Mrs. Kneely uses the kitchen to make quantities of meals when the need arises. Storms, a sudden illness encompassing many households at once, that kind of need."

The mother closed her gaping mouth but continued to grimace not taking her curiosity from him. For some reason she was apparently shocked by his father's name.

"He's Morgan's son?" said Mrs. Fitzjames as she twisted in her chair, practically shouting at her daughter. "Did you know?"

Miss Fitzjames glanced at him with a mixture of apology and concern, saying by way of explanation, "We've only just met for the second time." She had no desire to tell her mother about her earlier suspicions.

Christopher enlightened Miss Fitzjames with a grin before he sipped his tea, his right brow rising with his declaration, "The third time."

She smiled as she drew the china to her lips.

Silence reined, making him curious. "Why is the name Curran such a surprise?" He hadn't yet tasted the scone and wondered if he was no longer invited to stay. What could possibly be such an overwhelming surprise...or in the case of the mother, a shock?

Miss Fitzjames set her cup on the tray. He didn't miss the direct gaze she cast on her mother. Almost an affront as if to say, *be quiet.* He set his cup down and stood. "If you will excuse me, I need to get back to the infirmary. Thank you for the refreshment."

Miss Fitzjames also stood. "But you haven't tasted it." She wrapped the treat in a napkin. "At least take it with you. And thank you for walking me home. Don't forget your lantern."

He nodded to her mother and taking the offer, said, "Good evening, ma'am, miss." He grabbed the handle on the lantern and left.

With only a few stars, and a quarter moon to guide him, he bit into the biscuit and wondered what the *devil* had taken place with the mother. Was she edging into senility? Did she not want a man to show interest in her daughter? No need to concern herself on that score. He'd had enough of women to last a lifetime. However, he found he'd much rather think of Miss Fitzjames than Caroline Hammond. Blazes and damn!

The last half hour spent with Miss Fitzjames' bullying-mother his interest should be sufficiently doused. But a spark in the woman's daughter intrigued him.

Opening the door, he saw directly into his office. Dino was in his chair, swiveling it in a circle.

"What have we here? The image of a ghost?" He quickly strode into the room, as Dino spun for the last time, then stopped the chair and jumped out of it coming around the desk.

"I won't run away again, promise. You're too fine a bloke to leave without tellin' you."

"Where is the lad I've come to care for?" Christopher covered his mouth, pretending to hide shock.

Dino hugged himself with delight. "She was right, she told me you wouldn't raise h—, I mean be mad?"

Christopher got down on bended knee and held his arms wide. Dino stepped into the embrace. His small head nested against Christopher's padded wool jacket.

Somewhat consoled, Christopher inquired, "She?"

"The friend of Mrs. Cooke's. I would have come around, but she gave me a shove."

"Where did you shelter?"

"In a bloke's barn."

"Does he have a name?"

"Folks yelled for Dennis. He wasn't around much, but I think he lives in his barn. The house looked burned bad."

"That would be Dennis. I suspect other folks moved into the barn, too."

With a skeptical glance, Dino burst out, "Too many by my count."

"Well, the Constable told Dennis to share his barn with folks whose cottages had been damaged in the storm."

"I played kick ball with a couple of my friends from school. Yesterday was the best day since…since…" he gulped causing his Adam's apple to bob.

Christopher ruffled his hair. "It's fine, son. I accept why you ran, and I clearly understand why you've come back. I much prefer you home. Though you'll have to bunk in my room for a day or two."

"As long as you don't snort. I never heard such a racket as Dennis put up. His poor horse got so sick of it, he kicked up a fuss, stomping around in his stall. Most of the folks curled up in the hay tried yelling at him. One woman shook her husband till he woke, makin' sounds like Dennis, and had him push Dennis on his side so he'd quit. It was like listen' to a tune of snorts."

Christopher held up his hand as if to say *no more*.

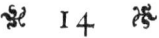

14

K rysta prepared a breakfast of pancakes and bacon for all occupants. Dino set a place at the table for Mrs. Cooke. Asia, who lay on the cot with his back resting against the wall, eyed Krysta as she bustled about the kitchen.

Christopher ate quickly and returned to his office with logs to enter and medicines to order from Mr. Talbot.

With no school today, Dino visited with Mrs. Cooke and her fascinating infants. He'd never seen one before, and two of them were double the interest. Kind of like looking in a mirror, the very same image. "How can you tell which one's which?"

"Something strange about mothers, we've a sense. If you look close, Patrick has a tiny crease on his left arm near the elbow." She urged him, "You can pull the blanket a bit and look. It's fine."

Carefully, Dino tugged the flannel, drawing it off a tiny left arm.

"Now look at his brother," she said from the chair.

As he withdrew the flannel, his face immediately brightened. "So, you know this one is Patrick, then?"

He covered them up and turned to Mrs. Cooke. Her smile was pleasant as she said, "May I ask about your mother?"

Dino hesitated a moment unsure of his memory. "I think she

had dark hair and dark eyes. Seems she smiled a lot. I mostly remember she smelled like sunshine and always let me have biscuits and jam. I think she got burnt once and someone else cooked."

Mona sucked in a breath and the lad glanced at her. He didn't seem remorseful in the least. In fact, his voice took on a note of sanctifying grace. His beautiful memory kept her alive, if only in his young mind. She could have cried. "I don't look like your mam, but I am one who needs a hug right now."

He folded into her embrace, patting her on the back. His little body sturdy in her arms. "Wherever your mother is, Dino, you can pretend she just gave you this hug."

"You're nice like she was. She wouldn't know me. I've grown a lot since I saw her."

"Mothers know, just like I know the difference between Patrick and Michael." She squinted at him. "You can be sure of it."

Later in the afternoon, after Christopher finally cleared his waiting room, he found Dino lingering in the office. Bending over the desk he whispered, "The babies were in her tummy?" and at Christopher's nod, Dino gushed, "Gorsh, she must have been big as a whale?"

A feeling of warmth came over him at Dino's childish question. He hadn't been entirely robbed of all his rightful innocence. "Babies begin as a seed and grow in the mom's belly. You began the same way in your mother's stomach. Same as every living creature on earth."

"How does the seed get in her?"

Oh, oh, he was on the brink of a *talk* he wasn't exactly sure he wanted to have with this young lad just yet. "Women are born with them. When the time is right, the seed grows."

Dino's brows rose into his olive-skinned forehead, his lips

pursed, as if receiving intense and secret information. Then he asked, "When do you think I'll get my room back?"

Blowing out a long breath, as if he had just dodged a hit with a sledgehammer, Christopher answered, "As soon as Mr. Cooke gets his roof patched. And I do believe that could be soon. You might wander over and ask if you could do anything to help him."

"Yes, sir, doc. Where's he live?"

"Above Browne's Dress Shop on Market. The Cookes live upstairs across the hall from your new friend, Miss Fitzjames."

"Would it be fittin' to knock at *her* door?"

"I wouldn't be surprised one bit if she invited you in." He drew a map for the lad. "Don't be gone long. And stay away from the fires, they can be quite dangerous."

The mop of black curly hair fell over his brow. His sincerity was evident as he met Christopher's gaze and said, "I will."

Moments after Dino's departure, Constable Waffer huffed up the walk to the front door and bounded into the office. "We found a dead man, way before the storm hit from the looks of it. We need you to take a look."

Christopher pulled on his waistcoat. "How did you discover him?"

"Cutting up the rubbish and hauling it to the fire. One of the men saw a boot and tried to pick it up, but a foot was attached to a leg, attached to a…"

"I get the picture." He grabbed his hat and they left.

Filthy and wet with their labors, the men had placed the body on a higher patch of grass near where they'd found him. The corpse was fully clothed, obviously a laborer with his calloused hands and well-worn clothing. Christopher's cursory search did not provide a means of death. No stab wounds, nothing to indicate a fight. The body had begun to decompose, so he couldn't begin to determine the possible cause of death. Several of the men held a sleeve to their nose at the offensive odor.

One of the men had gone through the dead man's pocket and

handed Christopher two scraps of paper—did that mean he could read—and a metal coin with a scrolled letter B etched on it.

Christopher scrutinized the rough wool of his clothing. Flaxen hair, a gray mustache and bushy brows. He decided the corpse's eyes were pale blue, though he wasn't certain due to the deterioration.

Waffer said, "What you thinkin', doc?"

"Let's get the body to the mortuary. Have Padhraig prepare it best he can for burial. If there are any wounds, he'll find them."

Waffer said, "Listen up a minute, doc. This is on the quiet, but there's been body snatchers at their fiendish business. You don't think this here fellow was one of their…?"

Christopher stared at the man. "Since when?"

"A couple of months. Maybe three."

"Which graveyard?"

"Both Christ's Church and St. John's."

Christopher shook his head. "Did Reverend Alcott notice something?"

"That's the devil of it. On my walkabout one night I found fresh diggings. Since then there have been eight more. The Reverend refuses to believe that could be going on in his parish."

"Even with your proof?"

"Until I dig up a grave and see if the body's gone, it's all circumstantial. And what with the blasted storm and now all this rubbish that needs clearing…" he scratched the back of his head.

Christopher offered, "I don't think this corpse was body snatching. This may be a question for Padhraig." Christopher's hat tipped when he bent over the corpse and he readjusted it.

In a hushed tone, Waffer said, "I'd like you not to mention this to anyone. My investigation is ongoing."

"You've got my word, constable."

Waffer rounded his shoulders his chin jutted. "I notice you seem mighty concerned about a dead body, doc. How come?"

Christopher's eyes squinted at the stocky constable. "Not a half hour ago you asked me here, do you recall doing that?"

A wind had risen and Waffer pulled the collar up. "You looked him over as if you had plans for the dead man. Body snatchers do nasty things. Cut open vitals and such."

Disgusted, Christopher growled at him. "Be careful whom you suspect, constable. I'm in the business of healing folks."

❧

The next day, Christopher headed off in the direction of McCarthy's Funeral Parlor. Padhraig was finishing up with old man McCleary's remains. His body was in the coffin and ready for burial. Schmitty's remains were on the table in the process of readying him for burial. Padhraig had a full house.

Christopher got to the point of his visit. "A body has been discovered decomposition well under way, the man died before the storm. Maybe a couple of weeks before. I might have an idea as to the identity, but I don't want to talk to his wife until we rule out murder."

Padhraig wiped his hands with a rag. "Ain't it a cussed thing. Who do you think it is?"

"Brandt."

Padhraig scratched the back of his head. "It would give his wife and daughters a lift to learn he hadn't run out on them."

"Keep me posted as to what you find, then I'll bring her down here. Hopefully she can identify the corpse once you determine the means of death. If it is him, he'll need a quick burial. He's past ripe now."

Padhraig nodded at the corpse on the table. "Your friend here will be ready tomorrow. Say about ten for the service?"

Christopher nodded.

❧

On their way to visit Mrs. Cooke, Renata's mother fixated on Mr. Curran walking her daughter home the other evening, and said,

"You are a bold woman, showing interest in him. Men take advantage of women who act like you." Her mother tugged at the veil of her hat with gloved fingers, a satisfied look on her wrinkled face.

Renata sighed. Her mother never tired of casting dark thoughts on perfectly innocent behaviors. "He is completely dedicated to his profession. I have no reason to consider him anything other than kindly in nature toward all people."

"And, handsome he is, broad shouldered, bright eyed." Her mother's dark assessing gaze slid up and down her daughter's well-groomed figure. "You aren't getting any younger. But don't settle on him for a catch. He's not in your society. Don't you forget his father ruined your father, caused him an early death."

Renata stated rather firmly, "If anyone caused my father's death it was Morgan Curran, not his son. And, I have not *set my cap* on anyone. Please get—" Renata stopped herself from stomping her foot in a childish fit. "You are so stubborn."

"If your father could hear you talk to me, he would roll in his grave."

"Considering his remains are in a pottery jar, I don't expect he'll roll anywhere."

"Harrumph." They bustled up along Forge toward the infirmary, all conversation at an end for now, for which Renata was grateful. Her mother tended to be civil when in company with others, and Renata hoped she had enough sense not to vent her spleen while visiting Mona.

After Renata introduced her mother to the women in the kitchen, Mrs. Kneely gave them her impression of the storm. "Mark my words, the English fairies invaded our poor island forcing the *Little People* who protect us to disappear amid a ferocious whirlwind."

Renata tried not to giggle at the fanciful idea. She directed her mother toward Mona's bedroom who appeared quite pleased to see them. "Look at my babies, Mrs. Fitzjames. It's lovely how much they sleep for me."

Her mother stood at the makeshift crib for several minutes mesmerized by the sleeping infants.

Renata said, "Your roof should be finished today or tomorrow. Mike had several friends helping when we left."

Patrick began to fuss, and Mona got out of bed and sat in the rocker as Renata handed the babe to her. "I think Patrick has colic he's been fussin' up a storm. Oops, I shouldn't say storm, should I?"

Renata's face brightened with humor. "We'd get squalls in Obidos, but I don't recall anything like this. It's comforting to know you're safe here with your babies."

Mrs. Fitzjames drew off her glove and touched a tiny pink foot that peeked out from the blanket. "He is lovely, Mona. You must be proud. Red heads, too."

"Doc says all babies eyes are blue at birth, then they change to the color they will be. But with Mike and me and Mary bein' blue, these little fellows will, too, most likely."

Mrs. Fitzjames shuffled to the only other chair in the room, a scowl forming. "I am deprived of grandchildren." Her attention focused on Renata.

"Such a thing to bemoan. Be happy you have an intelligent and delightful daughter."

Mona's generous compliment fueled Renata's ire against her mother. "Perhaps my mother would be willing to claim her maid's children someday."

Mrs. Fitzjames' narrowed gaze settled on her daughter. "If this is a jest, I am not sure how to take it."

Renata formed a conciliatory smile. "It was meant kindly, Mother. You dote on Lea, why wouldn't you do the same with her children."

Michael began fussing and Renata bent to him urging him to suck on his fist. His bright inspection fixed on the feather in her hat. "This one is docile as a lamb."

"Five days old, and I ken their differences." Patrick over her shoulder, Mona gently patted his back. "I'll be more than happy to be home. Mary's missin' me, and I need to be about my own things."

Renata said, "It's fortunate Mr. Curran has room for you until Mr. Cooke gets the roof done."

Mrs. Fitzjames cast a disgruntled glance in her daughter's direction. "Harrumph. There you go, inferring *that* man can do no harm."

Mona giggled. "Well, some things haven't changed."

Renata glanced at the ceiling as if calling on a higher power.

❄

Asia Malcolm was content with the cot in the kitchen. Whispers were Krysta had taken a liking to him especially enjoying his banter. Christopher was relieved to know the maid's affections had shifted to Asia. She took special care in cleaning his leg as the doc had shown her. The patient was all atwitter when she showered him with attention.

Mike Cooke finished patching his roof, arrived in the afternoon to take his wife and babies home. Soon after the Cookes left, Christopher took a few minutes from his ledgers to shake out the mattress and pillow and put clean sheets on the bed. Dino ran in from his errands just in time for Christopher to tuck in the sheet.

"All mine." Dino's voice held a prideful air. He opened each drawer to look at the new clothing, his palm brushing over shirts and stockings.

School would open again day after tomorrow. Dino was excited with the news and the prospect of time spent with the other lads and lassies, and even Master Carleton, if truth be known.

❄

For Schmitty's graveside service, Dino presented himself to Christopher. He dressed in short pants, long stockings, shoes, a clean shirt with a collar.

"Shoes, and no one insisted you wear them." Christopher glanced at Dino through the image in the mirror.

"Doc, this is really important. It's for Schmitty. Quit teasing me."

"Such a striking lad when cleaned up. Spit shined as my father used to say." Christopher reached for a double-breasted tailcoat. "Ready, then, are you?"

"Yes, sir."

"Well, let's give dear Mr. Schmitty a proper goodbye, then."

It was a rare day for autumn. No clouds with brilliant sun beating down on them. They walked to McCarthy's Funeral Parlor on Church Street, not far from The Church of Christ and the graveyard.

There were some people in Hawthorn Village who made it their business to show for every funeral whether they knew the deceased or not. As it was, three people were dotted about in chairs who could not have known Schmitty considering he was a sailor and brought ashore well into his sickness. Dino and Christopher stepped into the small parlor.

Christopher had already explained to Dino the *laying out* of the deceased. For the most part, families kept the bodies in their own parlors until burying. Keening and loud laments expended on behalf of the dead were the norm—that was the Irish way of sending off a beloved one. The belief being, the more sorrow displayed on earth, the higher in exaltation the deceased would arrive at St. Peter's gate.

"Do you want to view him?" Christopher pointed to the pine box perched on a table.

Without saying a word, Dino walked over. The stoic little man patted Schmitty's chest. Padhraig had put a clean shirt and pants on him, his hands and fingers cleaned of all grease and dirt, crossed over his chest. "He shaved. Looks like he got his hair cut."

"Do you recall meeting Mr. McCarthy?" At Dino's nod, Christopher continued, "He cleaned Schmitty for his laying out, so we will always be able to remember him this way."

"I think Schmitty would like it too. Do you think he knows?"

"I've no doubt." He gripped Dino's shoulder, giving him a little squeeze. "He was a good man to you. He's earned his reward in Heaven."

The small procession walked behind the box carrying Schmitty's remains to the graveyard, just a block up Church Street from McCarthy's Funeral Parlor. But for the trees lying along the paths, and buildings and houses still in disrepair, one could almost forget the disaster that had struck a few days ago.

Once situated at the graveyard, Reverend Alcott with bible in hand, read the 23rd Psalm, *The Lord is my shepherd; I shall not want. He maketh me to lie down in green pastures: He leadeth me beside the still waters. He restoreth my soul…*

Christopher concerned himself with Dino's reaction to the burial. The lad was taking the ceremony in with little outward emotion. It was unusual for him not to ask questions.

After the Psalm, the pine box was lowered into the recently dug hole. With all the rain of late, the bottom was a big mud puddle. Reverend Alcott asked Dino to drop a handful of earth on top of the pine box, followed by Christopher.

Reverend Alcott then asked Dino if he wanted to say something, and the lad looked up at Christopher.

"Miss Fitzjames said I could tell a story about him."

Christopher smiled. "A nice thought, I agree. Schmitty will be listening from up there." His gaze rolled upward, and Dino smiled at the very idea.

He took a step forward. It was the Reverend and two of his assistants, the doc, and two men with shovels off to the side.

Dino glanced up at Christopher and began. "Schmitty always saved a seat for me in the mess, sharing his bacon with me, too. He stood up to the cap'n when I tried to escape and took a lashing 'cause of it." He swiped moisture from his cheeks. "I knew he did it 'cause he was a real friend to me. The best ever."

Christopher couldn't help but notice the astonished look on the faces of the Reverend and his two aldermen.

Dino picked up another handful of dirt and dropped it over the box. "I'll come see you, Schmitty. I'm going to school now, so I can tell you all about it."

Christopher thanked Reverend Alcott. Dino swiped his hand of dirt down along his breeches and held it out to the Reverend as Christopher had done.

As they ambled toward home, Christopher noticed Miss Fitzjames looking in the window of the butcher's shop. He would have walked over, but Dino suddenly ran in the opposite direction and Christopher took off after him.

True to form, Dino, overcome with hurt and anguish, and without any idea how to handle his feelings, fled. Christopher was naïve in the earlier assumption the lad was beginning to heal from all he had endured in his short life.

The lad hied toward a copse to the south of the graveyard. He headed through dense growth, decomposing leaves, animal scat, and rotting wood, crunching sticks as he distanced himself from Christopher. The lad left a path easy for Christopher to follow, who soon found him standing at the water's edge of a small lough. Christopher knew it as a grand place to catch brown trout and perch.

The sun dappled on the leaves of birch and alder cocooning Dino in a bower of dark green with the water rippling in the light breeze. He stepped on a branch and Dino swung about. He must have fallen because mud splattered the whole of his new clothes. He'd swiped at his face smearing dirt across his cheek, nose and forehead.

Christopher's heart twisted. This child, this wild little lad, homeless, parentless, and now friendless, was the saddest creature he could imagine. And yet a resilience in him that Christopher could almost feel. He didn't advance on him, just stood, arms at his sides, eying the child. "I will always be here for you, Dino. I'm not going anywhere."

Dino swiped a wrist across his cheek. "I'm bad."

Christopher wasn't sure he heard him correctly. "Bad?" as he took a step closer.

"The cap'n said I was Satan's spawn. I know what that means."

His heart thumped a beat of utter pain. He was crushed with the devastation he saw on the child's face.

Christopher stated, "It's a fact evil people try to convince the ones they hurt that they are the evil ones. It's called subjugation. Redeye was attempting to defeat you. Then he could gain control of you. Which clearly, he was not able to achieve, or you would never have run away from him."

Dino stood very still listening to every word.

Christopher's throat clutched and he got down on one knee. "Come here to me, lad."

Dino walked into his open arms. His little body shaking with emotion. Christopher said, "You aren't evil. You're a miracle, a survivor."

Christopher could only imagine what was going on in his tormented thoughts. "The morning you showed up, and I saw you in bed with Schmitty, protecting him, I realized you had experienced goodness, not only from him but most probably from your parents before you were taken." His hands cupped Dino's shoulders and he looked into his dark brown watery eyes. "Their virtue and love overcame the evil Redeye forced on you. Right now, you're grieving the loss of someone who truly cared for you. But a funny thing about the gifts of true friendship, they are glued into our heart. No one has the power to take that from us."

Tears spilled onto Dino's thin cheeks, making little rivers of the mud. In a low voice, almost whispering, he admitted, "Schmitty knew what the cap'n was doing."

Christopher's heart clutched. "I would bet Schmitty tried to do everything in his power to protect you. Perhaps certain things you are not even aware of. You felt secure with him. He treated you with respect."

Dino nodded in the prevailing silence. A moment passed and he whispered, "He got whipped 'cause of me. Cap'n made me watch, and when I begged him to whip me and quit on Schmitty, he laughed. Said he knew I was a fool."

The disparity of the gentle lap of water to the mud shore and the rustle of leaves in the birch and alder against Dino's revelation made Christopher's stomach churn with acid. He lifted Dino's chin and managed to say, "You are as important to me as Schmitty was to you, son."

Dino said, "I feel the same about you, doc. It's why I came back."

Tears stung, and he gulped with an attempt to not become a blubbering idiot. His fingers tightened on Dino's shoulders. The cruelty in the world was mind-boggling. How such a wicked man lived was inconceivable. Christopher's faith allowed him to believe the pirate would eventually receive his just reward, and all would even out.

He got up off his knee and brushed dirt away. "Here's the gist going forward, son. You will never run away again. We..." his finger wagged to and fro between them "... you and me, will always find a solution. There isn't one thing that you and I together won't be able to fix."

Dino's somber face and pursed lips showed sincere agreement with a thoughtful and emphatic nod.

Christopher said, "I've got a confession." Dino's attention shot up, locking on him, waiting. "You've opened my heart to the truth of doctoring. You, and children like you, are one of the reasons I wanted to become a medical man and I had forgotten. I thank you from the bottom of my heart for reminding me.

"You've given me reason for renewed enthusiasm about my chosen path in life. I have rediscovered I'm proud to be a doctor. Thank you for helping me recollect my direction."

"Gorsh, me?" Delight was evident in his voice as he swiped his wrist across his wet cheeks.

"You."

As they made their way through the copse Dino's humming was a healing sound. A simple yet powerful exchange helped to tighten their bond. Christopher was reminded of the talks and walks he and his father exchanged when he was a lad about this same age. He was fully aware Dino had captured his paternal instincts. It remained to be seen how their relationship would unfold and deepen through the years. He was simply grateful they would have a future.

15

Smoke rose above Hawthorn from the direction where Billy-Boy and Carnahan managed the burning refuse from the storm. Villagers scampered from all directions toward the black spiral. Wheelbarrows and donkey carts loaded with debris, broken limbs not saved for home fires, and other accumulated detritus filled the track that led to the fire. It was well tended, and neighbors working shoulder to shoulder dug a trench so the fire would not spread out of control.

On the way to Mr. Talbot's, Christopher stopped at O'Bannon's Dry Goods. Enlisting the help of Nuala, Lady Rutledge, he asked if she would choose another set of clothing for Dino. He had not considered that when a young boy dirties his clothing, he needs a set for him, a set for the laundry, and an extra set, just in case.

She laughed heartily at his explanation. "You make a grand effort to give the boy a good home, Mr. Curran."

Christopher shook his head at the memory several days earlier of Dino's filthy apparel from his blouse to the shoes he wore. He said, "Darby washes our laundry and scolds me for the constant rush. She's the real reason I'm in need of more clothing."

Nuala was in the act of arranging linens on a shelf. "Have you any recent news from my daughter and son-in-law?"

Christopher handed her the last stack to be shelved. "The latest indicated they planned to be back at Rockmore Hall late autumn."

"Thank you." She patted the shelf. "I'm anxious to see Mairéad. I've missed her so."

"We'll enjoy their company before long, my lady. I'm looking forward to another pair of hands at the infirmary."

She looked thoughtful. "Do you really think he'll keep to his promise to help you?"

"It is his wish, though I understand it depends upon his great-uncle's health, and the assistance Lord Darnley may require at Rockmore Hall."

As she waved to a customer who entered the store and headed to the yarn section, Nuala said, "Lady Darnley invited me to a tea this summer. A fund raiser for the school. She looked younger than I recall. Lord Darnley made an appearance and looked exceptionally well. I would say he has almost fully recovered from his stroke. Two years ago, I believe. Time goes by so fast these days."

"Sounds about right. Before I forget, is it possible to have the clothing sent over? My next stop is the apothecary's, then the Black Pig to get an update from Padhraig."

"I'll take care of it this morning. A thought, too. I'll add a few extra items to Dino's package. Pajamas for instance, and an extra pair of pants, and a sweater for more recreational play than school wear."

His sense of relief was obvious. "Thank you, my lady. Wonderful suggestions. He will be delighted. He takes quite an interest in the other students making note of their dress, the books they read, and games they play at recess. He's very aware."

"I will help you in any way I can with your little ward."

Slapping on his hat, he gave her a nod. "I appreciate your kindness."

Not five strides down the street, he encountered Miss Fitzjames.

As she approached, he doffed his hat. "You've been avoiding us at the infirmary."

She glanced over his shoulder as if she expected someone. "My reason for visiting no longer exists."

"Would you care to have tea with me at Cashel's?"

"Is there something you want of me?" She looked captivating in a green felt hat with a tiny veil slanting over the tip of her little nose.

"Nothing serious. May I walk with you, then? I've something to thank you for. We walk, and I'll talk." Her struggle with the offer was obvious, was it the walking part or what he might have to say? It relieved him to hear her accept. "A short walk, then."

He led them in the direction of the Strand. A few benches lined the lough, shaded by rowan trees whose creamy white flowers were changing to bright red berries with the coming change in season. He also enjoyed watching fish jump snatching at bugs.

"I wish to thank you for taking time with Dino when Schmitty died. It was difficult for him. I noticed you at the burial. Your advice to the lad was thoughtful. You may not have heard him from where you stood, but he told a story of Schmitty saving him on one particular occasion."

Her gloved hands clasped at the short chain of her reticule as they walked. The tap-tap of her shoes made a light, dainty echo. The top of her hat came to his chin and he caught a peek at her lips, a pinkish color, full and smiling.

"There is no need to thank me, Mr. Curran. The child earns every bit of kindness coming his way."

"I'll agree about that. The lad hasn't a dram of self-pity. Nor does he speak ill of his past. Though several times he's mentioned something that startled me. Enough to know how dreadful it was."

He heard her breath catch. "Worse than I thought."

They reached a bench, and he offered her a seat. "The lad doesn't have a memory of a surname."

"You've given him yours I understand."

"Nothing legal at this point. He needs an identity at least until he gets older and makes decisions for himself."

Dismay creased her forehead as she related. "Dino told me why he left the first time. He was trying to protect you. He thought the captain would kill you if he suspected it was you giving him shelter."

"I did think as much. I searched and others kept watch. My hope was he would show up when he felt safe again, after the *Nomad* sailed."

Birds fluttered about, snatching at the few bright berries clinging heartily to the bushes. She lifted the veil of her hat, drawing it over the crown as she remarked, "You have been given the responsibility of providing Mona with twin boys, and you now have the responsibility of Dino. You're quite a man."

He heard a bit of a lilt in her voice as if she teased. Or mayhap accusing? "What are you saying exactly?" Perhaps he was foolish to ask.

Her eyes sparkled as she gleefully said, "Others might think you conceited."

"I didn't make the statement about twin boys. Their mother did."

"It's all the talk at the pub." She folded her gloved hands on her lap over the top of her reticule, a smirk on her pretty mouth.

He leaned in. "Conceited, am I? Apparently enough to want to kiss you." He was close enough a faint scent of honeysuckle wafted over him as he looked deeply into her shocked eyes watching them soften with his proximity.

Of a sudden the approach of voices was heard as two men carrying ropes and oars came around the rowan branches, nodded at them, and hurried on about their business.

The moment gave Miss Fitzjames enough time to regain her composure.

He reached for her hand, but she stood. "Good day, *sir*." A decided edge to her voice as if she meant to call him something else entirely.

He also stood. "I should apologize, but I don't feel any remorse for my remark." She enthralled him and it was clear to him all she wanted was to put distance between them.

He quickly changed the moment by answering her initial accusation. "I wouldn't call it conceit to admit enjoying the good will of Mike when he became the father of twin boys. But you and I both discern it was certainly none of my doing."

Her sarcasm rankled the air. "I've heard the gossip about your medical ways, and how some of the villagers avoid your infirmary. I think Mike did your reputation a world of good. A man's vanity being needy and all." On this note, she diverted her attention and made to leave.

Before she could take one step he said, "I've given the trio of monkeys at the Black Pig far too much authority over my feelings. It's my own fault."

Her wide beautiful gaze slanted to him from beneath the brim of her jaunty hat as she glanced back at him. "Monkeys?"

"I dubbed them monkeys because of their doom and gloom, all three of them, Carnahan, Danaher, and Mulroney. My personal critics, if ever anyone was so blest." He leveled his gaze on her face where a hint of a smile lingered. Was there a chance she liked him?

As if she could read his thoughts, she laughed softly and continued on her way leaving him to stand amongst the birds nibbling at the rowan tree berries.

Whistling, he set out for the Black Pig and was glad to encounter Padhraig behind the bar. "How's the latest corpse? Find anything suspicious?"

"As a matter of fact, he was a regular for years. You were right on, doc, about Brandt. We all thought he skipped out on his family. I found nothing suspicious. If I were a betting man, I'd say he was drunk out of his mind, stumbled, and knocked his head just right. The back of his head was matted with old blood."

"You wouldn't suspect foul play, then?"

"Not him. Say it was a person who didn't like his drink, I might. But knowing Brandt as I did, and the crack on his head, adds up to doing himself in. I'm surprised Waffer hasn't gotten involved, he's a nose for any corpse lately."

"Doesn't he now? I think I'm on his suspect list."

Padhraig, rubbing the bar top down, he didn't look up. "So, I've heard."

Christopher paused a moment, then suddenly wrapped the bar top with his knuckles. "Well, then, I'm going to get this over with. As far as the body goes, I'll have Mrs. Brandt identify it, and she can take it from there with you." He leaned in and in a low voice said, "The costs I'll incur. Send me the bill, but don't tell her I'm doing this. She'll think we are friends forever. Quite frankly I've had my fill if you know what I mean."

Padhraig gave him a salute, wet rag in hand slapping against his cheek. "Yes, sir. Have her come over about six tonight. I'll be back at the parlor by then."

His next stop was Evie Brandt's. She was alone in her dirt-floor cottage, knitting an infant blanket from the looks of it.

"'Tis a surprise to be sure, but we're all fine here, doc. Even our little mother-to-be."

Upon entering the small cottage, doffing his hat, he stated, "I've information about your husband. At least Padhraig McCarthy and I think he might be Mr. Brandt."

Her palm cupped her face. "Mother of God! Where is that bastard! I'll kill him if I get me hands on him."

"Well, that's the point, Mrs. Brandt. It's why I'm here."

Her eyes slowly widened her mouth sagged with the impossible. "What is it yer sayin', doc?"

"If it is your husband, then I'm sad to say he's passed." The shock struck every feature on her face causing him to rue his abrupt manner.

He took the chair next to her. "Some of the clean-up crew found a body under a pile of fallen rush down by the lough. It would appear as if he'd been there several weeks or so before the storm hit. I was suspicious when this was found in his pocket." He handed her the coin with the scrolled B on it.

She fingered the dulled metal. "This means he didn't run out on us, then?"

"If it's him, it would appear so. His remains were taken to the funeral parlor. If you are able, Padhraig would like you to come around about six o'clock to identify him for certain and make the necessary arrangements."

It appeared to him as though his unfortunate news had begun to sink in. Her cheeks paled. He felt a certain empathy for her, with what he knew about their marriage and the gossip at the Black Pig.

"Shall I call a neighbor for you? Are your daughters near?"

She came back from far away settling her sad resignation on him. "The girls will be back any time now. Doc, I almost hope it isn't him. I wasn't ready to lose him, just took a pot to his head one night when he came staggering in. He mumbled about me bein' cantankerous and took himself off."

As Christopher hurried down the lane, he mused over her remark *took a pot to his head.* He would let the matter lie. Any investigation was not going to bring her husband back. Her daughters were at home, one about to add a grandchild into the household. Life was hard enough; no reason to make it worse.

Bustling toward Nolan's Bakery, Renata needed to pick up two poppyseed muffins her mother specifically requested. Renata was afraid they would be sold out this late in the day. If not for meeting Christopher, she could have purchased them earlier.

Not meeting Christopher—what a foolish woman she was. Never kissed, and he had the audacity to admit he wanted to kiss her. And who was he? No one other than the son of her beloved father's archrival. A man he hated so much her father had demanded she bury his ashes as close to Morgan Curran's gravesite as physically possible. He hoped to *bedevil* his enemy through eternity.

Butterflies fluttered in her stomach. She tucked what Mr. Curran said deep away. She'd never have thought a declaration from the most handsome man she could imagine, would make her feel like a schoolgirl. His eyes twinkled with mischief. She'll take delight in unwrapping the memory and reliving the sense of him and his bold declaration.

Luckily, as she traipsed the steps to their second-floor apartment she was able to give her mother the last two poppy seed muffins from Nolan's.

"I gave you up for dead an hour ago." The grim set to her mother's jaw was not softened with the tea and muffins presented to her.

"Now, now, mother. I wasn't gone long. You know, not all the remains of the storm are cleared. I had to detour along the way."

"Harrumph." She washed the first bite down with tea. "You've got a cat's grin. What's to tell your mother who barely gets out and no one visits."

"Nothing really. I sat on a bench on the Strand for a bit watching the waves wash in and the birds feed, I'm glad they've returned. We take their song for granted but when it's gone, the cheery tunes are greatly missed. In the distance I caught a sail flagging in the wind as it passed into the Suir."

Louisa patted her mouth of crumbs and wiped her fingers of the delicious morsel. "We need to make our plans for your father's ashes. I want to go home. There is nothing here for us. It's time we are serious about returning to Obidos."

Renata noticed Lea hovering in the corner. Swathed in her veils, her dark gaze narrowed at both of them. She surmised Lea agreed with her mother about going home.

Christopher recalled the departure with Miss Fitzjames as she walked away from him. The gentle swish of her skirt, the dainty tap-tap of her shoes, the charming way she held her shoulders and chin. For a smallish woman, she walked with dignity and purpose. The look on her face when he told her he wanted to kiss her surprised them both.

Her response was appropriate, he deserved nothing less. With a flutter in his heart, he fancied what that kiss might have felt like.

Arriving home, he discovered Dino received the packages from O'Bannon's. He was in his bedroom laying the items out on his bed when Christopher came upon him.

Holding up a shirt and pants of soft flannel, Dino asked, "What do I do with these?"

"Sleeping attire, my lad. A product of modern thinking. They will keep you warm on a chilly night."

He exclaimed at the extravagance. "I already have clothes to wear."

"Ah, so you do. But if you continue muddying them up, you'll soon have to run about like a buck-naked stag. Darby doesn't wash every day now does she?"

"I get it." His soft answer crackled with embarrassment.

"Were you able to help Mr. Cooke?" Christopher shifted the books he carried from one arm to the other.

"He asked me to run errands. The babies are in a bed he made, kind of like what the babies slept in here but bigger. Mrs. Cooke had a friend over who helped with them. Wee Mary was on Mrs. Cooke's lap and cried when her mother wanted to get up. She stayed in the chair asking me to do this and that for her. When I got done, I knocked on Miss Fitzjames' door. She wasn't home, so I came back here."

"Before supper, will you run another errand for me?"

He nodded as his attention was on folding his new clothing.

"Come to the office when you finish up."

Christopher sprinkled sand on the short note, folded it, and used his seal. He wondered how Miss Fitzjames would receive his invitation to dinner and remembered the tilt of her lips as she smiled at him when she walked away. He could only hope she shared his interest in spending more time together.

He also wrote another letter to Ray Walsh, owner of the Curious Book Shop in Dublin. He was a school chum from Eton. Christopher asked him to send a copy of Johnathon Swift's *Gulliver's Travels*.

Giving both notes to Dino, one to be delivered to the post, and the other for Miss Fitzjames, he added, "Krysta found a scarf belonging to Mrs. Cooke. Will you return it to her when you stop by Miss Fitzjames?"

Dino was out the door in a flash. Christopher noted he wore his new shoes. His worries the lad would not take easily to wearing something on his feet was inconsequential considering he hadn't taken them off except to sleep, nor had he complained about blisters.

Asia Malcolm sipped on a cup of tea, his back to the wall. Christopher noted his good color and lively manner as he changed the man's leg dressing. "Healing nicely."

"I've got things to do, doc. A man can't spend his time lazing about?"

"A fracture takes longer. You will need crutches to get around for four maybe five months before the leg should be used. I want to see you regularly before I agree to it." Christopher placed his salves and bandages on the tray. "You are one lucky man. That was a smooth break, and your other leg shows no sign of infection. If you intend to walk without a limp into old age, you will heed what I say."

A grim shadow on Asia's face made it clear he didn't like Christopher's warning. Sometimes plain-spoken words are the most expedient, and surely send the proper message. However, Christopher could tell Asia wanted out of confinement of any kind.

Krysta took the empty teacup from Asia. "Is he fit to go home?"

He glanced at his patient. "Remind me where you live?"

"On the far side of the village past the Alms House, up on Church Street."

"How will you navigate on crutches from that distance?"

"We've got a cart, but I expect mam will keep me close to home."

Christopher asked Krysta, "Has she been to visit her son and I missed it?"

"You've been busy doc."

Asia said, "My mam blazes about like there's two of her—everywhere at once, will hardly leave me be. It's been grand stayin' here." His gray gaze swept over Krysta. "Special what with this lass and her conversation and all."

Christopher got it, all right. He felt mightily relieved to note Krysta set her sights on someone other than himself.

"There's no reason you can't go home. But mind Asia. You cannot under any circumstance put weight on your leg. You'll need to come in every day for me to change the thigh wound until it is healed." He laid a hand to Asia's arm causing the patient to look him in the eye. "You cannot walk on your leg until I say so."

Krysta dazzled with excitement. "Show me how to do it, doc. I'd be willing mid-day after I serve up lunch."

She blushed, and Christopher said, "If it suits Asia, that is a generous offer."

Thus, began preparations for Asia to be moved to his mother's cottage. Krysta planned to set off after lunch to his mother's and get the cart to take him home.

Not a moment later, Dino burst through the back door and reported the delivery of his note to Miss Fitzjames. He gave it to her mother who closed the door on him after she took it. He knocked on the Cooke's door. Mrs. Cooke was grateful for the scarf. He could hear the babies cutting up a storm and didn't want to hang around, though he'd been invited.

The turbulence from the storm calmed allowing everyone to go about their daily routines. After supper, Dino spent the next few hours reading the book Master Carleton had given him.

Christopher poured himself a libation from the closet in the hallway and walked out the back of the kitchen where he'd put a bench many months ago when arriving from Edinburgh. It allowed him a small sanctuary not far from the infirmary. His thoughts drifted over the events of the day as a hint of smoke assailed his nostrils. The restoration of Hawthorn Village continued.

Soon it would be time to plow the fields, tilling the necessary nitrogen into the soil by way of manure. He was grateful for so many reasons, not the least of which was Dino in his life. Someone for him to nurture and watch grow.

His mind drifted to a year ago and Caroline Hammond. A woman whom he'd once thought he could love. Their friendship ended abruptly, and he'd not looked back.

Now he was considering a spicy, smart and compassionate woman. Sipping his whiskey, he suspected she was capable of arousing much more than companionship. He was curious to see if Miss Fitzjames would accept his invitation to dinner.

With the evening coming on, a whippoorwill chirped its plaints, its brindled feathers kept him well-hidden. If Christopher believed in myths and folklore, the bird could be foretelling death, or marriage or woe. He knew few birds had spun such a crazed web of tales as the whippoorwill.

Pulling on his glass, allowing the blend to burn its way down his throat, he recalled a tale about the night-flyer often referred to as a goatsucker, because if a goat was nearby when they came out at night, the bird would fly to the goats milk and drink. Having never observed such a sight, he couldn't say if it was true or not.

After *that* thought, he ogled the glass from which he'd been drinking. A patient who'd traded a diagnosis and subsequent clean bill of health for his homemade poteen, had given it to him.

He summed up the events of the day. Asia now home thanks to a donkey cart. He assumed Krysta would be around less, too. Dino, now in possession of a more complete wardrobe, and proud of the loan of a book from his teacher. And Miss Fitzjames. He would sleep with a smile tonight and dream her response to dinner was a yes.

If it wasn't for Padhraig's comment about Waffer's gossip that Christopher was involved with body snatching, today could shine brightly in memory. Maybe he should keep an eye on the graveyards. It wouldn't hurt to take an occasional stroll late at night.

16

Mulroney bounded up the porch to the infirmary, yelling at Christopher. "Doc, Carnahan's son, Shamus, is burned, bad. He's callin' for you."

Christopher pushed back his chair as he stood, "Where is he?"

"Carnahan's carryin' him home."

Christopher reached for his bag. It was stocked with the usual, scissors, compresses, and several jars made up of medicinal teas and herbs he'd concocted specifically for burns. They were out the door in less than a minute.

"How'd it happen?"

Mulroney, a hefty sort, tried to keep pace with Christopher's stride. Wheezing, he managed to say, "Burnin' storm debris, he was tossing branches on it, helpin' with clean-up. Some of us saw it. Fluky like, a limb bounced back and shoved him into the fire, almost like an arm comin' out o' nowhere—shoved him smack into the fire. Happened so fast. He screamed, couldn't get his footing to get out. If it hadn't been for Carnahan daring to reach in and get 'im out, coulda been a lot worse, I suspect."

They reached Carnahan's cottage, where a small group gathered outside and made way for Christopher and Mulroney. Jeanne, Shamus' mum, held a bowl of butter about to slather her son. Lying out on his back on the table, he had a look of intense pain creasing his features. He appeared to fade in and out of consciousness.

Christopher was surprised the lad hadn't passed out from the intense pain. The burn to his chin, neck, chest and upper arms was red and blistery. Huge pustules already formed on the burned area.

Christopher gently asked Mrs. Carnahan, "Will you allow me to look him over before we begin with applications?"

She jerked toward him, fear and anger etched in the lines of grief about her mouth. She obviously had not been aware he'd arrived. "I've got to help him, I've gotta save my boy."

"We will do this together. You aren't alone. We'll heal him, Mrs. Carnahan. He will return to near normal."

She leaned in close, her teeth bared, as if she might bite him. Her mother's love balled into a great fear. "You can promise me that, can you?"

He took a breath. "I will stake my future on it."

"It's *his* future I care about, not the 'ell yours." She spit the words at him. Carnahan came up between them and put his arm about her shoulder. "Let the doc do his worst, then, ma. Our boy needs the stuff he's got in the bag he carries."

She jerked his arm off, wrapped her fingers about the bowl of butter, and dropped her gaze to the contents. "I hope you don't live to regret your promise, *Mr. Curran.*" She backed up against the wall at the head of the table where her son suffered.

Christopher asked Carnahan to clear everyone but he, his wife and Mulroney out of the room. Then setting his bag on a chair, opened, washed his hands with vinegar and wiped them dry. He uncorked a jar and asked Carnahan to gently lift his son's head to drink the contents. "Shamus, this is a cool drink. It will take some of the pain away as I clean your wounds and apply an ointment. Your mother and father are here and will help me care for you."

Within a minute or two, Shamus visibly calmed, his burned fingers no longer clutched, his feet relaxed, he moaned softly until it became a gentle snore. Christopher took out scissors and a small tweezer and began removing burnt flesh. It was miraculous the way the burns were in this area of his body and not his face. The only sound was an occasional groan from the lad, and his parents' labored breathing, as if they had run miles over the hills.

"I have clean soft linen in my bag we'll cut into pieces, my plan is to use camphor mixed with olive oil, and your butter, Mrs. Carnahan, to create an emollient that we'll spread on the linen and lay on his burned parts. We'll change this twice a day for weeks until the skin calms and boils no longer appear. Then we can change the strategy a bit."

He glanced up. She hadn't moved and appeared to hold her breath as her gaze locked on the bowl with her son's charred skin, terror etched on her face.

Carnahan said, "He's been a blessing from the start." The father owned and operated Hawthorn's forge. If anyone knew about burns, it would be him. He'd observed a few accidents in his time.

Christopher said, "He's going to be fine. Burns do take a long time to heal. But with his mother's care and yours he'll pull through."

She finally spoke. "You haven't bled him yet."

"He needs to heal. I believe blood strengthens. Bleeding takes the power from the body."

"It's supposed to take the humors out of him." She set the bowl of butter on a shelf with a clatter, crossing her arms over her chest. "Any fool knows that."

Shamus groaned, a bit livelier than previously, and Christopher knew the young man was rousing. Not responding to Mrs. Carnahan, he set the scissors and clamp down on a piece of clean linen and poured another draught. Carnahan lifted his son's head. "Drink Shamus, it'll keep the pain away."

Christopher asked for a clean bowl and a wooden spatula and began mixing camphor of olive oil and butter until it became a smooth salve the color of dark green. With Mrs. Carnahan assisting him he took a piece of linen, folded it then dipped the cloth into the solution. Very gently he brushed it over Shamus' chin and throat, illustrating to her the softness of his touch.

She mimicked his actions and they both covered the entire burned surface of his body, dipping and changing the cloths frequently, until the entire injured area was washed of char and dirt. Shamus hardly reacted at all. He was grateful the boy could be spared the misery of debriding and washing.

Perceiving the fear and suffering Shamus' parents were experiencing, Christopher was grateful to be finished. In the weeks to come the process would get easier. He hesitated to use opium continually, but the first few days it would keep him calm.

He packed his black bag and gave Mrs. Carnahan a pile of the cut linen. "I'll bring you more of the cooling ointment, too. Did you notice the ratio of camphor to olive oil to butter that I mixed?"

"I did." Her voice eased. Her son was calm, affecting her own emotions.

"Then I will leave this with you to mix more when this batch is gone." He gave her the jar of camphor. "He needs to be moved to a bed, where he can remain in comfort. Quickly if possible, while he remains under the influence of the drug."

Carnahan glanced at his wife and moved a chair over standing beside his son. "What do you think? Put him in our room for now?"

Exhausted, her weary gaze shifted to her husband. "Bring in the cot from the barn. Put it in the corner by the fire. I'll keep an easy watch on him, then."

Carnahan walked toward the door then glanced back at Christopher. "Guess we'll see you tomorrow then?"

"I'm at your call day or night. The drink I gave him won't last till morning. I left a small vial on the table for his use. He'll also need plenty of water, and whatever he may eat. I don't suspect he'll be too hungry for a day or two. I'll check in early tomorrow. Bear in mind these next few days and nights won't be easy for any of you. Have faith, you'll all pull through." Christopher nodded to the mother. Her entire attention was on her son spread out on the table as he was, with patches of linen covering the upper part of his body and neck.

Carnahan called to Mulroney to help him with the cot from the barn, apparently, it's where their son slept.

On his return to the infirmary, Christopher had been in such a rush he'd forgotten his hat and felt a bit undressed without it. It was late and he missed supper. Krysta would have left something on the sideboard. He hoped Dino was home. He wanted to make sure the lad was okay and had eaten a good meal. He wanted to hear about school, what special thing he'd discovered today. They had begun to settle into a nice little routine, sometimes including Krysta when she stayed through supper. The household was emptied of illness and babies now, calmer and more like a family. He enjoyed the sense of having someone waiting for him.

Rounding the corner on Chadwick, he literally ran into Miss Fitzjames and her mother. Out of habit, he reached for his hat, then looked at his palm as if an idiot.

"Missing something?" Miss Fitzjames inquired.

"I was in a rush when I left and forgot to put on my hat." He nodded to her mother. "Enjoying the evening, are you?"

"We are taking advantage of these pleasanter times." She hugged her shawl close.

Miss Fitzjames glanced at his bag. "From the looks of it, you've visited a patient."

He was about to respond when Mrs. Fitzjames caught sight of another couple walking on the opposite side of the cobbled street and nudged her daughter. "That's the one I was telling you about. Alice, she lives down the way from us. It's her husband born in Carrick."

Christopher said, "The Sutters. Nice folks."

Mrs. Fitzjames raised her chin and mustered her displeasure, "And, you'd credit them because…?"

"I've known them since I was a lad." Christopher's curiosity piqued at her harsh voice. At the same moment Miss Fitzjames' attention bent to her reticle, opening it to look inside as if she intended to disjoin herself from the conversation. Something was amiss.

"We've not a high opinion of Carrick-on-Suir," the mother's stentorian voice clarified the probability she had history in that village that enabled her to form an opinion.

"I'm sorry you feel that way." He shifted his bag to his other hand and wondered if she suffered from dyspepsia.

Her glint narrowed and her chin jutted. He'd put her on the defensive but considered she was quick to attack when opposed. Except he wasn't the one who began the conversation.

Miss Fitzjames took her mother's arm. "Shouldn't we be on our way? Lea will have tea ready."

Shaking off her daughter's hand, she glared at Christopher. "I've met your father. You've nothing to be so high and mighty about."

Miss Fitzjames gasped. "Mother, if you don't come with me this instant, I'll leave you here to make your own way home." She glanced at Christopher. "Please accept my apologies for her rudeness. I can't fathom what's come over her."

Christopher noted the darkening of her lovely face and gave a slight incline of his head. "I take it your answer to my dinner invite is refused, then?"

Her surprise was obvious, "I received no invitation."

"The lad delivered it yesterday."

She fastened a hard glare on her mother, who had glanced up the street rather than face her daughter and said, "No letter was delivered."

Miss Fitzjames, her chin set firm, glanced at her mother. Then asked him, "When do you suggest we dine, sir?"

"Tomorrow? I'll come by at six if that suits. I'll make arrangements at Cashel's."

"I look forward to it, thank you." She gripped her mother's elbow. "We'll be going now."

Christopher continued to the infirmary. Something was itching Mrs. Fitzjames. She could do with a dose of good nature like her lovely daughter who was gowned in a becoming shade of pale blue wool and wrapped in a plaid shawl. He chuckled thinking she took exception to her mother's connivance and may have accepted his invitation to dine to spite her.

The thought brought a smile to his face as he entered the front door of the infirmary and smelled fried perch.

A package wrapped in brown paper lay on his desk. The return address showing Dublin. He carried it into the kitchen and laid it at Dino's place.

Krysta was folding up a towel saying, "I've got to get on, doc. Can you handle supper and clean up after?"

Pouring himself an ale, he said, "Is your mother okay? Not sick?" He took a long swallow.

"She's fine, it's me wantin' some time to meself."

"Go on then."

Once Dino sank into his chair and tucked the napkin under his chin, his curiosity shifted to the package on the table. "My name is on this."

"Must be it's for you. Open it and find out." Christopher took the chair opposite and watched as Dino tore into the strings and paper.

His voice filled with awe. "It's a book. Gulliver's Travels," he said in a long-drawn pronunciation. His fingers ran across the leather cover. "It says Jonathan Swift wrote it." Picking it up he pushed his chair back and laid it across his lap. "Is it really mine? To keep?"

Christopher nodded and sipped his ale.

The wonder of a lad with his first property overcame Christopher. "The beginning of your very own library."

Dino stood up, book cupped safely in his elbow, and gave Christopher a big hug. A rare thing for him to do.

If he, Christopher, wasn't careful, he might get weepy. The lad was not demonstrative, except when he slipped his hand into Christopher's. This hug was a first.

"You will have to write your name on the first page and 7

September 1816. When you get to be my age, and you open the book, it will be as though an old friend is waiting to be read again."

"Is it okay if I put Dino Curran in it?"

"I hoped you would, lad. It's how folks will know you, after all."

❦

As the women walked back to their apartment, Renata churned with angst. "You are nasty and resentful toward Mr. Curran. And, you deliberately kept his invitation from me. Why?"

Louisa glanced at her daughter. "I'm tired. And, that man is a liar. He never sent you an invitation."

"Your antagonism toward the doctor or is it Carrick-on-Suir, perhaps both for all I know, reminds me of your cruelty toward my father during his illness."

Renata stopped walking. Her mother also stopped and glanced across the lane at a far-off hillside of dense forest. Mother and daughter were the same height, the only similarity between them.

Her parent had churned up a dose of vexation in her daughter. "Tell me, Mother, because I am confused by your dislike for Mr. Curran. Why have you animosity toward a man you've met two or three times?"

Louisa drew the shawl close about her neck. Evening was coming on. Waffer had already lit a few lanterns. "You are exaggerating my curiosity about him. The fact he was born in Carrick-on-Suir means nothing to me other than your father and I lived there for a few years before moving back to Portugal."

Renata dropped the conversation with her mother's last words on the subject. She knew the woman intimately. She was covering up something. What? What secret could she possibly keep that Renata would be unaware?

Lea opened the door to their apartment as they ascended the stairs. She must have been watching from the window. Wrapped in her shawl, she looked as though she'd been crying. When Louisa gained the final step and walked towards the girl, Lea embraced her with a sob. "I thought you left me."

Renata wondered if the neighbors could hear. The walls were paper thin. From across the hall, the twins could be heard when they woke to be nursed.

The maid's childish behavior bordered on foolishness in Renata's estimation. Both women were given to histrionics. Her mother coddled the girl, and together they walked into the apartment. Renata closed the hall door and hung her woolen shawl. They were whispering, her mother soothing Lea, caressing her cheek.

Renata had no desire to watch her mother humor Lea and said, "Goodnight." Neither acknowledged her as she escaped to her room.

It was dark enough that the lamps along Market glowed golden circles on the lane. She sat in the window for quite a while and allowed her troubling thoughts to drift as the stars began popping out, twinkling in the darkening sky.

Her wonderful papa, whose wisdom and love she missed so very much, gone to a better place. Her anxiety-ridden mother was a woman she could not appease. She required Lea sleep on a mat on the floor next to her bed. And Lea appears to be sinking into childhood becoming more of a burden than a maid.

Renata turned her focus to all the good in her life. Mr. Talbot's generosity that allowed her to use his back room gave meaning to her days. Her father used to say an idle mind is a jiggery mind. She found herself smiling up at the twinkling stars. "Your soul is up there, Papa. And you'll soon get your wish to *bedevil* Morgan Curran for the rest of eternity, or I'm not your daughter."

With her knees drawn up under her chin, she considered her mother's growing anxiety and the vow her father demanded. Could they be somehow linked?

17

Dino leaned against the door jam, arms crossed, watching Christopher fuss over his waistcoat after knotting his cravat. "Miss Fitzjames is special?"

"That she is, laddie. That she is." He grinned into the mirror as his gaze met Dino's. "I take it you have plans?"

"I'm going to Shamus'. Master Carleton says I need practice reading out loud. So, I'm going to read *Gulliver's Travels*. Shamus can't hold a book 'cause of the bandages."

"A marvelous idea. But aren't you already reading it?"

With spritely enthusiasm, he said, "It's okay. He's gonna blubber over Gulliver."

"Did I tell you I read it when I was about your age? Have you gotten to the part where…?" Christopher, at the mirror, tugged at his cravat one more time.

Dino stepped back holding up his palm. "Don't spoil it, doc."

"I won't. Do you recall where the Carnahan's live?"

Dino nodded and picked up a kerchief Christopher dropped, handing it to him. "Expect her to cry, do ye?" He giggled like a schoolgirl his voice a couple of years from lowering.

"Don't pester me, I'm as nervous as a cat on water."

"You're a catch, doc. I bet she's nervous too."

Christopher chortled. "Now where are you coming up with such ideas?"

"You get talked about at school. Seein' as how I live here, I get asked lots."

"Well, don't be giving away information about me. The gossips in town dig up enough, don't be giving them fodder about my private life."

"You think me a mutton-head? Don't worry about me." His chin rose a bit displaying confidence in his ability to protect Christopher.

Which delighted Christopher. "How do I look?" He rotated for Dino's inspection and grabbed his beaver hat off the dresser top.

"Like yer going to supper with someone special."

Within the half-hour, Christopher stood at the door to the Fitzjames' apartment. The maid, swathed in veils, admitted him then disappeared. Mrs. Fitzjames' rocked in her chair, pursed lips and scrunched brow. She acknowledged him with a condescending curl of her lip as he waited for her daughter. Which thankfully was quick.

She was a vision, a bright flower of a woman, clothed in the color of spring Irises with cream lace at the neck and cuffs. She greeted him with a shy smile. But it was her mother who inadvertently gave him a compliment.

"I thought you weren't going to wear your new gown?" said her mother. "You'd save it for a special occasion."

Her daughter tried to smother a gasp, looking askance at the ceiling. Christopher hid his mirth. After all, he was in little doubt her mother had a problem with him.

Miss Fitzjames held her shawl so Christopher could drape it over her shoulders, an intricately tatted lacey concoction matching the lace at her neck and cuffs. Her hair was pinned up and she wore tiny pearls in her ears. Picking up a beaded reticule, she said goodnight to her mother and walked out the door, Christopher in her wake.

The scent of musky sweetness was in the air. Folks burned peat logs against the September evenings. The night air thinned out with the onset of autumn. Changing leaves rustled in the gentle breeze, crunching under their feet.

As they made their way toward Cashel's, she said, "I apologize for her sharp tongue. Something's gotten into her lately. But she refuses to talk about it."

Christopher offered his arm. "Perhaps she's simply tired. Sometimes our elders lack the patience of their younger years."

"She's put out at me for stalling to fulfill a promise I made to my father before he died."

He waited for her to continue, and when she did not, he broached a possibility, "She frowned when I mentioned Carrick-On-Suir. I'm assuming the location might have something to do with the promise."

When she didn't answer, he added, "I don't mean to pry. But, if there is something I could do, I would be more than happy to help."

"It's a strange request," she said. "I'm not sure how to tell you without causing prejudice between us."

As they neared Cashel's, Christopher opened the door for them. Mrs. Cashel bustled from the kitchen, wiping her hands on an apron. "Short of help this evening, sorry. Just the two of you?"

"Yes, by the window in the corner if possible." Christopher stepped aside as Miss Fitzjames followed the owner.

She asked their preference of drink. As they waited, Miss Fitzjames made herself comfortable and Christopher set his hat on a shelf by the door. About half the tables were full, and he recognized almost everyone as they waved or smiled. Most folks in the village had at least a nodding reference to others. Because of this, it was easy to become a topic of conversation.

Tea came and Christopher recommended the mutton potpie. They ordered and Miss Fitzjames set her cup in the saucer and began where she'd left off. "My father was born and raised in Carrick-on-Suir. And from what I gather an entrepreneur of sorts. There was another man in Carrick who made life difficult for him, to the point where my parents sailed back to my mother's home in Portugal."

He leaned his arms on the table, giving her his full attention.

She added, "Here's where it gets prickly. My father delivered goods from the linen industry and fresh crops in Carrick to stores in Dublin. The man in question..." she looked down at her lap settling her napkin. "He built a toll road eventually running my father out of business over the cost of using it."

Christopher didn't flinch, but he had a fairly good idea the identity of the man and her subsequent reticence to mention him.

"This last year my father became quite ill. Which caused him to force a promise from me before he died. I was to bring his ashes to Carrick and bury them as close to the dratted man's burial site as possible. His intention was to *bedevil* him through eternity."

Christopher pondered the heft of her father's irrational request, but then chided himself for his own intolerance. Her earnestness was so captivating, he stifled a grin.

"Your silence on the matter suggests your bias."

"I'm listening with the intent to understand. I take it you are aware the identity of this man?"

"Most assuredly."

He reached across the table, touching her fingers. "Your father held a grudge for a good part of his life. Do you have any suspicions as to why, other than the one about the tolls on a road he traveled?"

"He said it lessened his income. I think I overheard conversation about my mother approaching this man on my father's behalf. But it was so long ago, and I was young. He and my mother were at odds most of their lives giving me the sense I was the only reason they stayed together."

Withdrawing her hand from beneath his she said, "You can have no doubt of my mother's hostility as you've been the victim of her caustic tongue on several occasions." She inhaled deeply, glanced at her lap then back to him. "She knows the man my father disliked for the better part of his life is your father."

"I thought as much." He tapped the tablecloth with his fingers. "That explains why your mother said to you 'he's Morgan Curran's son.'"

Mrs. Cashel arrived with their dinner ceasing their conversation. A serving girl set a dish of mashed potatoes on the table, butter melting down the mound of white fluff. A plate of biscuits fresh from the oven spilled their delicious yeasty scent.

Cutting into the crust of his potpie, he realized how hungry he was and thought back to the last time he had eaten. It had been almost noon as the morning began with a steady stream of patients with mostly mild complaints.

"The mutton is tasty." She gestured to his plate. "Yours?"

"Just the way I like it. I'm so hungry, it almost wouldn't matter," he added and forked a carrot dripping with gravy.

Between bites, she said, "I'm curious. Can you think of any reason my father held such an aversion toward yours? It simply doesn't signify toll fees would create such animosity."

He laid his fork across the plate and dabbed the napkin to his mouth. "My father was driven to succeed. An idea would come to him, and he'd dig into the finish, like the toll road to Dublin. There were many such projects over the years. He was well liked by his peers, but there were those who couldn't abide his forcefulness. My mother was not a happy woman. I never heard them argue. It was the silence that was deafening. My memory of them was their vast differences."

"Have you siblings?"

"Two older sisters, Molly, who lives with an aunt in Dublin, and Rose, married to James Hawley. They live at Lillybrook, in Carrick, with their five children."

"Oh my, you must miss them all. Are you able to visit often?"

He sobered at the notion. "Since setting up my practice, I haven't had time. Our dining tonight reminds me how nice it is to step away." He flashed a grand smile at her. "One I need to do more of, if you are willing?"

A blush crept up her cheeks. "I think that could be arranged."

"I might have to include Dino on occasion now that he is a part of my household such as it is. Do you have siblings?"

"No. It would have been lovely to have had a sister or brother. I used to ask my mother if she could *find me one,* until one day I realized my request was rather painful for her."

He fingered the stem of the goblet, swiveling it on the linen. "Could she not have any more children?"

"My guess is she was unable to after my arrival. My young self didn't realize her pain. She never talked about it." She patted the sides of her mouth with the napkin.

"Now, Mr. Curran, if you don't mind, please tell me more about your father. I'm intrigued as to why my father would harbor such animosity."

He took a moment to think. "I'd characterize him as stern. Moody. A taskmaster. But he deserved accolades for all he did to improve life in Carrick."

Miss Fitzjames pressed her elbows into the tabletop, leaning forward. Her forehead creased. "I have this sense my mother is keeping something from me. If I attempt to broach the subject, she changes the topic. It's silly to remember, but when I was quite young, I would ask about their wedding, as little girls do. She would abruptly change the subject. Early on I didn't question her change in mood, but as I got older, I realized she deliberately avoided my questions."

Christopher focused on an idea. "I'll write to my sister, Rose, perhaps she has an idea. It would be a start."

Her lovely features eased. "I'd be most obliged. Thank you."

"We can't have your father's ashes pining away on a shelf, now can we?"

Again, she treated him to her lovely smile, as Mrs. Cashel approached their table. "I offer apple pie and pecan pie." She reached for their empty plates.

Miss Fitzjames declared, "Pecan is my favorite."

"Bring two, please," he said as he relaxed against the back of his chair.

Then Miss Fitzjames peppered him with questions about the infirmary. What made him decide on the building? Did he think it to be a bit on the small side, especially with Dino in need of his own space? Talk ran the gamut of the village and the progress of clean-up after the storm, to the school Master and his teaching approach.

The evening passed quickly and Mrs. Cashel, having taken off her apron, came into the dining area and blew out lanterns on the vacant tables. Miss Fitzjames whispered, "I think we've overstayed."

Christopher of a sudden glanced about the room. "I hadn't noticed." Standing, he reached for her lacy shawl dropping it about her shoulders, then said to Mrs. Cashel, "Didn't mean to keep you so late."

"No bother, Mr. Curran. It's good to know you aren't all work." She gave them a veiled smile that Christopher swore meant something else.

They strolled toward her apartment as the stars were beginning to come out and the pale moon sat low in the east. Holding his arm out she tucked her hand atop. They walked slowly enjoying the peace of the moment. The moon streaked across her face highlighting the color of her skin like tea mixed with cream.

His awareness of her caused the cares of the world to fall away. "I wasn't certain of your reason for accepting my invitation."

Startled, she looked up at him. "You're referencing my mother's keeping your invitation from me?"

"Of course, I am. I couldn't help but think I was your revenge."

She lowered her chin, their walk slowed. "Yesterday I would most likely have agreed with you. But tonight, I am pleased to have spent a delightful evening with you. I've been concerned what you would think of our reason for being here. After all, it must seem rather unusual to come all this way and...well..." her voice softened and trailed off.

He stopped their walk and with his knuckle, lifted her chin to the weak lamp light that captured her glistening eyes. "You are lovely and charming. Any man would be honored to spend time with you. I would not presume to question your sailing to Hawthorn at the request of a dying man."

She took a step backward, her tone skeptical. "You don't think it foolish?"

A chuckle burst from him. "Hardly. I've never met a woman with the determination you possess."

"I don't believe you, sir. No one?"

His brow cocked and he shrugged. "Maybe someone, a long time ago."

She nodded thoughtfully. "Relationships are complicated. An example would be both of our parents."

His eyes traced the outline of her face. She possessed remarkable single-mindedness which caused him to wonder how she might view a relationship with him. "How is it you aren't married?"

❧

For a moment Renata lost her breath. "Are you mocking me?"

A cloud passed over the moon casting them into a duller light. He swept his coat to the side, clasping his hands on his waist, looking imperial from top hat, to polished boots. "Certainly not. I enjoy your company. How can I explain something I don't understand myself?"

His deep voice threaded itself between whisper and a touch of disbelief, that she could almost believe him. He was a cross between intelligent medical doctor, and charming boy-child, who, if she could believe him, desired to be with *her,* clumsy though he was going about it.

However, her skepticism made it vastly difficult to accept and she countered, "What is your game with me? I am not wealthy I have nothing of value. And there is the situation with our parents."

His dark eyes dug into her soul and she drew her shawl close. She was nervous, out of her depth with him, and suddenly felt foolishly insecure.

Her chin rose, she said, "You needn't walk with me. I'll see myself the rest of the way home," and practically stalked toward Market Street.

His baritone rumbled, "I think not. This is a special occasion if you recall. Your lovely gown, pearl drops dangling from your delicate ears, I'll not allow you to walk alone."

His manly voice tinged with mirth was not lost on her. He was humoring her, and she loved it; adored his teasing and attention. And, if she dared admit, the prospect that he wanted to kiss her.

18

The next day, at half-past noon Christopher strode into the Black Pig noting Mulroney, Carnahan, Danaher, and Mike Cooke all elbowing the table as they eyed him.

He headed straight to Padhraig who was stacking clean mugs on a towel.

Mike shouted out, "Doc, when you get a minute, I'd a word."

Christopher waved at him as he leaned in toward Padhraig. "What's going on down on the Strand?"

The bartender cast him a big smile. "Aren't you the one to bend my ear?"

"You've the pulse of the village. So, tell me."

He rubbed the counter with his rag. "Word's not official yet but seeing as how they walk the Strand measuring and all, it'll be out soon enough. Hawthorn Village is to be elevated to a port of some consequence."

Very pleasing information for Christopher, he asked, "I assume the quay will be rebuilt?"

"It'll have to be. The whole of the Strand will become a sight, wide enough to accommodate carriages as well. We'll have a Market House for incoming ships wares, all kinds of merchandise from Spain, China. No more leavings after Waterford folk take what they want. We're navigable for large tonnage ships yet have not offered easy access. Seems our village leadership has finally taken a cue from Waterford."

Christopher cocked his head toward the table of monkeys. "They should be plenty excited about this. It will bring steady commerce."

"You'd think. They've been whispering for an hour now. They caught sight of the topographers on their way here."

"Hawthorn's a good place to live, but poorer than most. It's apparent in my dealing with patients. I'm usually paid with eggs, a side of ham, all manner of barter. With ships allowed to unload, and merchants waiting on the quay. Our little village will begin to flourish."

Padhraig hung his wipes on a rack to dry and drew McGrath's mug off a peg without the customer having to ask. McGrath had plopped onto a stool at the end of the bar. Most of the villagers who were regulars had a mug of their own. Padhraig was pleased to show off how many regulars he had. Not one peg without a cup.

Christopher knew he wouldn't bring in a mug of his own.

Padhraig growled, "It's about time Hawthorn upped its image."

"Hey doc, I need to talk to you," Mike's raspy voice called out.

Christopher slapped his palm on the bar. "Guess I'd better see what's up."

As he approached the quartet, he caught conversation about body snatchers and the investigation that was keeping Waffer busy. At sight of Christopher they hushed and gave their attention to him.

"What can I do for you?" Christopher nodded to the three as he spoke to Mike.

"We've decided, the missus and me, you should be the twins Godfather. Sunday afternoon two o'clock at The Church of Christ. Reverend Alcott has agreed ye'd be a fine choice." He stood up and grabbed Christopher's arm, pumping it.

Dumbfounded, Christopher glanced around the table, the other three were grinning at him. Danaher said, "Come on, doc. Agree to it. We're waitin' on you to say so."

"Well, I'm honored." Christopher sought assurance. "You're sure?"

"'Course we are. Gave it a lot of talk, we did. You are a fine man and getting better at doctorin' every day now."

Ignoring the left-handed compliment, Christopher vigorously shook Mike's hand. "Thank you for your kindness."

Carnahan hee-hawed. "If it weren't for you, he'd not have sons. The whole village considers ye've fairy charms."

Mike jumped in. "I don't say yer perfect, I say ye're gettin' better."

Christopher cringed at their dismissive compliments. He focused his attention on the change of conversation between Shamus' father and Danaher, they were discussing the merits of enlarging the Strand.

Christopher waited until they finished before asking Carnahan, "You must be relieved at how well your lad is healing. I noticed a marked improvement this morning. If not for your missus' knowledge, he might not be doing as well. I've reduced his pain medication. A big step forward in the process."

Carnahan sucked on the end of his pipe and blew out smoke before he spoke. "The lad you took in's been readin' ta him."

Christopher's jaw eased. "For future reference, the lad's name is Dino Curran. It was his intention to share the book with Shamus hoping he would enjoy the story and put his mind to the adventure."

The trio respectfully fixed on Carnahan as Danaher stood having finished his pint and said, "Your wife's known for her healing powers. You'll get yer son back to normal." He slapped Carnahan on the back friendly like.

Christopher told Mike he'd look forward to Sunday and then left the pub. On his walk home he ruminated Waffer's threat to discover him as the body snatcher. While Christopher considered the implication a joke, it would not bode well for folks to even suspect he might be involved in such a nefarious act. He needed to take steps to clear himself of any inkling of suspicion. He needed to find the villain himself. Maybe tonight he'd wander a graveyard.

Back at the infirmary, he busied himself with making tea and snatched a couple of biscuits Krysta left on the sideboard taking the tray to his office. Dino was in school, and he was free of patients.

Time to write a letter to his sister inquiring about their lives in Carrick. What she might recall, especially when he had been away at school. Were their parents happy? Was there discord between them? Was there ever mention of an Ian Fitzjames? If so, what was the relationship like? Friendly, or did she think at odds?

Dino slammed his way past the infirmary door running down the hall to the apartment in back. Done with school for the day, he obviously had plans for what was left of the afternoon. Christopher followed him to his room. "How was school?"

"Master Carleton brought an owl for us to look at up close. When it fluttered its wings, they were *huge*." He held his arms out as far as they could spread.

"Was it an eagle-owl?" Christopher had on occasion seen them. "They're aggressive and have been known to eat the little red deer."

"Master Carleton said it had a wingspan of six feet. He had it chained in his cart and then let it go after we talked about it. Gorsh, if it eats deer, it could eat…" his brows rose as the thought popped into his brain, "…me."

Christopher ruffled his wavy head of hair, grinning at the shock in his voice. "It could, but highly unlikely. You aren't out and about in the dark, and it only hunts at night, and then usually in the forest. Besides, I know that eagle-owls don't like lads. They are particular for the red deer."

Dino gave him a long doubtful glance. "Are you teasing me?"

"Would I do that?" He raised cocked brows at the child.

"Doc, stop that."

"If you insist." He glanced around the bedroom. "Should we get a desk in here for you?"

Dino shook his head. "I like it in the kitchen else I'd miss out on Krysta's treats."

"We certainly can't have that." He grinned at the lad. "A lack of cookies is detrimental to one's mental sharpness."

Dino glanced sideways at Christopher. "Darby would say you are full of blather."

Chuckling at the retort, he inquired, "Are you reading to Shamus this afternoon?"

His voice aquiver, Dino said, "Gulliver was captured by midgets, and now he's going to a place called *Brobdingnag*." He grabbed his satchel adding. "Shamus made me promise I'd be back today."

Christopher shook his head at the lad's enthusiasm for the classic story. To be read such an adventure is probably the light in Shamus' day.

"I've two letters for the post. Will you drop them off on your way, please? And don't be late for supper. You needn't eat at their table. Mrs. Carnahan doesn't need another mouth to feed."

Dino stopped at the door, a look of doubt on his face. Christopher immediately realized what he implied. "I said that all wrong. It's not about you being a pest, it's about a mother overworked with the care of Shamus."

"You mean his mother does it all because she's not sure you're a good doctor?"

"I probably deserved that," Christopher chortled. "Yes, you've captured the exact meaning. And, once again startled me with your sharp insight. Now get on and enjoy the time with your friend."

As Christopher watched Dino walk off, book cupped in his elbow, Mr. Brandon, his landlord, came up the walk, "Ah, Mr. Curran, glad to catch you."

"What can I do for you, sir?"

"It's more what I...what we would like to do for you. Miranda hopes you will attend dinner with us tomorrow."

He had already made excuses twice now since renting this building from him and so he could not, in good conscience do so again. "It will be a pleasure," he said, much against his desire.

As the front door closed, he sat back in his swivel chair contemplating the whole of the time spent with Mr. Brandon and his daughter. Sighing, he wished he could have had a dire reason to have said otherwise.

Krysta stood at the door to his office. She carried a big bowl and was stirring the contents, unmindful of the mess dripping on the floor. "I've a soup today. Rabbit, onions and carrots. I'll leave it in the pot but swing it off the fire. Biscuits are on the sideboard under a cloth."

"Sounds delicious. I'll wait for Dino."

"I'm on my way to Asia's place. His mam invited me to sup." She whapped the spoon against the bowl splattering some of it.

"What's in the bowl?"

"My ma gave me this recipe for mutton pudding. I thought to take it over to Asia's mom to help with dinner." He reminded himself she was underpaid and knew her way around the kitchen, so held his tongue.

"Thank you for taking care of us, Krysta. I hope you enjoy your evening."

He was about to finish documenting today's activities in the ledger when she added, "Darby stopped by today looking for ye. Her husband's been off the boat a week. He's an infection on his ear but won't come by. She's worried it'll get worse but can't make him come to you."

He set the pen aside folded his fingers over the paper. "I'll take a walk after supper. I appreciate you're telling me."

"Oh, well, not tonight. They've got plans and won't be in. But Darby said tomorrow night would suit them." About to enter the kitchen, she hummed a tune. He thought of the young and carefree lives, then wondered why, as he was nearly ten years younger than Krysta who was in her mid-thirties, did he feel the elder?

Two hours or so later, Dino bounded into the kitchen as Christopher laid out spoons and napkins. "I got invited to stay for supper." His face happily lit.

"I take it you're not hungry." He filled a glass with cool milk.

"I told her thanks, but I had to get back home and sup with you." He grabbed up a glass and held it for Christopher to pour milk.

Bowing their heads, Christopher said a little prayer, put the napkin on his lap then ladled soup into a bowl for Dino, and another for himself. "Mrs. Carnahan must like you."

Dino picked up his spoon giving the question some thought, said, "She likes that I spend time with Shamus."

"You're a thoughtful lad. He'll most likely be a friend forever."

Teething his lower lip, his eyes narrowed.

"What's on your mind, lad?"

Shaking his head, he blew on the broth in the spoon.

"Did something happen at Carnahan's?"

"When you said he'd be my friend for life—" he paused. "does that mean like Schmitty was till he died."

"Yes, I would say so. People come into and out of our lives all the time. Some folks stick. I think Shamus will be one of those for you."

"'Cause we'll live here forever?"

Christopher thought of the life this child had already lived in such a short time. "Folks can be friends and live in another village, works for many all the time. But, yes, I expect us to live here forever."

Dino grinned and slurped the cooled broth.

A twelve-year old lad with a friend, can't beat that combination. Christopher buttered a biscuit. "Was Shamus able to stay awake for *Brobdingnag?*"

Enthusiasm infused Dino's voice. "How could anyone sleep. A man seventy-two feet tall? And a farmer who thinks Gulliver's the odd one and makes folks pay to see him. We read to the part he got sold to a queen. We only got some of it read. Shamus kept asking me to read certain parts again and again."

After their meal was done, they cleaned up, and Dino declared he had homework, Christopher offered to help, but he asserted his growing confidence and independence. "I've got this, doc. Master Carleton gave me extra spelling to work on. It's easy but takes time."

"Are you the only one who gets extra work?"

"Meg gets the most. More than me. I think he likes us, so it's not a punishment."

It became clear to him what Dino and Meg had in common. "Master Carleton is challenging you both to learn more. This is good to hear, son. Makes me proud of you."

Later in the evening he heard Dino attempting to whistle. The sound warmed his heart, he could recall his own attempts at the same age. Never did master it though. The result was a lot of breath with little tune.

The next evening Christopher presented himself at Brandon's door, carrying a bottle of wine that had been a gift from one of his patients. He couldn't account for the taste but didn't want to appear empty-handed. As he intended to stop at Darby's home before returning to the infirmary, he brought his black bag with him.

"Come in, doc." Presented with a corked bottle of white wine, Brandon asked, "Did you put this up yourself?"

"I'll confess it's from a patient and I've needed an excuse to open it." His daughter walked into the parlor untying the apron at her waist. "It is good of you to dine with us, Mr. Curran."

"The pleasure is all mine." Her father poured three glasses and distributed them.

She drew the glass under her nose. "A slight buttery scent. And, please, call me Miranda."

"I expect you to render me the same favor, Miranda. It's Christopher."

They held their glasses in recognition and sipped. "We are

having minty lamb chops, my father's favorite." A crash from the kitchen caused Miranda to set down her glass and excuse herself.

Brandon raised his brows at this and said, "She'll take care of matters from that quarter."

Christopher said, "I was looking forward to minty lamb. Can't say when I've had it last."

"I dare say, if she doesn't have a backup, might mean we have to trot on down to the Black Pig."

Christopher finished his wine and Brandon refilled both their drinks before Miranda returned.

She surrendered to a chair as sounds drifted from the kitchen. "All's right. Supper is as planned." And she took a long sip from her glass. Christopher was content there would be minty lamb after all.

The Brandons enjoyed a cozy abode made more so with the fire crackling, pictures on the parlor wall above a green divan. Two comfortable chairs perpendicular to the sofa, and tables with lamps flickering furnished the main room. The dining room off to the side was separated by an arch. Several plaques honoring community work hung on the wall opposite the fireplace. Altogether it was a handsome and inviting interior.

Christopher observed his host in his own element. What with signing documents and the few meetings to draw up the contract for renting his property and the necessary changes to build it into an infirmary, he had been unaware of Brandon's calm side. Usually, he was a fiery bundle of energy.

Christopher looked at his half-full crystal, "This isn't bad, a tinge of sweet without being overly so."

"Do you recall who gave it to you?"

"It was in my early days here, and names were running together."

"What's it been, four months, five?" asked Brandon.

"Nearly five. We opened in early June."

"Did you say you had a partner?" Brandon set his glassware on a side table and gave Christopher his full attention.

"Yes, and I recently received a letter from him. Jonathan, Lord Tremaine, he and his wife are touring the continent. They should arrive sometime this week sailing in from Calais." The thought of his old friend relieved the growing tension caused by lack of assistance at the infirmary, he could also begin to think of expansion.

"I recall their wedding. A splendid affair. Do you get to Rockmore Hall often?"

"A time or two, quick visits. The Earl and Countess are looking forward to their granddaughter and Lord Tremaine settling in the area."

Miranda, who had been listening to this exchange, asked, "Are you familiar with the name Mr. Baker, Simon Baker. A lawyer in Waterford Village?"

"Is he the same Mr. Baker who involves himself in our Alms House fund raising?" Christopher asked.

A blush spread upon her cheeks, her voice flustered, as if she hadn't expected his enthusiasm. "Why, yes, he is."

Brandon glanced at his daughter, a look of incredulity on his face. "How would you know him?"

"From charity work with the Women's Aid Society. I asked Christopher because he is in the medical profession and I wondered if they knew each other." The blush had not diminished as she explained her interest to her father.

Christopher downed his second wine and found himself easing in her presence. Her attention toward him was for information regarding another. Perhaps he could do something to bring them together.

Dinner was ready and they moved to the dining area. A maid carried in several platters of steaming food, a lamb pie, chopped potatoes, leafy greens, and squash.

Mr. Brandon drilled his daughter. "Why would you pester the good doctor with information about Baker?"

"Father really, I inquired of Christopher because I was sure they would have worked together a time or two. Mr. Baker appears a rather nice man, giving of his time to the children's society. Simple curiosity, 'tis all." Shrugging her shoulder, she took a bite of the pie.

Christopher thought she might be hiding behind that bite of pie. Could it be Brandon was interested in Christopher for his daughter because he did not know her interest lay elsewhere? Christopher enjoyed the remnants of his meal as he was pleased to think this. The oatmeal cake dripping with a caramel sauce was a bonus. He needn't concern himself about dodging an invitation to dinner if invited again.

His next stop was Darby and Sean's cottage. Sean opened their bright blue door. Stepping over the threshold, Christopher said, "This is the mountain coming to you. I understand you'd rather suffer than seek help?"

Sean cast his wife a dark look. "She's always at it. Never changes, will she?"

"Well, let me have a look in your ear and discover if the walk over was worth my time?"

With nighttime upon them, Darby twisted the stem on the lantern increasing the light and held it just so allowing Christopher to look in Sean's ear. "The first I'd say is clip your ear hairs, it's like a jungle in here."

Sean tried not to hee-haw, but his shoulders shook with the bottled effort.

"I take it your latest catch was worth the effort?"

"Yup."

As Christopher plied his instrument, he mentioned, "I've a bit of good news for you. Looks like a market house on the Strand will be approved."

Sean was surprised. "I wondered what folks have been whispering about. I'll be damned to 'ell and back."

Darby barked, "Shush that kind of blaspheme or you'll be goin' there."

Christopher cautioned, "Don't move, you might feel

something." With a tweezer and a little tug, he drew the tweezers up and held it to the lantern light.

"What the 'ell?" Sean squinted, not sure what he looked at.

Darby leaned over the doc's shoulder, "Is that what I think it is?"

Christopher said, "And what might you think?"

"A stink bug."

"A damn beetle livin' in my ear?" Sean shuddered to think of it.

"Well you make it mighty comfortable for him with all that gray hair hanging in your ear." Christopher tried to hide the grin on his face.

Darby patted the doc's shoulder. "You are a wonder."

Christopher said, "Use some salt and warm water, and cleanse it a time or two for the next week. Should clear up what might be the beginning of an infection. You know how to do that?"

Darby nodded. "Seen you at it time and again. Easy enough. Thanks."

He stood outside their little cottage knowing he was only a block over from Miss Fitzjames. Clenching his fist, he itched to knock on her door. But the possibility the door might be slammed in his face caused him to move along the lane toward his own place. It didn't keep him from thinking of her on the walk home.

Moonbeams were in and out of cloud cover, and a thought came to him about the monkey's in the pub earlier today. He reached Market and walked toward Christ's Church. This is one of the cloudy nights a body snatcher might make a move.

He set his bag on the front stoop of the church and stayed to the shadows as he glanced out over the graveyard. The night was quiet, not even crickets ticking. Not noticing anything out of the norm, he walked slowly alongside the church building and crossed the street to St. John's graveyard. A bit larger than Christ's Church.

He listened for sounds. The night air was thick with mold and the rustle of leaves on the stone path.

Of a sudden a screech rent the air and a scraping of branches against each other the near woods followed. Animals, still it caused a hair-raising sensation to skitter down his back. He was imagining someone creeping up on him and shook the silly notion.

Satisfied no body snatchers were about this evening, he walked out of the shadows and up toward the infirmary.

19

Sunday morning dawned lazy with a heavy mist hanging over the village, curling low in the lanes. As soon as the sun warmed the land, the mist will scoot like a startled cat.

Today Christopher would be anointed Godfather to the Cooke twins.

With Dino's curiosity about the twins and the Sacrament of Baptism, Christopher needed to assure him he was most likely baptized as an infant having been born in the overwhelmingly Catholic Sicily.

As they approached the stone church, they noticed the steeple on the back lawn still awaiting the crew to hoist it onto the roof.

Dino spotted Mrs. Cooke with one of her babies and ran toward her. Christopher stepped into the interior of the church. Because of the missing bell tower, a canopy was spread above the font where the ceremony was to take place.

The last time Christopher stepped inside was a year ago when he had taken the time to look Hawthorn Village over as a possible home for the infirmary. He had noticed the pews were not segregated by position, wealth, or the size of their donations. It made an impression on him.

He glanced at the pulpit of black oak probably carved by one of the original parishioners, then made his way to a small group of folks to the right of the nave near a doorway that led to Reverend Alcott's office.

Miss Fitzjames was in animated conversation with Mike Cooke and the Reverend. Gowned in lilac with matching feathered bonnet and shawl, her smiling face tilted to Mike. Christopher chided himself—of course she lived across the hall from the Cookes. She had cared for Mona daily after the births, so why wouldn't she be here? Her difficult mother stood to her side.

Mike immediately stretched out his hand as Christopher approached. "Thank you for agreeing, doc. You'll be sharing the Godparent honors with Miss Fitzjames."

Their glances met and she smiled. He figured she'd been made aware it would be the two of them.

She greeted him. "I hope all is well with you and Dino." Her mother stepped closer, and he had the distinct feeling it was to listen to their exchange. Fortunately, Reverend Alcott carried his Sacred Oils and Holy Water to the Baptismal font and called everyone to step close.

As if on cue, Michael and Patrick began fussing. Mona patted the infant she carried walking slowly toward the altar rail. Miss Fitzjames immediately approached her and took the infant in her arms. Christopher felt awkward, and he wanted to blame it on Mrs. Fitzjames presence, quickly shaming himself for the thought.

The Reverend stretched his arms in welcome. "We are a community of Godly Christians who will become part of the Cooke twins' extended family." He glanced about. "Godparents please take your place next to me."

A dozen or so folks from the village shuffled near, a goodly number of faces he recognized from the Black Pig. He saw several who had visited the infirmary. Dino put his hand in Christopher's and tugged for him to stand next to Miss Fitzjames, which he did.

Her arms full of one of the infants, she murmured to Christopher, "You need to take Michael from his father."

Stupidly, he felt as if in a fog and reached for the infant. Mona said, "He'll calm, it's his fussy time right now. Jiggle him a bit, he'll be fine."

Holding the infant as Miss Fitzjames held Patrick, he rocked Michael gently. With a tiny fist to his mouth, Michael fixed Christopher with a pair of serious eyes as if contemplating how he was going to make this as difficult as possible. For the moment, all appeared tranquil. The Reverend droned on in the background as Christopher prayed Michael would remain content.

Dino whispered, "You'll do fine, doc."

Christopher felt Dino patting him on the back. Who was the baby here? He tried not to chuckle and met Michael's intense scrutiny.

Reverend Alcott began, "Will the Godparents please step forward." He gestured to the font filled with Holy Water, which was placed opposite the altar and held separate with a wrought iron railing symbolizing the Rite of Baptism was as sacred as the Holy Eucharist.

Each with an infant, they stepped near the Reverend. "Parents, Mona and Mike, come near please."

Christopher felt the tiny body stretch rigid; Michael's face flushed the color of beets. A wail the likes of something to wake the dead rent the nave with a resounding echo.

"He is awake for his christening, good," said the Reverend with humor, and placed a symbolic white cloth, embroidered with Michael's name and a cross, on the now squirming babe. Christopher tried to comfort him with a rocking motion, but Michael was having none of it. Mona reached over to pat her son.

The Reverend continued by dipping his right thumb into the bowl of sacramental oil and making the sign of the cross on Michael's forehead. Feeling the warm skin of the reverend's hand, the infant twisted his open mouth as if seeking nourishment. When his needs were not met, another wail resounded.

Meanwhile, Christopher glanced at Miss Fitzjames to his immediate right. All smiles and with a contented infant in her arms, she raised her brows as if to say, *some of us just get lucky.*

How an infant could create a sound that reverberated off the domed ceiling and circle the walls was mystifying. He continued to rock him, whispering into his ear which was magical for a moment or two. Then the infant was discerning it wasn't his mother's voice and let out a wail putting the earlier one to shame.

Christopher kept his focus on Michael's red blotchy face rather than look up. Dino patted him on the back and whispered encouragement.

The group of friends and neighbors craned their necks to get a good look at the goings on and he felt like a bumbling gobshite. Jiggling Michael, he mimicked Miss Fitzjames cooing to Patrick. Nothing distracted the Reverend from his prayer book, who asked for indulgences for the parents, godparents, infants, and those in attendance.

The new sound Michael made was more like a raven on the hunt, and the titters from neighbors prickled his ears. Neither medical school nor life prepared Christopher to soothe a hungry infant. The babe managed to stuff his fist between his pink gums, his little cheeks red with dissatisfaction and his frustration fixed on his new godfather, when he would prefer to be in his mother's arms.

After the Sacramental oil was applied to Patrick's forehead, the parents and godparents were asked to uncover the babies' heads and hold them over the baptismal font, where Reverend Alcott, poured cold water over their foreheads.

Christopher couldn't be certain, but he thought he noticed Reverend Alcott's delight when both babies, shocked by the cold water, screamed to high Heaven. "In the Name of the Father, and the Son, and the Holy Spirit, I Baptize thee with the Christian names of Michael, and Patrick."

Everyone clapped with joy and Mona took Patrick holding him high, as did Mike with Michael.

The Cooke's announced tea and scones at Cashel's, and the procession made their way over to Strawberry Hill. With a great deal of relief, Dino held Christopher's hand and led them toward

Miss Fitzjames and her mother before Christopher realized what the scamp was doing.

He nodded to Mrs. Fitzjames and said to her daughter, "How did you know to choose Patrick over Michael?"

She flashed him a mischievous grin. "Instinct."

Mrs. Fitzjames mumbled, "Men don't understand infants. Even a high and mighty doctor who thinks he knows everything, doesn't." She stabbed the ground with her cane. Christopher was grateful it wasn't him.

Her daughter said, "I'm thinking your approach to infants is medical, rather than paternal."

"I'm an uncle. I've held babies before."

She inquired, "How have you been?"

Placing a hand on Dino's shoulder, he said, "This youngster is nearly a full-time occupation. Food and homework seem to be a priority."

Dino slid from under Christopher's grip. "Tell her you burned the pancakes and we still had to eat them because you had folks waiting in the outer room."

Christopher chuckled and ruffled Dino's hair.

Miss Fitzjames asked the lad, "What did you think of the ceremony?"

"I was worried the doc couldn't handle Michael."

Mrs. Fitzjames harrumphed, stabbing the ground with what Christopher consider an extreme thrust, with her cane. She had a way of terrorizing him, which in his adult rational brain he tried to reason could not be true.

He opened the door to Cashel's and let everyone file in. It pleased him Miss Fitzjames had taken the initiative to secure a table with Dino and her mother, leaving what he assumed was an empty chair for him.

With a cup of tea in hand, Reverend Alcott approached Christopher. "You carried on like a professional father, Mr. Curran. Just between you and me, the Cookes have a bit of different personalities in those boys of theirs."

Still gloating over her success as a godmother with a silent infant, Miss Fitzjames said, "Mr. Curran handled himself well considering Michael was on the verge of a real squawk."

"On the verge?" Christopher sputtered. "That ten-pounder gained the attention of everyone in the church. Acted as if I pinched him."

Mona, cradling a sleeping Michael in her arms said, "A full belly, and he's off to the land of nod. Wish all children were as easy to care for."

"Really? I wouldn't have called it easy," said Christopher. Everyone within ear shot laughed remembering the sight of the doc juggling an infant who wanted his mam.

Christopher complimented the mother. "You were meant to have twins and counting little Mary. You manage very well."

"Thanks, doc. Some day when you get married and have a houseful, remember to say such to your own wife. She'll be needin' to hear it."

Mrs. Fitzjames her head cocked in Mona's direction, listened to their exchange. "Ah, but that won't happen to my Renata. She has plans for a future that do not include marriage. She's to be a medical woman."

Christopher glanced at Miss Fitzjames as she stood next to the Reverend. "I'm not surprised. Your daughter's service at the infirmary has been acclaimed by not only Mrs. Cooke, but Asia with his broken leg, and Krysta when the storm did its worst."

Miss Fitzjames cheeks were almost red on her creamy olive skin. He could tell she was flustered over the compliment. Her gaze settling darkly on her mother, who harrumphed.

Christopher was nonplussed that Miss Fitzjames intended to work in the medical profession. She hadn't mentioned a word of it at dinner the other evening.

The Cookes readied themselves to leave. Their young daughter was beginning to act up, and the babies, who had their own unique routine, would be fussing within the hour. Miss Fitzjames glanced at her mother. "I'm going to carry a parcel for Mona, so will walk with them back to the apartment."

"I haven't finished my tea, and I wanted a word with Mrs. Kneely."

"Fine, then." She stood, taking up her reticule.

Miss Fitzjames followed the Cookes from the diner, Christopher close behind. "Do you mind if I walk with you?"

The look she gave him was of complete surprise. "Do as you like, sir."

"Let me help with that package." He reached over and took it from her.

She inquired, "Where is Dino?"

"A school friend who attended the baptism with his family invited him to their house for the afternoon." He slowed his step to match hers. "I wanted to tell you I've written to my sister asking about a feud between our fathers. What she might remember if anything."

"Should prove interesting to learn of the disagreement or whatever it was that occurred." Her stride was no-nonsense. She was in a hurry to catch up to the Cookes.

Shoving his fists in the pockets of his buckskin breeches, he asked, "Would you consider dining with me, again?"

She asked, "And why would you want that, Mr. Curran? I recall making myself quite clear. My promise to my father is uppermost. My mother has taken a rather keen dislike of you and makes no secret of it. I am well past the age for courting." She stopped in her tracks, scowling.

He slowly tipped his chin to better look at her almost causing his hat to slide off. "I'm keen for a challenge?"

His absurdity almost made her laugh, her gloved hand covered her lips but could not completely hide the hilarity bubbling up. "I'll grant you are the most stubborn man on earth."

He shrugged. "Have dinner with me tomorrow. It's your company I want. I'm not asking you to sign your life away. Humor me. I'll call for you at three."

"Isn't that early for supper?" Pursing her lips, she tried not to confirm how utterly irresistible she found him. His square jaw framed a flirty smile, short sideburns the color of rust, amber eyes fused with humor. No good would come of this, they were leaving soon after her father's burial.

"Maybe it's to be at a special restaurant?"

She couldn't resist one more bit of challenge. "What is it you wish to discuss?"

"Your interest in medicine."

He liked the way her smooth brow scrunched into a question. He said, "Your mother mentioned it in Cashel's."

She recalled the conversation. "There's nothing to discuss. Like all dreams, it's a longing that will most likely never bear fruit."

He stood on one leg, cocking the other, and folded his arms around the package. "I don't see a problem. I'll do all the talking about medicine, then."

"You are the most outrageous man I've met, Mr. Curran. And if dining with you will put a stop to your nonsense, then yes, call upon us at three."

She started after the Cookes when he added, "My invitation does not include your mother. No disrespect intended." He gave over the parcel to her.

Picking up her lilac-colored skirt to navigate a puddle, she glanced over her shoulder. "Tomorrow at three."

☙❧

Christopher could see Constable Waffer pacing in front of the infirmary as he came around the corner. What now? He approached the man with impatience. If ever there was a nuisance, like a fly you'd swat but not kill, it was the constable. Waffer met him halfway along the walkway.

"This is unexpected. What brings you to my doorstep?"

Waffer stuck his thumbs in his waistcoat and teetered on the balls of his boots, blocking Christopher's attempt to get into the infirmary. "There's been another desecrated grave last night. But I think you know all about it seeing as how you were there."

Christopher nudged his beaver hat up and squinted at the constable. "And what makes you think I'd be anywhere near a grave last night?" As he said the words, he recalled his deliberate casing of the burial site. Damn and blast!

Still trying to stand tall on the balls of his boots, Waffer leaned in. "What do you think I found near the crime scene? Solid evidence you were doing your dirty work. Just as I suspected all along. This is going to cost your license. Sure as 'ell."

"I was on my way from seeing a patient. It was dark and I thought I'd do a little scrounging."

Waffer's grin showed off a stained set of mismatched teeth. "Really? Folks hardly think of you as a doc, and now you want to try your hand at catching body snatchers." He leaned in, bringing with him a foul breath. "You know what I think? I think you've fixated on dead bodies bein' a man of medicine. I'm keeping your black bag as proof. There's those about Hawthorn think you are capable of digging up what you already killed.

The constable jabbed a dirty finger into Christopher's chest. "I'll solve this business and prove you the guilty one." He swaggered down the lane.

Who would think him capable of digging up graves? And, what he *already killed*? What the damnation did that rattlebrain mean by that?

He hardly slept a wink thinking of Waffer's damning threat. But business first. Christopher put medical items in an older black bag, needing to replace the one Waffer confiscated. It served no purpose for him to dwell on the constable's irrational conclusion about why he was in the graveyard.

Through the window, Christopher watched a rider securing his bay to the post and then bounded up the steps.

Krysta answered the front door then entered doc's office. "A letter for you. He's to wait for an answer."

Christopher was delighted to recognize Tremaine's wax seal and tore it open. The essence of the missive was the Tremaines had arrived yesterday and taken up temporary residence in the upper floors of Rockmore Hall.

Tremaine was bringing Lady Tremaine into town to visit with her mother, Nuala, Lady Rutledge, and he would like to take the opportunity to meet up with Christopher at the infirmary.

Christopher penned a short note welcoming his friend and business partner back to Eire, and that he would be at his disposal tomorrow.

Moments later, Dino stuck his head in the office door. "I'm home," he said, and continued on down the hall.

"That's it? That's all you have to say?" As the lad's footsteps padded down the corridor, Christopher shouted, "Dino—come back here."

The lad had the silliest grin on his face when he returned.

Christopher grunted. "How did school go? Was Master Carleton pleased with your essay?"

Dino shrugged. "Couldn't tell by his expression." He allowed a long pause, then with a big grin added, "But he wrote excellent on it."

Christopher groused, 'You sure do draw out the moment." He gestured for the lad to give it over. "Let me inspect this masterpiece."

Dino drew it out from behind and sheepishly grinned with satisfaction.

"This calls for a celebration, and I have it on good authority —" he tapped a finger to the side of his nose—" that Krysta baked your favorite cookies after you left this morning."

In the kitchen, Dino pulled out the jug from the cooler and poured goat's milk into the two glasses. Christopher pushed aside the curtains hanging from the sideboard, and not finding the tin with cookies, opened the door to the pantry. Shuffling tins and jars about he didn't locate the treats. Puzzled, he growled, "I believe that woman has a new hiding place."

Dino replaced the jug in the cooler and with hands on hips, in imitation of Christopher's stance, glanced about the kitchen. "She's wily, like a cat."

"They've got to be here somewhere?" He grinned at the lad. "We need to think like her."

"Not likely to happen. I've heard so much nonsense come outta her there aren't enough cookies to make me want to think like her."

He laughed so hard his stomach hurt. "Son, you have the wisdom of Solomon. I couldn't agree more, but right now, I want to eat at least three of those cookies and wash them down with a cool glass of milk."

"She hides stuff in the hall cupboard."

With a frown, Christopher moved to the hallway, hand on a closet knob. "You mean in here where I keep my ledgers and books?"

"Yup."

The moment he opened the door, the aroma of cinnamon and butter icing hit him. "Well, I'll be. Cunning she is."

By the time a few of the cookies had disappeared, they decided Krysta was going to be furious if she had baked them for a reason like the church bazaar or the school fundraiser. "'Cept," said Dino, "I'd of heard if there is a fund raiser."

"What does Shamus think of Gulliver's Travels? What part are you reading now?" Christopher scooped a finger of frosting off his cookie and licked it.

"His mom gives him that therapy you taught her, how to move his arms and such. He isn't taking any of the pain medicine and sleeps a lot when she's done. Reading's gone slow. I'm going over to catch him up on the part about the land of giants and Gulliver as small as the Lilliputians were to him. Gulliver's afraid, but his keepers are nice. I only read to the part where the King is angry. I wanted to read more, but then I'd just have to reread it to Shamus, so I made myself stop."

"What do you think happens to the King?" Christopher swiped up crumbs from the cookie he just ate.

"I hope he gets what's coming." His grin was filled with hopeful revenge. "Mrs. Carnahan asked me to stay for supper tonight."

"Is that wise to spend so much time with him if he's in discomfort?"

Dino rolled his eyes as if the doc was expected to understand. "It's his idea I read to him. I figured that he struggles so I go slow. I hold the book up and point to the words, then he kind of says them, but his chin doesn't move all that well yet. But I hear him whisper."

"Eating with the Carnahan's works because I've asked Miss Fitzjames to dinner."

Dino cast him a sly smile. "I'm glad you like her."

Christopher bit into the last cookie he would allow himself, almost choking over Dino's approval.

The lad leaned over and slapped him on the back. "You'll mind yer manners at table with her, right?" A silly grin on his face.

Christopher squinted and jutted his lower jaw. "You remind me of my mother. Maybe you're going to be a teacher someday, like Master Carleton."

"I want to be a doctor, like you." Dino pushed his plate away and crossed his skinny brown arms on the planked table.

Caught unaware, Christopher had to get a grip on a sudden flood of emotion. A minute ticked away, then another. "It's obvious to me that you are capable of becoming anything you set your mind to. I'll make a promise. If the desire stays with you through your younger schooling, I will make sure you go to university and pursue whatever career you might be interested in."

A look of pure delight brightened Dino's face. "If it's doctoring, I won't let fellows badger me like those at the Black Pig."

Christopher could only shake his head at one more of the lad's insightful pronouncements.

❦

Earlier in the day, Christopher had paid a visit to Grogan's in hope of renting a suitable vehicle for dinner with Miss Fitzjames. Grogan had a sly look on his unshaven face when Christopher said a buggy for two. Wiping his work-worn digits on a leather apron, Grogan slumped his way into the stables and showed him a rig with a flexible hood fit for one horse. It wasn't very fashionable, but he pointed out it could be used by the doc for making his calls.

To Christopher's way of thinking Hawthorn Village's

population size didn't call for the use of a conveyance. "If it's all the same, I'd like to rent this just for tonight."

Relieved that Dino would be with the Carnahans for reading and dinner, Christopher looked in his clothes press for something suitable to wear marking this as a special occasion.

Dressed in his usual doeskin breeches, a pair of black leather shoes with black silk stockings, and a snazzy red waistcoat, he felt ready for taking a lovely woman to supper. Pulling up in front of the apartment on Market Street, he called to a lad standing nearby. "Tend to my horse, and I'll have a sixpence for you."

The bare-foot urchin took the reins, "Aye, gov'."

Christopher took the stairs two at a time.

At his knock, Mrs. Fitzjames opened the door a crack. "You." Followed by a disgusted harrumph. "Might as well come in. She's one to keep you waiting, and not out there in the hall." She reentered the room as he stood in the open doorway.

He stepped inside the apartment, took off his hat and walked to the window overlooking the road below. The horse and buggy in full view. He smiled at Renata's mother. "How are you today, Mrs. Fitzjames?"

She grimaced as if his question soured her. "No need for small talk. I'm not for her going off with you, but little I can do about it."

Miss Fitzjames' entrance took his breath away. She looked radiant in a dark blue silk, long sleeves ending in points at her wrists, square neckline trimmed in ruffles of the same color, and her luxurious, shining hair pinned up with a lovely small hat in red with matching plumes and veil.

He was speechless as she lifted a red shawl and presented her back for him to drape it over her shoulders. She then drew on short matching gloves. "I hope I didn't keep you waiting?"

"You are worth every minute." He wasn't certain but thought her mother groaned. "Shall we be on our way, then?"

Miss Fitzjames brushed her lips across her mother's forehead.

Christopher noted the elder looked out the window without responding.

Outside on the boardwalk in front of Mrs. Browne's Dress Shop, Christopher drew out sixpence for the lad minding the chaise, who bit into it before running off.

She inquired, "I'm guessing we aren't dining at Cashel's."

He put down the step and assisted her into the seat. "I'm not sure if this is to be our last outing, I thought I would plan something special."

Casting him a side glance, she said, "And will that decision be up to me or you?"

"You, of course. I already know how I feel." He snapped the reins sending the gray mare into action.

Grasping the side brace of the chaise, she looked off in the distance as they took Church Street and headed east. "We aren't dining in the village?"

"It's such a beautiful day I thought we would drive into Waterford. I'm hoping you've not been to the Mermaid's Inn, not far from the Bishop's Palace. We can stroll the Mall before eating, or after, whichever you prefer. I also have a package I need to deliver to a friend."

As they took the main road to Waterford leading away from Hawthorn, the expanse of rolling hills spread out before them. Sheep grazed in the distance. She watched a pair of hawks sailing the skies. "I wonder how the shepherds protect their flock. They can't possibly be everywhere."

"Hawks don't eat sheep, but something caught their attention. The collies have spotted the hawks and are as aware of them as you are."

"Might I inquire who your friend is?" She glanced at him with a mischievous glint.

"Edmond Rice. A man who cares is the best way to describe him. Cares about our county and the children most especially. He established a school to educate poor Catholic boys."

"Would I be correct in thinking you are somehow involved with his endeavor?"

He snapped the reins, keeping the mare to a constant pace. "I offer my services when necessary. His enrollment is upward of two hundred boys. His goal is to teach them not only literature and numerations, but how to behave as useful members of society. My role is quite small and not nearly as dedicated as the others. My offering is medical in nature."

"I have a sense you are being modest. With that many students, I am sure sickness and injury prevail."

"If I had time, I could write a book about the scrapes and mishaps of young boys. But as I do not have that kind of time, I've written some guidelines for Rice to keep in mind when assessing the need for medical attention."

"From what you've told me, I think Dino is very lucky to have fallen into your life."

Ignoring her compliment, he pointed to the right. "If you look over that way, you'll capture the outskirts of Waterford. The building poking through the treetops is called Reginald's Tower built by the Vikings. You couldn't have missed it when your ship sailed up the Suir."

Clouds gathered in the southeast darkening the sky. A light mist had begun to fall as a precursor of what was to come. "We might get wet. I was hoping to walk the quay and show you the waterfront."

"A little rain won't hurt."

"I agree, but only if it's misty or less." He glanced heavenward. "Those clouds are sending a different message."

They rode in silence for a bit, then Christopher teased, "I've noticed you don't shy from adversity. Though with your mother, you bend, when others might be conflicted over her remarks."

Her attention focused on two riders off in the distance. Finally, she responded, "She's...um...difficult at times. I try to keep our relationship on level ground. Though it's gotten worse since we arrived in Hawthorn."

"Perhaps it'd hard for her to be without him. Adjusting to a new way of life at her age could be a challenge."

As he navigated the bend in the road, a ray of sun caught her full in the face, her lovely bow-shaped lips spread in a smile. "According to my mother life is a challenge. You may be right."

As the chaise brought them to the outskirts of Waterford, Reginald's Tower began to share space on the horizon with the Bishop Palace's handsome cornice, and the shining spire of Christ Church Cathedral. Those structures and others dotting the skyline made up what was referred to as the Viking Triangle. As they closed in on the village, travelers began to appear, some leading pack mules, or riding them. Carts filled with baled hay, and folks, bundles over their shoulders.

He pulled the chaise up to a stable and negotiated with the owner before assisting Miss Fitzjames down from the high seat. Tucking his package under his arm they strode toward Mayors Walk drawing up alongside a limestone building four stories high. A dark carved door in the middle, with a brass knocker was three steps up from the brick road.

Christopher mentioned, "I don't expect to be more than a few minutes."

Lifting the knocker, he allowed it to bang against the brass plate, they could hear footsteps within. A young man, dressed in livery, opened the door.

"My card. Is Mr. Rice at home?"

The young man invited them into a pink and gray marbled foyer, with several thick carpets, quite stylish. "I'll see. Wait here, please."

In less than a minute, Edmund bounded out of his library. He was always a man to show high energy.

They shook hands as Christopher said, "May I present Miss Fitzjames, sir."

Mr. Rice gave her a short nod of interest as Christopher added, "We've come over for dinner, and I've wanted to bring this to you." He held out the package. "You will find a list of ailments and their prescribed cures. Your staff should be capable of implementing the procedures. I expect it might save you time and coin if your staff are comfortable taking care of some things that come up more frequently."

Edmund's bushy brows topped a long face, prominent chin, thick lips, and a ready smile. "You are a man of your word, I'll say that." Judging the heft of the package, he said, "Feels like you've given us a good quantity of what we need." His attention shifted to the woman. "And you, miss, are you interested in medicine to the same degree as this young man?"

"Right now, I'm content to study herbs." She turned her attention to Christopher. "I do agree Hawthorn is lucky they have Mr. Curran."

Christopher's face lit up. "Miss Fitzjames is vastly interested in herbal medicines to the point she's set up shop with Talbot. I also discovered she'd like to pursue medicine."

Mr. Rice offered, "I understand someone of your gender has recently enrolled in Trinity Medical School. You would not be alone. And I'm sure you've already discovered many rich areas in Ireland's soil for your herbal studies." Without waiting for an answer, he asked Christopher, "I heard Hawthorn's damage from the storm was mostly in trees and flooding."

"It could have been worse. News was Waterford took the brunt of it saving our little village."

Edmund nodded, his mind obviously on other matters.

"We won't keep you."

Edmund executed a courtly bow to Miss Fitzjames. "It is a pleasure making your acquaintance. Please accompany my friend the next time he ventures this way. I'll be sure to have tea for us. Forgive me. I'm distracted. Next year's curriculum is…well, it's not going as well as I'd hoped. I can hear it calling to me as I complain."

Miss Fitzjames smiled at the older gentleman. "It's been a pleasure, sir."

Outside, a light mist had begun. Opening her parasol, Christopher held it above them.

Many citizens were about, all walking with purpose. Quite possibly to evade the coming rain. Brick buildings lined the walkway on both sides of the cobbled street. Several blocks from the quay, homes were built as though one long building. Separated by a lintel, door and one window facing the road. Flower boxes hung from most windows.

The River Suir was visible as they made their way down a proportionately broad space between the apartments, rows of Elms fenced with a stone wall completed the quaint look.

Christopher beckoned to the right. "Bishop's Palace is over there. Later, after dinner, I thought maybe we could stroll toward the river, depending on the rain. The Bowling Green would ruin the hem of your lovely gown."

She flashed him a smile as he led them along the pavers, he added, "You are benefitting from years of older sisters bullying me to be thoughtful."

"Oh, come now, Mr. Curran. You can't pretend to be put out. I think you care deeply for them both. It must be wonderful to grow up with siblings."

He closed the parasol and guided her toward another lane. "I was concerned that you would heed your mother's rebuff of me."

"For that I apologize. Her manner isn't a result of our meeting. As you suggested earlier, she does find life challenging. And, we are cramped a bit, with her maid, Lea."

"Have you written to the Parish in Carrick-on-Suir about your father's burial?"

"We wrote weeks before leaving Obidos. And I haven't apprised them of our arrival or where we are living."

"What keeps you from doing so, if you don't mind my asking?" They reached the end of the Mall and he directed her around the corner and up the next street, which was much smaller, with establishments and houses thick-tight together in an orderly fashion.

It was a moment of thoughtfulness before she answered. "If I'm going to be truthful, I will admit to feeling at peace in Hawthorn. For the first time in many months, perhaps more than a year. I fear, after burying his remains, my mother will demand we leave for home immediately."

"It's your home, too, isn't it?"

"Perhaps I've more of my father's Irish heritage than my mother's. I feel so at ease here. We've settled in rather quickly with neighbors. Mr. Talbot has been a great mentor teaching me about the chemistry of herbs and medicines." She cajoled, "A few of which might interest you."

He stopped them outside a dark-stoned front with a bright blue door and shutters on the leaded windows. A window box overflowed with maidenhair fern and purple heather. Above the window was a bright blue sign painted *The Mermaid's Inn*. "I hope you've an appetite. I'm ravenous. All I've eaten since breakfast were cookies and milk."

With a hand to her back, he directed her inside the establishment. "Table for two, please," then followed an aproned lass to a corner table next to the window overlooking the street.

After Miss Fitzjames chose a fish pie made of scallops, bits of lobster, and oysters in white wine dill sauce, Christopher, ordered a potted smoked mackerel he knew to be in season right now.

She lifted her tiny veil up over the brim of her jaunty red hat and removed her gloves. She was a puzzle. As lovely and delicate as she appeared, he knew her looks to be deceiving. Her strength was evident in the decisions she was forced to make; the promise she made to her father, and constantly tending to her troublesome mother.

He asked, "How are you getting on with Mr. Talbot? Did you know he studied in London?"

"I've begun to realize he is quite learned. Insightful." She opened the napkin and placed it on her lap. "The village is fortunate to have him as the apothecary. One does wonder what would have drawn him to such a small place after living in a bustling metropolis."

The server brought them glasses of water and after quenching his thirst, Christopher said, "I believe London's air weakened his lungs. Did you know he's originally from Hawthorn?"

"He did say something or other about the storm as if he was quite familiar with the land. The reason Hawthorn was struck by the storm's rage is because it's situated on the south side of the river and facing east. The location makes Waterford and Hawthorn vulnerable."

"Talbot's a bit of a philosopher, amongst his other capabilities. Hippocrates has written that a healthy city must open to the north and east with mountains to the south and west."

Her eyes flashed with mirth. "You've drawn the disparity between a metropolis and a small village before. I take it you much prefer village life?"

He said, "There's something to be said about green rolling hills, and white clouds that a larger city simply can't boast. London is a good example, black smog and lack of infrastructure. Edinburgh has the same issues." He leaned in arms crossed on the table. "Tell me about you and your life in Obidos."

"Oh, well, not much to tell. We live in a medieval village surrounding the foothills of the Castle of Obidos with a view of the Atlantic Ocean far off in the distance. For generations, my mother's family has owned a silk farm on a sizeable bit of land."

"What caused you to become interested in medicines and herbs?"

Shrugging her shoulders, she pondered a moment. "My mother's sister, Tia Agatha attended classes at University and would take me along. Once I discovered certain elements relieved pain, I was mesmerized. My father was plagued by gout…"

"…and you discovered the saffron plant?"

Her lovely features widened into a smile. "Not only my father —my mother used to prowl the house at night. Once I discovered the use of Mandrake, it certainly made a difference for her."

If he shared a roof with her mother, he might be inclined to put it in her morning tea. It was obvious she loved her parent and fully intended to care for her the rest of her life. Shame on him. He tucked the nasty thought away, asking, "Has Talbot been of any help?"

She brightened with an eager dose of delight. "Considerably. His enthusiasm for some of my papers is greatly rewarding. He is too kind sharing his passion for medicine and is becoming a friend. I wonder why he never attended medical school; he certainly appears knowledgeable enough."

"I believe he did. But I think he left before finishing." Christopher knew enough of the stressful dynamics of family for Miss Fitzjames. He could understand the void Talbot filled with her interest in medicinal herbals. Talbot was a bit of a surprise, too. Finicky and exacting as Christopher knew him to be, his offer to assist her was a bit out of character for him. He refrained from mentioning Talbot was let go from university for his lack of scholarly enthusiasm.

He sat back and listened as she talked of her passion for herbs. "You should come into the back room next time you need cures. Mr. Talbot's given me a table to store my things. It's a perfect place, far more than I could have wished. As we do not plan to settle in Hawthorn Village permanently, I find it quite comfortable for a time."

"Are you really so sure your arrangement is temporary?"

"It's mother's wish."

He leaned in, tenting his hands. "Tell me what your long-range plans would be if it were only you?"

The sparkle in her eyes was replaced with a frown. "That is impossible as it isn't just me. I'm enjoying a lovely afternoon, and right now what happens in the future is of no concern."

"Well, then, after we sup, I want to show you the quay from Reginald's Tower to the bridge." He glanced out the window framed by lacy curtains and potted plants. "If the mist holds off." And added, "An Irish native from Boston built the quay a couple of decades ago. Out of American oak, too. It's a delightful promenade such as you won't find elsewhere." His hand stretched across the linen, his fingers touching hers. "I should not have pried into your future. I get carried away."

The look she gave him was almost heartbreaking, a mix of sadness and expectation. "You've asked nothing wrong, Mr. Curran. Your attention makes me think of what might have been in my life, and what is no longer possible."

A bit surprised at this negativity, he declared, "Anything's possible."

Her little chortle held an uncertain ring.

The waitress brought their dinners. Conversation interspersed with bites of scallops, smoked mackerel and sips of a white wine.

The mist cleared as tea finished. A bright sun lowering in the west crested across the sky spreading pinks, oranges, and lavender into the heavens. They strolled the quay, away from the brick and mortar Tower built sometime in the early 11th century by Reginald the Dane.

A sudden thought came to him. The quarrel he'd witnessed between Talbot and Martin, both with medical backgrounds. What if they were involved somehow in the body snatching? It was almost too easy. Yet he felt a niggling of possibility. With Miss Fitzjames working in Talbot's backroom, he hoped he was wrong. Her safety was far more important.

As they walked the quay, people from many cultures hawked their textiles, fruits, breads, and perfumes, He enjoyed her enthusiasm as she browsed each display. And in several instances, asked questions of the vendors about their goods.

"There is talk the tower might be renovated into a prison. Waterford has a lot of pride in the beauty of this harbor, nothing like it in all of Ireland. The quay itself is a mile in length."

Wistfully she said, "I wish my mother could enjoy a place like this. It might take her outside herself for a while. Give her something worthwhile to ponder.

A gust of wind caused Christopher to hold the brim of his hat for a moment. "I expect you are a mixture of all kinds of feelings, your heartfelt obligation to your father, a daughter's duty to her mother who must be quite sad in her own right. After all, she's saying a final goodbye to her husband."

Renata fell to contemplation. Her crepe gown swished with each step. Ringlets rested about her shoulders and glistened in the lowering sunlight. "Theirs was not a happy marriage. A lot of tension. I was rather startled when my mother announced she would accompany me on this odyssey."

Christopher inhaled the briny scent of fish. Ships at anchor rocked in the tide. "My parents hardly talked. I would have preferred some emotion, even if it meant an argument."

She peeked up at him from beneath the brim of her hat, her lips quivering with mirth. "Well, then you might enjoy being neighbors with the Cooke's."

He laughed outright. "From the little I witnessed the evening of her delivery I can only imagine what goes on day in and day out."

Miss Fitzjames' eyes sparkled with mischief. "They live an honest life. He says what he thinks, and she responds in kind. And, if their household thrives, who am I to say naught. Little Mary is the brightest and happiest of children."

As they strolled the wind pushed foam and sprinkles of water over the boardwalk. He asked, "Do you ever think of being married—I mean do you wonder what your home would be like with someone of your choosing?"

Her eyes widened, and she gushed, "I can't conceive of it. I would never want to live as my parents did. And, at my age, I think it's safe for me to say I won't have to worry a jot about it either."

His gaze slanted to her. "At your age?" A blush blossomed on her cheeks and she offered him a false smile.

He added, "I think you are at a perfect age, Miss Fitzjames. I would have you no other way. Please accept my apology for making it sound otherwise."

She kept up her stride and said, "As you wish, Mr. Curran."

"As long as I've stuck my foot in it, allow me to inquire about your avoidance at Cashel's after the baptism."

She stopped and faced him as pedestrians brushed past. She pressed a palm against her heart. "I must apologize. You were a perfect gentleman and did not deserve my sharp tongue. I was disconcerted about something my mother said and allowed it to get the better of me. Now I must beg acceptance of my apology."

"I'm relieved it wasn't something I said or did."

Mischief was in her tone. "What is unusual is the use of my sir name. I should think we could dispense with such formality." Shrugging her shoulders as his eyes squinted, she added, "Really? I think we've become friends and I should like you to call me Renata."

He bowed his head slightly, "Thank you, Renata. And please call me Christopher."

In the sweet moment, someone cursed, "Move yer bloody carcass." and Christopher led her by the arm from the center of the quay, laughing as they moved.

He said, "My partner is back from his travels on the continent. They are settled in at Rockmore Hall. He's looking forward to the changes at the infirmary."

"When you say partner do you mean he'll be working with you in the infirmary?"

"For a time, yes. Tremaine is second in line as heir apparent to the Darnley title and land, after his father. Our intention is to build a bigger facility. What I use right now is leased from Mr. Brandon. It's obvious it isn't ideal. Tremaine will be involved as he has the time to devote." A thought struck him, and he continued, "I believe you've met Nuala? Proprietor of O'Bannon's? She is Tremaine's mother-in-law."

"Many thanks to her, I've been able to have some dresses made. She happens to be one of the few people my mother enjoys. Nuala and I have visited on several occasions."

"Then you know how unassuming she is. She prefers to be called Nuala, rather than by her title, Lady Rutledge."

Renata smiled at him obviously thinking of Nuala. "She is a lovely woman. And, her daughter and husband, how long have they been abroad?"

"He graduated last December, and they've been traveling ever since."

"I take it Lady Tremaine must have been at university while he finished his studies."

"Yes. They married just before his last term and she accompanied him to Edinburgh."

"Hmm. Lovely for her to have shared that experience."

He couldn't agree more.

They reached the part of the quay where oak bridge came into full view. Seabirds on the hunt swarmed across the Suir, splashing into the river hoping to catch their supper. A dozen ships with masts furled swayed in the gentle roll of the tide. The panoramic sight across the river to the rolling hills in County Wexford where huge homes nestled in the landscape was quite different from Waterford's side of the Suir with all its commerce.

Renata said, "You've settled yourself in Hawthorn, and I wonder why you wouldn't have done so in Carrick-on-Suir, considering it's where you were born."

He inhaled a whiff of her lavender and wanted to touch her, fold her in his arms. Her question deterred his thoughts. "Tremaine and I saw the need for a doctor in Hawthorn. When school lads at Eton we would talk of our dream. Hawthorn's villagers have this mindset Waterford is the premier place to live because it is situated on the Suir and is as old as Croesus. Hawthorn was a more natural village situated on the lough with direct access to the Suir. And we liked the folks."

"I would think Hawthorn a quieter and more stable kind of environment."

He smiled down at her. "Exactly why we chose it. Though I must say, if my infirmary is any indication, by weeks end, I can usually number at least half a dozen patients are off the ships as opposed to villagers."

"Give it time. The villagers will come around and realize how fortunate they are in your choice."

He smiled at her encouragement. "Thank you for the endorsement. But the villagers are a humbling mix. Most times I enter the Black Pig, it's like walking into the strap my father used."

"It can't be that bad." She glanced upward at him. "As smart and clever as you are, it appears uncharacteristic of you to allow those smirky elders to get to you."

He blew out a puff of air and tried waving off the compliment. "I admit since Shamus has begun to heal they've eased off me a bit."

They began strolling again, this time to a park near the wooden bridge. Shady oaks and elms provided a lovely canopy where a group of benches beckoned. Maidenhair fern grew wild bordering the slates on the path, two-lipped Irish eyebright peaked out now and then amongst the fern. Pink and purple heather covered the hills beyond.

Christopher led her to a bench and separated the tails of his coat as he sat next to her. His gaze swept her face, lingered on her lips, and hungrily lifted to her questioning regard.

჻჻჻

Renata breath quickened. Would he kiss her? He once said he wanted to. The air between them filled with energy. He captured her with a piercing inspection then leaned in gently touching her lips with his, tenderly brushing them over hers. Her breath came swift as he clasped her arms drawing her into an embrace that sent blood thrumming in her ears. Casting the world aside she melted into him opening her lips allowing his deeper kiss.

The spread of his palm beneath her bosom around her side and up her back weakened any reservations. Replaced with a yearning so strong, she barely understood the gravity, the thrumming, the most pleasant warmth of his nearness. Drawing back slightly, sliding her cheek against his, she clung to his arms calming the storm and waited for her heart to unruffle, her breath to slow. When had she begun to long for him?

His voice was low and intimate as he whispered in her ear, "I apologize. I shouldn't have—"

Her gloved fingertips settled against his lips, hushing him.

He drew her away enough to look into her eyes. She leaned in pressing her mouth against his and felt the flex of his muscled arms through his tailcoat. He encircled her in an embrace once again. A murmur bubbled in his throat as he took her back to the heaven from where she'd just come reigniting the yearning. The urgency of his lips overpowered her, demanding she follow his lead into passionate senselessness.

Their kiss could have lasted an hour, but when it ended, it could have been a second. His warm palms cupped her face, chastely brushing his lips on her nose and forehead. "I don't want to let go of you."

She traced his lips with the tip of her glove. "Nor these *devil* lips of yours," she teased. A blush crept up his neck, and she delighted in the realization he was as giddy as she.

Renata sat back against the bench. Christopher followed her interest as she glanced at the treetops the lowering sun colored the sky peeping through the canopy of leaves. He reached for her hand and gently removed her glove pressing the soft skin of her knuckles against his lips.

Later, as the bright moon led them back to Hawthorn, and the lanterns creaked with the movement of the chaise, the truth settled upon her. Her mother must not know of this wondrous interlude.

At one point they startled a herd of small red deer as their legs and antlers rushed into one long image as they took flight over the road.

Renata knew her life's intention was to care for her mother, to bury her father's ashes, and to return to Obidos. Christopher blurred the dedication to her family. His physical attention awakened her yearning to the point she rued her spinster's age, felt pity for the woman who was honor bound to tend her parent. A knot in her throat reminded her she had a duty to perform.

She glanced at Christopher's profile as he held the reins, snapping them every so often, his strong jaw set in calm satisfaction. She guessed he was content right now. Her gaze rested on the russet curls brushing against his white cravat. His broad shoulders seemed capable of overcoming life's trials and tribulations. His strong hands desiring to caress her, make her feel safe.

Dear Mother of God, what was she thinking?

She must leave him be and settled herself to simply bask in his company, the clean fresh scent of him, the gentle yet robust nature of who he was, and the wonderous fact he alone held the power to capture her heart.

Dank musk stirred in the evening air. An occasional night owl or bat in search of prey, whisked through the ebon night. This would seem such a normal and lovely evening to share with a husband. Afraid to glance at him, that he might notice longing on her face, she settled on the far distant forest of trees spiking the darkening sky. But her mind could think of nothing else but the comfort he afforded her with his friendship…she could not…dared not consider anything more.

E arly morn dawned with an explosion splitting the air and shaking the ground. Christopher jumped out of bed and slipped into his breeches, shoved his feet in boots and ran out the front door of the infirmary where a brilliant glow came from the direction of Grogan's Stables.

Dino stood on the doorstep rubbing sleep from his eyes. "What happened?"

"Stay put, son. I'm not sure." He grabbed his bag and a shirt then tore onto the lane. The acidic scent of sulfur in the air.

"I'll help." The lad followed Christopher outside.

Christopher spun about. "I couldn't bear it if anything happened to you. Give me peace of mind and stay where you are safe." He shoved an arm into his shirt as he ran toward the glow. Several other concerned fellows joined him along the way.

Old bearded Grogan, thrown back against a hay mound, face blackened, appeared a bit bewildered. Another haystack afire and the walls of his shed used to repair carriages and such, blown out, scattered like the leaves of an oak shedding in the autumn.

A haystack fire against the orange and pinks of dawn cast a disastrous scene in morbid light. Danaher and Mulroney were industriously retrieving tools and such from the perimeter of the fire. Christopher ran directly to Grogan.

One glance told him the man was disoriented. Perhaps more because of the explosion than his age, although he was up there in years. Christopher took the elder's pulse and questioned, "What happened?"

"Not sure," Grogan's gravelly voice choked.

Constable Waffer ran towards them. "What happened?"

Grogan wobbled his head toward the constable. "Not rightly knowin'"

Christopher satisfied himself Grogan appeared to be in no immediate danger. His search of Grogan's limbs fortunately found nothing broken. "Can you stand?"

"With some help, most likely." Grogan extended his arms, and Christopher pulled him up. He was shaky on his feet and clung to the doc's arms. "Give me a bit. Dizzy I am."

"Take your time. I'm not going anywhere."

Waffer took in the scene, his lantern jaw agape. Mulroney ran over with a stool and tin of water. "The shed's pretty well gone." He glanced at the old man. "Yer damn lucky you old coot. Where were you when it blew?"

The constable walked toward the shed, now fully engulfed in flames. The red glow licked the dark sky, and Christopher knew this was probably not going to bode well for Grogan, who stunk of liquor.

Christopher helped him onto the stool and took the tin cup from Mulroney ordering Grogan to drink.

He took a long swig, spit it into the air, swiped his mouth and barked, "Where's me good stuff, I'm not wantin' this." His beady little eyes glistened, affirming Christopher's earlier thought.

"I got me powders mixed." His arm jerked up as he waved in the direction of the blown-apart shed.

Mulroney shouted at him, "You old fool, could a got yourself done in."

Christopher took in the exchange and inquired of Mulroney, "What powders would he be talking about?"

"Sulfur, charcoal. He most likely added something to it, would be my guess." His large face was red from the glare of the fire. He growled at Grogan. "Yer a damn fool, old man. Got the whole village in an uproar." He leaned in close. "Even got the law here. You'll be lucky not to end up in the gaol."

His concern being Grogan, Christopher hadn't taken notice and glanced at the fringes of light cast by the fire. A good-sized crowd watched the haystacks and shed burn. "What had you intended by mixing the powders?"

Grogan sheepishly cast his attention to the ground. "I was thinkin' to mix up a wee bit of the black powder and increase the size of my pond..." a belch of pure alcohol wafted over Christopher as he leaned in. "I would a brought it down there..." He pointed to the pond in question. "But as you ken, I didna get that far."

Danaher's voice could be heard encouraging folks to go home. "The fire will burn itself out. Grogan is fine. Go on, now. All's well."

Christopher leaned in as close to Grogan as his sense of smell could tolerate and barked, "I've a mind to toss you in that pond, sober you up, and give you over to Waffer. A week behind bars might be just what you need." He knew he got the old fool's attention when Grogan's hairy jaw swung back to him.

Beside himself with Grogan's irresponsibility, he warned, "You could have killed yourself don't you know that?"

Mulroney said, "Doc, he won't remember any of this. When he wakes sometime later today, he'll think the banshees paid him a visit."

Waffer, fists pocketed, casually strolled back to them. "I suspect this might have been set. What do you have to say about that, Grogan?"

The old man rolled his focus to the constable, then blinked and shook his head. "Payin' me a visit are you, then?"

Christopher gave him a good shake. "The blast woke the village, you damn fool. He came running just like the rest of us." Christopher asked Waffer, "Help me get him to his bed?"

Waffer barked, "Hold on, doc. I need some answers. A fire like this doesn't start itself, now. Tell me what's going on here, or I'll let him spend more than a week behind my bars."

Grogan shrunk back against Christopher and Mulroney who each had an arm to begin the trek to his bunk. "I gotta take a piss."

Waffer shook his head. "He's bloody drunk." Glancing over at the shed, he ran to it getting as close as he could and took a long iron pole and prodded about the edges of the fire.

Mulroney said, "He's looking for signs of a distillery. You've done it this time, old man. Your goose is gonna get cooked, I'm thinkin'."

"Let's get him to bed." Christopher led the way.

Grogan fumbled with the front of his pants. He could hardly stand. Christopher didn't want Grogan pissing on him. "Come on, do your business inside, not out here."

Waffer yelled at them, "Hold up there, doc, Mulroney. I've got questions." He jaunted across the yard. The shed was almost gone. Daylight loomed on the horizon revealing many of the folks who preferred to stay and witness the outcome of Grogan's folly.

Grogan opened his cod and pissed a steady stream. Christopher and Mulroney were ready to catch him if he lost his balance.

Then they took Grogan to his small abode, little more than a lean-to built against the north wall of the stable. They could hear Danaher and several other men, settling the horses on the other side of the thin wall.

Just as they laid the inebriated man out, Waffer stomped into the room. He glared down at Grogan, swearing, "If I find evidence of a still, I'll slam yer drunken self in the gaol." Spittle flew from his words as he pointed a finger at the man. Grogan was already snoring, and a wet spot was spreading on the front of his breeches. He wasn't quite done.

Christopher shook his head. "He nearly got himself killed."

Waffer said, "He'll wish he had when he wakes."

Christopher said, "I don't think you'll find evidence of whiskey making, constable. It appears to be a miscalculated judgement on his part."

"He's drunk," Waffer said. "I'll buy it's accidental. And whiskey makin' is an offense."

Mulroney chimed in, "It's not an offense to drink on one's own land."

The constable glanced from Christopher to Mulroney. "I'll be back later in the day when this dies down. My investigation will be thorough and surely I'll decide what's what then." He sent a scathing glare at Grogan who snored, his lips fluttering with the sound. "Bah! Drunken sot." And walked out.

Mulroney said, "You go on home, doc. We'll stay till it's out and keep a watch over the old man."

Christopher hadn't walked ten yards when Waffer, who had obviously waited for him, was on the attack. "Where were you last night?"

He glared at the constable, whose height came just about to Christopher's shoulder, and said, "Why?"

"Up to your heathen mischief in Waterford by chance?" Waffer stopped walking and stood in front of Christopher preventing him from going on his way. It wouldn't have been hard for Christopher to brush him aside, but he decided to humor the man.

"You gloat about knowing so much about me, why don't you know I was at dinner at the Mermaid's Café. And, by the way, where's my bag? Seems you should be done looking over the contents by now."

"Busy, are ye. No wonder it's been awhile since the graveyards have been paid a visit. I've got me eye on you, doc. I'll prove it's you before the first snow flies."

"You have no right to keep my bag." Christopher's brows scrunched with ill humor.

"It's evidence you were at the graveyard. I'll keep it until the trial."

Christopher tried not to laugh. "Trial? You're daft. All you have to go on are some grave sites that've been raked over. No corpse found disturbed as yet. Is it you think I'm checking pulses on dead bodies?"

"For a man claims he's innocent, you're gettin' all fussed up." With that Waffer tucked his thumbs into his vest and walked off with a jaunty swag. "In the end I'll getcha."

On the walk back to the infirmary, Christopher mulled over a slew of names he thought fit the stubborn jackass constable. He was a burr in his saddle, a thorn in his side. Back in his own kitchen, Christopher watched Dino shuffle from his bedroom yawning. "You smell like smoke?"

"I probably do." He sipped a mug of tea. "Grogan blew up his shed."

"Wow, what a sight that must have been. Wish I'd gone." Dino padded to the cupboard taking out his jar of jam and placing it on the table. "What was it like, a big kapow boom, then what?" his small fist punched the air with youthful vigor.

"The kapow boom is what woke everyone. Ended up destroying his shed and burned down a couple of haystacks." Christopher set his mug down. "Krysta won't be in until mid-morning. What'll we have then, pancakes or bread and jam for breakfast?"

Dino flashed a smile and with eager anticipation said, "How about pancakes, jam, bread and bacon?" Dino added two peat logs to the fire and swung the griddle as Christopher reached for a bowl, spoon, flour, and eggs.

Wrapping one of Krysta's aprons around himself, Christopher said, "Well, I'll get cracking. Don't want you late for school."

Dino washed his face, dressed, and came back into the kitchen to set plates and mugs on the table. Bacon sizzled on the griddle, filling the kitchen with its meaty, smoky flavor. He began telling of a canon backfiring on the *Nomad*. Two tars flew into the air never to be seen again, and the fire took hold of the deck and ropes before it was put out, as Cap'n Redeye shouted orders to blast the other ship closing in on them.

Christopher stared at Dino, his thoughts swirling with images of what this child had endured in his short years. Struck with such an intense emotion, he bent down on a knee and gripped Dino's shoulders, looking him square in the face. "The bravest thing you've ever done is seek refuge under my roof."

Dino placed his small palms on Christopher's shoulders, meeting his gaze. "Your backdoor was open. You were an easy target."

Christopher got up off his knee, chuckling. "If that's what it takes to get help around here, I'll have to keep it in mind."

After breakfast, Dino gathered up his books and grabbed up the luncheon sack Christopher prepared. "See you later, doc."

Christopher called after him, "Have a great day, son," as he gathered up the dishes, piling them on the sideboard for Krysta. He considered how Dino's use of the language had changed from the idioms of tars to schoolroom usage. He recalled one of his mother's favorite sayings, *all things in good time.*

Readjusting a list of medications from yesterday's patient diagnoses, he began another of needs for his next visit to Talbot's Apothecary. He decided to make a move on Talbot, too. See what he could stir up about Martin. Darby came in the back door, calling out good day wherever ye are, and he answered from his office.

"I've brought clean linen. Must be a slow time for ye, doc. Not so much to return to ye." Then her notice fell on the pile in the corner. "Oh, spoke too soon, didn't I? That'll teach me to hold my shush."

His head shook with the wonder of the woman. "I believe you are capable of entertaining yourself all day long."

"'Tis a good thing, I'll say, what with that man at my place comes and goes as he pleases, leavin' me to settle all our business."

"Sean? A fisherman's life isn't a walk in the park."

"Are you sidin' with him, then? Cause I'd just as soon leave your dirty linen ta someone else."

He stood up, took the pile from her arms, placed it on his examining table, and said, "You need a cup of tea and some of Krysta's biscuits. She thinks she hid them, but Dino knew where. There might be a few waiting just for you."

Krysta arrived to see the two of them chatting and devouring her latest batch of apple walnut cakes.

Caught in the act, Christopher brushed off the front of his waistcoat, stood, and said, "I think I'll get back to my desk." Both women eyed him as if he were a naughty child. "I can't help it if you make irresistible treats. Oh, and lest I forget, I need a brew of barley water. You can put it in the container labeled as such on the shelf in the office."

Right then the bell at the front door dinged. A mother, and her child approximately ten or thereabouts, came in. "Doc, she's a lump on her throat, but she ain't sick, no cough nor fever."

"Your name, please."

"I'm Sandra me daughter's Emma. Sandra and Emma Thornton."

Christopher lifted the girl onto the end of his examining table, a sweet little flaxen haired child sucking her thumb, which he pulled from her mouth. Recognizing the child had a goiter, he asked, "Does Emma like her potatoes?"

"Funny you askin', doc. She won't touch em."

He lightly prodded the swelling on her neck. "Is it hard to swallow?"

She scrunched up her lips as if trying to remember, then nodded. Her bright blue eyes widened to the point it reminded him of the big marbles he used to play with at her age.

He said to Mrs. Thornton. "She has a goiter. Nothing to be alarmed about, but it can be the body's way of asking for more iodine in her diet. Potatoes are a good source, but also do you or your husband gather kelp?"

"He does. Feeds it to his animals, he does."

"Well, you should also feed it to your daughter. Her thyroid gland needs the iodine from the ashes of brown seaweed. Sprinkle it on her food. I've got a jar in my pantry. Wait a minute."

He came back in the room, handed the mother the jar, and requested she bring her daughter back in one month for a checkup. "The goiter will take time to reduce. More than a month for sure, but I'd like to assess her anyway in four weeks."

"I'm much obliged, doc." She nudged her daughter's arm. "She's most precious, glad it's an easy fix," and presented Christopher with a jar of honey, explaining the hives were her own, and the bees took nectar from the fruit trees all summer long, pridefully acknowledging that everyone around for miles wanted her honey. Christopher walked them to the door. In the same moment, the postman walked up the short lane to the infirmary, waving a letter.

He immediately recognized his sister's handwriting and closed the door to his office, eager to digest the information without disturbance.

Dear Chris,

It is lovely hearing from you. We miss your wit and humor, although your nephew Morgan, seems to take after you in that regard. His serious father has drawn the comparison, putting me in hysterics and kindling the regret I feel not spending time with you. The wit and humor I mentioned, you will surely need a dose of as my answers to your questions will no doubt bring you to a sad understanding of our parents.

He leaned his forearms on the desk as he had begun to read. But her first paragraph caused him to drop his arms to his lap and sit back against his chair taking a short breath to still a rise of anxiety.

You were, of course, at Eton during the tumultuous occasions our parents had intense disagreements. Molly and I never talked to you about those occurrences because I suppose we felt you could do nothing about them, and we were in great need of your humor (aforementioned) and distractions.

Your brow is most likely scrunching in that famous scowl of yours, but do not, please, dear brother. Molly and I were old enough not to be scarred by the goings on, though I suppose Molly's never marrying, and you practically dedicating yourself to medicine and may never marry, could be considered residual damage.

Getting on with what I know, our father had an affair, and the woman started increasing. Mother discovered the truth. The woman was married to a man our father disliked. Something to do with business or other. There was a terrible scene on the steps of our home in which Molly and I heard almost the whole argument. Not only had our father had an affair with the man's wife but he ruined the man's business having to do with transporting goods to Dublin, or some such. It's hard to recall with so many years passing on the incident now, and our parents long gone. Basically, the men could not stand each other. The woman was of Portuguese descent, and her husband, who I understand was Irish, carried her off to her family in Portugal to have the child. Apparently, the woman and her husband had been estranged for many months, when she conceived with our father. All this heard as we hid behind a drape at an open window. It was years later our mother confirmed all this as she confided in me before she passed.

I know nothing of the child, and I can't recall if I ever heard the name of the woman. It goes against our upbringing, but as much listening at closed doors Molly and I indulged in, you would think I could recall more than I do.

I hope this answers your questions. Our father wasn't the easiest of men to live with. I do believe our mother loved him, in her fashion. Perhaps this will explain the cool atmosphere of our home the times you returned to find it so. It wasn't you it was what occurred between the two of them. Mother never did forgive him and there was never any talk of the child, even during mother's telling us shortly before she died.

Please keep me informed should you come our way. We've had the family home added on to in the last few years, what with the growth in our brood. I think you will like what James has done. You might recall his dreams were to become an architect. This nurtures those earlier dreams.

Much love, Rose

Christopher reread the letter several times. His gut wrenched at what he learned. And a horrific thought sunk into his heart.

Had he fallen in love with his sister?

Krysta came to the door with his barley water, and he barked at her to leave him be and shut the door. Dismay swept every fiber of his body. He folded the note carefully and locked it in the drawer of his desk, as if the knowledge it contained burned his hands. Burned his mind, seared his heart black. Unbelievable! Unthinkable!

His immediate reaction was to get outdoors, and he passed through the kitchen in riding boots, gloves, and crop. "I'll be gone a while." He didn't wait to find out if Krysta heard him and lunged down the steps of the porch.

Grogan's stable seemed to have been put back in some sort of order since the fire. Without asking Grogan how he was getting on, he pointed to a black Arab. "I'll take her."

Grogan mumbled, "Ye've not been ridin' since before the fire."

"Well, things change," he growled.

"Still upset with me, are ye? Can't say as I blame ye, doc. Pure foolishness on me part, don't mind sayin'." He saddled the Arab and led her to the front of the stables where the doc paced back and forth.

"Havin' the constable rag on me about a distillery scared the *bejesus* out a me. He wanted to put me in the gaol, didja ever?" His voice squealing with the injustice.

Christopher had little he could say, but Grogan was leaning on him in a frail way—emotionally. "I guess it was the lesser of two evils, you were bent on enlarging your pond rather than making whiskey. Powders and drink do not mix."

"I most likely won't do such again." He winked at Christopher and gave over the reins.

Christopher jumped in the saddle the mare danced sideways until he jerked on the leather and looked down at Grogan. "As long as you stay sober, your thinking will carry weight. You could have died. Others could have lost their homes."

Grogan shook his grayed head. "Truth be told, doc. I'm a changed man, I am."

He grunted and spurred the mare to a run. He didn't care what direction only that it took him away from the desk where he laid the life-changing missive. He'd read it again, though he knew it to be Renata whom the woman carried, *his father's illegitimate child, his half-sister*. There were too many consistencies with Renata's story to think otherwise. *Blazes and damn!*

Of all the possibilities in the world for fate to play its hand, why in the name of blazes did it have to be this? He could never touch her again never kiss her. It would be a horrid sin. His heart squeezed with regret and remorse. He defiled her, and himself.

Digging his boots into the Arab's sides, he hoped the wind would blow the ugly truth out of his mind, and his heart.

He'd fallen in love with her, and she'd become as precious to him as his own sisters, but in another way. His anger roared, and the Arab reacted with a quickened pace. The cooler air of autumn blew past them as her stride sent them across the rolling emerald hills.

An invitation to tea was delivered to mother and daughter Fitzjames from Nuala, Lady Rutledge. Her daughter, Mairéad, Lady Tremaine, wished them all to meet.

Mrs. Fitzjames was stunned with excitement over the invitation. Donning her best bonnet, all Renata could do was pray her mother wouldn't make the visit a challenge.

Known to denounce other titled personage in Obidos, Mrs. Fitzjames had an obsessive desire to be accepted by the very people she admonished for their excesses.

It had rained during the night and the Fitzjames women avoided puddles as they made their way, parasols in one hand and lifted skirts in the other. A reed-thatched cottage with a red door and matching red gate was the only house on the block. A stone fence enclosed the neat abode. An elegant yellow-wheeled curricle tied to the post suggested Lady Tremaine had already arrived.

Renata, having heard the doctor talk glowingly of Lady Tremaine, was delighted for the opportunity to meet her. With introductions around, Renata thought her lovely. Her dark auburn hair stylishly piled high on the back of her head and laced with a ribbon of soft yellow. Renata considered she was several years younger than herself. The four women assembled around a table in the sunroom. The maid laid out tea and biscuits.

Lady Tremaine poured and passed cups to her mother's guests. As she handed Mrs. Fitzjames her refreshment, she inquired, "I understand you are acquainted with Mr. Curran who is also a boyhood friend of Tremaine's."

Mrs. Fitzjames sputtered, "I hardly know that man. You need to direct your question to my daughter." She blew gently on her tea.

Lady Tremaine smiled as her lovely gaze fell on Miss Fitzjames. "Are you visiting, or planning to make a home in Hawthorn?"

Though not addressed, Mrs. Fitzjames insinuated herself into the conversation. "We are here to fulfill a request of my dear departed husband." She cast a side-glance at her daughter and hastily continued, "We must remain in the village until then." A few crumbs from the biscuit dotted her bodice, and she daintily gathered them up and put them in her mouth.

Nuala, Lady Rutledge inquired, "Is it a matter we could perhaps assist with?"

Renata tore her gaze from her mother and settled on their hostess. "It's been more a matter of time than anything. As I am part of the effort to restore the interior of the church since the storm. I have been occupied with that effort."

Mrs. Fitzjames again interjected, "She also likes weeds."

Lady Tremaine giggled as she glanced at Renata. "Weeds?"

Ignoring her mother's sarcasm, Renata said, "I'd not realized it, but Ireland has a preponderance of healing herbs I've not found in Obidos. I've decided to collect and catalogue as many as I can."

Her mother coughed into her glove. "There is another matter, very upsetting to me, that has occupied her time."

"Mother," cautioned Renata, "please."

Lady Rutledge glanced at her daughter, Mairéad. "We might guess at your meaning, Mrs. Fitzjames, and shall make no further reference to the matter." Her unusual green eyes slanted toward Miss Fitzjames with a wink.

Renata felt heat creep up her neck and tried not to glare at her mother, who nibbled contentedly at another biscuit.

Mrs. Fitzjames asked of Lady Tremaine, "Have you always lived in the vicinity of Hawthorn Village?"

"I have. No matter if or when we might travel abroad, Ireland will always be home. All the people I love are here."

Mrs. Fitzjames glanced across at Lady Rutledge. "You raised her with a sense of duty to never consider leaving you. It's a daughter's moral responsibility. You have a right to be proud of her."

The ladies sipped their tea, giving Mrs. Fitzjames more time to insert her ideas of motherhood. The feathers in her hat bobbed as she said, "Renata is a dutiful daughter. She will live with me until I die. And I wouldn't think of denying her the privilege of such tender care."

Mairéad, Lady Tremaine, set her tea aside. "Miss Fitzjames, I promised Mr. Curran I would show you my mother's garden. He apparently is aware of your interest in herbs. My mother enjoys growing a vast number of them. And, for once, it is a day without mist."

Renata was relieved to put distance from her mother's attitude. She hoped her mother wouldn't show her *other* side to Lady Rutledge.

Lady Rutledge leaned toward Mrs. Fitzjames. "I'm interested in travel. Please tell me about life in Portugal. Do you live inland or along the Atlantic Coast?"

The two young women walked down the hall to the kitchen and out the back door.

With a mischievous twinkle, Lady Tremaine asked, "May we dispense with formality? I would like you to call me Mairéad. And may I call you Renata?"

Pleased to be less formal, she nodded. "I would like that, Mairéad, thank you."

"Well now, Renata, I am most curious as to how you and Christopher met. He is very special to Tremaine. They've been friends since schooling at Eton."

"Christopher said as much to me. I could tell their friendship is of long standing. As to *how* we met, we bumped heads at the apothecary's shop."

Mairéad bent over to pick a late blooming daisy and chuckled. "I knew it had to be an unusual introduction. His heart was broken, and he wasn't likely to go looking judging from Tremaine's terse explanation."

Renata offered, "Christopher mentioned a previous connection. He appears to have recovered."

Her eyes twinkled with mischief. "I agree. When we lived in Edinburgh, I made Tremaine promise if he saw *that* person, he would point her out to me." Mairéad stopped walking and put her hand on Renata's arm, "And, didn't the occasion occur one day. Tremaine pointed her out walking across the avenue. My focus was on her until she turned a corner. Mind you, I'd only met Christopher a time or two before my marriage. You, my dear, are far superior in looks and comportment."

"It shouldn't matter, but I confess it does." The compliment thrilled her.

Mairéad said, "Men don't think details are as important. But we women do. I certainly learned this first-hand the way I was raised."

Renata asked, "What do you mean *the way you were raised?*"

"Until I married, I lived my life in a convent, surrounded by lovely women dedicated to Christ."

"Not what I expected you to say." Her breath stalled.

Lady Tremaine explained her upbringing with many mothers and how she happened to be put in a convent. "My grandfather likes to think he rescued me. Tremaine says I am a caterpillar who came out of its cocoon."

Renata touched her arm, and with great sincerity said, "I shall never forget your remarkable life. But I do wonder how you felt about your mother leaving you in the convent."

Downcast, Mairéad sighed. "It makes me sad to think of my parents in their early marriage. It was kept secret with the penal laws and then my father's death. I can't fault her reasoning. And though I didn't know her from many of the other people seeking a hot meal, she visited the convent on occasion. I believe not knowing who she was at the time allowed me the freedom to be content."

Renata said, "It is hard for me to understand what you experienced. I see you together with your mother and sense a great love."

Mairéad asked, "What about you?" They began strolling again. "I suppose you've led an exciting and exotic life in Portugal before you came to Ireland."

"My father was born in Carrick-On-Suir. As a lad, he traveled ending up in Obidos to work on a farm owned by my mother's family. They grew grapes and silkworms. When my parents married, he brought my mother back to Carrick. After a disastrous failure of his transport business, they returned to my mother's people where I was born."

"And now you've come back."

"My mother alluded to it in the parlor. My father passed away and made us promise we would bring his ashes back to Carrick for burial. We haven't done that yet, but the time is coming when I won't be able to stall her any longer."

Mairéad reached out a hand to Renata's arm. "I am so sorry. Is it you are saddened because he is gone?"

"I came to terms with his passing. He was sick for quite some time." Her shawl slipped from her shoulders and she adjusted it. "I'm discovering I don't want to live in Portugal any longer. I want to stay in Hawthorn. I rue the day my mother demands to leave."

Mairéad hugged her. "You don't know how to approach your mama, do you?"

Renata drew in a low breath and gathered strength from her friend's enduring understanding. "She has always had difficulty accepting another's view, especially mine."

She stood back from Renata and said, "I support your decision and if there is anything I can do to help, promise me you will come to me."

Renata met her dark gaze and saw friendship blossoming. A selfless harmony of spirit between them. "Thank you. I may take you up on bolstering me if it comes to that."

When the two friends entered the parlor, it was quiet. Lady Rutledge was seated in the parlor. Mrs. Fitzjames, also seated, dabbed at her lips with a napkin. The air stirred with tension.

Renata said, "I hope we didn't keep you waiting?"

Mrs. Fitzjames' voice was definitely defensive. "We mustn't overstay our visit, my dear." The *my dear* accentuated with strain. Renata could feel her shoulders droop with disappointment. What could she possibly have said to Lady Rutledge, the loveliest of women? Removing her mother from their presence was imperative.

"Thank you for a grand afternoon." Renata leaned into Lady Rutledge. "Perhaps she's tired."

"I heard that, and I am *not*." Mrs. Fitzjames rose out of her chair almost effortlessly considering her bulk. Swiping at crumbs, then gathered up her gloves and reticule marching to the door.

Awash in humiliation, Renata cringed. "Thank you again for a lovely tea, Lady Tremaine. It's wonderful to meet you after hearing so many nice things about you." Her mother harrumphed from the small foyer.

Yet Renata continued, "Lady Rutledge," and lowered her voice to barely a whisper. "She's not at her best today. I apologize for our abrupt departure." Glancing at Mairéad, she added, "Thank you for the walk in the garden. It was lovely."

Both women saw her to the door. "Please give Christopher our best when next you are with him."

Wrong thing to say. Despite her bulk, Mrs. Fitzjames rotated on her heel and marched away from the three of them growling out, "I'll wait outside where the air is fresher."

Renata's lips pursed. A headache was forming. "I am so sorry to end such a lovely afternoon with disagreement."

Lady Rutledge came to the rescue, lowering her voice, "Never you worry. Sometimes age doesn't treat us kindly."

Renata was greatly concerned her mother's acerbic tongue might come between them. She asked Mairéad, "I do hope we meet again."

"I've no doubt of it. Tremaine and Christopher are such good friends, why not you and me? It's been a pleasure getting to know you." Mairéad glanced over Renata's shoulder. "It looks as though your mother is leaving on her own."

She sighed. "Goodbye, then." And fled down the path to catch up with her peevish parent, leaving the ladies to wave from the open door.

۞

Several blocks away, Tremaine and Christopher inspected the infirmary with an eye to its inadequacies in caring for the needs of the villagers.

The men, tall and broad-shouldered could have passed for brothers except for Christopher's russet hair, and the sprinkle of freckles across his nose, and Tremaine's flaxen hair and hazel-blue eyes. They were easy in each other's company, a good fit they used to say at school.

"What do you think of the location?" Tremaine asked.

Christopher leaned against the sideboard in the kitchen. "I like the location and the building. It's the size that's insufficient. Brandon is encouraging us to stay. I'm not sure about his willingness to expand. We haven't space for patients needing long care, especially those who have dirt floors and sleep three to a bed. It's not a sanitary environment in which to heal."

Tremaine glanced into Dino's bedroom. "This is where the lad sleeps?"

Christopher nodded.

"I'm not surprised you took him in. You've always had a soft spot for those in need." He glanced over at his friend, "What was the name you gave that food charity you created for the rag-tags roaming the streets near the university?"

Christopher chuckled. "Bairns Pantry. Haven't thought of that in a while." He raked a hand through his thick hair. "What's your assessment of looking for a new building, as opposed to expansion?"

"Let's see what Brandon comes up with first. Although I think this location probably suits you quite nicely. There's land aplenty right here. A full block of it."

They walked the perimeter of the property. The building sat on the northeast corner, sharing space with Cashel's Inn and Tea Shop around the far corner of the southern portion of the block. It was one of the larger parcels of land in the village.

Christopher agreed, "I'll talk to Mulroney. Do you recall him? He runs Hawthorn's printing press. He also sits on The Church board and might be willing to help with raising funds. But, before I bring him into our plans, I'll pay Brandon a visit and get his reaction to selling, using a long-term payment system. Or his willingness to expand the building."

"The infirmary may grow to a size where we will need a board of advisers. That would surely be advantageous for someone like Mulroney, and Brandon, too." Tremaine clapped his friend on the shoulder. "It appears our dreams are taking root. Let's celebrate."

Doubtful, Christopher raised a brow. "Tipping a pint in the Black Pig after they realize you have a medical degree is a challenge. Your title might exempt you—at least to your face, anyway. Their hubbub is somewhat of a curse for the rest of us."

Tremaine's teeth gleamed with his grin. "I would think if anyone could get someone's approval it'd be you old chap."

"It's more like bringing change to well-intentioned people who have done it another way for generations. But I've got my toe in the door."

Tremaine clapped him on the shoulder again. "Paving the way for your chum, are you. I'll also pay homage to your stubbornness almost to the point of dumb optimism."

Christopher shook his head. "Quite a compliment. Reminds me of all the times we spent after class arguing the professors' points."

"Show me the way to the pub, let's bend our elbows a bit. Let me witness this so-called curse."

"Well, maybe I should call it bickering, it's more like what they do."

As they strode toward the pub, Christopher asked. "Have you heard the rumor I may be jailed for desecrating graves. Body snatching to be precise."

That brought a hearty laugh. "Surely you're jesting."

"Not according to the constable. He's got proof I was there. Someone's digging up graves."

He turned a hard look on Christopher. "The lads at the Black Pig, the constable—I'm beginning to wonder about you. What kind of proof?"

"It's stupid of me, but I left my black bag on the step of the church when I took a walk through one dreary night. For my own satisfaction you understand."

"The constable found it. And that's why he suspects you. Perfectly logical." Tremaine sighed. "As I see it, there is only one thing to do, catch the diggers yourself."

"Which I intend. But it has to wait until I handle something else first."

Tremaine shook his head. "I won't ask. The life you lead is beyond probability."

As they continued toward the pub, Christopher realized he hadn't thought of the letter in his desk since Tremaine walked into the infirmary. An ache nestled in his heart that he could not share. There was only one person he dared confide in, and telling her, which he must, would be the killing of a dream.

For once in his life, he had thrown caution to the wind and embraced the company of an extraordinary woman, who shared his feelings. His pursuit was fated to end badly, and a few pints would not change the outcome.

23

"I've been here five minutes and have yet to understand why you summoned me? What was so urgent?" Renata's voice pled, "You are causing me great worry."

Christopher stared out the window of his office taking the coward's way out. Dumping the shocking news on her with his back to her, she wouldn't notice his shame. He could think of nowhere else to have this conversation that would afford them privacy. Dino in school, and Krysta gone for the afternoon.

"Something's terribly wrong, isn't it?" Renata's voice edged with growing concern.

He cleared his throat. "I'm not sure how to think of it, unbelievable nonetheless."

He heard the rustle of her skirt as she stood.

Lest she came near, he quickly said, "There's a letter on my desk. It's from my sister. You need to read it."

"Christopher don't do this to me. Look at me." A tinge of fear shadowed her voice.

"Read the letter, Renata." His voice sounded thick, arms dangled at his sides, fists clenched. He girded himself against… what…the truth? He could hear the shuffling of the pages, heard her gasp and the sound of collapsing into the chair.

She shuffled the last page, then folded it. He forced himself to look at her. At the shock that would be on her lovely face.

Her shoulders drooped her fingers wrapped over the fold of the letter. She glanced at him utterly bewildered, her eyes clouded with disbelief, like she didn't understand what his sister wrote.

He took refuge in glancing at the shelf full of medical books. He'd read the letter for three days, read and reread it looking for anything other than what was written.

Renata whispered, "I can't believe...all this time and I had not an inkling my parents...I can hardly fathom this." Her fingers ran along the edge of the fold. "But the circumstance and timing is exactly what I do know of them." Her wrist bent to her lips, crushing her shock.

For the next few minutes silence filled the room. Outside a carriage rattled by, the whirr of conversation drifted in the air as people strode past. Life goes on, even if the possibility of love is crushed by the truth of another generation's sins.

Like reaching for a lifeline, she asked, "Could your sister be confused about the facts?"

It pained him to look at her. He wanted to comfort her, hold her in his arms. But his feet were anchored by shame. "Rose would not tell me these things if they were not the truth as she perceives it."

"What happens to us?" Her voice so soft as if she'd lost all effort to communicate, her face paled.

A surge of anger gripped him. "Us? Blazes, woman, do you not know what—" one hand raked his hair, he put words to the horror. "Blazes and damn—we're...." He choked it out, "We're brother and sister."

Using the arms of the chair, Renata stood on shaky legs and gently laid the folded letter on his desk. She kept her face averted with the help of her hat brim. In a tight voice, barely a whisper, she said, "It seems appropriate to learn of such crushing family news in the privacy of your office. The Hippocratic oath you took means no one will ever know but us."

Silence stretched out as both of them realized there was no future for them.

Renata's surge of anger spewed forth. "My mother knew, didn't she—this certainly explains her dislike of you." Legs trembling, heart weighted with sorrow, her thoughts muddled, she gathered her gloves and reticule and left.

❦

Yesterday afternoon after Renata left him, he tried to work. Tried not to think. Through the night his tortured thoughts kept him from sleep. His father had not been much of a role model, distant with his feelings and consumed with his work. But he was the patriarch of their family. The picture of his father and her mother turned him cold, numb.

He needed distraction and thankfully it came in the guise of a meeting with Brandon and Tremaine in the infirmary. Discussing the possible expansion of the existing building was the topic.

Right off, Christopher sensed Brandon's negative attitude.

Tremaine mostly kept to himself, offering little to the conversation as they walked through the existing structure. Christopher knew Tremaine wasn't going to ruffle Brandon's feathers just yet.

Finished with explaining the needs, both men waited for Brandon's assessment. He glanced about the kitchen. "This room appears ample as is." He walked over to the only door off the kitchen and opened it. "Who sleeps here?"

"It has multiple purposes. Most recently, Mrs. Cooke's delivery. Before that, a sailor dying of sleeping sickness. Right now, a young lad, Dino, calls it home."

Brandon glanced at Tremaine. "Are we running an orphanage?"

Tremaine was about to answer when Christopher said, "I'm Dino's guardian."

"I don't recall you mentioning a lad as part of your household when we hired you."

Christopher's patience was running thin. "Shall I hand in my resignation?"

Tremaine put his palm up. "I don't think it's come to that." He faced Brandon. "The lad began as a charity case, and Christopher's benevolence toward him has become a guardianship."

Brandon didn't back off. His thumbs tucked into the sides of his waistcoat, he sucked on his teeth. "We hired one man. No family. I'm talking about square footage with a monetary value placed on it."

Already angry at the world, and if he was honest, seeing Brandon in the same light he thought of his father, Christopher forced a false passivity on Brandon. "Not a problem, sir. I'll be packed up and out of here by morning." He gave a nod to Tremaine and walked down the hall to his office, firmly shutting the door.

Within minutes, Tremaine knocked on the office door. Not waiting for an invitation, he walked in, Brandon in his wake.

"See here, Christopher," Brandon said. "I certainly wasn't entertaining that you should quit. Hawthorn needs you. I can get a little testy about money, I'll grant you that. I'll have a builder see what he thinks about enlarging this place. And get his quote."

Christopher eyed him with disgust. "Don't you ever hint the lad is a problem or so help me God, you'll wish you hadn't."

"As to that." Brandon's chin jutted. "I apologize. It was insensitive." He stuck out his hand and it was a very long moment before Christopher shook it.

Tremaine said to Brandon, "We appreciate your listening to our proposal and look forward to your decision."

Pushing his hat on, Brandon left the two of them as he walked out the front door.

The air was strained, and Tremaine sought to change the atmosphere. "Will we see you at the Black Pig tomorrow?"

Irritation feather his words. "What's tomorrow?"

"A few of us are getting together to celebrate Mulroney's birthday, a surprise for him." He eyed Christopher. "Don't tell me you've forgotten?"

Rubbing the back of his neck, he shook his head. He had absolutely no interest in a celebration of any kind. "I guess I had. Didn't realize he had a birthday coming up. What time?"

"Teatime. Fiveish I think."

Christopher collapsed in his chair.

Tremaine asked, "Is something bothering you? You were distracted through the entire proposal."

"Nothing to concern yourself with." He placed his pen in the ink bowl.

"Wouldn't involve Miss Fitzjames would it? Mairéad couldn't stop talking about their delightful visit. I gather her mother is quite different in nature."

Deadly serious, he intoned, "You have no comprehension the depth of your statement."

"I hate to leave you in this state, my boy, but I've got duties of my own at Rockmore. Will you be attending Mulroney's birthday party tomorrow or not?"

"I'll drop in, but my attitude is pretty sour right now."

"That I can see. Go for a ride, always seems to clear the air."

Christopher practically jumped out of his chair, sent it in a bit of a twirl as he did so. "I'll walk out with you then and see if Grogan hasn't rented out that little Arab. I need to check in on him anyway."

"You must be referring to the explosion."

He nodded.

"What was it, a distillery, or something else?"

"The drunken sot attempted to make his pond bigger with some powder, but he lit it before he got it to the pond. Damn near killed himself."

The Arab cantered toward the open hills beyond Hawthorn in the direction of the Knockmealdowns. Christopher wanted to empty his head—clear his heart.

He hadn't slept the last few nights. And attempted to put Renata out of his mind but wasn't certain how to do that. He also avoided questioning Talbot about the argument with Martin that he witnessed.

Christopher dug his heels into the Arab's flanks hoping the wind would wash the whole of it from his thoughts. "Blazes and damn!"

Drawing near a stream, he loosened the mare's reins and took in the verdant countryside, crisscrossed with stone walls, sheep nibbling at clover, and a lovely blue sky with nary a cloud for distraction. His vision of the future had begun to include Renata.

He contemplated her pain. Dedicating herself to her mother's care, fulfilling her father's last wish. She deeply cared for her family. Adulteress and adulterer, her mother, his father. It must have broken his mother's heart. Knowing Renata as he did, she would find it difficult to reconcile her mother's behavior.

He kneed the Arab and moved on through the copse kicking up acorns and stones. His father was a surly, irascible man. He tried to remember how his parents got on but didn't recall a lot of trauma in their home. His memory of his sisters was filled with the latest fashion, boys, and secrets.

Admittedly, his head was in a book most of the time.

Wrens took flight from a small copse. Skittish, the Arab side-stepped and he calmed her with a pat on the mane. The flock soared in cloud formation weaving in and out of an array of patterns until they disappeared from sight.

As the Arab moved along a path that followed the creek, they came upon a cliff overlooking a lush valley dotted with clusters of sheep. A falcon sailed on the breeze high above the rolling hills.

He couldn't undo what his selfish, narcissistic father had set in motion so many years earlier with a woman who didn't deserve her daughter. It was shocking to think of her as his sister.

Listless and unfocused, Renata barely kept a civil tongue with her mother. Her heartbreak bloomed achingly. She sought refuge in her room smothering her anguish in the pillow. The tender sweet love that might have been her future with Christopher crushed by her mother's infidelity twenty-seven years earlier.

Of all the men Renata could have met, and indeed, had met, who were interested in her at one time or another, not one of them fascinated her like Christopher. Had the innate draw been sibling attachment?

Devastated by the anguish in his voice and the shame clinging to his handsome face, she could do naught but grieve.

Eventually she refreshed herself then entered the parlor where her mother rested in a chair cupping fresh brewed tea in her gnarled hands. The sun streamed through the window casting her in a glow. Renata saw it as an omen.

Lea was as useless as a person could be. She refused to go to the market alone. Complained in a little child-like voice about the weather, the rain, the apartment. The only time she appeared content was when brushing her mistress' hair, caring for her gowns, or buffing her nails at bedtime.

Renata took up her shawl and hat. "I'm going for a walk."

In the hallway, she almost choked on a gasp, and ran down the stairs, the pain in her heart spurring her on. She would have been denied the comfort of her father with this heartache. He would have had his own cross to bear.

The next morning for a moment when she first woke, she was filled with expectation. Just for a moment her heart warmed.

Then an axe chopped it away with the truth.

Mona knocked on the Fitzjames door. She was cuddling one of her babies, little Mary sucking her thumb and clinging to her skirt.

"Just a reminder about this afternoon—Mulroney's party at the Black Pig."

Renata was about to excuse her presence at the gathering when her mother came up from behind elbowing her out of the way. "How are those babies? I don't often hear them cry." She glanced at Renata. "Ask her in, don't stand there like a ninny."

"I can't, Mrs. Fitzjames," Mona interrupted. "Busy as a bee, I am. Just wanted to make sure you knew of the party for Mulroney, about five at the Black Pig. Everyone will be there, mustn't miss it. Food aplenty to celebrate his fifty years."

"We'll take advantage of your kind invitation Mona, thank you," said her mother.

When she closed the door, Renata glared. "I won't be going." Lea lurked in the hall eyes bright with interest, probably understanding the irritability in her voice.

Her mother's face screwed into a snarl. "Oh, yes, you will. Something's happened with *that* man. Got what he wanted did he? I'm not surprised, mooning after him. You're a wilted rose, past your prime. Should have followed my advice years ago when Señor Carrasco was interested, but no, you shoved him away like the plague. Now, you're my spinster daughter."

Renata bit her tongue lest she spew out damning truths. This woman had the nerve to accuse her of—she spun away biting her lip. Lea had moved closer to the edge of the hall, enthralled with their argument. Which caused Renata to wonder about the girl's inability to understand English.

"Daren't defend yourself, eh? Let me tell you what you'll do, like it or not, missy. You'll present yourself and hold your head up. Let no man tell you, you aren't fit company. Sour looks and all, you are a hard worker, and smart, I'll give you that. Some men want what goes on in the bedchamber as the most important thing a woman can give."

Surging with repulsion, Renata suppressed her feelings and stood at the window.

"You needn't get uppity, I'm still here even when others toss you aside. We'll go this afternoon, and we'll have a gay time of it. You've never believed me, but I do have your interests at heart. Wasn't just your father who cared."

Thinking she might give up the contents of her breakfast, Renata ran into her bedroom and slammed the door. It was all she could do not to argue against her mother's irrational assumptions. Her crude and suspicious thinking, warped beyond common sense, was unbelievable.

One thing of which Renata was certain. Watching Christopher with Dino and with his patients, and the way he handled Krysta when her work was sloppy, he exhibited more care for the individual than for himself. She knew his heart to be pure and honest.

Forcing herself to keep tears at bay, gasping for a calm breath, Renata remembered his goodness from the first they met, bumping heads. It was easy to allow Christopher close, to spend time with him, confide in him because he made her feel safe. He made her feel as though she mattered.

With smothered resentment, her eyes squeezed shut, and her palms spread across her chest. A shuddering breath left her weak with longing of what could have been. Dear Mother of God, Louisa Fitzjames was a monster—it is why she hated Christopher from the beginning. She knew all along they were siblings.

Somehow Renata would put one foot in front of the other and see to her daily routine until she could come to grips with the loss of Christopher.

Five o'clock came early. Christopher leaned on the polished bar top along with five others. Mulroney slapped him on the back almost sending him to his knees. Christopher said, "For an old man, you have a mighty heavy swing."

"I've never had a birthday celebration in my life. I'm bolstered with excitement."

"Your name is on this one." Christopher shoved a pint at him and gestured to Padhraig to give him another.

Under his breath, Mulroney said, "I'd not a clue I had what it takes to rouse so many in my honor."

Christopher jested, "Don't fool yourself, it's the food. That and some of these fine people might want to make the front page of your paper."

Lord and Lady Tremaine made their way through the crush of well-wishers toward them.

Mulroney said, "Before I forget, old man Haggerty is setting the type for the article about the infirmary."

Surprised, Christopher asked, "You've heard from Brandon, then?"

"Not exactly. I told Haggerty to do it before he gets into the swill. Once he starts, he's good for nothing for a day or two. Last I saw of Brandon he was dithering between selling and the expansion. Kind of like the weather, he is. But I can't see why he would reject our proposal. It's for the good of the village. It will bring a dignity to Hawthorn to have a wardroom, and a proper examination room."

Christopher was doubtful. "I hope Haggerty knows better than to print it until we hear from Brandon."

After a long pull on his mug, Mulroney said, "He will."

Christopher nodded as he reached for his pint off the bar top. He scanned the crowd for Renata and didn't see her. The heavy carved door to the pub opened bringing with it a wet, cold blast from the outside, refreshing the stale smell of wet wool, and muddied boots. A small group entered, Renata and her mother, Mona and Mike Cooke. Darby and Sean right behind them.

Renata's gaze cast downward, which meant she spied him immediately and was unsure how to greet him. She looked miserable. Mrs. Fitzjames was in high spirits from the look of her. Something elated her, she was usually out of sorts. It made him wonder what kind of marriage she and Mr. Fitzjames must have had.

A devil of a business. He pulled on his ale and glanced at the couple who'd come up to pay their respects to Mulroney, but Christopher's interest was on Renata listening to Padhraig tell one of his tales. Her slender carriage and seemingly conversant interest was given away by the sadness in her eyes. How to recreate their relationship into something other than what it had been might never happen. He wasn't going to solve anything until they adjusted to the idea that they were half-siblings. A shiver ran down his spine at the thought, and he finished off his pint and gestured Ian for a refill, hoping no one would need his services this night.

Renata stayed close beside her mother but found it extraordinarily difficult to keep from watching Christopher. Her heartache worsened. She would never forget the feel of his arms about her.

Mrs. Fitzjames' nasal voice interrupted her melancholy. "Get me a thimble of whatever that woman in the big hat has."

Renata would have to approach the bar where Christopher stood with a mug. Suddenly she realized her mother was rubbing her face in her discomfort. Because she thought Christopher had compromised her.

"I will not."

"Harrumph. Is it you don't want to rub elbows with what's-his-name?"

Renata turned away from her mother and approached the table where Mona and Mike sat. "May I?"

Mike pulled a chair for her. "Surely, Miss Renata. We'd be glad if your mother joined us, too. I'll pull another for her."

"I believe she has other plans." Renata sat, drawing off her gloves, and slipping out of her shawl.

Mona was full of interesting tidbits about Mulroney. "He is a well-liked man. As was his da who started the press and died young. As a youngster, Mulroney spent a great deal of time at his da's side and felt capable of stepping into his shoes."

Mike added, "Did a fine job of it now, didn't he?"

She twisted in her chair a mite to glance at Mulroney who was at the door greeting villagers. A cheerful man, he was always ready to help others. Most of whom end up as a story in his newsprint, *The Tattler*. Aptly named, so Renata thought and found herself grateful for changing tables if for nothing more than the conversation.

Christopher and Mulroney had worked on several charitable benefits together, but it wasn't always so. Renata recalled Christopher referring to Mulroney as one of a trio of monkeys inhabiting the Black Pig. A bane on his existence his first few months of living in Hawthorn. She glanced at them now, friendly and laughing together. Things do change over time. Casting a glance at her hands, thumbs twirling in her lap, she could only hope.

"Nice to see you Mona, Mike. How are the twins and Mary?" Renata's gaze flew upward, locking on Christopher, hoping her dismay wasn't apparent.

His beguiling smile melted her heart. "I hope you are well, Miss Fitzjames."

Not trusting her voice, she nodded.

Mona spoke up about her children. "We are all doing fine, doc. Thanks to you. Left them in the care of their Auntie Doris who is visiting us for a bit. This is a treat gettin' out. Gets to be stifling in our small place what with October's rain settling in."

Christopher moved on to the back of the room where some men without wives had gathered. Merriment roared and mugs clinked. Renata glanced about for where her mother had settled, finding her at the table with the woman who wore the black hat. A thimble of something in front of her, Renata drew in a breath of relief.

Two ladies set up a sweet table with sponge cake, and scones with jam and cream. The centerpiece being Barmback, an Irish cake with bits of nuts and fruit.

Padhraig lighted a candle in the middle of the table that

flickered cheerily as the helpers peppered it with a few presents, forks, and plates.

Mulroney's delight was obvious as a few of his male friends tried to sing, *may your glass be ever full, may the roof over your head be always strong. And may you be in heaven half an hour before the devil knows you're dead.*

Someone in the room yelled, "What's the devil want with a good man."

Someone else answered, "He'll never make it, he's too full of blarney."

A chorus of chuckles and well wishes bantered through the room,

Renata was grateful Christopher had stopped by their table, knowing the change between them was as hard on him as it was on her. All the tomorrows to come would be her life as it was before they met.

৩⊱৯

The front door of the infirmary rattled. Someone was banging it. Christopher jumped out of bed shoving his feet into his breeches. By the position of the moon it had to be at least two a.m. He reached the door and drew it open.

Waffer with one fist in the air aimed to knock again, his other fist wrapped around Dino's collar.

Christopher grabbed Waffer's hand releasing Dino and shoved the lad in behind him. "What's going on?"

Waffer's face was in shadow, but the glee in his voice was obvious. "Caught him grave robbin' I did. Go on, ask 'im."

Christopher swung about facing Dino, whose face was as somber as a dead man. "I wasn't. I promise. I was investigating." Dino put his hand on his slim hips, stance wide. "I tried to tell him, but he wouldn't listen to me." Nodding toward the constable, he added, "I saw two men lurking around and would have told

Constable Waffer if he hadn't started yelling at me. That's when the two men ran off."

Christopher had no reason to discount Dino's tale. He said to Waffer. "Looks like you missed your chance to catch the body snatchers."

Waffer, a lighter tone to his voice, asked Dino, "Are ye able to describe them?"

The lad took his time. "They were tall. And wore small hats that covered their eyes. I think one was older than the other. I think he had a limp. One of them was Earl. I know that much."

Snorting like a bull, Waffer reached for Dino, Christopher stepped in his path. "Don't even think it. The lad stays with me. This is his home."

"I'll get a warrant." Stubble growth and his war jacket from Vinegar Hill were part of who this man was. Dedicated, no doubt. A fool, no doubt about that either.

Christopher crossed his arms over his chest and looked down at the stocky man. "The lad's given you all the information he knows. You'll have to bring the whole of County Waterford to my door before I give him over to the likes of you. Now think on it, my good man. A twelve-year-old and two grown men in the yard at night. Why would you take the lad? Was he the only one you could catch? Or have you in it to implicate me?"

The air puffed out of Waffer as he grimaced. "This isn't the last of me, Curran. I know you are part of the corpse digging. Everyone knows men like you use 'em to learn by. I'll get you one way or t'other." With that, he turned on his heel and stomped down the steps.

Closing the door on the last of the constable, Christopher turned to Dino. "Anything you want to say to me?"

His brown eyes wide with astonishment, Dino slowly shook his head.

"What made you do such a fool thing?"

"I heard you talking to Lord Tremaine. And I wanted to help."

Clearing his throat, Christopher asked, "That's what you get for eavesdropping. Are you hungry?"

"I have a test tomorrow. I'm tired."

Christopher got down on a knee and cupped Dino's shoulders. "I know you wanted to help me. But these men could be dangerous. I don't know what I would do if I lost you."

Dino's cheek rested against Christopher's shoulder. "I don't know what I would do if I lost you. The constable scared the wits out of me. Jumping out of nowhere like a banshee, screaming at me."

Christopher's shoulders shook with hilarity. "He does look a bit like a banshee now that you mention it."

24

January 1817

C hristopher, Tremaine, Mulroney, and Brandon came to an agreement back in the fall, the week after Mulroney's birthday. The work had begun the next day. A mild fall and winter allowed the men to work through October, November, and December. With the winter fast upon them, and the land fallow, farmers offered their assistance, and many hands made the work go fast.

The addition to the infirmary, the wardroom boasting four beds would be completed with the addition of two windows. Krysta was thrilled with the larger working space in the kitchen making her work much easier. The smell of new wood and paint were almost a perfume of order and cleanliness.

Patients increased. Christopher's mordant humor assumed the increase was due to inquisitiveness rather than any real medical complaints.

Dino was excited with his new bedroom, one room down the corridor from Christopher's bedroom rather than in the back off the kitchen. The new placement gave the lad a real sense of possession and belonging, plus, he'd been involved in drawing up a picture of the bookshelves he felt necessary, and which quickly began to fill with reading material Dino finished these last few months. Gulliver's Travels occupied a very prominent place on the shelf as his own first book, ever.

The lad was becoming quite the scholar for such a young person, perhaps driven by Christopher's influence. Though doc would be the last person to pat himself on the back. It was Darby who drew the comparison when every other day she popped in to take soiled linens, as the increase in patients grew at the same rate as the addition was built.

Darby knocked on the doc's door. She spied him through the crack. "I've come for the linen."

He looked up from his writing. "How are you this morning?"

"From the dower look on your face, I'd say a mite better'n you, doc." She set her basket on the floor. "Ye've been keepin' your distance from the kitchen of late. Anythin' ta do with that scatterbrain?"

He shook his head of the nonsense. "I haven't a clue what you're talking about."

Darby closed the door and neared his desk. "That gal is after you. She promoted you ta legal with the infirmary all fixed up. She sees a future and wants you as her beau."

"Krysta? What nonsense is this? She set her cap for Asia. Much to my approval I might add."

"Ah, doc, you're blind as a bat. That twitter brain has plans for you. Told me herself, she did. I'm here with a warning. Doin' my duty seeing as we are on a friendly basis. As long as I'm at it, how come you're down in the mouth lately? Krysta thinks Miss Fitzjames has cleared out of your life and you're an opportunity to be had."

Dumbfounded, he sat back in his chair and processed Darby's words. Was there a modicum of truth in what she was saying? He ignored her reference to Miss Fitzjames.

"I've suffered many cups of tea with her. Believe me, doc, she's got plans for ye." Darby gathered up the pile of soiled linen and stuffed it in her basket. Done with her task, she looked at him. "Just thought you should know. Forewarned is forearmed."

He untangled himself from the chair and stood. "I've been buried in work and the renovation. You were my first friend in Hawthorn, Darby. And have been a help to me and this office ever since, for which I am grateful. I appreciate your concern. But you needn't worry about me."

Basket in both hands, her plump stance determined, and doubt furrowing her brow, she almost made him laugh at the absurdity of her warning. Yet realized he hadn't experienced a good jest in months.

"You might be foolin' yerself, doc. But you're not foolin' me. I've got to get back. Sean's off the boat right now, and as big a task as any woman doesn't need. I rue the day I took on a fisherman."

Christopher came around his desk and put his hand on the doorknob, his other on her shoulder. "Thanks for caring and being a friend. It means more than you know."

Darby left with her bundle and Christopher rummaged through the papers on his desk when the unmistakable stomp of boots from the nether region of the kitchen charged down the hall and within seconds Mulroney stood in his doorway.

"I've come by to check with you on the shed. Have you decided its placement?"

Christopher and Mulroney had become fast friends over the winter with the enlargement of the building. There hadn't been a week gone by that Mulroney didn't mention the new infirmary in one of his columns. Which was most likely related to the increase in patients.

Christopher stood, "Let's have a look." As they passed through the foyer, patients whispered amongst themselves. He'd been unaware of their arrival so involved was he in his paperwork. The room immediately quieted. Christopher said, "Give me a few minutes, I'll be right back."

As Mulroney and Christopher made their way down the hall,

the whispering between his waiting patients flared almost to a crescendo. In a low voice, he said to Mulroney, "Something is up, I can feel it in my bones. Do you feel it?"

"Me?" Mulroney's lantern sized jaw swung to the doc.

"Come now, you've got an uncanny sense of the village. If anyone has the pulse of these folks, it's you." Christopher opened the back door and they walked onto the porch, and down the steps. For once it was a day without the biting sleet that plagued them of late. The winter was mild enough, the sleet never built up on the lanes, melting into mud instead. He supposed Mother Nature was holding back on a fierce winter after the storm she sent back in August.

Completely ignoring Christopher's remark, Mulroney pointed to the copse where the little garden lay dormant. The remains of grasses and plants and other scrub tangled with a coating of milky rime where the sun hadn't reached. A sprig of bright green caught Christopher's attention and he reached down plucking the defiant stem. "Now, here's a bit of luck." He held up a four-leaf clover.

Mulroney offered, "Maybe it will come in useful what with your leaving the waiting room almost full." His nod bent toward the infirmary.

Christopher quipped, "Amongst them I might just get something involving a medical need." They walked a bit further into the brush where a bench, dormant ivy vines twined about the legs, was no longer hidden amongst the bare hawthorn bushes and elms.

"We could build it here allowing privacy to the garden. The infirmary flanks one of the busiest lanes in Hawthorn. Might keep the cart rattle down a bit. I could add a trellis on the wall for the ivy to grow."

"Sounds like you've solved the problem. I'll get on back. Shouldn't keep the good folks of Hawthorn waiting."

"Go on then, I'll poke about and let the contractor know you're fine with it."

Renata's scrap of loveliness through the cold winter were the invites to Nuala, Lady Rutledge's home, which included Mairéad, Lady Tremaine, who imparted a wealth of news about Christopher, Dino, and the additions to the infirmary, as Mairéad heard it from Lord Tremaine.

Today began the same as yesterday with Renata at Mr. Talbot's Old Town Apothecary in the back room. Late in the fall she had strung up plants to dry though the winter.

Drawing in the sweet scent of lavender, she intended to crush mustard and hawkweed first but needed a ladder to get to the withered herbals.

The front doorbell tinkled as one of Mr. Talbot's customers entered. The mumble of voices in the front of the shop always sent a shiver as she listened for Christopher's. On three separate occasions she had heard him talking to Mr. Talbot.

This customer was a man's voice she didn't recall hearing before. He sounded angry. She thought she heard a loud bang on the counter. Both voices lowered hissing in anger. Her curiosity roused, but it wasn't her business.

Instead, she wondered where Mr. Talbot had put the ladder. Solving her immediate problem, she drew a chair up to the table, stood on it, then stepped on the tabletop directly below the herbs. She heard Mr. Talbot's angry voice and a slam of the front door. She considered getting off the table to inquire about the ladder when the bell tinkled again.

Reaching for the hawkweed she grabbed the ties that bound it loosening them from the nail where it hung. Glancing downward, she stepped around a tray filled with jars and reached for the mustard. It wasn't quite so brittle.

At the same moment she heard Christopher's voice and reached for a beam to steady herself. The tray and all its contents clattered to the floor. Mustard and hawkweed drifted from her clutch as she reached out. The dried bundles crumbled, and detritus fell in her face and hair causing her to sneeze, which caused her to lose her grip on the beam.

The men rushed in, and Christopher caught her in his arms as she swayed toward the floor.

"How long have you been dancing on tables?" The rumble of his voice mixed with teasing brought her instant joy.

She blinked rapidly, swiping at her face inches from Christopher's. "Saving a damsel in distress is my favorite thing to do."

She sneezed, again and again, thinking it was *her* favorite thing, to be saved by him. He settled her on her feet and pulled a kerchief from his pocket handing it to her.

Mr. Talbot reached for the shards of pottery that was once a tray and what was left of the hawkweed and mustard. Christopher brushed the top of her head, and the brittle organic scraps scattered everywhere. She sneezed again, and again putting the kerchief to good use.

Mr. Talbot placed the bits of pottery on the table. "Looks like an enterprising business was in the making."

She waved at the herbs dangling from the rafters. "I thought I would start my powders."

"Why not use the ladder, then?" Mr. Talbot inquired.

"I couldn't find it and you were with a customer. I climbed on the chair and then the table…"

"…and became dizzy with the effort," finished Christopher.

"It was more the dried petals in my eyes."

The bell rang again, and Mr. Talbot excused himself.

She couldn't take her eyes off him. His handsome face and russet hair partly covered by his top hat. It was going to take the rest of her life to get over him. It was a reminder of what was never going to be.

Though a dutiful daughter, her anger at her mother's duplicity surged. She had been able to keep her true feelings in check, but looking at what she could not have, brought the anger back with a vengeance.

Christopher's attention was on papers scattered across the table. It was a mess with jars, pistol, churning cups, labels, an open notebook. Swiping her hands on her apron, she inadvertently backed up to a small table topped with a washing bowl and tipped it over splashing water and shattering pottery.

She palmed her cheeks and felt like an idiot.

Christopher tore his attention from the paper he was reading, "Are you all right?"

Her lips parted as her heart thumped. Slowly her palms drifted down. "I…yes…it…"

Renata and Christopher's gazes locked, his with a twitch at the corner of his mouth. Nervous, she swiped her hands on the apron again, not knowing what to do as a lump tightened her throat. The sheer manliness of him weakened her knees.

Unconcerned with the mess and spilled water, Christopher waved the sheaf of papers in the air. "This is your work, isn't it? Your interest in herbals? Quite impressive. Will you show me what you're working on?" His voice, interlaced with excitement and wonder, eased her awkwardness.

With no thought to the mess on the floor, she said, "Slipslop."

He chuckled, and her heart skipped a beat. He said, "You're making ptisans, then?" And plucked another sheet from the pile of papers, shaking off the dried-herbal detritus.

Mr. Talbot poked his head through the curtain. "Is everything all right in here?"

Humbly, she said, "I'm terribly sorry. I've made another mess. I'll take care of it." Talbot nodded and retreated to the front of the shop.

She glanced at Christopher. "Teas have soothing power. Mixed with certain spices and gruels I believe it increases the merit."

Clearing his throat, he said, "You've done a remarkable amount of research." He glanced over the piles of paper on the table.

Renata reached for a broom and pan. "You must have a far more urgent place to be, Mr. Curran."

He put the papers down and offered, "Let me help clean this up," and began picking up shards of pottery.

Every inch of her responded to his presence. She forced her attention to the mess she'd made, shoving it with the broom into a pile.

"It's back to Mr. Curran is it? I thought our friendship was beyond formality of that sort. I've missed you greatly, as has Dino. He asks about you frequently." Her heart skipped a beat at his declaration. He found a pail and rag and began sopping up the water.

Shrugging her shoulders, she continued sweeping, and bit her lip to stay a rush of tears.

He stopped mopping up the mess. His deep voice low and hesitant. "Is it possible we can still be friends?"

Her sweeping motion stopped, she slowly met his gaze, as a low breath escaped. "I would like that, Christopher. Very much." Biting her lip didn't stay her misty eyes.

His smile turned the chamber to sunshine. He swiped a palm across his mouth almost as if he could feel their kiss. She looked away at the thought, shamed by it.

☙❧

As Christopher walked back to the infirmary, he mulled over witnessing Mr. Martin, his face blotched with rage, slamming his way out of the shop. Christopher caught the action through a split in the drape. Raised voices in the outer room are what got his attention. Talbot appeared mottled with anger, himself. It occurred to Christopher these were the two men who quarreled in the alley not too long ago. Could it be they were the same two men Dino saw in the cemetery the night Waffer nabbed him?

That evening at supper in the newly enlarged kitchen, Christopher and Dino sat at a sturdy maple table, planed, sanded, and stained in Mulroney's barn. Eight people could sit comfortably. It would now accommodate patients who were ambulatory. Krysta had fancied it up with a doily in the center.

She left chicken pie with potatoes and gravy. String beans from the cellar. She must have had extra time before leaving because an apple tart cooled on the sideboard.

Christopher inquired about Dino's schoolwork; the lad always had something of interest to impart. His answer wasn't forthcoming because he was busy chewing. Perched on the rim of his platter was a biscuit slathered in jam. He did have a fancy for jam, right from the beginning. The thought caused him to smile.

"Did you tell me you received the best grade on the essay about the counties in Ireland?" he asked as he lifted the watered ale to quench his thirst.

About to take another spoonful of gravy and chicken, Dino paused. "I got them all. The only other one was Meg. She thinks that makes me her boyfriend."

He guffawed. "Well, that kind of thinking may never go away. You'll just have to learn to control it. Always be kind but have friendships on your terms. What you want."

Dino nodded as he pulled off a piece of thick crust with his fingers and popped it in his mouth.

"I've a notion about something." Christopher set the mug down.

Dino quit chewing, swallowed, took a sip of milk, and said, "You and notions."

This lad would be testing him through the years to come. Surprisingly, he liked the thought. "Do you have a birthdate?"

A cloud of doubt covered his dark brown eyes, he shook his head.

"You need one. How else will we know to celebrate that you were born?"

"I'm here, aren't I?"

"Christopher chortled. "We need a date. Master Carleton thinks you must be twelve and as a doctor evaluating your size, I agree. Though Master Carleton also thinks you are knowledgeable enough to be more mature than that. Yet your voice shows no sign of changing, and most probably there would be other indications if you were older." He leaned against the back of his chair. "Six months ago, when you arrived, you thought you were eleven or twelve then. Remember?"

The lad nodded, but never quit eating.

"If we use that as a measure, and add in Master Carleton's thoughts, and mine, let's assume you are twelve. If we do that, we need to come up with a date for your thirteenth birthday."

Dino swallowed and his small Adam's apple bobbed. Those liquid brown orbs shone with wonder. He placed his slender arms on the table and gave Christopher his full attention. "You pick my birthday."

"I think you should. It's going to be forevermore the date of your birth. And, traditionally, you will always receive a pie and maybe even a gift on that date."

Dino's eyes widened. He seemed to puff up taller. "How about tomorrow?"

Christopher shook his head. "Krysta won't be baking another pie that quick."

Dino asked, "Can I pick the day we met?"

Overwhelmed with sudden emotion, Christopher gulped back a surge of compassion. His intention was to give this child a life, a chance in the world. Much to his surprise, he was the one receiving. "I would be honored. But we could also choose from one of the other days when you showed up after running away? Let me see, you skipped out two or three times?"

Dino's black brows scrunched. "Doc, don't tease me."

Christopher couldn't stop the laughter that spewed.

"I apologized to you. Miss Fitzjames said that was the proper way to mend my fences."

"Mending fences is it? You near broke my heart, lad." The mention of her in this delightful conversation saddened his mood, and he forged ahead, "Right. You did, and I won't tease again."

"Promise?"

"Well, I'll give it a good try. Sometimes I need to hold it over you, to remind you never to run again."

"I promised never to run again." His voice was infused with intent. He swiped at the milk on his upper lip.

The sincere and resolute pledge struck Christopher. "Then I can do no less than promise to never discuss your running away again."

Dino groaned. "You just did."

Laughing, Christopher withdrew to his office and brought back his log. "The date I saw your dirty foot under my bed was June 3. The official date of birth will read June 3, 1804. Country of birth will read Sicily. And your name will read Dino Curran." Closing the log, he asked, "How does that signify with you?"

"Like I'm really a real person," Dino said as he slathered jam on another biscuit and opened his mouth wide for the sweet, tasty treat.

25

The next day, Tremaine knocked and opened the door to Christopher's office. Writing, he looked up from his desk and greeted his friend. "This is unexpected?"

"Should you ever be so blest to marry, you'll be laughing out the other side of your mouth. I've been on several husbandly missions and decided to take some time for myself. How about a pint at the Black Pig?"

Christopher's brows lifted. "I'd like nothing better, but I just cleared the waiting room and need to log the medical issues."

"The *devil* take it. Come on. With your attention to detail, I'll wager they'll still be swimming in your brain when you return." Tremaine nervously tapped his hat against his thigh. "I've better things to do than watch you make entries in a log."

Christopher didn't need much prodding and grabbed his hat, flipped the sign in the window to *closed* and stepped outside.

"When did you put that up?"

"When I had far too many complaints." Their strides matched, and he mused, "I feel like I'm playing hooky. Brings back memories of Abernathy."

"He won't be swatting a ruler across your knuckles now."

"That good old first year in prep. We were rustics."

"Were we not! The only thing we had to concern us was *not* riling the old man and his beastly dictums."

"Makes me think what I should eventually do for Dino's schooling. On the other side of the coin, he's had no home for most of his life. I'm inclined to think he's better off right here."

"I'd agree. It's obvious he adores you." The wind flapped at their great coats, tails flying behind. A heavy mist began to fall, bringing with it a chill.

Christopher nodded. "Quite a responsibility."

"What does Miss Fitzjames think?"

Christopher slanted a look at Tremaine as they rounded the corner toward the pub. "Why do you ask?"

He shrugged his shoulders. "Aren't the two of you an item?"

"We're friends. Friendly," he stammered. "She's sailing for Portugal."

"I didn't know that." He eyed his companion. "Sorry in fact. You seemed quite comfortable together, as if you'd known each other a long time."

Christopher gulped. Tremaine came nearer to the truth of their relationship than he could have known.

Approaching the pub, the mellow sweet tones of a concertina floated through a window cracked enough to allow pipe smoke to escape. Doors were shut against winter's chill.

Tremaine opened the ancient blackened door and stood aside as Christopher entered. He blinked against the dark interior until his eyesight adjusted, Tremaine came up behind.

Cheering and clapping greeted them. A sign hanging from the shelving around the upper perimeter of the room read *Thank You for being our DOC* in big red letters.

The concertina stopped playing and someone shoved a mug at Christopher spilling foam on his cuff. A prickly sensation swept through him. This was for him? Blazes and damn!

Carnahan stepped forward, waving several sheets of paper. He welcomed Christopher to an afternoon of thanksgiving in his honor. Christopher's glance traveled the pub, into its nooks and around the shiny bar, finally settling on Renata and her mother. He nodded when he found her. A light blush rose on her cheeks. For some reason it mattered a great deal that she was among the crowd.

Tremaine took their top hats and great coats, leaving Christopher to greet his fellow neighbors and friends. Danaher slapped him on the back. "Ye've finally done it doc—the approval of the dependable folk of Hawthorn."

Before he could take a breath and answer Danaher, Mr. and Mrs. Cooke, daughter and twin sons came forth. "Without you, doc, wouldn't have 'em." He wanted to correct Mona, caught himself and thanked them for coming.

Much to his surprise Krysta, arm entangled with Asia Malcolm's, stepped to the table. "Now you ken why I wasn't at work this morn. I helped with the cookin' here. 'Tis an honor workin' for you, doc. Gotta say, I set me cap for you, I did. Just wanted to show how much I esteem you."

Everyone who overheard Krysta snickered and hooted, followed by shushing as she continued, "When Asia asked me pap for permission, I had to make a decision. You lost, doc. But I think yer a right good bloke. Someone'll come along to take yer fancy."

"Thank you, Krysta." He looked Asia over. "You appear fully recovered. You look healthy."

"Got me a good woman. I ain't sorry you came in second best." His grin showed a few vacancies in his row of teeth.

Christopher sipped his pint and leaned into Tremaine. "How long have you planned this?"

"My only responsibility was to get you here. Village folk began planning several weeks now. Word is they think you're the best thing since bacon, according to Darby."

Christopher leaned in taking another gulp of ale to hide his snort, he spoke low, "It wasn't always so. Took a while to earn their comfort."

Mr. Brandon leaned near, his face intense as he asked, "I hope you are as pleased with the infirmary as I am. I assume you will not be going anywhere now that you've a place to really call home."

"Dino and I are quite comfortably situated thanks to the renovations. It's already proved its worth with an increase in patients." Brandon appeared to ease up as if he'd been worried.

He nodded and moved on when Mr. Dooley stepped up to present himself to Christopher. "Cart's not broken down since you paid that home visit, doc. Else I wouldn't be here today. I'm showin' support for ye. I am." Stiff, bushy gray brows lifted with conviction. "Me love's in the corner, shy as she is."

Christopher followed the arm pointing to the back. "Give her my best then." And grabbed Dooley's hand with a firm shake. "I'm glad to hear my patient didn't need to reschedule."

Dooley blinked, taking a minute to figure out what the doc meant, perplexed until it hit him the cart was the patient. He gestured to the food table. "Think I'll get a bite."

Mrs. Kneely and her daughters, Greta and Mary, waved at him from behind the bar as they helped Krysta set out more dishes.

Darby, for once accompanied by her husband, hugged Christopher. "I'm so proud of you. Thankful to call you a friend, I am." Sean grabbed Christopher's hand pumping his arm. "You've pulled this old town together, friend and foe alike come out for you. You are a good man, doc, and much deservin' of this. Darby said so since the first day."

Christopher could have blushed at the high praise. "Well, the infirmary wouldn't be up to par without her consistent help. Especially when I first arrived. I could not have survived without her assistance."

Her round face blushed and eyes twinkled with his appreciation.

He took her hand, holding it in both of his. "I am most sincere when I say, you've been a true friend. I was in a daze the first few months, and you, with your solid wisdom of Hawthorn's ways guided me. I'll always be grateful."

Evie Brandt with her two daughters cozied up to the three of them, and Sean said, "I've a pint waitin'. We'll leave you to the Brandt's, enjoy your party, doc."

One of the Brandt's, the younger he thought, Cassie, decidedly increasing. Her arm was entangled with that of a tar, who appeared to be right off a ship. "I'd like you to meet me son-in-law, Mikeal. Married ta Cassie, he is, and presentin' me with a grandchild in due time."

Pleased as punch, Mrs. Brandt lit with pride. Christopher greeted Mikeal, who gave the appearance of being unaware though he smiled. Christopher considered he may not know much English, if any at all. If so, does he realize his situation, the lone male in Mrs. Brandt's household? He wished the lad luck, plenty of which he was certainly going to need.

The door to the pub opened washing the interior in a cold blast. Master Carleton marched in with students in tow. Dino and Shamus right behind their teacher. The whole village had gone to a great deal of planning to carry this off. Touched, he felt a blush to his cheeks.

Master Carleton lined up his pupils and announced they were going to sing, with the concertina, bodhrán, and fiddle as accompaniment. Master Carleton allowed the tuning of instruments then tapped his stand with a baton.

"Cut the hubbub folks, we've a song to sing, written by my students and dedicated to Mr. Curran." And as the noise leveled off, he raised his arms high, and began the limerick set to music.

Our doc, honor in him itchin' beneath the skin
Full of wisdom and willin' ta care was he
Our healer brought himself ta Hawthorn's looney bin
And heartfelt gladdened he did were we

Taken unaware, Christopher was flabbergasted. The song continued as he glanced at cach student, one by one, settling on Dino in the front row. The lad was beaming and singing with all his heart. The lyrics were quite special considering they were written by children.

> *Pills for this, creams for that, he's got sense*
> *A red-headed man, healin's his skill*
> *The villagers of Hawthorn will spend a pence*
> *As it's many a folk he'll see and not cost a banker's bill*

The chorus done, parents and patrons clapping, Dino strutted over to Christopher. "Were you surprised?"

"So, you knew? And kept the secret? Impressive, my lad."

Dino giggled, obviously mighty pleased. "Did you like the lyrics?"

"I'll want you to sing that again when we are home, so I can ponder it a bit longer."

Dino introduced two of his classmates. It was clear their attention was riveted on the table laden with goodies. "Go on before everything's eaten." No sooner than the words passed Christopher's lips they scooted to the food table.

Ladies Tremaine and Rutledge, came through the door, once again casting a brittle cold into the pub. Tremaine must have been waiting for them because he had been standing by the door. About to cross the room in greeting himself, he noted Renata and her mother nearing the women. A stab of memory came to him at his father's perfidy and his long-suffering mother. He still hadn't quelled his longing for Renata, who was adorable in a deep blue gown, her raven-dark hair tucked up with pins.

He gave them a minute to say their hellos, then with forced composure joined the group.

Renata, a soft expression on her lovely features said, "No one deserves this more than you, Christopher."

Lady Tremaine agreed. "Just proves that all the bragging I heard from Tremaine this past year wasn't just boasting about a good friend." She squeezed his arm, with a teasing look then glanced about the room. "I've never been inside, but the sign has always intrigued me."

Mrs. Fitzjames piped up, "Lady Tremaine, your husband has had an advantage some have not."

"I'm sorry, I don't think I understand."

"Mr. Curran's friendship with Tremaine has undoubtedly softened the edges of his demeanor, allowing him to acquaint himself with the behavior of a real gentleman."

Renata glared at her mother, reached over and shook her arm. "Where in Heaven did that come from? He is as honorable a man as any. You should apol—"

Tremaine overpowered her scolding when he called out, "Attention please. Mr. Carnahan has a few words."

Tremaine showed his wife and Lady Rutledge to a table set aside for them. Miss Fitzjames a firm hand on her mother's arm, pushed her to their table.

Christopher took a deep breath and was called to stand near Carnahan for his presentation. He noted the retreating Mrs. Fitzjames. Her wrath toward him hadn't appeared to lessen. The look on Renata's face was one of pure misery.

Carnahan began by settling his papers in order and proceeded to read, "We are assembled here today to draw attention to our practitioner, Mr. Curran, who has proven himself these past months with his know how, and kind manner.

"My wife and I are among those who are grateful for the way he cared for Shamus." He pointed to Shamus sitting next to Dino and his school mates. "There sits me lad, with only a bit of scarring to show for it, and a head full of knowledge having learned to read during his months of healing." His bright eyes settled on Dino for a moment.

Christopher, along with everyone else, glanced at Shamus, his arm still a bit stiff of movement as he patted Dino on the back. Their classmates tittered and snickered good-naturedly as pipe smoke swirled about their heads. He could almost envision the lads in the future, grown men sitting in this same pub, elbows bent to the gossip of the day as they sipped their pints.

Carnahan carried on. "It is with pride we tell you doc, everyone in this room, and a few who could not be here, pitched in on the changes at the infirmary. We've no outstanding bills. You needn't worry your income will have to stretch."

Amazed, not because of the money, but that these folks cared. He was a trifle unsettled at their generosity. Most in the room cked out a living as best they could.

Carnahan wasn't finished. "Doc, we want you to know, from now on it's to be called Curran's Infirmary."

A roar of clapping and a high-pitched whistle rent the air. Behind the bar, Padhraig raised up a mug, saluting him. Scanning the crowd, Christopher's gaze fell on Renata, clapping along with the rest and a bright smile on the face he had grown to adore. Her mother still as a stone, a grim, hard glare fixed on him. He winked at her causing her to recoil.

Christopher clinked a spoon against his mug, and the noise calmed. "I'm deeply honored to have so many of you here to celebrate Hawthorn's new infirmary. It is your building and belongs to Hawthorn Village. Thank you for allowing me to bring my learning, and yes, my pills and creams—so eloquently sung by Master Carleton's students—to this wonderful village." The students chuckled, and he heard the whistle again.

"Your kindness and generosity are overwhelming. I certainly didn't expect this when I came in for a pint." He nodded toward the kitchen area. Krysta and Mrs. Kneely appeared to be in a heated discussion from the looks of the long wooden spoon waving in the air. "There's a buffet laden with tempting food, please enjoy yourselves."

A man's voice, clear as a bell, from near the kitchen called out, "Soon's the cooks settle down, you mean? Sure as 'ell ain't safe right now."

An uproar of guffaws and sniggers caused Krysta and Mrs. Kneely to abandon their argument. Bafflement dawned as their attention shifted to the open space between the kitchen and the outer seating area where folks were stuffed shoulder to shoulder.

Krysta's and Mrs. Kneely's faces reddened. The spoon disappeared and both women's focus settled on the immediate business of serving up what proved to be a delicious buffet. It dawned on Christopher why Krysta had been taking so many days off.

Constable Waffer came up to Christopher as he waited in the back of the room for everyone to get in the buffet line. "Saw the grave you dug up last night. The mother of Mrs. Cashel. You didn't leave her be for two days, didja. I'll be arresting you this week. Wanted to wait until this was over and you received the last nice words folks'll have for you."

Christopher turned to him. He would have liked to pick him up by the lapels and shake him good. Instead, he smiled. "Do your worst then. Because I think I know the real perpetrator and it won't go well for you if you arrest the wrong man. Now will it?"

Mulroney edged himself between the two. "Sorry to interrupt your whispering lads, but—" he turned Christopher toward the buffet table, "—you are needed at the bar to open some trinkets folks brought."

⚜

Renata overheard her mother in conversation with Nuala, Lady Rutledge. "He's got himself all puffed up."

Lady Rutledge countered, "We had a doctor, a Mr. Martin, who believed in bleeding. As luck would have it, his young associate, Mr. O'Reilly, subscribed to the opposite cure. The incident involved Lord Darnley. You can be sure the doctor who bled his patient was escorted from the sick room. Mr. Curran came to us with the latest knowledge of medicine and in a short time has proved his worth."

Renata watched as her mother, obviously disgruntled,

spluttered, "In my day, bleeding was required to vent humors from the body. Did his lordship pass then?"

"Oh no, robust as can be." Asserted Lady Rutledge fighting a grin.

Mrs. Fitzjames scoffed and set her gaze on the long table laden with slices of mutton pies and mouthwatering cruasach delicious on the steaming potatoes. Plates of Barmback, Carrageen pudding and the staple dulse-soda scones, were at the end.

Not to be deterred, Lady Rutledge added, "Perhaps you don't realize Mr. Curran graduated head of his class at Edinburgh Medical University."

Mrs. Fitzjames burned a steely look at her. "Was it he who told you that? A man who brags his own success is suspect to my way of thinking. You've been hoodwinked, Lady Rutledge." Bulk and all, she pushed herself up from the table, slowly making her way to the buffet.

Lady Rutledge sighed and Renata sat down. "Allow me to apologize. Regrettably, she is antagonistic to almost everyone."

"Are you spared her hostility?"

Renata's gaze settled on Nuala as she pursed her lips and slightly shook her head. "Never."

An hour passed quickly for Renata as she exchanged lively conversation with Mr. Talbot; except for one item of devastating conversation where he suggested Mr. Curran was in trouble with the constable. Talbot had hinted Constable Waffer called Mr. Curran a ghastly ghoul and that a wooden shovel had been found in his shed. According to Mr. Talbot apparently anyone knows body snatchers use wood because they are quieter than metal shovels if they should scrape a rock. He had also imparted that it is a known fact, medical men use cadavers upon which to practice their profession.

Having gathered all this readily imparted information from Mr. Talbot, Renata was torn between the impossibility Christopher would be involved in such a ghastly endeavor, and the intensity with which Mr. Talbot appeared to know the truth as he spoke it.

As she and her mother walked in the sleet-driven evening away from the Black Pig, her mother's strident voice eclipsed the sound of the weather. "Why did you leave me alone at that table? I am hardly acquainted with anyone in this horrid village."

Renata muttered something, eager to settle her parent's rising ire.

Huffing, her mother barked, "It's rude to mumble."

Renata stopped, her hand on the umbrella, and glared at her. "You understand rudeness? How odd. Because you spewed to anyone within listening your disdain of Mr. Curran at his *own* party."

Her mind in a whirl from the suggestion Christopher was a ghastly ghoul to her mother's whining, she stepped up her pace eager to arrive at their apartment where this conversation could unfold. Yet, distress ate at her and she spewed, "Why did you make it a point to be there when the man being honored is someone you can't abide?"

"I wanted to eat." Mrs. Fitzjames sounded a bit winded now that her daughter had caught up and *she* had to keep pace.

"You've ordained yourself to believe you can sit in judgement of others, when…" She bit her tongue.

The woman barked, "When what?"

She ignored her mother as they reached Chadwick Lane and rounded the corner. The husky wind blew the scent of salt in the air. Clutching their wraps, they came to Market and with the full blast of the wind, leaned into it with a vengeance as they pushed ahead until reaching the doorway to their upper apartment. Once inside, the sound and force of the blow lessened, and they climbed the stairs.

Renata shook off her cloak and hung it, unpinned her hat and set it on the shelf, and unwrapped the scarf from about her neck with an acute sense of purpose. The time had come, and she faced her mother with tight fists and anguish in her heart.

"I know you were in a relationship with Morgan Curran. Is that why you dislike Christopher so much?"

Louisa stiffened as she glared at her daughter, "How dare you confront me like I've done something dastardly. I take it that man told you?"

"By *that man*, do you mean Christopher? Because the information came from Morgan's daughter in a letter. Do you deny it?"

Her mother fell into the rocker setting it in motion. "Why

should I? A rotten husband I had. His only concern paying the toll to Dublin, keeping his delivery business alive. He hated Morgan for that, felt it was deliberate."

"A man doesn't build a road and put a toll on it because he doesn't like another. There's more to it. And I want to know what it is." Renata stood off to the side, arms folded as if arming herself against her mother's denial.

She took note of her mother's coy behavior as Louisa picked at her skirt, murmuring, "You think you know everything."

Renata scrutinized her mother. "Enlighten me, then."

Louisa's arthritic hands clutched the arms of the rocker, the gnarls and thick veins showing her age. "I was sick of listening to him and decided to meet Morgan, plead with him. I had to shut Ian up one way or another. I was greatly surprised to find Morgan was a charmer. Even sweet to me."

Louisa lifted her chin, inspecting her daughter. "I was prettier than you at your age. You wouldn't believe it now, but I was. Ian's apathy and disregard for me had my mind wandering over the years back to that time with Morgan. I was young and wanted to be in love, be loved, not worry how to pay the bills."

Her voice perked up. "Morgan was a spender with plenty of coin, he bought me pearls from Spain." Her thumb and forefinger pressed a pleat in her skirt as she drifted off to those memories.

With her arms crossed, Renata leaned against the wall coldly assessing the elderly woman; the mother she could never quite figure out, now becoming clear. Selfish, not interested in making a life with her husband, working against him. Uncaring of the odds he faced.

"He beguiled me." She puffed.

Renata was startled from her thoughts as her mother rambled.

"Flattered me with words and tokens. I felt so pretty and desired."

"What about your vows? You were a married woman."

"Ian's apathy and disregard drove me to it. I was young. I wanted to be in love."

"How can you blame *your* husband for what *you* did?" A flutter of Lea's veil in the shadows caught her attention.

"You didn't know him; he was different with you." She gripped the arms of the rocker with her knotty fingers.

Renata pushed off the wall. "It broke my heart to learn the man who made me feel so important, wasn't…." Her voice faded as she considered what she had learned from Rose's letter. It sickened her.

Her mother suggested, "It's likely why you insisted on bringing his ashes to Carrick. Guilt!"

Guilt? A surge of hot anger riled her to boiling. Her poor father endured the ultimate betrayal from his wife. He had been cuckolded. "I am sorry he had to live with me, and I wasn't his."

"What are you talking about—you stupid girl?"

"You needn't bluff your way through this. I've learned the truth. Morgan Curran is my father."

Louisa's confrontational grimace slowly changed to sly shock. "What would give you that idea?"

"The letter from Christopher's sister, she knew you were pregnant and had an affair with her father. She remembered how anxious her mother became when she learned the truth. The letter stated my father returned with you to Portugal before the child was born. Though you were the one to commit adultery he wanted to protect *you* from the disgrace of it all. He had the decency to accept me as his daughter."

Louisa shifted in the rocker, adjusting her skirt. "You've no sense of what it was like, living with a loser. It changed him."

"He denied you nothing. It's always been as you wanted. I refuse to get swept up in your web of whining, and *oh poor me*. I won't live another day under the same roof as you."

With a conciliatory tone, her mother whined, "I don't know how I'll get on, alone."

"You pamper your maid. Give her a real chore, like getting your meals."

The veil sailed out of Renata's view. She figured Lea backed into her room and closed the door, indicating to Renata she understood the language better than she pretended.

"That poor child doesn't know the first thing about running a household."

Renata huffed. "I'm beginning to understand why you didn't want to come here. I might discover your infidelity. In my heart, Ian will always be my father. You treated him disrespectfully for as long as I can remember. Right now, I can't abide being under the same roof with you."

She left the parlor and pulled a bag from under her bed packing as much of her clothing as she could manage. She walked out of her small room and saw her mother still in the rocker.

"You'll leave me on my own? I haven't eaten, have you forgotten? We left early."

"Your willful actions cause me heartbreak in more ways than you will ever know. And I grieve for my father. He must have suffered a broken heart because of your selfishness." Her gaze drifted to the maid, Lea, who obviously was still interested enough to listen to their parting. "Require more of her." Renata nodded in the direction of the maid. "Make do with her or fend for yourself."

Hand on the door, Renata closed it firmly behind her. Once in the hall, she fought back the tears that were wont to fall now that her anger melted to anguish. Nauseous, she leaned against the wall grieving for the man who raised her and loved her. Cementing her resolve to accomplish his dying wish, she suddenly realized his ashes were in the apartment.

She jerked the door open. Lea was bent over her mother, her dark fingers stroking her mother's face, crooning to her. Renata grabbed the urn from the shelf and left the apartment without a word.

A sense of relief washed over her as she walked down Market toward Mr. Talbot's shop and whispered a prayer that he would be amenable to her living in his work room.

The night air slipped about the streets around the lamp posts. She could barely see through the mist. Constable Waffer had lit the lamps, for that she was grateful. Mr. Talbot would have closed for the night because of Christopher's surprise party. She had no desire to walk into the Black Pig, carrying her valise and urn, and ask him for the key in front of others.

She knew Mr. Talbot's apartment could be reached by climbing the stairs that ran along the outside of the building. Tucking her bag in the shelter beneath the stairs, she was surprised by a voice calling out.

"Is that you, Miss Fitzjames?"

Backing out of the cubbyhole, hugging the urn, Mr. Talbot was standing at the foot of the stairs. She said, "I was about to knock hoping you had arrived from the party."

"I'm very surprised to see you about on such a night as this." Moisture was dripping from his top hat.

"I've had a falling out with my mother and hope you will allow me to stay in the back room until I get myself sorted out."

"Certainly." Clearing his throat, he dipped a forefinger and thumb into his waistcoat and pulled out a key. "It's not as clean as I would like."

"I'm so grateful, that is no bother to me. Besides, I'm the one who made a mess." She ducked back under the stairs and pulled out her bag.

"Let me help with that." He took it from her eyeing the urn in her other arm and unlocked the front door to the apothecary shop allowing her to enter. "It'll be damp tonight. I'll get a few logs for your fire. It's good to be inside, is it not?"

"Very much." She rubbed her damp gloves together.

He scratched a match and lit a lamp. With the light they both glanced about the back room of his shop. "The chest in the corner is full of blankets and sheets. My cousin stayed here for a few months not long ago. Knowing her she will have tucked some lavender in with the linens."

Renata smiled. "I'll be just fine, you needn't worry. And I'll be able to assist in the shop if that would be to your liking. I'll be quite cozy here. You are helping me out of a bit of a bad circumstance. I appreciate your generosity very much."

The wind rattled the window, and somewhere along the street a shutter had loosened and banged against the building with gusto. It was not yet raining full out, slightly pinging against the panes.

"The key unlocks both the front door and this one back here." He nodded to the door on the back wall. "Are you sure you'll be all right down here?"

"I have everything I want."

"I'll knock at the back door with some logs, then I'll go on up." His gaze fell to the urn she hugged. "Is that what I think it is?"

"My father's ashes."

"Ah, then you won't feel so alone?" He hadn't wiped off a few drops of water from his glasses and the candlelight twinkled off them.

Smiling, she realized the monumental decision she'd made and felt contented.

He brought enough logs to get through the night and bent down starting the fire when the front door opened, and a voice called out. "Talbot! Are you back there?"

The door shut and footsteps could be heard crossing the shop closing in on the backroom. In a loud voice Talbot said, "I'll be right there."

"I'm here now."

Renata was unpacking her bag in a corner where the chest stood. A man, taller than Mr. Talbot and very well dressed, availed himself of the warmth from the fire. Talbot was on one knee adding logs. "Waffer is sniffing around. You've got to stop him—"

Talbot shot up gripping the iron. "Not now."

"I'm the one giving orders." The man leaned into Talbot his gloved hands fisted.

Talbot smoothed out his voice. "Allow me to introduce you to Miss Fitzjames." And extended his arm toward the chest where she stood.

Renata gave a nod, a frock in her hands partially folded. "How do you do, sir."

Talbot said, "I think all is well down here now. I'll leave you to it, Miss Fitzjames. And goodnight." With that he replaced the iron at the fireplace and strode out of the room, the tall man in his wake.

She glanced about the space as she heard the front door close and his key locking it from outside. Their voices dwindled as she heard them climb the outside stairs to Mr. Talbot's apartment.

The one lamp in the backroom cast a golden circle on the table and reached across the braided rug to where the bed stood waiting for her to dress it with sheets and blankets. Her herbal ledgers were exactly as she had left them two days ago. The urn received a prominent space among her jars on the shelf of herbals.

Snuggled beneath the eider cover, the lantern off, and the rain pelting the siding and windowpane, she allowed her thoughts to traverse over the afternoon. Christopher's face full of delight as he thanked each of his guests. His countenance glistened with surprise and sober delight. She guessed it took him a while to digest that most folks had finally taken to him. How she loved that face. And why not, he was her sibling.

Her father had taken care of her financially several years ago when it was clear she wouldn't marry. He had given her independence. She clung to it now.

Her mind whirled with future possibilities. She had family here. Could this be one of the reasons her father insisted she bring his remains to Carrick? It wasn't the first time she had this thought. He knew his wife's weak character and mayhap had guessed how things between mother and daughter might unravel? That had to be the answer. He somehow suspected this might happen.

The room was dark, the moon barely able to cast more than a feeble drab gray through the window high on the wall. She was a long way from Obidos, having left behind servants, beeswax candles, dinners prepared by a cook, and a personal maid, just to name a few luxuries. Aside from losing her father, and learning of her mother's perfidy, she was more content than she could ever remember.

The heavy mist changed to a downpour, and she grew sleepy with the rhythm of rain on the windowpane. Would her life calm, would it ever be a semblance of order and comfort?

Her last thoughts were of Christopher. No matter what else should follow in the wake of her discovery, he would always care. He was that kind of man, not unlike Ian, whose memory she would hold dear until the end of time.

After everyone left the Black Pig, the Tremaines gave Christopher and Dino a ride to the infirmary. Lady Tremaine asked for a tour of the facility.

The carriage pulled up and after the footman turned down the step, the four of them darted into the infirmary, barely allowing the footman to cover them with an umbrella.

Christopher offered tea, but his guests were sated from the buffet offered on his behalf, so he showed them the office, with added shelving, the addition of the examination room built onto the existing building; and glass cabinets neatly filled with medicines, bandages, and miscellaneous paraphernalia of the medical profession. The examining table was padded for comfort with a step stool for patients to use. A small desk stood in the corner where he could take notes. And a filing system attached to the wall to organize the papers. A three-sided screen hung with linen to offer privacy.

"What do you think? A huge improvement, right?" He was mighty proud of the work that was done.

"You are in your glory, my friend. It will be a pleasure working with you from time to time."

Lady Tremaine had been whispering with Dino, and queried,

"Is this all? I was under the impression a lot more work had been done."

"Follow me." Christopher led them down the hall. "This is my bedroom, unchanged."

A few feet further, and Dino piped up, "This is my room."

Her ladyship inspected everything. "You must be quite the reader, Master Curran. You have a good many books. You could be a lending library. Your clothing is neatly hung." With admiration in her voice, she said, "I'm impressed."

He proudly said, "Thank you."

"Do I recall that Mr. Carnahan said you taught his son to read?"

Obviously pleased to be called out on that score, he beamed, "I made a friend for life."

"I can believe it. You gave him a powerful gift teaching him to read."

Christopher and Tremaine had wandered on down the hall that led to the kitchen, and the large addition of the ward with four beds a table and chair by each bed, and storage. Lady Tremaine and Dino followed. Christopher was explaining how he planned to keep patients who weren't physically able to go home.

"A cellar beneath the kitchen was enlarged and much easier to access now with stairs rather than a ladder. We'll be able to keep foods and go to market every other day or so. We'll buy in quantity as we have the need. Though I must say, many of our patients pay in kind. Honey, fruit when in season, bread, meat, and even some staples."

Lady Tremaine walked about the ward. "I like this idea. You've set up the infirmary to assist a number of folks who might not otherwise seek a doctor."

Dino whispered to Christopher that he had schoolwork to finish and bade goodnight to the Tremaines as he retreated to his room.

The three adults sat at the table in the kitchen mulling over the afternoon's event. "I noticed," said Tremaine, "a good deal more villagers have given their approval than I thought possible. Your party was a success."

Lady Tremaine added, "There was one woman I was glad to see the back of, I can tell you."

Christopher arms on the table, leaned in, "Let me guess. Mrs. Fitzjames."

"You must know I met her at Nuala's a while ago. She's free with her opinion of others."

"As I'm one of her targets, I won't ask you to repeat anything."

"Keep a stiff upper lip. I've a feeling this will pass soon enough."

Tremaine laughed. "My wife always looks to the brighter side."

Christopher wished he could lift his heavy heart. The rain had finally given up, but a damp chill hung in the air. He got up and put some coals on the fire.

Tremaine eyed him seriously, his lips pursed in thought. Christopher waited for him to say what was on his mind, but he was not forthcoming, and Christopher didn't want to hazard a guess.

Lady Tremaine's leather-gloved hands were folded atop the table. "Is it my imagination or has something happened between you and Miss Fitzjames?"

"Egad, Mairéad, is this our business?" said Tremaine.

Christopher spoke up, "It's quite all right."

Ignoring her husband, she asked, "Has it anything to do with her mother?"

Tremaine said, "Honestly, how can you be so prying?"

Ignoring her husband, she added, "The woman's problematic. Renata is perplexed as to how to manage her."

Christopher idly folded and refolded a napkin then offered, "She's presented quite a serious problem which Renata and I need to come to grips with. I can't say anything more. Just—well, yes there is a situation."

Lady Tremaine's eyes filled with concern. "We will pray for

both of you to ease this from your hearts. We are your friends Christopher, in good times and bad."

A lump caught in his throat. "Your concern is appreciated. Thank you both."

Tremaine said, "I noticed the constable was in attendance. Has he lightened up on you?"

"He informed me this evening I would be arrested this week. But I've my doubts. I won't be losing sleep over it you can bet on that."

27

A jingle from the apothecary's bell in the front of the shop drew Renata from her task. Mr. Talbot had left her in charge. "Mrs. Brandt, good morning. May I help you?"

"I heard you were assisting poor Mr. Talbot. He's simply too busy. Good of you." Setting her reticule on the counter, she pointed to a black jar on the shelf. "I believe to be that one."

"Have you a name?"

"Camphor oil."

"Your daughter not feeling well?"

Mrs. Brandt weighed her answer. "Cassie has a case of the nerves, what with the baby coming on and all. I thought it might help."

"Do go easy then. We don't know how it affects the child she carries."

"I'll take care. I've a tab with Mr. Talbot and good day to you."

Renata recorded the sale and intended to spend a few minutes on her project in the back only to hear the jingling again. As she neared the drape separating the two rooms, she saw Christopher in the outer room and wavered on going through.

His smile was instant the moment he saw her. "I knew it

would be a matter of time before you worked for Talbot. He's a wily one, most likely taking advantage of your medicinal expertise."

Renata wore starched over sleeves that kept her gown's cuffs from dirt, and a full-length white apron she hoped gave her the look of a professional. "Quite the other way around." She stood by the counter.

He came close, his brows furrowed. "Something's not right. Can I help?"

His sympathy almost made her cry and she snapped, "It's no longer your affair." She swiped at an imaginary spot on her apron. "Though I appreciate your concern."

He leaned in, cupping her elbow. "If I can help you, let me, please."

She waited a long moment considering her, him, them. The air sputtered out of her, and she had no desire to push him further away. "Have you time for tea?"

"I have all the time in the world for you." His personable features lit with regard as he removed his beaver hat and bent his head a tiny bit toward her.

Following her to the back, he sat in one of the chairs as she set out cups, sugar, and a small plate of scones. A kettle steamed over the fire and she poured water into a pot, a strainer filled with leaves was nestled in a cozy.

She took note of his gaze scanning the bed, obviously fixed for sleeping, and her hat and coat that hung from a hook, her bag in the corner.

He drew back narrowing his gaze on her. "Are you living here?"

She drew in a breath and placing the kettle on the arm swung it over the fire then wrapped the teapot in a cozy. "I've been here a week."

"What happened?" She pursed her lips as he pleaded, "Tch, Renata, have you forgotten who I am to you? Let me help you. If anything, it will give me ease and perhaps you, too." He crossed his long legs and cupped his hands over his knee as his gaze searched her face.

It was not easy to think of this man as a brother from what she had begun to envision of him, something much more than a sibling, for sure.

She carried the steeping pot to the table and sat across from him stacking the papers aside. "It all came to a head at your party. My mother wasn't at her best and said some things I could no longer ignore. When we arrived home, I lashed into her, accused her of the affair." Her brow rose as she gave him a knowing glance. "She didn't deny it. In fact, she maligned my dear father as the cause of her going elsewhere for companionship."

Finished, she cast him a clouded glance ache filled her heart, and confirmed, "I will always think of him as my father."

"As you should." He stretched his arm across the table cupping her hand.

She slipped hers to her lap and continued, "Then she began refuting the accusation, probably realizing what she had admitted. It was then I told her I had proof I was Morgan Curran's daughter. She immediately accused you of telling me. I said it was a daughter of Morgan Curran who wrote the letter."

Christopher's features grew somber, waiting.

"She gave me a queer look like she gets sometimes when an idea comes to her."

'What would give you that idea?' she argued.

"I told her the part in the letter where the two men argued over the cost of the toll road, then the couple left for Portugal in disgrace, with the woman expecting Morgan's child."

"What did she say to that?" He shifted in the chair.

"She was bitter. Then melted into a dramatic mass of self-pity."

Cool enough, he sipped the tea, then set it on the saucer. "I'm curious, how does it happen you are here?"

"When I originally inquired if I could set up my things in his back room, Mr. Talbot asked if I would be available to help him out. I hadn't agreed to it at the time."

"He's needed an assistant for a while."

"The night of your party, after confronting her and then her admission, I found I could no longer stay under the same roof. Her deceit—what she did to my father and to us. I packed up some things and came begging to Mr. Talbot."

He leaned in. "I wish I had known."

His greenish brown eyes fixed on her in a way she thought she saw a mixture of hurt and sympathy. "I must have looked like a drowned rat. You recall it rained that night? Mr. Talbot was most gracious. Of course, I also told him I would certainly help out with the shop."

Refilling their cups, she added, "I haven't been back to the apartment since. I left my mother in the care of her maid, Lea." She held the teacup midway between the table and her lips. "She's a sly girl. It came to me of a sudden she understood every word we said. She's pretended all these months not to know English."

Christopher set his cup in the saucer and for a moment glanced at the papers strewn on the table between them. He took a deep breath then asked, "How does Talbot treat you? Is he kind? Respectful?"

"Why yes. Very. What an odd question."

He met her gaze and held it. "He's not shown any strange behavior in your presence?"

She set the cup down. "There was an odd incident my first night. A man came in through the front door and found Mr. Talbot setting the fire for me. He was quite angry. He shouted at Mr. Talbot saying things like... 'Waffer is sniffing about. You must stop him.' I could tell Mr. Talbot was very much out of sorts with his intrusion. He tried to quiet the man, who countered that he was the one giving orders. His hands were fisted like he might strike Mr. Talbot.

"Then in an about face, Mr. Talbot introduced me to the man, but oddly never said his name, just mine. As the fire was catching on, Mr. Talbot said goodnight and the two of them left. I could hear their footsteps on the outside stairs."

"Would you recognize the man if you saw him?"

"I think so. He was dressed fashionably. Quite elegant. Taller than Mr. Talbot." His asking fanned her curiosity. "Why do you ask? Tell me what is going on?"

The smile he presented was forced, she knew him well enough to know the difference. His fingers tapped on his knee. "Nothing to bother you about." He took in a long breath, and added, "Not too long ago I saw Talbot arguing with a man outside this shop who would fit the description. If it is the same one, they have a contentious relationship."

⚜

Christopher left Renata and strode up Stephen's Lane, crossed over to Forge and entered the county gaol. Waffer was sitting at his desk tossing a ball in the air and catching it.

When Christopher charged in, Waffer sprang to his feet and the ball bounced along the floor. "Surprised me, ye did."

"From the looks of it, not a moment too soon."

Waffer looked him up and down. "Have ye come to confess yer filthy doin's with the poorly dead folk?" He scooped up the ball off the floor.

A hearty laugh escaped Christopher. "I've come to give you the names of the perpetrators."

"More than one? That's interesting. And how have ye come by these names?" He began tossing the ball again as if anything Christopher had to say was of no account.

"I suspect Talbot works for a Mr. Martin, who used to practice medicine in Hawthorn. Martin was dismissed when doctoring Lord Darnley several years ago. I would think, being let go by the Darnley family caused his reputation to suffer. I've heard he is writing a book about anatomy. Which makes me think he might need cadavers to authenticate his writing." Christopher braced his shoulder against the one jailcell in the room, arms folded across his chest.

Waffer quit tossing the ball and sat up in his chair. He weighed the information then squinted at Christopher as if taking his measure.

Christopher added, "And if you recall, there were two men in the graveyard who ran away when you nabbed Dino."

Waffer sucked in his bottom lip. "I might be a fool, but I'm going to trust ye."

Christopher glanced at the iron bars he leaned against. "You won't be locking me up?"

"That depends."

"Miss Fitzjames gave me a description of the second man. Taller than Talbot, elegantly dressed which could describe Martin."

Waffer frowned. "For the last six months, graves have been disturbed in our two graveyards and several in Waterford. It's a particular body part that's been missing in each case. My notes show that within two days, sometimes three, after burial, the graves have been desecrated. I planned to stake out a watch for the next several nights at St. John's Catholic Church. Little Missy Carmichael died of influenza two days ago."

Christopher closed his eyes a moment nodding. "A sorrowful thing when a child passes. As can be expected, her family is taking it extremely hard."

Waffer grunted. "The body part they've been takin' is the head."

He gaped at Waffer. "The book on anatomy Martin is writing is about the brain."

"Looks like ye might be on to something, doc. Talbot and Martin it is then."

❀

This was the second night Christopher hid behind a bank of mist covered yews affording him a direct line to the plot where Miss Carmichael was buried. Yews were folklore meant to drive away devils.

Waffer hid on the opposite side behind a large monument. The wind was brewing up cloud cover rotating the moon through light and dark. Both men were staked out and hunkered down for a long wait. Waffer planned to make the first move with Christopher as backup. Waffer insisted on waiting until they were done digging as proof of their intent.

Almost as if on schedule, Talbot showed up with a shovel and rope and began digging. An hour or more passed and Martin wasn't anywhere in sight. Talbot had dug far enough down his head was the only thing about him visible. Christopher heard the clunk of the wooden shovel as it hit the wood of the coffin. He concluded Martin was the brains and Talbot was the brawn of the corpse defilers.

Christopher found it most difficult to envision Talbot cutting off Missy's head. He almost tore out of hiding to beat him to a pulp. The distinct sound of prying the lid off alerted him to what was next…where the hell was Waffer? Of a sudden an object flew out of the grave landing on top the dirt pile and rolled down the edge.

Blazes and damn…he'd chopped off her head.

"Move and I'll run ye through!" Waffer growled as he stood over the grave, a seven-foot pike at Talbot's chest.

Christopher had kept an eye out for Martin and not detected any sense of a fourth man. He walked toward a line of angled headstones. A shaft of moon slit through the clouds. With Waffer's pike pointed at Talbot who was climbing out of the hole, Christopher grabbed him and swung a mighty jab at his jaw knocking him over. He dug his knee into Talbot's back and tied his hands together. Then jerked him to his knees facing the sharply honed pike.

Talbot's chin fell to his chest still gasping for air.

Christopher walked off toward the pile of dirt looking for the child's remains that had been tossed. His gut churned with anger and remorse that he hadn't stopped the desecration.

The stench of death and the ground heaving with generations of dead upon dead buried beneath him, he searched for the head.

When he appeared once more, he slid into the grave and opened the lid of the coffin and placed a stuffed doll back in Missy's arms. And assured himself her head had not been touched.

Talbot spent the rest of the night locked up under the watchful eye of the constable who delighted in telling the chemist, "If they don't hang ye, ye'll spend the rest of yer life in a rat-infested black hole, that much I'm certain of."

Christopher made a quick stop at the apothecary shop to enlighten Renata of last night's deeds. Shocked at the news, Renata would temporarily take charge of the shop, until arrangements were made to replace Mr. Talbot.

She said, "You're questioning me about Mr. Talbot makes sense now. You were worried because you suspected him of this horrid crime?"

Christopher took off his hat when he stepped inside. He stayed the impulse to take her in his arms. "I have only a minute. I was fairly certain no harm would come to you. If anything, I thought Talbot was quite interested in you. And, if I alerted you to my concern, it would cause you worry. If I didn't alert you, only I would worry. So that was the path I chose."

He pushed his hat on and ran out the door. He was meeting Waffer, who had knowledge of where Martin lived; they planned to take him into custody and didn't want to waste any time.

Christopher and Waffer proceeded to Martin's abode. He lived in an old wooden framed, three-storied home on the outskirts of Hawthorn on the old road to Kilmeadan. They tied their mounts in the distance and readied their weapons as they advanced on the building. A dense growth covered their approach as they quietly made their way.

Their approach was at the back where a portion of the home was only one story, close enough they could hear conversation.

It appeared Martin was not alone. He had an accomplice to assist him. Christopher held his flintlock pistol at the ready. Waffer his trusted musket in hand, they crashed open the door.

For a moment, Christopher was momentarily stunned. Then his years in medical school brought him back to the reality of studying and practicing medicine. A shelf to his left was lined with glass jars each with the embalmed head of a person. It was the most grotesque and bizarre sight he'd ever seen outside a laboratory. He wasn't certain he'd ever seen anything like this even in a laboratory. His gut roiled with loathing that a man who took an oath to uphold the ethics of medicine, would stoop to desecrate a corpse.

Waffer waited a moment too long, being as stunned as Christopher, before he pointed his musket at Martin's chest. The younger man was bent over a table where a head with long black hair was placed. He had already peeled off the scalp. And, with a saw in hand, appeared ready to remove the bone. He raised the tool as a weapon. Martin inched away and grabbed up a hammer.

Christopher pointed his weapon at Martin. "I'd rather see you hang for what you've done. But move and I'll shoot you dead."

With a hair-raising scream, Martin lunged at Christopher who pulled the trigger killing him.

The younger man fell to his knees begging for mercy. Waffer shoved the barrel of his musket into his back ordering him to lie down. Christopher tied his hands and hauled him upright. Waffer kept the musket aimed at him.

In the days following, Martin was buried, and his accomplice was taken before the resident magistrate and sentenced to twenty years. Waffer felt justice had been served. If Talbot wasn't hung straightaway, he wouldn't be seeing the outside of his rat-infested black hole in Dublin's gaol for years if ever. The younger man, Bart, was also hauled off to Dublin's gaol.

28

"Hmm." Christopher put a dash of sugar in his tea and stirred. "I've wondered, what is your birthdate?"

He inadvertently brought a smile to Renata's face. "'91 on the Fifth of May." She glanced across the table at him. "Thinking of giving your sister a gift, are you?"

"I'm wondering about the timing of your birth and your mother expecting Morgan's child. I would also be interested in the date they arrived in Obidos."

She glanced up from the cup of warmth. "She didn't deny she was with child when I talked to her."

"And, according to my sister, she was. I'm not disputing it was Morgan's. What if she gave that child to someone, and then became pregnant with another—you? What if?"

Her gaze searched his face for the longest time, filtering his questions. "But—that would mean—"

"Exactly."

The silliest grin broke out on his face. She cautioned herself to not believe what he was suggesting. "It was so long ago."

He stood, the day was early, not yet past noon and it wasn't raining, rare for January. "I'll ride to Carrick and ask my sister of the exact dates."

"But…but you could write? And your patients?" She was beyond bewildered at the prospect, the possibility, but mostly at his sense of urgency.

"I want the truth, and I want it *now*—not two, three weeks from now."

She was stunned and began shivering. Her breath caught.

Her distress was obvious.

"Come here to me my darling." His arms opened and she melted into him, sobbing. He held her until the storm quieted, his large hand tenderly cradling the back of her head against his shoulder.

The heavy timber of his voice calming, assuring, "I will love you whether we are sister and brother or husband and wife. Rest assured no matter what I might discover, we will be friends at the very least of it."

He wiped the tears from her cheeks and kissed her forehead. "Will you be alright for now?"

She sniffled into his kerchief and nodded.

"I must go."

"Be safe, Christopher. Take care." Her tremulous smile quivered. She placed her palm on his cheek. "Thank you for the comfort. I needed to know you will be in my life no matter what the outcome."

He grabbed his hat; the look on his face spoke volumes. "By the by, we share the same birth year 1791."

She watched him leave as he darted through the drapes and out the door. It was obvious she hadn't firmly discarded love as she had thought. Nor had he or the truth wouldn't be so urgent.

⚜

Christopher walked into the back of the infirmary. Darby was exchanging the linen. She seemed chipper. "That was some doings last week, doc. The food was plentiful, and more folks showed than I thought might. You're a right good man, doc. I've always known. Now the rest of the village does, too. More so now with nabbing the men who dig up corpses."

He shifted on his stance, uneasy with her compliment. "I've got a situation and need some help. Krysta has taken a few days off."

"I think she might be plannin' a weddin' if gossip means anythin'. I'll be glad ta step in." Her ample arms bent with fists into her waist.

"I need to get to Carrick-on-Suir quickly and won't make it back tonight."

"Say no more. I'll take the lad home with me. Sean planned to clean out his boat later; maybe Dino can be of some help."

"Tell him not to worry. I'll inform him of all when I get back. And, Darby, I'm most appreciative for the nice things you say." He took a deep breath and barged down the hall into his room. Quickly changed into buckskin breeches and riding boots, he threw a few things in a bag. Opening the front door, he made sure the sign read *closed* and took off toward Grogan's.

"I need a post horse." Christopher glanced about Grogan's stable looking for the black Arab.

Bushy-browed Grogan looked up from tending a roan, her tail slapping him in the face. "Will this one do?"

"I need the Arab," he said and nodded toward the third stall down.

"Aye, but I like her, too. If it's a post horse you need, I'd want her back. You comin' back, right?"

"Sometime tomorrow, most likely."

"Where you headed, then?" He came out of the stall and put the brush on a shelf.

"Family business up in Carrick-on-Suir."

"A good day's ride. I'll saddle the Arab, then. You'll want to plan for Mooncoin as yer first stop. Remind Old Sam for me to take good care of this one," Grogan threw a rug over the Arab's back. I'm thinkin' yer next stop'll be somewhere near on six, seven miles beyond. Not much up that ways 'cept a tavern with post horses, but you'll see it."

After leaving Hawthorn, Christopher skirted the west end of Waterford and headed for the bridge. The locals referred to it as Timbertoe. It spanned the River Suir, where he and Renata had walked the quay after dinner at the Mermaid's Inn. He sighed at thought of that evening and the glint of a promising future.

The clip clop of hooves on the wooden bridge was just the beginning of a three-hour journey before he reached the first post and exchanged the Arab. It was going to be a long day.

The sun was sliding down the hills in the west when he arrived at his sister's home. When his parents were alive, his room had always been on the top floor.

And it's where his sister had put him now. Tired as Christopher was, he glanced about as memories invaded the space. He was amazed at how tall the trees had grown.

Rose and James lived here with their brood of five. Christopher had been greeted by a swarm of excited children. It had been too long since his last stay. On his way down to dinner, he was greeted in the parlor with a dark red wine.

Placing a kiss on his sister's cheek and nodding to James, he offered, "My nieces and nephews are growing. It shouldn't have surprised me they are all sizes." He sipped the wine. He had so much to tell and didn't know where to begin.

Rose smiled at him. She was always calm no matter the situation. "Bring us up to date, as your last letter was short. Does your visit have anything to do with my answer?"

James piped up, "It surely does, I ken it on your face. Does it bear well, or bode ill, then?" Scottish, James always dressed in his green plaid kilt for supper. Not so many decades earlier, he would have been killed if found wearing it.

As he took a seat across from the two of them, Christopher challenged, "I'll let you be the judge of which. First off, I've taken in a lad, Dino, a runaway from a ship where he'd been captive since the age of about four or five."

Rose was shocked by the revelation. "You have a big heart, giving him a sense of family and a home. I'm so grateful there are people like you."

James added, "I agree, the lad couldn't be in the care of a better man. Is this the only way we're to get nieces and nephews then?"

Christopher set his whiskey down as the butler announced supper. He took his sister's hand and placed it on his arm as they walked toward the dining room. Over his shoulder, he answered James, "That possibility may depend on what more Rose is able to tell me about our parents."

Doubt creased his sister's brow. It was James who tended to see the humor in situations.

The meal was comprised of mackerel, a chicken pie, candied yams, and a corn mash. "Quite a table. In my honor?"

Rose quipped, "Only you would ask, Mr. Humble himself. You've cook to thank. When she heard there would be three for dinner, word got about quickly it was you. We've missed you terribly. Couldn't you tell by the greeting from the children?"

His brother-in-law asked, "I'd like to hear the *bear well* or *bode ill* story. Can we get right to it?"

James, a decent man deeply in love with his sister, was educated at Dublin University. Since their marriage he had acquired mills in both Carrick and Portlaw. And, recently he had been appointed to the council in Carrick. He was respected for his honesty. Christopher knew it was a love match between James and Rose.

Christopher laid his eating utensil down and said, "I've met someone."

Rose gasped, a smile spreading across her features.

James offered a slow smile. "Ye've been bitten. This being the *bear well*, what's the *bode ill* to tell, then?"

Christopher flashed him a grimace. "When I wrote to you, it was because...well, let me begin at the beginning. I've met someone I am very fond of, Renata Fitzjames. She and her mother arrived from Portugal late last summer with the express purpose of burying her father's ashes in Carrick's graveyard."

Rose was stupefied. "No! Is it you think there is a connection between Miss Fitzjames parents and the man and the wife, who were expecting? Is the wife the woman who had the affair with our father?"

"It appears so. The woman is Renata's mother, Louisa Fitzjames. She's admitted she had an affair with Morgan."

"Ahh…" His sister laid her palm against the front of her burgundy gown.

He added, "When Renata presented her mother with the information in your letter, she admitted to it."

"Oh, Christopher, you've fallen in love with…"

"Don't say it. Let me finish. What we knew is what you wrote —the woman was expecting when she and her husband sailed to Portugal."

Her pretty brow furrowed as she looked him in the eye. "I'm so sorry." Sincerity clearly etched on her face.

James asked, "Do *you* believe Miss Fitzjames is Morgan's child?" His gaze instantly shifted to his wife.

"Well," said Christopher. "I don't want to believe it. But what we know certainly points to the truth of it. 'Tis the crux, the whole of it. Renata could be a sister rather than what I was wanting."

He smiled at Rose. "Let's hope the truth lies in your diary."

Their food had grown cool with the exchange. James toyed with his silverware, his fingers moving them this way and that. He was obviously deep in thought.

Christopher questioned, "I'm curious if you remembered the date this happened, when the Fitzjames left for Portugal?"

"It should be easy to figure out. Unlike our sister, I kept a diary. Nosy thing she was, always trying to find it and read what I'd written."

"I wondered how you could recall everything you wrote in your letter. A diary? You wrote of Morgan's affair?" Christopher's skepticism clouded his question.

"No, no. I wrote of the loud argument, so young, and so shocked was I. I still remember it. No one *ever* shouted in our home, remember? It was quiet like a tomb most of the time. I would have written about all that shouting, the curse words, and our father flailing his arms at Ian Fitzjames."

"I'm grateful for your attention to detail, Rose. Hopefully, your diary will have the answer."

Glancing at his wife, James asked in a rather hesitant voice, "Do you still write in your diary?"

She snickered. "Everything, my dearest. Every night, yes."

Christopher rolled his eyes as their humor spread across the linen.

Dessert was jam tarts and apples. Fresh food this time of year was rare. If it wasn't stored in the cellar, put up in jars, or curing in the smokehouse, they managed without. The house was quiet but for a few indistinguishable shouts from the children's wing.

"Nanny's hands are full right now," said Rose, "Lucille and Mary are of an age when sisters hate each other and love each other within minutes over the silliest things."

"I don't remember you and Molly fussing at each other. Why was that do you suppose?"

"The times perhaps. Conventional wisdom on child rearing now is quite different than when we were young. According to Nanny, it is thought children should be allowed to express themselves. When we were this age, we were to be seen but not heard. Don't you remember?"

"I might have had my head in the clouds most of the time."

"More like a book. You were called the worm behind your back," said James.

He glanced at his brother-in-law. "I was well aware of the name, I just ignored it."

With a grin Rose warned, "Nanny will be bringing the children into the parlor for a visit before they go off to bed. They are eager to see their uncle."

"May I peek at the baby?"

"You may. We will stop by the nursery on the way up. He's in the care of Nurse Pratt."

Later, once the children had their fun with Uncle Christopher, he peeked in on Norman, who was fast asleep after nursing. He knew better than to wake a sleeping infant. Staying only a minute, Christopher took the stairs to his third-floor room.

Not much later, Rose knocked on her brother's door. She showed him the diary from the autumn of 1789 and into the new year. The books were dated according to the school year, not the calendar year. "Shall I read this to you? Or do you want to read it for yourself?"

He chose to read it himself.

"You'll want to begin on this page." She pointed a finger at her childish comment about the fight on the steps of their home.

...mama is in her room crying, nanny told me to leave her be. Papa is yelling at a man on the front steps. A carriage awaits, the bay has four stockings perfectly matched. Papa wants the man to leave Ireland and go back to Portugal. His face is red like the beets from supper. The man shouted at Papa that his wife was carrying a baby, but I can't see the baby just the woman's skirts through the open door to the carriage...

...I wonder if she got the baby in time for Christmas. A baby is better than a doll. Maybe mama will get a baby for Christmas.

"What Christmas would this have been?" His concern caused his voice to waiver.

"The date is imprinted on the front, autumn 1789 to summer 1790. The Christmas would have been 1789."

The breath gushed out of Christopher. "There is no doubt of these dates?"

"None. What does this prove?"

"That I am *not* in love with my sister."

Her brows high with mischief, she said, "But I am your sister, you had better love me."

"You know how I feel about you, dearest, but I am not *in love* with you."

She groused, "I've simply got to meet this extraordinary woman who has captured your heart."

He closed the diary and handed it to her. "Put this in a safe place, should I need to show Renata proof."

"I've had this under lock and key all these years. Is that not safe enough? And what do you mean *show her proof?* Does she think you a charlatan?"

His hair fell across his forehead and he brushed it back, impatient to get back to Hawthorn now he had the truth. "I suspect you'll judge for yourself when you meet her."

"How long do I have to wait?" She pouted.

Almost giddy, he picked her up and twirled her about. "Rose, you've made me a happy man. You and your diary." He set her down and kissed her on the top of her head.

"Fairly soon. And I'll have a lad with me named Dino, who snuck into my home and hid under my bed." He grinned at her, happy as he'd been in a long time. "He ran a few times, but always came back. But that's another story."

She gave him a slanted look. "It's this Renata Fitzjames I'm curious about."

"I don't plan to ever leave her side again. She will surely be with us."

Her hand on the doorknob, she glanced over her shoulder. "I suspect you'll be leaving early. Do have breakfast before you go running off. James will want a word or two, as will the children. We simply do not get enough of you." Before she opened the door, she added, "Miss Fitzjames must be quite a woman. I don't recall when I've noticed you this happy. Maybe the time when you caught your first fish. Funny to think of that right now, isn't it?"

Hands on his hips, he teetered on the balls of his shoes. "Life is curious. Mine of late has been miserable. Yes, sister, I am happy, indeed. And eager to deliver the good news to Renata."

He had left immediately after breakfast. It was late now, raining most of his ride back to Hawthorn. He retrieved the Arab in Mooncoin. She was rested and ready. Half-hearted shards of sun dipped low in the horizon as he made his way across Timbertoe Bridge heading toward the apothecary's shop. He was soaked and a bit sore not having ridden such a length in a long time. But his spirits soared allowing discomfort to fall away.

Reining in the Arab outside the apothecary, he muttered. "I'll not be long and get you to the stable and some sweet oats, just be patient." He took two steps at a time and stepped inside. He saw the lamp light edging the hem of the drape that separated both rooms.

Renata had her back to the window at the far end of the room. She slowly faced him, almost afraid to know what he had to say. Like she had held her breath the entire time he was gone. "I hoped you would come."

He walked directly to her, gathered her in his arms, and kissed her full on the lips. His hand spread to the back of her head, holding her as if he would never let go. It took her a moment to soften. He'd been too abrupt, but he needed to kiss her, dreaded the thought of never doing so again. Raising his lips from hers, he looked deep into her quizzing green orbs.

"We are not related in any way, my dearest. But I hope to rectify that as soon as possible."

"It has taken me a moment but is the only conclusion I could consider when you kissed me." Closing her eyes, she waited for another.

Tender, loving and filled with relief they could be together, the physical closeness was hard to let go. Slowly, so slowly his cheek rested against hers, his arms held her securely. "Marry me, my love. I never want to think of losing you again."

⌘

"You overwhelm me with a kiss, a marriage proposal—when there are problems galore. For one there is my mother who lied to me, to *us*. What to do about her? Most importantly, I need to understand how you've learned we aren't related."

His thumbs were softly rubbing the top of her hands, and he withdrew them. "All I could think about was conveying this information to you. I am a bit impetuous, sorry."

"My darling Christopher, please don't keep me in suspense, tell me what happened at your sister's."

"She's kept a diary through the years. It is clearly documented in her ten-year-old hand when the argument ensued between our fathers. I've read it, down to the date it took place."

Renata was stunned.

"It's the dates we were after. The argument in her diary took place February 1790, and your birthdate is May 1791. It could not have been you your mother was carrying."

"I'm concerned about the truth. And my mother fabricates and twists to suit her own means. Honestly, Christopher, right now, I am worried my birth date is not correct."

"But why would she change your birth date? What would be her point?"

"You know her so little, it's hard to explain. I was quite surprised she wanted to accompany me to Ireland, she forced herself on me."

Renata placed her hands on his face. "My dear, dear darling man. I am being cautious because I know her. She's not like you or me. Bear with me in this. I need to confront her, get at the whole truth. And, because I want to spend the rest of my life with you, I need her to convince me we are not related by blood. I also want to know why she would deliberately lie about something so important."

He covered her hands and drew them into a prayer-like fold. "I don't want you to go alone."

She took a deep breath. "I prefer it. It won't be nice. She'll have her back up and liable to say anything she pleases."

"When will you talk to her?"

"It's too late now." She cast a glance at the window, a few stars not clouded over sparkled in the dark blue.

"I agree. It's wise to sleep on it. Tomorrow we'll clear this up."

He withdrew his hands from her. "As much as I would like to stay and talk this through some more, I need to get the Arab to Grogan's she's earned a bag of oats and a dry stall. Will you come directly to the infirmary when you are done?"

She nodded, already deep in thought of the visit she planned.

He repeated, "Renata?"

"Hmm."

"Promise me you will come to me directly. I won't be able to think of anything else until I speak with you again."

Her palm lifted to his cheek. "My darling, yes. I will."

The next morning, Renata woke after a night of troubled dreams. With all her heart she wanted Christopher's discovery to be the truth. What an extraordinary way to find the dates. His sister diligently keeping a diary of their lives. A child's perspective is usually different than that of an adult. She gave herself an astonishing gift, chronicling their lives.

Planning to arrive at ten o'clock, her mother would have eaten and be rocking and looking out over Market Street at the comings and goings of the neighbors. It was a busy lane because of all the commerce, and it occupied her.

She prayed her mother would be honest. As cunning as she had proven to be in the past, Renata would have to coax it out of her, not confront her as was her want.

Opening the door to the apartment, just as she predicted, her mother rocking, her attention on the lane below so she would have known Renata was on her way up. "Good morning, Mother. How are you doing?" She hung her wrap and set her reticule on the shelf.

Louisa cast an ominous look on her daughter. "Come to see the old feeble woman?"

Lea walked into the parlor. Her ever-present shawl covering her hair, arms folded across her front. She leaned against the wall her face unreadable.

Louisa barked, "My legs are cold."

Renata waited for Lea to tuck the blanket over her mother's legs. "Are you getting out at all?"

Louisa picked at a smudge on the blanket. "It's hard when she…" nodding toward Lea who had gone back to the corner of the room "…doesn't feel comfortable with the skittery Irish language."

"The weather is quite agreeable this morning. We could go for a walk?" She sat in the chair closest to her mother.

Louisa's disgruntled manner spread to her voice, "I don't feel like going out."

"Shall I make tea? I brought a basket of your favorites poppyseed."

Lea straightened and murmured something as she swiveled back to whatever she was doing down the hall. Renata was glad she left the room. The maid held an influence upon her mother that irritated her; though she readily considered it could be her own bias. Lea hiding her understanding of English was another matter. It was calculated and intended.

"Poppyseed is my favorite."

Renata placed the basket on her mother's lap. Her gnarled fingers pulled back the covering over the white, crusted delights. Besides poppyseed, she knew chocolate shavings and nuts were another favorite. Louisa wasn't disappointed. A soft *aah* of delight, and she plucked one taking a bite.

Renata watched her as she reached for a second biscuit and decided to make tea after all. The kettle blew steam, her mother ate a third biscuit, and Lea had not peeked into the parlor. Settling the tray with a steeping pot and two cups on the low table, Renata asked, "Is it possible for us to be friendly?"

Savoring her biscuit, Louisa didn't answer right away. Swallowing the bits, she finally said, "You want to move back, is that it? That *man* finished with you?"

Renata forced herself not to react to the insult.

Of a sudden Louisa hauled her bulk out of the rocker and stepped toward Renata, shocking her.

Instant rage colored her mother's face, the basket of remaining biscuits scattered over the floorboards. She pushed a finger into her daughter's chest, crumbs flying with her words. "It's all about that man isn't it? You ignorant fool."

Sweat broke out on Louisa's face. She appeared irritated, out of control.

Frustrated, Renata breathed deeply, searching for calm to talk to her parent. "I'm here because I need the truth. Why did you allow me to believe I was the child you carried when you left Carrick and returned to Portugal?"

Narrowed slits accompanied her answer, "Think you've figured it out, have you?"

"Are you telling me I was that child?"

Louisa retreated to her rocker and plunged into it, setting it in motion. "Worried you've had your legs wrapped around a brother, are you?"

Her mother's vulgarity stung her to the core. She leapt from the chair, flew to the door, hand on her wrap, overwhelmed by the possibility they were siblings. Shattered by the pain of it.

Yet her mother had lied before, and her only hope was she lied now. Who was this woman? When did she become so dreadfully bitter? Why hadn't this side of her mother sickened her before now? Deep inside she knew the difference. It was personal now. And her beloved father was gone, he had always smoothed out the roughness between the two of them.

The truth had to come out—it held the power to change her life forevermore.

Gathering some sense, she spun back to the room. Her mother rocked to and fro, a wicked smile on her lined face. Was she deranged? Renata's stomach lurched with anxiety.

It wasn't just Ian who hated Morgan Curran. She was beginning to think her mother hated him, too. Was it because he banished the spoils of his infidelity when he discovered she was increasing with his child? If she, Renata, was Morgan's daughter, why would her mother hate him? If she wasn't, why was her mother so bitter?

Louisa nodded toward the shelf where the urn had set since their arrival from Portugal. "You took his ashes."

"Your adultery no longer gave you the right to him."

Sarcasm twisted with her mother's words, "I wondered why I felt better. Like a black cloud lifted. Good riddance I say." The tone of her mother's voice shriveled the skin on Renata's arms.

Wanting answers, she forced herself to sink back into the chair, and in as calm a voice as she could muster asked, "If I am Morgan's daughter, why not just tell me outright? Why all this hinting and game playing?"

Her mother's face blotched with anger. "You think you can love *that man* and scorn me for my love of his father?"

Renata glanced at the empty space on the shelf, no longer able to abide her mother's mottled features and the sarcastic slant of her mouth. "How can you compare an adulterous relationship and a relationship between two single people? Where is the justification?"

Did this all come down to...jealousy? Disgusted, she could hardly look at her parent. "Answer me, did you lie about my birth date or did you not?"

Renata hoped for a flicker of truth and fastened on her mother for a reaction, desperate to discover something. Her future depended on believing what this woman had to say.

It was a long moment that grew to minutes. She distinctly heard the word *bitch* muttered in Portuguese. Lea had been around the corner this whole time with her ear to this unbelievable discourse. Whatever her mother's answer, one thing she knew— Christopher would care about her forever. Wife or not, he would care. Renata firmed the decision to stay in Hawthorn no matter the outcome of this discourse. Her father brought her here, and here she would stay. Calm and fearless in the face of her mother's bitterness she waited.

First came a deep sigh, then her mother's voice, low with a

hint of resignation. "It was a troubled carrying from the beginning. A woman aboard the ship warned me others miscarried with the same spotting and cramping I experienced. Within the week, I lost his child, the only thing I had of him, and I lost it." The memories dredged from the past brought a sorrow to her voice. She didn't have long to wait when her mother began again, "Months later I allowed your father into my bed and you were conceived."

Renata sat on the edge of her chair with hands clasped in her lap. "I've known you to be a liar. How can you expect me to trust you after deliberately allowing me to believe I was the child you carried when you left Carrick-On-Suir?"

"I knew what you were about when you asked. I saw what was happening between you and *that* man. I had the power to keep you apart and I used it." Shrugging her shoulders, her features melted into a wicked smile. "You're not as smart and clever as you think you are."

Renata didn't know whether to believe her now or not. She was deliberately evasive. Her whole life with this woman had been disordered, and anxious. A jumble of emotional outbursts at any given moment over trifles was a common occurrence.

Her mother set the rocker in motion, and casually mentioned, "I gave birth to you and banished your father from my bed forevermore." The words slipped out of her as if she had just asked for a cup of tea. Devoid of emotion, not unlike ewes that can forget within seconds of birthing their lambs and need to be taught to care for them. Her mother was no better.

A screech and a whirlwind of skirt and veil bounded around the corner of the hall. Lea threw herself at Louisa's feet, sobbing, clawing at the woman's skirt, crying out, "I am yours It is me. I am yours. You told me."

Louisa's arthritic hand soothed Lea's bowed head. She whispered endearments, proclaiming nothing would change. Her love was forever.

Though she suspected Lea knew English, it still came as a shock. Her mother cast her a mean glare as if to say *look what you've caused,* and then began hushing Lea, promising her treats if she calmed.

The three of them spent a month aboard a sailing vessel, and Renata had never witnessed anything like this. Certainly never in their home either.

Her mother's arms wrapped about the sobbing Lea. She stood, and the two of them walked toward the hall, her arm about Lea's slender frame. "Hush, child. It's going to be better now. Hush, sweet girl. You *are* mine forevermore."

Her mother returned to the parlor some minutes later and sank in the rocker.

Renata waited for some clarification, desperate to believe what she said about her birth date was the truth.

As if in apology, Louisa admitted, "She needs me. I am all she has. I alone can comfort her." Unmindful of the strewn biscuits, she mushed them with the rocker treads.

"You've led her to believe you are her mother."

A defining silence followed, Lea's muffled sobbing from the room down the hall and the rocker crushing the crumbs the only sounds. Stunned, Renata looked askance at her mother, waiting.

Her mother's head bowed as she looked at her knotty hands, tears trailing down her leathered face. "You were your father's child, never mine. We were…we are so different. I found Lea in an orphanage and brought her to live with us. She is grateful, loves me for it." She blew her nose on a cloth and continued, "She calms me, makes me feel beloved."

Somewhere deep inside, Renata might have already suspected. "Is she your child?"

Her mother didn't answer, nor did she raise her chin in acknowledgement.

Overwhelmed, Renata cringed. Her voice sounded tired as she spoke. "I remember you going away when I was eight. A hush fell over our houschold that was impenetrable. It lasted for months and then you suddenly appeared. Years later Lea was brought into our home to be a maid you could train, but she was so very young, and you played with her rather than show her how to become a servant."

Her mother shrugged but said nothing. She had no need. It all made sense that Lea was her daughter. The girl fit perfectly into the mold of her mother's needs.

Renata had understood at an early age the entire household soothed the frazzled Mrs. Fitzjames, always leapt to her demands. With great relief, the young girl, Lea, and her wondrous ability to calm their mistress, was eagerly welcomed.

Glancing at her mother's bowed head, the push of her shoes off the floor to keep it in motion, Renata didn't begrudge her mother someone who doted on her. For as long as she could remember her mother was self-absorbed, always exhibiting a desire for her personal comfort.

Clearing the speculation about her own parentage was a relief. Renata wasn't crushed realizing she had been replaced or rejected. That had slowly occurred through the years, unlike a sudden slamming of the door.

She said, "Thank you for telling me the truth of my birth."

With a sardonic cough, her mother said, "You wouldn't want to go against the laws of incest now, would you?"

That remark hurt, but Renata held her feelings close. If she clung to anything in this moment, it was that she and Christopher were not siblings.

"I know what goes on between the two of you. Doesn't surprise me. It's the Irish in you, like your father you are." She fiddled with her handkerchief twisting it. "I must go home. I can't stand it here. Lea begs me to leave, and I won't deny her anything. I've already looked into passage."

Biting back a woeful sinking in her heart, once again Renata wasn't surprised. "I'm happy for you and your maid. If you apprise me of the date you sail, I'll be there." She stood up, picked up the fallen basket she'd borrowed from the shop, leaned over and kissed her mother on the cheek. "If you need anything, I'm staying at the apothecary shop."

With that said, Renata slipped into her wrap, picked up her reticule and closed the door behind her.

For a moment in the dark hallway outside her mother's apartment, with the aroma of bay leaf and rosemary, the unmistakable scent of lamb stew filled the corridor, she braced herself against the wall and took a deep breath. Her heart felt bruised. It remained doubtful if her mother would send for her before she sailed.

29

A day without rain, but February was fickle, and low dark clouds sailed across the horizon. Christopher leaned against the rented chaise. A coachman tended to the horse as he waited for Renata to leave her mother's apartment. He assumed it might not go well and wanted to be supportive. As she stepped down from the building's outer stair, her ashen face melted his heart. The moment she noticed him her pace quickened.

He met her halfway in the lane. "Bad was it?" Guiding her to the chaise, he opened the door. When she took one last glance at the upper window, she caught her mother's image, Lea soothing her face, kissing her cheek.

Christopher assisted her inside reaching for her hand as he settled into the space next to her. "Speak to me."

She was still, her voice barely above a whisper. "I hardly know where to begin."

He knocked on the separation for the driver to move out along the lough toward Waterford, then placed his right arm along the back of the horsehair bench and gave her all his attention.

She kept her gaze on the passing countryside. Her rigid demeanor softened as the chaise gently rolled. His worry churning, he held himself in check. She gave him a watery smile and placed her hand over his. It was enough for the moment.

A few minutes of the cloudy, peaceful countryside, Renata let out a sigh. "It appears my birth date is correct, which is wonderful news for us. However, in the ensuing conversation, I discovered my mother replaced her affection for me quite a few years ago. Apparently, I was too mindless to understand that she had."

He bent close to better hear her soft tones. His hand fell to her shoulder. He wanted to soothe away her downheartedness. Lethargy was not in Renata's character. She was one of the most alive and exciting women he'd ever encountered. Witnessing her dejection rattled him.

"I'm here for you. After all, *macushla*, I just heard the best news—you are to be my wife."

She cast him a weak, watery gaze, and reached for his hand.

Darker clouds gathered in the west perhaps filled with rain. It was cold enough to have sleet. The magnificence of Rockmore Hall and its beautiful hilly park loomed up as the carriage gently rolled in the direction of Waterford. "How did you know?"

"An unfortunate guess. The little I do know of your mother led me to believe the visit would not end well." His arm curled around her shoulder encircling her in a hug. "I assured myself you have strength to rise above the nettles." He tipped his chin glancing at her. "Besides, we've not been out together for a while now, and I miss you."

❦

"My mother admitted to miscarrying during their sail to Portugal. Months later she and my father reconciled. It was then I was conceived. You would think that alone would be wonderful news, wouldn't you?"

"I suspect you've more to tell?" His voice was low and soft like a caress.

"She accused me of favoring my father over her." The carriage lurched and his hand curled around her arm. She continued, "She's leaving, has never taken to Ireland from the moment they began married life here. Then there is the maid who begs her to leave. She's already looked into passage."

"How do you feel about that?"

"Troubled. She is my mother; I am her only child. Well, that's not quite clear. I believe Lea to be a love child of hers, born when I was eight and brought into our home as a maid for her to train when she was about five."

Christopher gently turned her in his arms. The comfort of his warmth and attention loosened her sadness. She wept for all the years that were wasted and for her father who, with great dignity, lived with a woman who did not love him.

Christopher slipped a kerchief between her fingers. The roll of the carriage and the cradle of his embrace were comforting.

He whispered *macushla* again. She had never been called my darling and felt cherished. It almost erased her mother calling Lea *sweet girl*.

Christopher lifted her face and kissed away tears. "You are a salty one." Brushing his lips across her cheek, he said, "Hmm, tasty."

She quirked and bubbled wiping her cheeks with his kerchief, then blew her nose. "I love you. Yes, I will marry you."

He drew both arms about her, kissing her forehead. "It's a good thing I didn't hold my breath, I'd be keeled over by now since it was yesterday, I asked."

◌⋙◌

Three days later, Christopher sat at his desk having just sent off a letter to his sister, informing her of his betrothal to Renata. And that they would be arriving with Dino next week, Monday.

A knock on the infirmary door brought him to his feet.

"Mr. Curran? Mr. Curran, are you here?" He knew that voice and wondered why he was so blest. Almost wishing he had a back door in his office, he opened his door and stepped into the hall.

The woman thumped her umbrella on the floor and ready to shout out once more before realizing the doctor had appeared.

"Mrs. Fitzjames, what can I do for you?" He stood in the doorway of his office. Should he invite her in or was she simply to drop some of her acidic comments and leave?

Her chin at a haughty angle, she inquired, "I hope you are alone, and we can indulge in a chat."

Extending his arm, he allowed her into his office and closed the door as she took a seat directly across from his desk. "I take it, this isn't about an ailment of yours?"

"I am fairly certain my daughter has amused you with our conversation of several days ago." At his nod, she continued, "She wouldn't have kept her mouth shut, especially with you."

"Your point is what, Mrs. Fitzjames?"

She rearranged the closed parasol in her other hand. "I am leaving this miserable place. We travel on the morning tide. The *Lisboa Lady* is anchored on the Suir. Renata asked if I would so inform her."

"Then why are you here and not at the apothecary's shop?" He leaned forward, arms across his desk. She was a puzzlement with all her fury and indirect innuendos.

Shifting in the chair, she mumbled something he didn't catch.

"Is there something I can do for you, then, Mrs. Fitzjames?"

He distinctly heard her foot tapping the floor. She was nervous. His usual reaction would be to put a person at ease, but this woman didn't deserve empathy. Instead, he waited for her to come to whatever fitful decision with which she warred.

She stared at the wall behind him, saying, "I never wanted to come here. A lot of bad memories for me. Tomorrow cannot come quick enough. I may owe you an apology and I've come to give you one if it is so."

"I can't think why you would have need to apologize to me. What I do know is, Renata deserves a sincere expression of regret from you." He wanted to say much more, but bit back the urge. He was deferring to a self-indulgent woman, allowing her to get to the place in her heart where he hoped she could do right by her daughter.

Mrs. Fitzjames fiddled with the strap on her parasol, then rearranged her skirts before finally speaking. "I don't want to leave without a goodbye between Renata and me. In all probability, we may never see each other again."

He let out a long slow sigh. "She will be grateful you wish to say goodbye. Renata is suffering from your last encounter. Shall I take you to her?"

She stood so fast considering her girth, he was taken by surprise. "It will be enough that she come to the quay in Waterford. I look forward to saying farewell to her there." Gathering up her reticule and parasol, she made to go. "I don't like scenes. They drain me."

The memory of his broken-hearted darling sobbing in his arms after the encounter with this woman still bothered him. To think a mother could disregard her daughter's aching heart bothered him greatly. It was all he could do to be civil. "I'll pass on your invitation."

"That should suffice." As she shuffled out, the point of her parasol thumped into the floor.

❧

Just before the first hint of dusk, Christopher and Renata strolled Stephen's Lane. Two feathers on her blue felt hat stirred in the light breeze, a matching shawl about her shoulders.

"You look quite fetching. What is the occasion?" Her arm twined with his.

"Most likely peace of mind. My world is righting."

"I intended we dine at Cashel's, but heard they closed against the public. Something to do with a cart load of family descending on them. How do you feel about the Black Pig?"

317

She teased, "You'll take me to a place where you are not comfortable?"

"Carnahan's and Mulroney's fund-raising and the party made me realize I had to become a regular, until then I was a fellow passing through. Besides, lass, I want to show you off as my prize. I'm a lucky man after all. But, I've something to tell and wish to get it out of the way before we get where we might be overheard. Your mother paid me a visit this afternoon. She leaves for Portugal in the morning and would welcome you to the quay in Waterford for her sendoff."

Renata stopped walking and looked up at him. "Really?"

He noted the delicate contours of her face and the wonder of the unexpected. Whatever was going on in her heart, he prayed she could accept the inevitable departure of her parent.

Renata's voice was guarded. "She chose the quay because it's public. She wants a formal parting, no scenes."

"She did admit they drain her."

"It's not in her to think of how they drain others as well."

Continuing on toward the Black Pig, scuttling north on Stoney Batter, he said, "I'll arrange for the carriage and pick you up about seven. That should give us plenty of time to arrive before the *Lisboa Lady* sails."

The next morning, the sky looked pleasant with bits of sun peeking through a few dark clouds. Dino was off to school, and for once Krysta had shown up early enough to put breakfast on the table before he left.

She whistled the while she fussed, and Christopher considered Darby was correct in thinking she and Asia were marrying.

It took the better part of an hour for Christopher and Renata to arrive in Waterford. They left the vehicle with the coachman. Her arm through Christopher's they made their way on the crowded pavers slippery from the morning fog. Empty donkey-drawn carts awaited the unloading of the vessels in the Suir.

People milled about, setting up vendor carts and hawking their wares in the misty, damp morning. They strode toward several folks muddled in conversation, then came upon a tea parlor and through the window found her mother and Lea at a table for two.

❦

Renata looked dismayed. He coaxed, "Put a happy face on it. You'll never regret these next few minutes with her. Perhaps you can put some sunshine in her heart. She is conflicted. I don't think she understands how hurtfully she affects others."

She heartened. "You are too good for me."

"You could be right." He grinned. "But we'll figure ourselves out."

He'd put a smile on her face easing her constitution for the minutes ahead.

As they entered, Lea shot up from the table and hastily retreated to the back of the shop. She stood in a corner, arms crossed, a grimace on her pouty features.

Renata approached her mother, touching her shoulder. "Thank you for letting me know of your departure, though I'm surprised at the quickness of finding passage."

Louisa patted a napkin to her mouth. "I mentioned I'd been planning, didn't I?"

Renata nodded. She had no desire to begin a contest of wills.

"I couldn't go without at least making you aware." Her mother rattled the cup in the saucer as she set it down.

"May I sit?"

"We haven't much time, the dray will be coming."

"I won't stay long."

Her mother shrugged and bit into a light-brown scone. Some crumbs dribbling onto her bodice.

Renata looked at her parent, trying to put this parting someplace in her heart to recall as a fond goodbye, certainly without a grand display of emotion. "You must be excited to finally go home?"

With a mouth full of her treat, all her mother could do was nod.

"Have you any thoughts on Father's ashes?" Renata asked.

Washing the scone down with tea, she cleared her throat and in a hearty voice said, "Throw them in the gutter, or down a drain. He forced you to make a promise to bury him next to Morgan Curran. He used you to carry out his vengeance against me. I no longer care about any of it. I told you the truth after all these years, and all I want to do is leave this godforsaken island and go home." She nodded to the back of the restaurant. "That poor girl is beside herself with misery. She cries all night long."

Renata suddenly realized that Lea was the single person on earth who could draw her mother's attention off herself. She smiled, and ignoring her mother's last remark, said, "I'll write to you what I decide." Renata clenched her reticule. "Mother, I'm sorry. For everything."

Louisa's eyes were so dark they reflected like mirrors, with deep wrinkled corners and grayed lashes. She stared at her daughter. "Do what you want. I don't care about that jar or its contents. Morgan stole my heart long ago. Your father wasn't man enough to capture it."

Pain hit Renata like lightning. She suddenly understood that her mother would never change. She was excessively and exclusively concerned about herself. She was so filled with love of self, there simply wasn't room for anyone else in her heart, except perhaps for Lea.

Christopher was coming toward her, a twinkle in his eye, and a smile. Her lifeline.

He put a protective hand on her back as if guarding her. She forced herself to meet her mother's dark glare. "I pity you, Mother. Your hateful moods became a great burden for those who would have loved you."

She twisted inside Christopher's arm, and he bent over her, asking, "Are you all right?"

She whispered, "I'm fine."

Christopher guided her away from her mother as the fog thinned.

The sun slowly brightened the morning. Her heart thrummed, and she took a deep breath. Christopher's hand rubbed over hers where it rested on his arm.

"If you've no other plans for the next few hours, I know of a scenic drive along the road to Portlow? We'll follow the Suir upriver and pass Rockmore Hall. Further upriver there's an old castle, most call it dark castle—rumored to be haunted—and further on another old castle built by the Normans that was remade into a convent. Sacred Heart Convent a refuge for Catholic nuns."

After handing Renata into the waiting carriage, he sat next to her and informed her, "This road will take us past the convent where Lady Tremaine spent her first seventeen years before Lord Darnley knew she even existed."

"Diverting me, are you?" She gave him a sly glance from beneath lowered lids.

His grin was apparent though his gaze was directed out the window as they passed the west end of Waterford. "Not nearly so far up as the convent there is a haunted castle, dark and dreary, bats in the tower, moss everywhere."

She joined in the mood he was attempting to create. "Moss, hmm, I could take some samples if I had tools with me."

"Never fear, miss. I try not to leave the office without my bag. I'm sure I have what you might need to scrape up this or that."

"I can't think of anything more exciting than scraping moss from a rock at dark castle."

He shook his head and ran a hand through his hair. "Ironically, I believe you."

She squeezed his hand.

The carriage passed Rockmore Hall off in the east. The copper tip of the dome twinkled in the sunlight. The Palladian front boasted eight columns. "This is where the Tremaines call home."

"Most of the trees were taken down in the storm, otherwise it would show to even greater advantage." With a finger under her chin, he raised it so she would look at him. "I've one more surprise." His eyes rolled to the back of the conveyance.

A basket filled with goodies and a blanket. "You've brought a picnic and it's February."

"I considered that, and we can indulge in the carriage, or take it into the cold, damp castle where moss and bats linger. Your choice, my love. I'm here to make your day brighter."

She laughed at his absurd plan. "Damp castles, bats and a picnic basket. Hmm. I'm delighted with the prospect of spending the entire day with you." She grabbed his lapels drawing him near, and just before kissing him, said, "You are exactly what I need."

Several days later, Christopher, Renata and Dino were on their way to Carrick-on-Suir to visit his sister, Rose, and her family in the home where Christopher had been raised. They set out early in the morning with expectations of arriving in time for a late supper.

Full of enthusiasm for his very first carriage ride, Dino could hardly contain himself when the coachman rolled up in front of the infirmary and began roping their bags on the back. His first question was predictable, "Can I ride on top with the driver?"

It almost pained Christopher to deny him, but common sense prevailed. "You might divert the driver's attention, and once the carriage moves, it will prove to be bitter cold. I would feel much better if you were inside with us."

The lad jumped into the interior and took his place next to the window, Renata and Christopher opposite. Dino appeared content waving at neighbors in the lane as they passed. With at least five hours of riding and a post stop before reaching Lillybrook, they settled in for the journey.

It was near nightfall when their carriage drew up a long narrow road lined with oaks to a Georgian structure of pinkish brick, three stories, and smoke curling from several chimneys. Surrounded by a lovely park and old stately trees, Renata was enthralled.

"What a grand home to grow up in." As she said this, Dino pulled his eyes from the book he was reading and glanced at the estate.

"It's big. Did you ever get lost?" He had twisted around in the seat to get a better view as they approached.

Christopher tousled Dino's hair. "I knew every nook and cranny early on. Lots of hiding places. I'm sure my nieces and nephews will show you every one of them." His gaze fixed on the structure, his thoughts on the past.

"Did Morgan build it?" Renata asked.

"No. The part he added can't be viewed from this perspective. That would be the four acres of walled gardens behind the manse filled with exotic fruits, figs, nectarines, and such. My parents called it Lillybrook because they also filled the garden with lilies near a brook running through part of the land. My mother's favorite flower."

They were greeted by a small crowd gathered in the front. Dino fixated on the group of children about his own height.

Their arrival ended any sense of dignity when the children, Lucille, Mary, Morgan, and Ella, encountered Dino. Christopher loved the onslaught of hugs and kisses; though he had to admit, the children were far more interested in Dino than either he or Renata.

As the eldest son, Morgan stated rather firmly to Dino, "We are six in number, but Norman can't walk or talk yet, so he's in the nursery. We've instructions to take you to the classroom. Nanny Patricia allowed us to bring you up. We've been on lookout from our schoolroom window."

Dino's eyes glinted and he eagerly looked to Christopher for permission. "Go, enjoy. But watch out for Morgan, he plays tricks."

The moment they headed up the stairs Christopher could hear Lucille say, "We dine in the nursery. You will eat with us. I'll introduce you to Nanny Patricia. She is going to let you sit with us during lessons as long as you are here."

"I missed school today," Dino replied.

Lucille, the eldest said, "You might wish you were back in Hawthorn when Nanny Patricia gets done with her lessons."

Lucille struck Christopher as a little Rose, organized and ready to answer most any question. He chuckled to himself, anticipating that Dino was going to enjoy the visit very much.

Renata was quite taken with the *en masse* greeting—children, adults, footmen, the butler. Rose took her by the arm and escorted her into the marbled and mahogany paneled foyer. Footmen disappeared with their bags. She caught the tag end of children scampering up a sweeping staircase to the classroom.

She felt an immediate camaraderie with Rose, who was almost the same stature as she. Though Rose's blue eyes, light brown hair, and lovely, unblemished, silky white skin was so different from hers.

Rose said, "It's been a long time coming in my brother's life. He's finally brought home someone he feels special about." Rose's warm greeting eased her. She hadn't realized how tense she'd been.

James, quite handsome and with an engaging smile, was dressed in a green plaid kilt. He reached out a hand to Renata. "Welcome to our confusion, Miss Fitzjames. I am truly pleased to make your acquaintance." James nodded in Christopher's direction. "We've waited a *longgggg* time for this."

Christopher cocked a brow at his brother-in-law. "Really?"

Rose patted a green silk settee and Renata joined her. Christopher said, "Oh, oh. The moment I dreaded, filling Renata's ears with my past."

His brother-in-law, chuckled, "The heat's off me with your arrival. I will enjoy myself now she's targeting you."

As it was way past tea, James served something stiffer to Christopher and the two men wandered over by the large bank of windows overlooking the rear of the home. The dark clouds had taken over the sky. An angry wet system was encroaching.

The women enjoyed a cherry cordial. Rose asked Renata if she was tired from the carriage ride.

"Not at all. It was enjoyable. My mother and I arrived in Hawthorn Village early last summer and I've not had an opportunity to travel until now."

"Is your mother still in Hawthorn, then?"

"She sailed for Portugal several days ago."

Rose's voice filled with sympathy. "Has her leaving left you in despair?" She suddenly fluttered her hands. "I'm far too nosy, forgive me."

Renata said, "No. I don't mind. We've always had a difficult time of it. She's doing what she must."

"Well, then, I won't concern myself on that point." She sipped her cordial then said, "Supper will be the four of us. We dine within the hour. There is no need to change unless you would be more comfortable."

Rose was delightful and thought of everything and everyone. Renata agreed, "Considering the lateness of our arrival, I'm fine, thank you."

Supper was roasted goose with potato stuffing, large slices of smoked ham, green beans soaking in a wine sauce and sour-dough bread.

The sweet wine, candles flickering, beautiful landscapes of the surrounding area brightening the walls, and a home filled with family—no wonder Christopher was eager to arrive. Merry chatter filled with stories of their history made Renata feel as if she stepped into a family that she had been a part of all her life.

Though Renata knew the strife that had gone on within these walls long ago, obviously James and Rose had put their stamp on this generation. The four chatted in a most merry way.

With the tug of friendship and acceptance, she marveled how her life had changed and would continue to do so, all because of Christopher; her warm, intelligent, and very capable man, who for some blessed reason wanted to share the rest of his life with her.

C hristopher placed his empty goblet on the linen, clasped Renata's hand, and clanked his fork against the crystal. "Announcement time—we have come for two reasons. This adventurous, warm and brilliant woman has consented to become my wife."

Rose beamed. "I had hoped."

James' brisk rolling Rs thickly accentuated his rebuke, "You're rather blunt...no preamble, simply laid it out on the table like a sack of coal."

"I've no practice as to how it's done." Christopher's delight at catching them off guard glowed in the twinkle in his eyes.

His dear sister said, "I congratulate you, dear brother, on this lovey lady's acceptance."

James finished his wine, patted his mouth with a napkin, and said, "I'd a notion the minute I saw her." His glance slid to Renata. "You are sure? He's not got you beguiled?"

"He charmed me, won me over." She cupped Christopher's chin. "I'm happier than I could ever have imagined."

Rose inquired. "Did your visit a month ago clearing up some history have anything to do with this decision?"

Christopher eased back into his chair, toyed with the stem of his goblet. "We were under the delusion we were half siblings. The not knowing was devastating."

Renata reached over, slipped her hand in his. "It was horrid. The hopelessness of what we knew, and my mother didn't help the situation a'tall." She glanced downward, sighing. "It's in the past now, but she wasn't truthful, led us to believe I was the child she carried when she and my father left for Portugal."

Rose asked, "Were you able to make peace with her?"

"I didn't realize the guilt I carried for her unhappiness. Though I knew on some level it wasn't my doing. She is happy to be going back to Obidos. And—" turning to her beloved said, "—I am thrilled for our future to unfold."

Christopher squeezed her hand in comfort.

James said, "Life has its lessons for each of us. Your mother needed to be the center of everything and forgot she needed to be a nurturer. I suspect your father took over that role."

Rose giggled. "At the moment he is reading a paper on applied analysis of behaviors."

Christopher jumped in, "Allow the man his interests, Rose. He's always been deep into scientific studies of behavior." He glanced at his brother-in-law. "Take it easy on us. We've had a harrowing week."

James returned a fraternal glance at his brother-in-law and winked as he drew on his wine.

Christopher said, "There's something else needs an explanation. Renata and her mother came to Ireland to honor her father's dying wish." He glanced at Renata who had grown quiet, "Do you wish to tell them?"

Rose and James turned surprised glances at her as Christopher took up his glass and sipped. Renata said, "Ian, my father, hated Morgan for building a road and putting a toll on it. He said it ruined his business. This was before my mother had her affair with Morgan.

"I'm not sure, but I think, initially, my mother's intent confronting Morgan was to talk him out of the toll. Perhaps their involvement began then. She admitted to me of an affair and she got with child. And, certain it was Morgan's as apparently my parents had been separated." Renata, quite unlike herself suddenly had the need to gulp down rising emotion. "Sorry."

Puffing out a long breath, she began again, "My mother shifted her attention to Morgan. As you know she was carrying his child. They did return to Portugal. And she miscarried during the sail. It was some months later she warmed toward my father, and then according to my mother, I was conceived.

"I knew nothing of my mother's adultery. I only knew my father's outrage over the road and the toll subsequently blaming Morgan for the loss of his business. He obviously knew the child she carried hadn't been his. But he never shared that with me. I was quite close to my father. He extracted a promise before he passed last year to bury his ashes as close as possible to Morgan's burial site so he could bedevil him throughout eternity."

James slammed his palm onto the table causing the silverware to dance on the linen. "I'll be double damned. Sign me up, give me a shovel."

Rose's scathing glance fixed on her husband, and with a rising pitch in her voice asked Renata, "And your mother is aware of this, and welcomes it?"

"She announced I could toss his ashes in a ditch for all she cared."

Christopher added, "Mrs. Fitzjames withheld information from Renata. It was only when faced with your letter of the fight on the front steps that the truth came out. Mrs. Fitzjames allowed Renata to think she was that child—"

"And you believed you were brother and sister," asked Rose.

"Exactly," nodded Christopher. "Bless you for keeping a diary, or we wouldn't be here today announcing our forthcoming marriage."

Silence fell over the foursome, until James admitted, "Count me in to assist in any way to achieve his wish, Renata. I for one, enjoy the image of someone settling the score after all the ways

Morgan distressed and tormented, not just your father, but others as well."

Christopher was left with the notion James was one of Morgan's victims, but he would leave that herring untouched.

James asked, "I'm curious where your father is at the moment, Renata?"

"What!" Poor Rose swiveled from one catastrophe to another. Her palm drifted from her face to her bosom.

"His remains are in a jar, Rose," said her brother.

"Oh, thank the Almighty," she whispered, fanning her face. "I thought…well, no matter what I thought."

James offered, "I'll grant that Morgan loved his children. I think he loved his wife in some fashion. But his ethics were not in line with his family life. Watch out if you ever wanted to cross him, you'd the devil to pay. I kept my distance in our early years together. No need ruffling my father-in-law."

Rose answered her brother's earlier question. "You were at prep during the time our father caused so much upset in the household. You were spared."

"Sorry you had to lean on Molly. She kept to herself so much, she might not have been a comfort."

"I believe we are better friends today than we were as children. She's quite content with Aunt Mildred, who still runs her household at ninety-three with little help from Molly."

This exchange gave Renata a sense she was among family. She *was* more her father's daughter than her mother's. The larger picture of being here in Ireland quickened her mind, spoke to her of home.

Christopher changed the subject asking James, "I'm curious, are you familiar with the procedure for burying someone?"

As a footman removed an empty plate, James leaned in. "If we bury him next to Morgan, I should think we won't need anyone's approval. The plot belongs to the Curran family. You remember, his memorial is surrounded by a patch of land with a wrought-iron fence. I think we need go one late night and dig up a section and bury the jar." He glanced at the women, "What say you both?"

"If we own the plot, why do you have to sneak around?" Rose, too, leaned in, clasping her hands on the linen and whispering should the servants eavesdrop.

"Reverend Holland lives behind the church, adjacent to the graveyard. Is he going to allow us to dig a hole and put a jar in the ground, Curran ownership or not? He's a pain...excuse me. He riles me with his nonsense. I think it would be easier to go in at night, dig the hole, say a dignified prayer, cover the hole up and be on our way. No fuss."

Rose declared, "You won't see me prowling a cemetery late at night, not for any reason." She glanced across the table at Renata. "Sorry, I simply can't be a party to this."

Renata said, "I share your sentiments. If he wasn't my father, I wouldn't consider traipsing through a cemetery at night either."

James piped up, "Will you require a headstone? Because that may change things a bit."

"Absolutely not." Renata stated. "We already etched a memory of him on the wall inside the vestibule of our church in Obidos, with the understanding we would carry him back to Ireland."

"We've come prepared to spend a few nights with you," said Christopher, "so you name the night, James."

"Tomorrow night. It promises to be somewhat cloudy which will work to our advantage." Because of his big grin, and rubbing his hands together, it was easy to catch James' enthusiasm for such a nefarious foray.

The next morning, refreshed from a good night's sleep irrespective of the horrendous lightning and roll of thunder, Christopher met up with Renata, Rose, and James at breakfast.

"Such a brute force last night. I'd forgotten how fierce they can be in Carrick."

James responded, "Not like in Hawthorn? How's that? We experienced the tail end of a horrendous beating back in August. Surely you must have sustained some damage?"

"My guess would be Carrick sits on the Suir where Hawthorn is shielded by Waterford to some degree. Or, it could be I'm so used to them in the village, I just don't notice anymore. We had one death in August, when the chimney caved in on the poor bugger. We also survived a list of injuries, roofs torn off, and sodden filth everywhere."

"I think you probably didn't have a moment to yourself," Rose piped in before taking a bite of toast.

Christopher clasped his hand to Renata's. "It actually afforded us an opportunity to discover one another after a rather disastrous first meeting. She was a volunteer during the crisis." Gently, he pushed a lock of her dark hair fallen from its pin behind her ear, receiving a beautiful smile for his effort. "You look rested, I'm glad."

Conversation blended to plans James had for Christopher. The men were going to look over a building he was interested in purchasing as an investment. He wanted Christopher's opinion.

Today was Rose's day to deliver baskets of food to the ward in their village. She invited Renata to join her.

With an hour before Rose planned to leave, Renata visited the schoolroom eager to see how Dino was getting on. She peeked in before entering, Dino sat between Lucille and Morgan fully engaged in a lesson on geography.

Her gentle knock drew all the children's attention from Nanny Patricia and her pointer on a map of South Africa.

The eldest, Lucille, got up from her chair. "Did you miss Dino at breakfast? Our meals are brought up to the nursery. Mother thinks we can be unruly at times." Obviously, Lucille was a chatterbox.

"I overheard you yesterday say your meals were taken in the school room." Renata glanced at Dino. "I wish to see how our lad is doing." She cast a smile his way.

Dino exalted, "Nanny Patricia is a lot nicer than Master Carleton."

Morgan poked him from behind. "Currying favor, are you? It won't work on Nanny Patricia."

Nanny spoke up, "Morgan, I heard that. Mind your manners young man."

Renata leaned over Dino's shoulder. He was attempting to draw the map of South Africa.

Lucille held her palms together. "We love to play games if you want to join in later. We would enjoy having you. Nanny would say three o'clock in the playroom." Renata's gaze swept over the children, settling on the youngest, Ella, who jumped up and down.

"Your mother has invited me to assist in her charity work, but if time permits, I intend to visit you later."

Nanny gave them permission to escort Miss Fitzjames down the hall. Ella, who appeared to be about four, slipped her hand into Renata's as they made their way to the top of the staircase and watched as she descended. She heard their whispers and giggles and was delighted to watch five sets of hands wave at her. A wide grin on Dino's face confirmed he had settled in quite nicely.

In the carriage with Rose, Renata said, "Dino is having quite the time with your delightful family. They all appear so grown up and quite serious about learning. How long has Nanny Patricia been teaching them?"

"Lucille was two, and Morgan just born, when she came to us about eleven years ago from a distant aunt of James who had passed. She'd been in the aunt's service for years and years. She's a jewel, the children love her."

"Dino gave her high praise."

"Christopher has always had a big heart. He told us how he took the boy in. Honestly, Renata, I am so happy for all of you. God has a hand in this, and you fit so perfectly into each other's lives." Rose gave her a long side-glance. "I wish you the happiness I have."

Renata felt a rush of thankfulness. "That means a great deal to me, Rose."

It was early afternoon and the adults convened at Lillybrook from their various excursions. Renata met Christopher on the stairs. He explained, "I was on my way to the nursery."

"The children would be overjoyed. But they are having lunch now, then a walk outdoors. Lucille, Morgan and Dino are joining us for the evening meal."

Christopher drew a finger along her cheek and across her lips. "Rose loosens the reins a bit when I'm around."

A flash of heat spread across her face, which she had trouble ignoring. "They...the children..."

He chuckled. "I want to kiss you."

She stepped back from him. "Someone could come upon us."

He reached for her hand and pressed his lips in her palm. "Now, what were you going to tell me?"

She lost her line of reasoning and took a moment to recall. "The children act as if we are near royalty invited for supper, Lucille and Mary were giggling over what dress to wear."

He placed her arm through his as they began to descend the stairs.

A sudden rush of three children, Lucille, Morgan and Dino sped up behind them.

"Whoa, there," barked Christopher. "What is this all about?"

"We're going on a treasure hunt. The first one who finds it gets to keep it."

"We won't stand in your way. One thing before you leave, what is the treasure and who hid it?"

Morgan flashed his uncle a grin. "This was Nanny's idea. She said it was something in a place where it shouldn't be, in the garden beyond the labyrinth."

"Well, get going then and good luck."

The trio scooted toward the kitchen and his attention fell to the woman with her hand on his arm. A beautiful warm-hearted woman. "I want to show you something, if you have a moment or two."

He led her into a paneled library. The drapes had been pushed back brightening the room considerably. "The portrait is of my father." He closed the heavy paneled door behind them. "I wanted you to see his likeness before we commit our deed tonight."

"Do you think he will rise up and chastise us, then?"

Christopher grinned. "Gad sakes, I hope not. I'd faint dead away."

"You look just like him, you know. Was he as tall as you?"

"We were quite similar in height. I think his shoulders were broader."

"You have the same regard. Though yours is kinder."

He drew his arm about her shoulders bringing her against him. "You have sweet thoughts, *macushla*." He drew her into his arms. His large hand on the back of her head drew her close.

⚜

On tiptoe, she leaned in, her arms reaching upward fingers threading his russet waves. The kiss deepened as every fiber of her being responded to him. Her pulse raced taking her breath, drawing her under the spell of his warmth and enduring security. She couldn't imagine life without him. The thought almost brought her to the brink of fear.

His warm breath brushed her cheek as he drew away and cradled her in his embrace. His rough voice whispered, "I love you."

Her eyes stung and she tightened her arms about his shoulders. "I couldn't bear to lose you."

His voice held surprise. "Why would you think you would?"

"I don't want us to end, ever. I hurt just thinking of it." Her arms tightened more firmly.

She could hear the smile in his voice as he said, "I'm not going anywhere without you, darling. You aren't the only one with a fear of loss."

If it weren't for their fathers, they wouldn't have met. She glanced again at the portrait hung high over the flickering fire, and thinking of her dear father whispered, "Thank you."

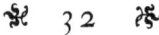

With James in the lead, Christopher and Renata skulked toward the graveyard. A chilly night and a light drizzle made their endeavor sloppy and vastly uncomfortable. A staggering conclusion was at hand for Renata.

Christopher hefted a shovel; James gripped a lantern to guide their steps. Renata tightly clung to the jar with her father's remains and walked between the two men.

James pointed to the old ruin of Ormond Castle its shape barely discernible against the dark sky. The Church of Ireland stood not far from the grounds of the old castle. The night was dark with cloud cover, but not cold enough to bring snow. Renata thought she heard bats.

James' burr, never more pronounced when he said, "Here we go." They strode up a short hill, the outline of tilting gravestones barely visible. It was like looking into the mouth of a giant ogre. "Good thing about the drizzle, most folks won't be about including Reverend Holland."

Renata hugged the jar against her breast, whispering thoughts of love and telling her father her promise would soon be fulfilled. Her mother's heart of stone reinforced Renata's determination.

Christopher placed his hand on her elbow. "Careful of the roots."

"If it weren't for my father's wish, I would be sitting by the fire with Rose finding out all about you as a young boy."

He chuckled. "Then I thank your father."

"Psst, psst." James held a finger to his lips and pointed at the church. The Reverend lit a globe, he's heard something.

The toe of Renata's boot caught on a root; Christopher's large hand steadied her.

James dimmed the lantern in hopes they wouldn't be observed. A definite sense their behavior was bordering on sinister caused Renata's skin to prickle.

Awed by the silhouette of Morgan's monument that must reach at least seven feet in the air, Renata chuckled at the thought of her father bedeviling the man.

James unlatched the lychgate. Metal scraping against metal rent the air, sending a flurry of some sort, probably bats, into the night, leaving only the whap of wings.

Christopher whispered to James, "Last time I saw that gate, it was festooned with wedding flowers for you and Rose."

"Really? Now?" James agitated voice shushed him. "Bugger mist, bats flapping, and God only knows what all, and you can recall that?" James shook his head and pointed to his left. "We'll dig over there." He placed the lantern on the ground about four feet from the monument. His voice low, he asked, "Is this close enough for eternal *deviltry*, Renata?"

She could have mustered a nervous laugh if their mission wasn't provoking. "Yes, it's perfect." Glancing about the area she noted another light in the reverend's home and wasn't sure *perfect* was the right word.

Hugging the jar of ashes, she realized she would live the rest of her life in Hawthorn and not so far from this spot. *Papa, I hope you know about my lovely Christopher. I have never been happier nor more content. I'm getting a young son, Dino, too. Thank you for insisting that I bring you back home where you belong. And, where I belong.*

Christopher hissed, "Who are you talking to?"

"My father. I'm telling him about you."

James whispered, "Ye'll give us away with your chatter, lass."

The sound of shovel to earth caused her to glance at Christopher. He bent to another plunge of shovel into the rain-soaked dirt, releasing the scent of wet moldy earth. Within minutes, he had dug a small hole twice the depth of the jar, and offered, "Would you like me to place it in?"

James shuttered the lantern, whispering. "Don't move. Someone, probably that dratted Holland, is looking through the window in this direction."

Renata fell to her knees, kissed the jar, and slid it into the hollow. Barely able to discern anything, her nose inches from the pit where she'd dropped her father, she shoved the loose muck into the hole. Then inched about on her knees and continued filling it until the ground felt even. She then placed what felt like a piece of sod on top, patting it down as best she could without raising her head and alerting the reverend.

James hushed, "He's moving away."

"Quick, get out." James added, "I fear he may be shuttering his light to better catch us."

Renata slipped on the muck, lost her balance, fell backward, and slid down the far side of the hill, biting her lips lest she cry out. She came to a stop against a rock and bushes. It was pitch black, except for the few stars far above. She could move her legs and arms. But she was practically upside down and couldn't manage leverage to get up. She was stuck.

Christopher's voice was low and cautious; she couldn't make out the words. He probably wondered where she'd got to.

James' whisper was filled with dire warning. "Don't move. He's come outside his door." Clouds drifted off the moon casting the graveyard in a pale luster, and his horse voice cracked, "Duck."

A minute passed. The rustle of leaves, several swooshes—probably bats. An owl objecting to their intrusion. The reverend made no move to come closer.

Finally, Christopher's frantic hushing, "Are you hurt?"

"No."

James whispered, "Shush. Blazes, he's walking toward the lynchgate."

Foul decay assaulted her. A creepy sensation ruffled her skin.

Dew dripped on her face from the branches. She must be in a bog, it felt like spongy moss beneath her head and shoulders. The earthy smell of decomposition, she hoped was not animal scat, or a dead animal. Perish the thought, she breathed through her mouth.

James murmured, "Damn and hell. He's right for us."

The owl hooted again. They were said to symbolize protection and wisdom. At this moment, she hoped that was true. Then she heard its wings flap as it took flight.

Not a sound from the men. The owl hooted once more. Something shuffled through the rotting floor of the woods near her head.

"Who goes there?"

That must be the reverend. She guessed he's practically on top Christopher and James. What a mess she's brought them to.

A nudge against her leg, a wet nose sniffing her skin where her skirt road up. It took every ounce of nerve to still a shriek. Terrified, she kicked her leg, and instantly heard the scampering of a small animal, several small animals to be exact.

"Your mischief isn't allowed here. Whoever you be, be gone." That must be the reverend. He'd not taken notice of the men, yet.

Then his voice changed. "Aha, foxes. Nothing for you to sniff at here. Scoot."

The air blew out of her. It must have been foxes scenting her, and she had scared them off when she raised her leg.

A very slight aura beamed off the top of the hill from whence she'd fallen. Which meant the reverend was up there near the edge of the drop. Please, please do not slip and fall. She could have giggled at the thought of him sliding downward ending up next to her. They could have a nice little chat.

If the reverend caught her two conspirators, they would bear the brunt of mischief in the graveyard. If only that man-of-the-cloth would be done with his inspection and toddle off to his cottage they would be able to look for her.

Wet seeped into her clothing. Christopher and James were most likely hiding behind gravestones.

"Renata, say something." Christopher's voice came from some distance.

She hushed, "Christopher, oh thank God."

"Blazes and damn. Where are you?"

"At the bottom of the hill."

James whispered, "*Damn*, did she fall in the creek?"

"God, I hope not." Then in a loud whisper he said to Renata, "Keep talking so I can follow your voice."

"We did it, didn't we! I hope my father already knows where he is. Do you think he does? What an accomplishment. I'm at the bottom, partially covered by branches, I think. Wedged by some big thing. I can't get up. I hope Rose has some warm chocolate waiting for us, cookies would be nice—I'm down here under a bush of some kind. I'll keep talking until my breath runs out. You should be near—Christopher I'm a mess and wet and smelly—"

A flash of pale moonlight spread across the green, the bottom of the hill in deep shadow. She saw Christopher's outline against the dark sky and whispered loudly, "I'm straightaway."

"Say something else."

"Down here under a bush."

He swiveled in the direction of her voice sliding down the muck. James stayed on top keeping a lookout on the reverend's retreat.

Christopher reached for her, his warm breath on her face, his hands circling her arms. "Are you hurt?" Kneeling in the muck, he realized the white that drew his attention were her petticoats drawn upward exposing her legs.

"I don't think so. Just filthy and stuck."

He lifted her to the point he could put his arm behind her and under her legs, raising her. Her wet and muddy clothing made her twice as heavy.

He buried his face in her neck. "My darling girl."

James came down the hill at a quick jog. "How is she?"

"No broken bones."

"Of all the misfortunes, this is horrid," she gasped.

James grabbed up the shovel and held tight to the lantern. "If the reverend returned to the rectory, he squelched his lamp. But he's not outside his door, that much I know. Follow me around the base of this hill, that should get us to the far side of the church."

They slunk away from the graveyard. Reaching the old castle, James said, "Stay to the grass, it's quieter."

Christopher set Renata on the ground, and the three bent low and stalled under cover of trees waiting for confirmation they had not been discovered.

Renata sucked in a breath, hoping against hope the reverend would not discover her father's resting place on the morrow.

In a hushed tone Christopher said, "I think your father is having some fun right now with the cloud cover gone."

James slapped a hand over his mouth, hiding a chuckle. "Or, it could be Morgan, irritated now that his arch enemy has moved in."

"Shush, both of you," hissed Renata.

"A chair in front of the fire, an Irish blend in hand, what more could a man ask for right now?" Christopher agreed with James.

"I'll be wanting a good soak, and a drink of some of that Irish blend. But if you get us caught, I'll never let you forget this night," she chattered through clenched teeth.

Both men chuckled softly. James punched a soft fist into Christopher's arm. "Did you hear that threat?"

Christopher said, "Something tells me we won't ever forget this night no matter what. At least we didn't make a mull of it."

A snapped twig, a bat taking flight, they stopped in their tracks. James looked in the distance the outline of the rectory barely visible. A faint glow from within proved the reverend's location.

"Here's our chance," hushed James. "Be careful, I don't want to light the lantern just yet." He added, "A stroke of luck when that fox and her pups scampered across the graveyard. Took the reverend's attention off the moment."

"They sniffed at me." She cried, tripping on a root. And again, fell face down in the mud.

Renata was shivering and Christopher wrapped her in his coat and scooped her up in his arms.

She sighed, feeling safe.

Out of sight of the church now, well past the old castle ruin, James lit the lantern.

She nestled her cheek against Christopher's shoulder and said, "I think my father might not want to *bedevil* Morgan. With our marriage, they will become friends."

Christopher responded. "You're saying this was all in vain?"

She snuggled her filthy face into his neck and relaxed in his very capable arms. "On, no. None of this was in vain. Life is wonderful."

Don't miss
A Break in the Clouds
Prickly Hawthorn Village #3
Coming early 2021

Don't miss out on your next favorite book!

Join the Satin Romance mailing list
www.satinromance.com/mail.html

THANK YOU FOR READING

Don't miss out on your next favorite book!

Join the Satin Romance mailing list
www.satinromance.com/mail.html

Did you enjoy this book?

We invite you to leave a review at your favorite book site, such as Goodreads, Amazon, Barnes & Noble, etc.

DID YOU KNOW THAT LEAVING A REVIEW...

- Helps other readers find books they may enjoy.
- Gives you a chance to let your voice be heard.
- Gives authors recognition for their hard work.
- Doesn't have to be long. A sentence or two about why you liked the book will do.

ABOUT THE AUTHOR

Karen Dean Benson gained a love of history from travels that took her into many different cultures around the world. A voracious reader from an early age, she loves research, history, and tales of complicated lives. Her stories, woven against the backdrop of a by-gone era, present numerous plot twists.

Her first series, *Ladies of Mischief,* is about women who find themselves enmeshed in mischief and mayhem spiced with charm in the 18th and 19th Centuries.

Her second series, *The Prickly Hawthorn:* Southern Ireland in the early 1800's where the inhabitants of Hawthorn Village's lush emerald hills and breathless azure heavens find adversity and acceptance along the banks of the ancient River Suir.

She lives with her husband Charlie in Florida on a golf course.

www.karendeanbenson.com
http://freshfiction.com/author.php?id=40966

facebook.com/Author-page-for-Karen-Dean-Benson-1415121542104941

goodreads.com/karendeanbenson

bookbub.com/authors/karen-dean-benson